Alistair is a creative practice tutor specializing in youth and disability arts. He also works as a visual artist, a musician and has written for stage and radio. Alistair graduated from the Goldsmiths University MA Course in Creative and Life Writing.

To my family with love

Alistair Roberts

RHINOCEROS OR THE BEAST'S BIOGRAPHER

AUSTIN MACAULEY PUBLISHERS™

LONDON · CAMBRIDGE · NEW YORK · SHARJAH

A CIP catalogue record for this title is available from the British Library.

ISBN 9781398461895 (Paperback)
ISBN 9781398461901 (ePub e-book)

www.austinmacauley.com

First Published 2023
Austin Macauley Publishers Ltd®
1 Canada Square
Canary Wharf
London
E14 5AA

Rest your head in my lap, Ode, and tell me how it began.

Anna, your face is as clear inside my mind as it ever was held in my hands.

Shh. I know, Ode. Story. Please.

Yes.

The child was starving. He had left his mother in their hut. She was swarmed with flies. He followed a rhinoceros beneath the bitter sun. It paused. The boy waited, breathless. At last he found what he had been searching for. A warm, fat, rhinoceros turd. He stuffed it into his mouth. His stomach sang with the joy of filling.

Where are you, Anna? I thought my cheek rested on your thighs.

I am sat here with my empty arms, Ode. But I shall be patient. Don't come rushing to me. Wait till your back is bent with age.

Yes.

Promise?

I promise.

The story, Ode.

My father, Ysoun, still a child, and his father, Akebe, stared at the near silent village. There was no smoke. There was no smoke because no one was cooking. And there was no cooking because there was no food. And everyone was sleeping in the middle of the day, because they had no liveliness. And there was no point foraging because the last green things left in the land, were the tips of the high leaves that only the giraffes could reach with their long black tongues.

Some in desperation had rummaged in the dry soil to unearth the bitter cassava. And not taking the time to pummel the poison from its rootish flesh, they instead stuffed the tuber raw behind their lips, mashing down with shaking teeth and swallowing in brackish gulps. For a while, they felt a fullness in their bellies, but then the toxins spread through their joints and veins and the full suffered the same agony as the empty.

The sky was wide and clear. The dust slept.

'Son,' said Akebe, 'we, the Kikuyo, our beloved tribe, are at the end of all reserves. There is no food or water to be found within the borders of our lands.'

'Can we not find a new earth to sustain us?' said Ysoun.

'Our enemy, the Wollof, barricade the pass as they have done for centuries. You know that they will not let us venture beyond our soil.'

'Our warriors are brave men, Father, let them kill the Wollof and be proud again.'

'Our warriors are so starved they have gone blind. I do not wish to give the Wollof the satisfaction of witnessing our defeat.'

'Are we to die and be forgotten then?'

'Our spirits will live here free after our bodies have rotted in the ground.'

'Father, we should not submit and we should not surrender. Is that not what your taught me when you encouraged me in sport. Did you not say I should always strive to win? Why are we submitting? Where is our courage and our strength? You did not raise me for this. I love and know you, Father. This is wrong.'

There were tears in my father's young and tender eyes. And there were tears on my grandfather's cheeks also. For he could see no hope. What could he do when he could see no clear path in front of him? How could he direct his tribe along a road invisible? He felt his failure keenly. His failure to find magic in the dust. His failure before the eyes of his tribe, his wife and his son. He said these things to himself a thousand times a day. He could not hold back the bitter winds that poured through the gorge and swept away the soil. He had no dominion over the sky to make it rain.

He was the most respected man of his people, the Son of the Son of the Son of, stretching back to the beginning of time, ordained as leader, absolute in decision, the conduit between the earth and spirits. And yet how useless he was. His voice unheard by the ancient dead. His command of the earth ignored.

And his son, stood beside him, crack lipped and withering. How many more days did he have to live? And how painful it would be to witness the loss of the boy, and yet he could not bear to leave before the son and spare himself that vision.

'Son, when time offers us no other choice, we shall take your mother's hands, and enter the world of the spirits together. And we shall do so with our heads held high. We will find better joy in that world than we have found in this.'

'So the Kikuyo are to be a spirit tribe, Father?'

'As we were before the first firing of the sun. We descended at its first warmth, and the world blossomed around us in celebration at our arrival. Now it is time for us to return. Maybe this was a thing ordained. Our destiny.'

'Will we ever return to flesh and earth again?'

'When is it time. The universe works on a scale of time that human minds cannot comprehend.'

And at that my grandfather flung his arms wide and raised his chin to the blue and screamed his spirit cry. And even with his dry and hungry mouth, and with no spit to grease his tongue, his voice echoed across the land of the Kikuyo.

'If we are leaving this earth, we shall do so with all the pride that has always marked our tribe.'

Then they saw a small child heaving into the bush and collapse.

There was a rhinoceros moving close.

'Come, we should not leave the child lying in the dirt,' my grandfather said. 'We should carry the body home. If the parents are still alive we shall let them mourn. If they are already dead we shall lay them all side by side.'

As they approached they saw that the rhinoceros was nudging the body with the side of its chin, as if the child were only sleeping and the beast wanted to wake it and say, do not sleep in the middle of the day you lazy calf, there are errands to run for your mother, friends to be played with.

'Has the rhinoceros come to watch us die?' Ysoun asked his father. 'Does it want to see the last of us before we are forgotten? Is it sad or gloating? Does it wish our land for itself?'

The rhinoceros raised its head, stared at the boy Ysoun, and with deliberate weight approached.

And it is strange to think of one's proud father as a boy, scared and pissing himself before a mute beast. He could not take his eyes from the pointed horn. He was too weak to run.

'Be still. It has neither the nature nor the cause to harm us.' said my grandfather. 'There is no need for fear. Not when you are with me.'

'I am never scared with you by my side. Not even when we are all about to die.'

As Akebe went to put his flesh before the flesh of his beloved son, between the horn and his boy's heaving chest, the beast stopped and knelt before the child.

Above them, newly risen, a bank of thick, black, cloud poured across the sky. A herd of giraffe bolted among the high trees.

9

The rhinoceros flung back its head and snorted. Ysoun flung his arms around Akebe's waist. And then the sky above opened, and glory, it began to rain.

The beast did not move to hurt them.

'Father, is this madness or a dream?'

'Son, I have no idea why the beast kneels in respect before you.'

'If it has purpose it should kneel before you, not me.'

'It chose you, Son. And I will not question it.'

'Father, did the rhino hear your call?'

'Never before have they let themselves be commanded.'

And still the beast kneeled before them. Patient as a supplicant. Before a nervous and excited child and his astounded father.

'Father, what if the spirits of our dead have taken root in the mind of these beasts?'

'Let us first return this child to the village,' my grandfather said. 'We will try and make sense of this later. Come.'

He placed the dead boy in the entrance to his family home.

'This is not time for condolence. Come let us speak to your mother.'

They walked quickly through the rain to their own dwelling.

'Wife,' he called, 'it is raining.'

'I know,' she said coming to the door. 'I am already preparing to wake them from their torpor.'

She had a copper pot and a wooden spoon. My grandmother drummed and my grandfather spoke the clear truth.

'This is not a dream. It is raining. We haven't seen rain for a hundred days. Raise yourself.'

And then my grandfather heard a strange singing over and above the sound of the downpour plashing against the dry ground. In the distance the heaving body of a giraffe lay on its side.

'Are there to be more surprises for us this day?'

Akebe left his wife in charge of the rain.

The giraffe lay on its side, it's belly ripped wide, its leg slashed below the knee. Standing to the side stood the rhinoceros that had knelt before my father. Blood dripping from its horn. And beyond that corpse they saw another two giraffe carcasses and another two rhinoceros. Proud executioners.

'What strangeness is this? The rhinoceros does not eat of the flesh,' my grandfather said.

'Father, I think this meat is intended for us. The beast want us to survive.'

Above them the sky raged and rain coursed across their shaved skulls and down their coal black chests and backs.

'Come, Son, let us share our news.'

The villagers, on hands and knees, were moving with the last of their energy, dragging pots and pans, and bowls and cups, out into the pouring rain. Or simply lying there on their backs with their mouths wide and brimming.

'Sharpen your knives,' my grandfather commanded of them all. 'This day, this hour we shall eat meat again, raw and warm. And the rain will pour down upon us and we will celebrate that we have been saved from extinction.'

After a week of storming rain, the ground was soaked, and green shoots appeared each morning, and we plucked them for their sustenance and flavour. And each day the rhino killed, so that we could eat of meat.

And sitting around the carcass we jabbered.

We are blessed.

On that day, balls of light poured across the sky and the air exploded in the clouds. Did you see it!

The natural order to the world has changed.

And for this there is a reason.

We, the Kikuyo have been chosen.

And if we are chosen we have to make ourselves worthy. We have to find our place in history.

Our tribe is destined for greatness, not extinction, I knew it all along.

Teenage girls removed the offals of the beasts and carried them back to the village to boil.

So there was water and there was food and there was talk.

But my grandfather pondered how was this destiny to be made manifest? What should they actually do?

With their pots full of fresh rain, and the green shoots of wild onions simply popping out of the ground like welcome guests, would it not be too easy to simply dream of great adventures whilst getting fat on flesh and snoozing throughout the day?

My grandmother had cured a giraffe bladder and stuffed it with dried grass.

'Make a game with this,' she said. 'You have a full stomach, but you are becoming lazy.'

'We could throw it at each other's heads,' said my father.

'Could you not be more inventive? Why not see how far you could kick it? Put two twigs in the ground and try and kick it between them.'

'Would that not be too easy?'

'Then have another boy standing between the twigs trying to stop you.'

And so my father had kicked the ball hard at the other boy stood between the two sticks and smashed him in the face. Blood was pouring from his lips. Then the rhino came to my father again and simply stood there before him.

'It wants you to tickle its ears,' said one friend.

'No, it wants you to pat its head,' said another.

'No, it wants you to snog it,' said the boy with blood pouring from his mouth.

'Is it a boy or a girl?'

'Have a feel.'

'Fuck off.'

'It is you,' said my father, 'you have come to visit me again. I have not seen you since that first day. You kill the giraffe for our bellies and then you retreat into the bush. You are never around here for us to thank you.'

And my father went down on his knees before the Beast and then in further prostration put his forehead to the soil as the boy with the split lip began to laugh behind him.

'I anoint you as Mphuno,' said my father. 'A Beast as worthy as yourself should be named. And that name should be spoken with a human tongue.'

The Beast stared at my father and began to trot in circles.

'It is going nowhere.'

'It is waiting for direction.'

'A circle is a journey that never ends,' said the boy with blood on his tongue.

'What the fuck does that mean?'

'It means something man.'

And then my father knew what to do.

'It wants me to ride him. It is a male, and he will take me on his back. And together we shall be invincible.'

'Yeah right.'

'You climb on that and he'll just buck you.'

'You want a mouthful of dust.'

'No man has ever rode the rhinoceros.'

'Just fucking watch me!'

And my father was the first to ride the Beast. With a wild braggadocio, teen and tall, astride the rhinoceros's neck with the young girls screaming and wriggling their hips and dancing on their toes.

It was a sight, a circus, but where could it lead? So the boy can mount a rhinoceros! But all he does is ride around to impress the girls. The rhinoceros kills the giraffe. We eat. Is that not enough? We should respect the beasts, not ride them for sport. The Gods have granted us great favour. If we do not respect this gift it will be withdrawn. And we will be back to being fucked.

They were a mile outside the village. My father riding and a girl on foot behind him, her lips peppered with dust.

The rhinoceros halted suddenly and my father was almost dismounted in surprise.

Mosaa, the girl who would become my mother, caught up quickly.

'Have you lost control?'

'No, of course not.'

Ysoun could feel the heartbeat of the Beast, the vibrations through the hide. The proud creature turned its head slightly to the East and began to move. My father could feel the animal's impatience.

'It is going to bolt at any moment. This is to be an adventure. Come with me. Ride behind me.'

Already she was a girl alone, far enough away from her home without permission or chaperone. Her only company a boy she was not related to or promised to. It would be so easy to be punished for her audacity. To be a girl was to never be alone and yet always lonely.

My father offered his hand and she took it and she swung herself behind him and put her arm around his chest and squeezed his arse with her thighs and breathed in his ears.

'Where are we going?'

'Mphuno has picked up a smell that excites him.'

And my mother breathed in the fragrance of my father's sweating neck and thought that Mphuno and herself were similar in their intoxication.

The animal had picked up the scent of four Wollof warriors. They were heavily armed and trespassing on Kikuyo land. They would kill my father, put his head on a stick, gang rape my yet to be Mother, and then drag her back to their lands to be a slave for the rest of her life.

'I have brought you into danger,' Ysoun said. 'I shall try and turn the Beast around.'

'You will not. This is no accident. Ysoun, I have never seen one of these arseholes before,' Mosaa said, no trace of fear in her voice. 'They are ugly. They are not handsome like you.'

The Wollof goggled, pointed, laughed and shouted scornful words about the sight of a boy and a girl upon the back of a Beast. And in my imagining I wanted to hurt them. These will be my parents you dumb scum. I will remember this when you are pleading beneath us.

'They think that we are playing a childish game,' said Mosaa. 'I don't like to see them mocking you.'

'News of our communion with the rhino must not be known to them. They will tell the others of their tribe. Our secret will be revealed and it will be my fault.'

'You did not bring the rhinoceros here. It brought *you*. It has its own reasons.'

And then the rhinoceros charged. There was no instruction on my father's part. The four warriors watched the approach in rude and adolescent amazement. The hysterical, cock sure shock, of those that think they will live forever.

'Do I have leaves or grass about me?' Cried one. 'Has it come nibble me? Bring it on you dumb, fucking dumb boy on a dumb fucking Beast. I will be fucking your screaming girl as you spit out the last of your teaming blood.'

The first fellow was gouged from crotch to belly, the second tripped and his skull pounded to dust. The third and fourth went down wailing but unseen from my fathers's view. And all the time he kept his grip around the neck of the Beast and my future Mother kept her grip around the waist of the boy she was to marry. Until it was all over, and the moans had died away, and they found themselves staring down on four broken enemy.

'It wanted you to know,' said Mosaa. 'And it wanted me to see.'

'I do not understand. What did the Beast want me to know?'

'That it can kill your enemies. Just think,' she said. 'You can ride them and they can kill.'

'Why am I the only one to be shown these things?'

'Because you have been chosen. And you will lead your people to great conquests. Next year when I come of age, I will marry you. For I think that I am blessed also, and our children will be heroes.'

My father slung the bodies over the back of his Beast and he and Mosaa returned on foot. And as I imagine, already in love.

'Does the sight of death disgust you?'

'I am not feeble. Women see more death than men. Three of my sisters died before they could spit.'

They took the bodies with them to prove the truth of their story. And on the outskirts of the village stood one hundred rhinoceros in a marshal line.

Mphuno tossed the dead bodies from his back in front of their rank and the beasts raised their horns and blew their breathe across their thick black lips.

My grandfather strode from the village gate to confront his son. The villagers, both men and women, boys and girls, followed in an unruly gaggle behind him.

'Ysoun, explain,' said my grandfather arriving at his side.

Mosaa's Mother came to her with a hand raised and a furious brow.

'Please,' Akebe said simply.

And my future mother curtsied and grinned and her mother forced a smile.

'Ysoun. Explain! The eyes of the village are upon me.'

'The rhinoceros took me, Father. I did not lead it. It took me to the smell of our enemy. Four of them on our land and foraging. The Beast killed them all without a sign from me.'

Mphuno cantered around the dead with all eyes popping at the sight. And his fellows began a strange dance, moving from side to side, their horns drawing circles in the heat haze, and then rising on their hind legs, briefly taller than the tallest of the tall tribe of the Kikuyo.

And then Mphuno mashed the ruined flesh of the enemy dead to utter pulp, and the villagers jostled to spit upon the mush.

'Ysoun. Why was the girl with you?' said my grandfather, his long fingers digging into his son's shoulders.

'She followed me. How was I to stop her?'

'Girls used to follow me too. All the time. It is hard to resist. I shall have to speak with the girl's father to make sure there is no offence.'

And Mosaa, my mother, still a girl, full of brim and playful haughtiness, sidled up close to my future father.

'Ysoun, can all the men ride as you can do? For if so, we will need saddles. It is hard to stay upright unless a person has you to hold on to. And how can every man hug you for their comfort and security? We can use the giraffe leather. My mother will help me and your family will never forget us.'

Her mother stared. She no doubt thought, that although a union with my father would bring great favour to her family, it should be done properly and according to custom. But of course everything was changing wasn't it?

Anna?

Yes, Ode.

You would think this was the beginning of the story, you might expect things to happen very fast after such extraordinary events. But no. That was not the case.

Then tell me, I am not short on time.

Each strong man found a rhino to bear him.

The women did not fight?

It is not our tradition.

Nor mine. But sometimes I think I would like to fight a man. Not a fine man like you, Ode. But there are many that I have met, where I have thought, you would look more handsome with a knitting needle through your eye. But enough of that. So, Ode, each strong man found a rhino that he could ride and you set off straight away to destroy your old enemy? Yes? For that is what I would have done.

No. My grandfather told the men to wait.

Men are not much good at waiting. They leave that to the women.

My grandfather said that they had to be prepared. He initiated the creation of our rhino-mounted army. The villagers thought six months, and we will be at war with our rivals. A year at most. But two hard and painful years passed with combat exercises from dawn to dusk. Strong, tall, boys as young as four were taught how to ride the beasts and how to hold a wooden sword.

But still no talk of conquest of the hated Wollof.

The teenagers became restless, the older men checked for grey in their pubes.

In private there was I imagine, much complaining.

A gang of them took my son when he was only seven and wandering lost. I have not slept these last ten years. I do not know if he is dead. But when I think of how they might have treated him if he were alive, I wish he were. To want your own son dead!

How long do we have to wait to fuck up those bitch's shit?

What was left of my sister to bury … Sorry I cannot speak of this without tears. Excuse me.

Only after two years did my grandfather gather all his people together to explain his vision.

Food was brought, fermented fruits and wines. The men came with their wives and children. They had painted their chests and cheeks. Unlike the Wollof we did not decorate our necks with bones and teeth. Our tribal mark was one simple and restrained gash between the eyebrows to the bridge of the nose.

My grandfather Akebe stood before them. My father Ysoun, two paces behind. Fifteen and married. His son, my brother, on Mosaa's lap, picking at his dusty nose. And me sat inside my mother's belly. Curled up nicely. Hearing my grandfather's deep tones through the fluid that I floated in.

The high-born women were perched on ceremonial stools. In respect of the order of this day they had woven grasses and dried cicadas into their hair.

'It was two years ago to this day that the rhino came to us,' Akebe began.

Wild cheering.

'The men and women of our tribe then numbered in their hundreds. But since that day more and more children have been born, and they don't die in infancy, they are strong and healthy. Our babies used to starve to death. But we have meat now. Two days each month, not one, nor three, but always two, by some magic beyond our comprehension it rains. And so we do not die of drought.

'I want to see the ablest of our young men grown into warriors. I dream of a day when I can survey an army of a thousand.

'For so many years we have been prisoners of our own geography. With a mountain range to the south that we cannot ascend because there is no air to breath at its summit. A river to the west that we cannot navigate because of the falling water that smashes bones against the rocks.

'For so many years we have been trapped by the hostility of our neighbours. They are more numerous than us. And they have in the past defeated and contained us. But now no more. We are new born now. We are the future. We will venture and adventure. But it will take time. This will test your resolve. A man who does not respect time, has no understanding of life. And so you will come to understand my meaning.

'Our Forefathers could see no way of escape from the trudge of absolute poverty and the barren aspects of our land that was only just sufficient to feed us if we kept our number low. We had to stay small and weak just to survive.

'We have for generations been fiercely proud of this land of ours. But can somewhere be truly called home if you can never leave it? Home should be a sanctuary, not a prison.

'But now the world of the Kikuyo has changed beyond measure in just two years. The city that surrounds this square is the product of the might of our men and women gorged on meat. A product of our new found hope. The beasts have assisted us in hauling felled trees and sledges of cool, wet mud. Our city is a mark of the success of our land and culture. But what about the further reaches?

'Who has not asked themselves, are there different skies elsewhere? How do other men measure against ourselves? How pretty are the women beyond the horizon?'

All knew that to be a joke.

'No match for us,' cried my grandmother and the circle of decorated women around her laughed. 'Stay home husband, you'll find no greater beauty in all the world than that which already lays beside you.'

Her gaggle sniggered.

'There will be no sleep tonight.'

'I shall put my child to sleep with booze on her gums and spend the night humping.'

My grandfather smiled indulgently and waited. The women quietened themselves soon enough.

'Is the world different beyond the gorge, or just a continuation of our own? We know that not all men have our colour. But do they have our courage and our dreams?

'Earlier this year,' my grandfather said, 'I traded with an Arab for a book. It is full of symbols I cannot read. And I will not learn to do so in my lifetime. But other's amongst us will I hope.'

And at those words, even though I was still unborn, I knew my destiny.

'We have been riding the beasts for two years now. Our bellies are full. I know that many of you are impatient, I know that many of you have thought to yourself, why are we waiting, lets us go and destroy the Wollof now. I know that in respect of my authority you have not voiced these thoughts, but inside your minds you are frustrated and impatient. Yes we could take the Wollof now and be done with them forever. But would that be the extent of our ambition? As a child I was abducted by those bastards. Enslaved. My wife has spoken of the scars upon my back. You all know the story of my escape as told by the Griot.

'But the Wollof lands have nothing of the grandeur our own. Our land is blessed by the spirits of our ancestors. They live in every tree and shrub. We hear their voices in the well. Our grandparent's lullabies whisper in the winds. Blossoms sing of young girl's dreams. Our teen boys pour thick white seed upon the ground when they think they are not being watched, and thick trunks spurt from our thin soil.

'What fucking use is the dry and spiritless Wollof land to us? Fuck them all!'

Even the youngest replied. Even if it came out as fudem, fkem.

'After becoming chosen are we merely to extend ourselves by a few meagre miles? No, we will not attack the Wollof this day. Nor this week. Nor this month. Nor this year or the next.

'The change in the nature of our beasts was driven by some spirit we have yet to divine. But I think they came to us with an idea for history. This great event, and all that has followed is meant to change the world. To change the history of man. Not just to solve some local squabble with another tribe and beat our chests like black arsed gibbons.'

My grandmother stood beside my grandfather, the rows of pearls around her long and slender neck. She kept a serious, but admiring face upon her husband.

'We will travel way beyond the Wollof lands.'

'Chief Elder Akebe, are we to go as far as the northern, coastal towns?'

'Elder, shall we plunder those fucking Arabs that like to trade in our black flesh?'

My grandfather smiled.

'No, we are going further than that.'

They looked at each other.

'Further than the sea?'

'We shall cross the water.'

'To where?'

'To Yurop. Everything the white man has, we shall take from him.'

The village was stunned. My grandmother's face showed no surprise. She knew the extent of her husband's ambition.

'But we will have to be prepared. And so I am to tell you of my plan and my decision. We will train our children for the next fifteen years.'

There were suppressed gasps.

'Elder, we will be old men by then.'

'Yes you will, but your sons will be young and vital. That babe on Mosaa's lap. He is my grandson. We will begin our conquest when he is fifteen and a ready warrior.'

And I was soon to be born into such revels. Was I expectant in the womb?

Was I un-aware of my un-growing deformity?

My mother had a workroom in the rear of our house. And as a child, I watched my mother work the leather of the giraffe. Her dextrous fingers enchanted me, yet I was also on the tenderest of hooks lest she prick her flesh and bleed.

'Women's work,' she said once, showing me the fine tools she possessed, the shelves of fine skins and fabrics. She looked at me, my face, and then her eyes slowly rolled along my withered arm.

'Still, Ode, what do you want to know about such things?'

My mother had perfected a device that reset broken bones to a perfect straightness. An exquisite contraption.

Young men in our warrior class were quite ashamed if they themselves had not snapped a bone by a certain age. So they trained even harder and with even less regard for their safety. Boys would say to each other, have you not worn one of Mosaa's slings yet? No? You cowardly shit! You fucking homo! You shall never become a man.

My grandfather had decided that new tactics would be needed. No one had ever ridden the rhinoceros into battle before. Sons trained from the age of four. They would know nothing else. They would think a blade or spear to be an extension of their bones. The rhino's spine, wrapped in fat and moving under the hide, would forever be the most important thing between their legs.

Warriors would rise with the sun and mount their beasts. Take the rhinoceros to the river and swim across together. Take their beasts to the low hills of the mountains to the south and climb until neither of them could breathe. They would take their meals in the saddle. And sleep on the backs of their beasts at night.

They would grow to be young men so imbued with the promise of great glory, that it would abolish the very concept of fear.

And my mother and her sisters would present their men with the very finest armour civilisation had ever known. Six month cured, and triple folded giraffe leather that could stand the greatest assault and yet, was light, and subtle and breathed around a warrior's body.

My father became the Chief Elder of the village when my grandfather passed to the spirit world. There he would be celebrated for the revival of his tribe. He would be in glory everlasting.

'Ode,' said my mother looking up from her work, 'in your Grandfather's book there are drawings of many fine and tall buildings across that continent. Your father has promised to bring them back to our lands, brick by brick, and rebuild their glory here so that I can see them for myself.'

'That is an endeavour due a queen, my mother.'

'I am a queen?'

'Of course. Have you not been told so?'

'By your father, yes, but that is a special thing between us.'

I smiled at the mention of my parent's happiness.

'There are fine metals there,' my mother said. 'We shall take them as our own and leave them mud and grass. We shall eat meat and they shall eat gruel. They shall run and we shall chase. They shall know confinement and we shall know freedom. And if it takes our fancy, we will sell *them* to the Arabs as slaves.'

'Mother, I fear that because I am useless, I will never see the great adventure.'

The Kikuyo say, one hungry mouth needs two strong hands to eat. If I had not been the Grandson of the Chief Elder I would have been put down at birth.

'Ode, you are to keep me company during this long campaign. Ode, I need you.'

'And I will stay here when the men embark on their adventure years from now.'

The first day my brother left home for training, before my grandfather's passing, my brother said: 'Father, can we not devise a thing that will let Ode fight with a single good hand?'

'Son, I think we might, but it would anger all the other boys, they would think our family's treatment preferential, and take it as an insult.'

'But, Father, who can be insulted by the Chief Elder? Grandfather's word is like God on earth.'

'And he has to be careful with his words as he has to be with his decisions.'

21

There was never any talk of my future. And so I did not think of it myself. I bit on the finger joints of my right hand, a habit that caused painful indents in my skin, but gave me pleasure and respite.

As full of imagination as I was, I lived at that time in the clear, tender, visible present.

By the time I was ten, we had built a city to match, in its own unique, Afrik fashion, those we had seen in my grandfather's one, well-thumbed book. If we were to live here before adventuring abroad, we would live as civilised men. And the city would be a place to return to with pride.

The birds, riding the currents of warm air above us, saw our city, Sixeko, as one vast red hexagon dominating the landscape. It was a place of mud walls and warrens. Our streets were built as concentric circles within. You could leave the front door, stroll through many excited conversations, pass quiet words of love, cooking smells, the whiffs of perfume, breast milk, wine, and return home without changing direction. Walkways like the branches of a tree led to the central square and the sacred well.

Those recently bereaved would say that they heard the voices of their loved ones ticking in the water.

Our food was cooked in communal kitchens. Men did not cook. I tried it once in secret, and ruined the flesh of a poor goat that deserved better love and attention after its slaughter. The girls, so swim and swain, served up to twenty families at a time. Our city was never quiet. We lived side by side. At night we snored and teethed as one.

The entrance of each family house was decorated by carvings cut into the mud across the lintel. Each unique to each dwelling. People would say, I live in the house with the two fish jumping over the frog.

Girls would conduct races, running on their hands with a dried gourd held firm between their upper thighs. This way great balance and strength was learned. And although I could not join in, and could not clap in joy, I could slap my thigh and holler.

I would have happily joined the girls huddled over their leatherwork, but I could neither cut nor sew.

I remembered a thing my father had said to me once. I had been watching the girls at play and tried to join in. They would not let me and I cried. One girl even spat at me before the other girls slapped her down.

Girl! What is wrong with you! He's the Chief's son. We can refuse to play with him but we can't spit at him. Shit!

My father had been a silent and distant witness to this. He took me by the shoulder and comforted me. Let me tell you something, Ode.

The following day I went up to one of the girls at play, she had a long thin face and a high forehead.

'Yesterday my father said to me, Ode, you are a blessing.'

The girl showed me her teeth.

'And my father is the Chief Elder and what he says is the truth, and you cannot disagree with him. So I must be a blessing and you have to agree and you can say those words to me if you want to.'

She ran away.

I turned to another girl, Naima. I had noticed that she was not especially popular with the other girls.

'I'm a blessing,' I said. 'But that girl that just ran away, she didn't understand.'

She smiled. She had a gap between her teeth that made her cute. It suggested a certain playfulness. I wanted to put my tongue between the gap and smell the glory of her face.

'Don't talk to my sister,' said a boy coming to stand beside her.

'You cannot speak to me like that. I am my father's son.'

'And that is all you will ever be.'

'What do you mean by that?'

'You will never be a woman's husband. A father to a son yourself.'

'Brother, shut the fuck up. Ode is the son of Ysoun. What will he say if he hears you speak like this? He will have you hung from a tree. You dumb shit.'

'Don't call me dumb shit bitch. Ysoun he is not here to hear is he? And Ode will never tell, because Ode has no balls.'

Her face fell.

'Leave him alone.'

'You fucking leave him alone.'

'I'm sorry, Ode. I must do what my brother tells me to. It is a women's life to be dominated by fools. But you are not a fool are you, Ode?'

And of course I could have told my father about this affront, and this girl's brother would have been severely punished for his disrespect. I could have told my brother and he would have slit that cunt's throat quietly under moonlight with no remorse or concern.

But I kept silent. If I were ever to reverse the insult that so many thought they could serve me with, I would have to do it on my own terms. And I would do that not by causing harm, but by becoming wonderful.

Ode, no child should be invisible to other children. Did you ever try and hurt yourself?

No. I would have been forced to spend a thousand years in a pit in the Neverlife if I had.

God states we should not kill each other, in that ghost-written book of his. Yet we do. And the priests bless the bloodshed when their earthly masters ask for it to be ordained. But why can you not kill yourself? Who is the criminal, who is the victim of the crime? Why does it anger him so?

Anna. That is a simple enough question to answer. The Gods give you life as a perfect gift. You cannot throw it back in their faces without offence. The Gods are as vain as us. And as easily insulted.

Ode, those lace wristbands I wore.

I never saw you in the light without them. A present from your grandmother, you wore them with respect.

I wore them with shame.

Anna, am I making this up?

No Ode, you are not, what I am telling you is the truth.

But, Anna, you are only a voice in my head.

No Ode, I am not. I am real. You know me better than any other person ever. I think that at times you know me better than I know myself.

And now you are a spirit or a ghost?

No Ode. You are remembering me. Remember?

I cannot forget you for a moment.

I am a compendium. As you might find in a fine library. Now tell me more about your city. Mine was full of filth, and the rich went around in carriages with herbs stuffed up their arses.

Noses, Anna. Noses surely.

It is a joke, Ode.

I do not understand.

The rich would say, I am so grand, even my shit does not stink.

You were grand and I never smelled a foul thing upon you.

That was because you were beautiful, and stupid, and in love with me.

I was the last of those two things for sure.

You were the first and last of that list you dumb boy. Come on, talk, or this tale will take forever.

Do we not have forever? Anna? Okay.

Any neighbour in our city may have entered another's house by simply wandering in and calling out a warm hello. But to enter the house of the Chief Elder, you had to be invited. And for many years, before I gave up hope, I would approach any pretty girl I saw at the market and say, with great solemnity.

May I invite you to my house? We have many fine foods. I could entertain you with a thrilling story. My name is Ode.

We all know who you are, Ode! Duh! How is your brother? When is he going to marry me? Always outside the city walls, tethered to his Beast. Fighting, training, eating meat, racing. But he is missing another education that only a girl or woman could confer.

I stayed at home. The only other boy of my age that remained in the city during the day was Fifu. He had fits. He did not want to be my friend. I am sure his parents encouraged him to gain my acquaintance, but he did not wish it. I understood. He did not want to admit his difference. By making friends with Ode the cripple, he would be twice-marking himself as an outsider. But his avoidance of me did him no good. He was regularly beaten up by gangs of girls. If he had a fit in public, they would open their skirts and piss on him.

One day each week the boys returned to their family homes for lavishing and coos. The teachers of the arts of war returned to their wives and made excuses for being excused, and daughter could you tend the pot awhile while I speak to your mother in private. *Speak* the girls would mouth unseen and grin. Have I not seen animals at play? Do the older girls not talk!

As my father and my brother told tales of all that had happened the week before, I seemed to almost vanish into the steam that rose from the celebratory cooking pot. The stewed giraffe meat, the spring onions, the slices of liver coated in molasses and steamed to fragrant collapse.

I was born into the age of the rhinoceros. I was born into the age of meat. I was born into the age of the green shoots that popped their heads from the soil, and through their own magic, helped clear our skins of blight and cleared the

25

sights of our eyes. I was born into a time that dreamed of war. I was born into the time that my tribe knew that they were chosen. I was born into the family of our Chief Elder, with the carved sign of a smiling sun and moon over the door.

My people were magnificent. And if anyone deserved to own the earth, it was us. Let us take it, from the weak, fat and the stupid whites.

My father once said to me.

'Ode, do you know why I let you live?'

'Because you loved me? Because I came from your seed and my mother's womb.'

'As you know, nature changed when Mphuno bowed before me. And when I saw you as a squalling babe with the one strange arm, I did not think, this is an imperfection that we cannot bear. I thought I have been offered another chance to accept the changes of nature. And this child shall be special and rewarding.'

'But, Father, I am not at all special. I can't even get a girl to kiss me. I can't even find a friend to share my time with.'

'Your mother finds you a comfort.'

'Yes, Father. But that is not the path to being a man.'

'Love will come to you, Ode. I think that when you find the right woman, it will be as special as that which exists between myself and your mother.'

Oh Ode, said Anna, stroking my skull. Your father knew us before we had even met. Sorry, I am interrupting. Continue.

'Don't let him know that I said this,' my father said, 'but your brother, will, I fear, struggle to find real love in this world. He is too keen to hurt. He is the finest warrior in training as befits the son of the Chief Elder. But he finds too great a pleasure in conquest and subjugation.'

'But is conquest not our aim, Father?'

'It is our aim to find ourselves worthy of greatness. We will take everything the white man has because they murder us and trade us like beasts, and for that they must be punished. But we are not to be thieves, but the seekers of retribution.'

'All the girls adore my brother, they buzz around him like flies on new found meat.'

'Yes they do, and he hardly even appreciates it. Love is better for being hard won.'

'Did you have to work hard to make my mother love you?'

'No,' he said laughing, 'I most certainly did not. She saw that I was the chosen one and just reached out and said you are mine. I had little choice in the matter. And I am forever grateful for having such little choice.'

I knew that from my earliest childhood, that I would never have a wife or child. But there was something inside me that gave me companionship. The voices that conversed within me. They were not spirits or ghost. They came from the parts of my mind that I could not map. If others thought that I was silent, it was because they could not hear the shadow voices in my mind.

I would study my father's one and only book. I could read it no more than he. And at that time I had never had any hope of doing do so. Each of the letters that I would grow to love were indistinguishable and meaningless to me then.

So I memorised the pictures. I filled my mind with things intangible. My mind became a scholar of things that I could not touch. My mind knew things that my fingers had no sense of.

Had I not been my father's son, and had the book not been my father's, I do believe other boys would have taken it from me, torn the pages from the binding and used the precious paper to wipe their shit and then thrust it in my face.

But, no. I was protected. The book was precious and I felt precious with it in my hands.

One day caressing it in the village square, sat by the talking well, Naima came and squatted beside me.

'Read to me, Ode. I have never heard words read from a book. This was your grandfather's, then your father's, and now look, you hold it in your own hands. I have heard it said that there is another world hiding between its covers. The world is small for a girl. Show me a bigger world, Ode?'

And of course I was a fool. I could have made up anything I wanted and been convincing. Instead I told the girl the truth.

'I cannot read it.'

'Oh,' she said. 'I thought you were clever. I know you are a cripple, but I thought you were clever.'

There was no way to explain, that however clever one might be, a boy still needed instruction.

'Naima,' I said. 'I *am* clever enough to know that any man would consider it an honour to be your husband.'

'Ode, no. You mustn't speak to me like that. You really mustn't.'

I returned to the pages.

Buildings. Machines I had no mind of, but which I perceived were weapons of the whites. And even as a boy I thought, all your devices, will fall before our might. When you encounter us, you are going to shit your britches. And you will rush to your great inventions, and wind them up, and prime them, and stoke and stroke them, and it will all be to no avail. For we will simply pound you into the earth of your fathers, where you can lie amongst the bones and your turnips and your onions.

In my mind, I brought to life the entirety of our grand campaign, giving voices to the characters, deciding their fates.

And no one had any idea of the size of the world inside my head. There was a drawing of a man having his arm sawed through which repelled and attracted me in equal measure.

I dreamed of finding a great physician, and promised him great favour if he could rebuild my arm. A miraculous operation that was completed by some Yuropan magic. Painless, instant.

And me perfect. A perfect image of my tribe.

At other times, quite perversely you might think, I imagined the surgery in all full horror. Our warrior boys were injured frequently and they never cried out. And so I pictured myself, with a calm face as the doctor had to cut into the flesh of my arm and saw out the bones and replaced them with new limbs made of gold.

While I cried not a tear. And everyone said, we are surprised at your bravery. Or they said, we knew all along, Ode, that there was a warrior's heart inside you. Do you want to come around to our house and chat shit? Do you want to flirt with my sister?

It was the tradition of our tribe that we had one great storyteller, a man we named the Griot and never knew the name his mother had bestowed on him. He held the library of our history in his mind and could project his voice across the entire lands of our tribe.

The walls of the city stood around us in their dark. I was sat with my brother by the well. The girls took quick glances of his face. A bat landed in a girl's hair and she screamed. My brother reached out, grabbed it and snapped its neck.

The Griot raised his hands and we fell silent. My father, the most powerful man of the Kikuyo, did so without hesitation.

Then it struck me, could I be a Griot? Would such position give grandeur to the constant stories in my head?

But I knew it was a hereditary title. The job would pass to the man's son. Even as the child of the Chief Elder I could not usurp that position.

The Griot's stories of the long before, were long in their telling, because our history is one of countless generations. It is given the respect of time. It could not be hurried. The men chewed herbs to help them see the Griot's words. My brother chewed freely. There were many girls around him.

I could not chew the herb for fear of confusion. But I could consume the stories. If I could learn to tell such tales myself, I might be listened to. I could not kiss any of the luscious lips of our fine young girls. But might I kiss their ears with words?

'At the time of Everywhen,' the Griot began, 'thousands of generations before the present days, men and Beast freely conversed. We understood each other. We shared a language.

'The animals knew that hunters needed their flesh. And it was understood that man would hunt animal, as animals in their place would hunt each other. Man could use his net and spear against the animals, and by rights and in all fairness, the animals would do anything in their power to defend themselves. Tooth and claw as the old saying goes.

'Each taking their part and art in death and injury, a balance was established. It was the way of the world and was known to have always been that way. And if it had always had been that way, then that was the way of the world. And if that was the way of the world, there was no need to question it or judge it ill.

'We kill to eat. We eat to live. Who can deny they want to live?

'Tooth and claw against spear and net. An understanding.

'And then. The disaster, the fall, the divide.'

We knew the story. We did not seek innovation. The pleasure was in the story's repetition. We knew ourselves by revisiting our history.

'And then man invented the weapon we know as the Uttomenge Ballista. Its design is thankfully lost to us now. This weapon allowed killing at a distance. Man no longer had to put himself in a position of danger to achieve his meat. He became lazy and greedy, first killing more flesh than he could eat, letting it go to rot, and then the great aberration, killing for sport, killing for pleasure.

'And the animal kingdom decided to wipe man from the earth for the breach of a contract that had lasted since the dawn of time. They amassed an army on the great plains of Suskina Frana, some hundred miles south of this land.

'One thousand Elephant, rhinoceri, Mastodon, Xerus, Veildebest, Giraffe, Baboon, Cheeta, Hog, Wild Dog, Jakel, Impela, even a swarming mass of tiny Klipspringer, Lyon, Porcupina, Sable Bull, Nyala, Topi.

'In the air, with sharpened stones in their claws, clouds and swarms of Quelea-Quelea and Vanga. The Stock Dove and the Laughing Dove. Laurel Pigon, Houbara Busterd, Guinea, Turaco, Black-Throated Coucal, Blue Malkoha, Pied Cukoo, Somebre Nightjar and Pallide Swift.'

'Not this fucking list again,' said my brother.

'Stripped Flufftail,' I whispered, 'Corn-Krake, Red Knobbed Coot, Nkulengu Rail, Ballious Krake, the Sheathbills, the Thick-Knees, the Plovers, Stilts and Avocets.'

'You've learned the list, Ode?'

'I like lists, Brother, it is fun to learn and remember things.'

'No it is not, Ode. Fun is fighting and chasing girls.'

'Shh,' said my mother.

'Sorry Mother, but does he not know of any other story?'

'The story of the fall is corrected by the story of the change and celebrates the majesty of your father and your grandfather. Does that bore you?'

'No, sorry.'

'All of mankind appeared that day to fight,' spoke the Griot, 'Animals, armed with horn and claw, with tooth and speed, with paws and weight, fleet footed to confuse the chase.

'They had number, and strength and speed, but the very thing that they had gone to war to protest was the weapon that they then had to face.'

'This is the better part of the story,' said my brother, 'even though I *have* heard it a hundred times before.'

And so the Griot continued with many gruesome details that my brother did enjoy. The slaughter of the beasts did not appeal to me. I never spoke of it for fear of being branded for my sensitivity.

'It was utter slaughter. Of the thousands of each species only two of each were left alive, one male and one female and they turned their backs on man forever. The contract destroyed. Man was to be avoided and ignored from that day forth.

'A hermit was sitting at his campfire talking to his hunting dog. Between them they were discussing rabbits, when all of a sudden the dog's contented whines and growls became unintelligible to him. And when he asked of his friend, what the matter was, the dog picked up his ears and looked confused.'

My brother leant over to whisper in my ear.

'What I never understood, Ode, is, did the dog chose to no longer speak to his master or did it just happen?'

'In the story Brother, nature is a single entity, multifaceted but indivisible. And every part of it manifests the nature of the whole. But the end of their communication is also metaphor.'

'Well that fucking clears it up, Ode. Hey if there's ever something else I don't understand, I know who to ask. If you understand this shit, then maybe you should talk it.'

'Be quiet both of you,' said my mother, 'show some respect, or I will have you both standing outside the house without your pants on.'

One of the girls overheard and giggled.

My brother was, I think, quite willing to be stood naked outside his house, as long as the girls would look, as he knew they would. He was at that time quite obsessed with his pubic hair and one evening asked for our comparison. Shit, Ode, your cock is bigger than mine. Shame you will never use it. He didn't mean to be cruel.

'Only one animal came out of the slaughter undeterred,' said the Griot. 'To small, too fast, too dangerous. The Mosquito. It survived and spent a thousand lifetimes feasting on the blood of man.

'Countless generations passed. We, the Kikuyo became weaker over time. Until one day, the rhinoceros like an emissary, from the kingdom of the beasts made new contact. He knelt before the son of the Chief Elder of our tribe and everything changed from that day forth. And that is not my story, it is yours!'

We were all on our feet hollering. Even my bored brother.

My mother began to sing and her entourage swayed and harmonised beside her. And in due respect, the Griot let her finish her song before continuing.

'Some people wondered, was the change particular to the rhinoceros? Might the other animals come to our service? Could they also come across the divide of consciousness and present themselves as willing partners in our quest?

'Sages studied other species, they lay in rivers and talked to fish. One man married a goat.'

My father led the laughter.

'Ode,' said the girl beside me, 'maybe that is what you should do.'

'Hey,' said my brother. 'Shut the fuck up bitch!'

'I was only joking,' said the girl and burst into tears. 'Sorry, Ode.'

I mouthed an obscenity at her. But it didn't make me any feel any better.

'People looked to the sky and read signs in bird migrations. Were the flocking shapes they made above us, messages, portends? Instructions even?

'There was no evidence and after a period of great excitability, it became clear that the rhinoceros was our only partner. All the other beasts and birds continued with their lives as if we did not exist. Did this discourage us? It did not. For we had been chosen.'

The water bubbled in the central square. It was the quiet time of day with the sun at its highest, itching to punish you. The Griot was resting under a tree and hoping to hear the sound of his son's voice in the tinkling water.

I went to sit before him on my knees.

'Ah, it is Ode, the blessing,' he said opening one eye.

I frowned.

There was a gourd beside him, with a leather stopper.

'Cassava juice?' I asked.

'The bitter kind. It gives me comfort. To have it there beside me and to say, I will not drink this for another day.'

'To drink that knowingly and die would be a sin against our traditions.'

'Then don't mention it. What can I do for you, Ode? Speak.'

'I want to be what you are.'

'And how old are you now, Ode?'

'Old enough to know what I want to do with my life sir. I know that the Griot always passes on his role to his son and ...'

I became embarrassed and couldn't speak further.

'Yes my son died nearly three weeks ago. It is a terrible thing for any father to lose a son. For a Griot it is worse. I have lost *my* blessing and I fear that my stories will die also.'

'Could you not train *me*?'

'You know that I could not. You are not my son and you would make a poor substitute.'

'I am the son of the Chief Elder, how can you say that to my face!'

I could feel the tears waiting, impatient. The rise of anger. And so I turned my back and quickly walked away, bumping into a servant girl who was carrying water in an earthenware jug that fell to earth and shattered.

'Are you going to insult me as well?' I screamed. 'Are you? Look at me.'

But of course the servant caste never did look at our faces, and they never spoke to our eyes. And yet despite her lower caste she was quite beautiful.

I thought to command her, take my hand and walk with me. And what a sight that would have been, with me overjoyed to have tender fingers wriggling against my palm, and the poor girl in tears.

And only later did I find out that she was beaten for the loss of the water jug. When I could easily have delivered her a thousand replacements.

'You are back, Ode. You see I am still alive. This gourd of bitter juice still stoppered beside me. I am sitting here caressed by the sounds of the water from the well, my old skin warmed by the mid-morning sun and all I can think of is clutching my boy again. But I know I will not be welcomed into the afterlife if I poison myself, because that will be seen as cowardice. And yet I cannot go into battle with the Wollof and be slaughtered because I am a Griot and not a warrior. So I will have to live many years beyond my desire to do so.'

'Then teach me sir, if you have time on your hands.'

'You know it cannot be so. Ode, we have had this conversation.'

'I will never be a warrior and now I am nothing. I wander the village, I walk in circles. I am not the blessing my father tries to comfort me by saying that I am. I am without use. Why can you not find it in your heart to help me?'

I could hear the whine and sulk in my own voice. I could feel the childish wetness around my eyes. I feigned the presence of dust about my face. Some unwelcome breeze coming along to taunt me.

'Did you not listen last time we spoke of this?'

'I will talk to my father,' I said. 'I will talk to my father and then you will have to do what I ask.'

'Do I? What if your father punishes me for not following his command? Might I not die of that pain and punishment? Would that not send me to my boy and all that I desire. You have no leverage over me child. There is nothing you can make me do. Go to your father, whinge and plead. But tell him straight that I will not do this, whatever anyone threatens me with. The job of Griot was to fall to my son and my son is dead and therefore, the position of our Griot is dead and cannot be replaced.'

'Who shall remember the Kikuyo's stories if not you?'

'I do not care, Ode. I am beyond it. Let the women remember in their prattle. Let the men remember in their boasting. Let the children play act out what they remember of our history, let them kick up dust. Me, I shall sit in the sun and hope for death.'

'And our tribe's stories die out with you.'

'Ode, your whining is irritating me. Fuck off before I slap your skinny arse.'

'My father would kill you for such an affront.'

'Good,' he screamed at me and stumbling to his feet raised his hand, not at my arse but at my face.

The servant girl I had bumped into a few days before made a goat like sound, put down the new jug she was carrying, and went to him. She put her hand on his raised arm. He looked at her and she returned his glance. A thing I had never seen before between the castes. But then the Griot was a caste of his own. A caste of one. Unique.

That morning in my priapic arrogance, I entertained the thought of taking a lower caste girl as my unwilling servant. And waking with an impatient prick, I spat on my fingers and rubbed myself to increase my pride. I went into the kitchen of our house quite naked. Two servant girls in their early twenties were preparing our morning meal. They were sleepy and giggly but they froze when they saw me naked before them.

And I knew I had done wrong.

I returned to my room and fucked my one good hand. Coming quite profusely, I rubbed the cream into my withered other arm as if the seed might make it grow well again.

'You are back again? Have I not already told you to fuck off? What fouler language do I need to speak to be rid of your insistence?'

'My father says persistence is a virtue.'

'So you have spoken to your father? And am I to be ordered to do that which is against my will?'

'No. Out of respect. I did not want you commanded to educate me. Or punished for refusing to do so. You are already pained, and I do not wish to increase your burden.'

'Do not patronise me, kid.'

'I wish the opposite. I want you to want to train me because you find it in your heart to do so. Because you find some worth in me. Do you find me unworthy because of my deformity? Maybe if we worked together we might make each other's lives a little more worth living. For we are both lost and lonely souls…'

'Ode, enough, that is very respectful and caring in a young boy. Even my own dead son would not have been so thoughtful of my feelings. I loved my boy more than my own flesh, but he had a mouth about him. He had the notion that he would be better served with a blade than a tale.'

'And I am desperate for story and useless with a blade.'

'Be careful boy not to put yourself above my son. I will not tolerate that.'

'Master, should we argue often if I were to become your student?'

'I would not be unhappy to do that. My mind needs occupation and if you can stir me then do so. I was talking to Irin, the servant girl.'

'What?'

'You are blinking, Ode? She has a name. I spoke to her about you.'

'You talked about *me*? The son of the Chief of our tribe. With a servant girl!'

'Why does that offend you? I saw your face when you knocked the water jug from her hands. You with a hairless chin and yet you still wanted to shag her. You saw beyond her caste.'

'Sir, I entertained no such thoughts.'

'Ode, if you are to be a Griot you will have to learn to be a much better liar than that.'

At which he smiled.

'I spoke with her and she said happiness is not always to be found resting beside your pillow. Sometimes it is lying under the soles of your feet. I cannot bring my boy back and I cannot die without disgrace.

'Ode, if we agree on this you will have to work every hour of every day on that which I teach you. Your training will be as hard and unrelenting as for those warrior boys. I will push you so hard, there will be times when you will want to kill me.'

I laughed.

'I will never kill anyone.'

'Ode, that is not a thing to be ashamed of.'

He took my hands in his.

35

'Ode, thank you for this chance. But you will never be able to replace my boy. With all respect I will never be able to love you as I did my son. But yes, Ode, it would give me the greatest happiness. And if by mistake I ever call you by his name, you will forgive me.'

I nodded.

'They amassed an army on the great plains of Suskina Frana,' I said, 'some hundred miles south of this land. One thousand Elephant, rhinoceri, Mastodon, Xerus, Veildebest, Giraffe, Baboon, Cheeta, Hog, Wild Dog, Jakel, Impela, even a swarming mass of tiny Klipspringer, Lyon, Porcupina, Sable Bull, Nyala, Topi. In the air, with sharpened stones in their claws, clouds and swarms of Quelea-Quelea and Vanga. The Stock Dove and the Laughing Dove. Laurel Pigon, Houbara Busterd, Guinea, Turaco, Black-Throated Coucal, Blue Malkoha, Pied Cukoo, Somebre Nightjar and Pallide Swift. Stripped Flufftail, Corn-Krake, Red Knobbed Coot, Nkulengu Rail, Ballious Krake, the Sheathbills, the Thick-Knees, the Plovers, Stilts and Avocets.'

My father was stitching a long wound in my brother's shoulder. He had been hurt in training. My father trained his warriors hard. A splitting of the flesh or a breaking of a bone was part of their education.

'Father, I have a favour to ask of you.'

I told him what had passed between myself and the Griot.

'If you are seeking my permission, Ode, you have it. I have never wished to hold you back.'

'Thank you, Father.'

'I can see some pattern in this I had not clearly considered before. Each of my sons have their own and differing destinies. Maybe you will find a time when the two of them are complimentary. In a few years your brother will soon be joining me in the conquest of the white man. We will have many tales to tell upon our return, but not the skills to tell them well. That job shall fall to you.'

'Should I not come with you then and see things at first hand?'

My brother cried out in pain.

'Quieten yourself boy. Eat your pain in silence.'

'Sorry, Father.'

'The first enemy a man must conquer,' I said grandly. 'Is the enemy of his own weakness.'

My father laughed and my brother huffed though the pain.

36

'Is that well said?' I asked.

'Ode, you are not the one bleeding,' said my brother. 'Words are easy.'

'Yes, Ode, it is well said,' spoke my father. 'You are becoming a Griot already and you have yet to start your studies.'

'So, Father, shall I come along to bear witness to our great adventure?'

'We will talk of that later, Ode.'

I was told to visit the Griot at sunrise. We sat opposite each other in the dim light, our knees touching.

'Ah, here comes the beautiful young girl that brings my breakfast each day.'

The girl entered quickly, laid the food before us and went to sit in the shadows. Not Irin, whose water jug I had broken, not by her height.

'Minds, like bodies must be fed to function at their best.'

'Sir …'

'Shh, Ode. We eat in silence.'

I wanted to say that I knew him as the Griot, but I did not know his family or his given name. I wanted to say that I thought my father the most wonderful of men, and who could challenge that? That I loved my father beyond all limits of culture and imagination, but that I wanted to prove myself worthy of his love and trust. I had been born a disappointment, but by application I could redeem myself.

We drank clean water and ate blood cakes with balls of pounded cassava and offal. We ate in silence, with the Griot looking right into my face with the greatest concentration.

I would rather have looked at the girl who waited to take the empty bowls away, but I knew this was my first test. Could I be expected to concentrate? Could I do what I was told without being distracted? Or would I fidget and become bored like the child I was? Many of us were wives and husbands at thirteen, fourteen. I did not have long to leave all childish things behind me.

I was determined not to fail, not to be thought of as an un-disciplined brat.

At last he spoke.

'To be a storyteller, you will need a keen eye. That girl who brought us food. She sits in the shadows and cannot be seen. Describe her.'

'I only caught a fleeting glance.'

'You are finding excuses, Ode. You had more than enough time. Think. Half a second should be enough to remember a beautiful girl.'

And so I took him at his word.

'She is beautiful, tall, slender. She wears a magenta skirt, a green shawl. She has risen even earlier than me this day to paint her face. She loves to be looked at and so she paints her mouth blue, she wears suns on her cheeks, orange circles with yellow dots surrounding them.'

The girl who was still stood in the shade and quite invisible to me began to laugh.

'Step forward Mwanda,' the Griot said.

She had no paint on her face. Her clothes were of an entirely different colour to my description. And she wasn't a girl. She was a grandmother. I felt sickened. Had I insulted her?

But then I looked at their faces. This was a game that they were happy with. I gathered my courage.

'I may have spoken in error in some ways, but I told the truth in the most important aspect. This woman is beautiful, as all women are in their souls.'

The woman and the Griot clapped their hands in delight.

'To tell a story, you must first believe it to be true yourself.'

'Even though you know it is of your own invention?'

'Yes, only when you have fooled yourself, can you fool others.'

'Our aim is to mislead?'

'Our aim is to make the audience believe the story to be true. For that is what they desire of us. That is the role of the storyteller. To provide a service. We are not attempting to cheat their minds. And if the story is well told, they will be entertained. And if they are entertained they will be enchanted. And if they are enchanted, they will remember. And if they *all* remember, then they will become one in thought and vision. And our race, our culture and our tribe will flourish. Such is the power of words that they can outweigh a thousand swords.

'And you must *see* the things you speak of. They must be visions as exquisite in their detail, and as clear in form, as the perfectly real and foul world before your blinking eyes. Then you place your listeners inside the world you have created.'

'Might they not complain?'

'Only if your skill is crude. You place them where you want them to stand, but you make them feel that it was their choice to arrive there. You make them believe that they are participants. That they are an essential component of the story. The daring deeds that you relate could not have happened without them. You make your listener a character in the story that you have created.

'You are only a boy. I should not expect you to understand such things yet. My son was fourteen when he died. Maybe I am going too fast for you.'

'The true storyteller disappears from his own words and the true listener steps up to take his role in the tale,' I said.

'Yes Ode, yes. Ode, come with me, I want you to watch how the other boy's fight. I want you to find the perfect phrase to describe each of their strikes and lunges.'

'I want to go with them on the conquest.'

'But you cannot, Ode. Your father spoke to me and asked me not to encourage you in such thoughts. I think he feared I might.'

'My father should have told me this himself. It is not right I hear it from you.'

'I am not your father, Ode, but I am your Master. You are not my son, but you are my Ward. No, Ode, your father cannot take you with him.'

'Because I am a deformity?'

'Your father cannot take you into a war because you cannot fight. You must know that, Ode. He would have to assign you a permanent guardian. No, you will stay with me and learn, and await their return. Ode, I have made a commitment to you and you must make an equal commitment to me.'

My shoulders slumped.

'I know. A warrior who had trained for ten years to fight would be insulted to be nothing more than my wet nurse. I am not stupid.'

'No Ode, you are not. You may be the smartest one amongst us, but you cannot protect yourself.'

Despite my jealousy, despite my overwhelming desire to be one of them and not one of me, the training ground was a glorious sight that thrilled me beyond measure.

There were more boys and beasts than I could count or estimate.

Many military dances had been devised and perfected. When I have looked into the sky and seen a flock of birds whirling and swooping, I have often wondered why and how, in their elaborate choreography and at that speed, they maintain their distance from one another and do not collide?

And as are the birds, so were the Warrior-Beasts. A perfect distance maintained between them at all times. A technique practiced with such dedication that it looked instinctive.

My mother had designed the leather saddles that strapped under the belly of the rhino. The seat itself was ridged at the rear so as to provide support for the small of the back and raised in front so that the rider spread his legs around the shoulder of the beast and gripped it firmly with his thighs. On either side of the saddle hung a form of stirrup. Unlike the Yurop stirrup that I had seen illustrated in my father's book, which was a sort of hoop, what my mother had designed more resembled a knee high and laced boot that literally tied the rider to his charge. There was no way to quickly dismount. Beast and rider were one.

Lashed to the backbone of the implacable rhino and encased in the cured and supple skin of the Giraffe, each warrior was an object of utter beauty. If I had been a girl, I would have flung my skirt from me and run around naked and wailing with joy.

The leather armour was sublime. The hides were soaked, cured and sun bathed for weeks. They were immersed in clear water and pummelled with round stones. And then hand oiled each day for a month until they achieved the most extraordinary resilience and suppleness. The giraffe hides, were ventilated by countless holes bored with the end of a sharp bone. Our warrior's armour was made from a triple layer of this soft skin, And although a well-landed and direct strike from a spear could leave a bruise or in some cases a livid splitting of the skin from the impact, the armour could not be pierced. This was discovered in training. It was a mark of honour to volunteer to be assaulted.

The warrior's armour was a second skin. Brown markings over ochre, the natural and differing shades and pattern of the giraffes themselves. Our warriors were man shaped, but animal skinned.

The hides hugged the upper body, graced the stomach and groin, and covered the forward part of the thigh and leg, making for great mobility.

The helmet was like a hood, from the top of the head reaching down to the shoulder, creating a protective cawl around the neck like a lizard.

The rhinoceros despite their thick and leathery skin wore the giraffe armour also. The outline between man and beast became no outline at all.

Fake riders and horses fashioned from twigs by the servants were set in lines, with bitter cassava heads, and endlessly sliced by our forces. We had no experience of metallurgy at that time. Our spears were fashioned from Palawnia wood, with slices of sharpened flint set and lashed into the tip. Lighter than a Yurop lance and very much cheaper and easier to produce, what might have seemed to outsiders as a crude instrument, were whip fast, brutally efficient, and if broken could be refashioned within moments.

'Do you want to come home with me, Ode? Shall we have some food together?'

'No Master, I cannot drag myself away from this spectacle.'

'Then I will have something sent out to you. And some water, your lips are dry.'

'Maybe they will let me eat with them.'

'I will have something sent to you.'

I waved at my brother but he was too concentrated in a complex physical manoeuvre to take heed of my felicity.

Turning at speed one Beast caught his paw in the open warren of a Rock Hyrax and toppling crashed on his side, crushing the leg of his rider. The Beast was righted, the moaning boy unlaced and carried home.

The servants unlaced the boots of the other warriors so that they could dismount. They poured under a tent of leaves, they settled down to goat kid curry, giraffe steaks and syrah wine.

Irin turned up with a pot of cold stew for me, a jug of water.

'My Master's food is not too good,' she said very quietly. 'He is poor.'

'Would you like to join me?' I asked her.

She stared at me. I pointed at the pot. She sat beside me and dug her fingers in, grabbing bony chunks of meat. I let her eat it all. Then she stood and took the pot away without a word.

'It was nice to sit beside you,' I said.

Later that day, the boy whose leg was crushed and the Beast that had fallen, were both set upon a pyre and burned side by side.

That night I told my father that we had to pay my Master each day in fine food. And my father was surprised to hear that we did not already do that. Neglect is sometimes merely forgetfulness.

Irin swallowed when I went into the kitchen of my Master's house. I spoke very quietly.

'Food from my father. May it please you both.'

A giraffe leg from hoof to thigh. She took it from me and held it as if she would quite like to find herself betrothed to such a prize.

I returned to my Master.

'For you.'

He uncorked the flagon. And poured himself a draft.

'Son, this wine is better than anything I have tasted before. It is a present from your father I presume.'

'I stole it. So it is in effect a present from me.'

'You have taken to stealing from your father? I would not want to be blamed for this change in your behaviour.'

'I am still aggrieved that he told you to discourage my courage.'

'A nice rhythm, Ode, but a poor feeling. I am drinking wine stolen from the Chief Elder. Ode, he would have my tongue cut out if he knew.'

'But he will never know.'

'I didn't take you for a thief.'

'I didn't take my father for someone who would let another give me the bad news that I was not welcome on the adventure.'

'Ode, there is something wrong with your gaze. Your eyes give you away. You are lying. You are not a thief at all. You are an honest boy.

'I am lying. He gave it to me to give to you. I spoke on your behalf.'

'When you make things up, always look straight at your audience. To a storyteller the semblance of truth is more important than the truth itself.'

'Why do Griots not write their stories down?'

'What? On paper, on skin? Do you think we should use squiggles of ink like the Arabs do?'

'Would it not be easier?'

'Why are you so fond of ease? And in any case I cannot read.'

'Could you not learn?'

'We have no written language of our own. You know that.'

'Maybe one day we will.'

'I would not like my stories written down, with fancy lines of black snakes squirming across the surface of paper or skin. They would cease to be mine, and anyone that could read could steal them from me. No, if you think this way you have not understood the way of the Griot. You have annoyed me now. Go home to your father.'

'Shall I come back tomorrow?'

'We will see.'

'Might I venture,' I said as carefully as stepping on feathers, 'that last night you dreamed of your beloved boy.'

He looked at me as if he wanted to kill me. I stepped back, so aware that I had gone too far. Aware that my arrogance and pretentions sometimes took me to places that infuriated others.

And then he began to cry.

'Yes Ode, I did. How did you know? Were you there to watch me? I did not notice you if you were.'

We had eaten. Giraffe flesh, slow cooked in berries, ash and black pepper. To aid in our digestion we went for a walk around the exterior wall of the city. It was the first time I had left the interior of the city without a bored warrior walking paces behind me as my protector. Watching out for the cripple. It is an honour to serve our Chief Elder in any of his whims. But it is not a thing to talk about over the camp fire and a good piss up.

The Griot held an umbrella of dried ferns above us both. Our shadows moved before us. My shadow hands were flitting like birds. Yet I was sure that my real hands stood still, dutifully hanging at my sides.

'In the world of the storyteller, the warrior must be exalted above all other men. It is the Griot's job, his vocation.'

'Then I shall aspire to that status and by assiduous graft become that which you describe. You will be proud of me, and so shall my father and my tribe. Master, you are showing me my future. And this is a great relief, for I feared I would die of loneliness and of my lack of usefulness. Unloved, forgotten. But by remembering the deeds of war, I will be remembered myself as the rememberer.

'I shall use words to make our warriors respected as the greatest men that have ever lived. I shall say to my brother, you have made yourself a great man, but I, Ode, who cannot even work a spear, shall make you even greater.'

'Will you not do the same for your father?'

'Yes. But I could not *tell* him that I strove to improve him. No. It would be an impertinence.'

'But then again what is a warrior?' said my guide flicking a stone that had lodged in his leather sandal. 'A man with a weapon that goes to another village and instead of offering brotherhood, kills others just like himself, rapes their sisters, and bonds and shackles those fit enough to fight to be worked to death or sold.'

'I do not understand. You say it is the role of the Griot to praise the warrior caste. And then you find fault in their dedication and their honour? In saying such things, you defame my father and my brother. I may be your student, but that cannot be allowed to stand.'

'So will you have me punished, Ode?'

I looked at his face and he was enjoying a private smile.

'Master. Are you testing me? Are you looking for weakness in my heart? Or a lack of resolve in my mind?'

'Ode, we may say, there was a great victory that day, but we must also remember that many of our brothers were left for carrion upon the ground. Many women would never hear their sons call them Mother again.

'Stories are models for life but they must also be entertainments. We have our adventure stories, but we also have our stories of instruction. These I read to children and you will learn to do the same. You remember Andede?'

'Yes.'

'Do you remember the story of Andede and the wild dog?'

'Yes, master.'

We were sat in my room, the sun driving through the sky-light and making a shimmering square on the wall. My master always asked for two cushions to sit upon. He complained that he was born with a skinny arse. He had a fragment of Kola nut stuck between his front teeth.

'Andede found a wild dog,' my Master began, 'the dog had broken its leg and in compassion Andede made a splint from twigs and vines and a compress made from mud and the animal limped away gratefully.

'Some months later when Andede was at the river gathering water he felt a presence behind him. He turned on his haunches to espy a gang of wild hunting dogs. The animal he had saved was amongst them, fully recovered now. They were hungry. Andede was small and sweet. They sniffed the smell of his young body and approached with salivation.

'I saved your life,' Andede said to the one creature that he knew. 'Why do you come for me like this. Tell your brothers that we are friends.'

'We were friends when we were alone,' said the dog, 'Now I am part of the pack and I must come at you as the other's do. This is my tribe, my clan, my family. I cannot go against such things. Go into the water before we eat you. And they chased Andede into the water and he drowned.'

'But Andede appears in other stories?'

'Andede lives and dies many times, Ode. The Griot can raise the dead, we have the power of life and death.'

'Ode, Now it is your turn to tell me a story. You know the story of Andede and the lion? You have heard it enough times in the past, let us see your art of recall and your verbal skills.'

'The was a boy, Andede, and one day when he was playing at the outskirts of his village, he found a lion cub. The cub's foot was trapped in a space between hard rocks, and Andede eased the foot from the trap and the cub began to roll around on its back and showed Andede its belly.

'You must be hungry, said the boy and the cub licked its nose. Andede went back to his village and found some bones which he brought back for the lion cub.

'But his mother saw him take the bones and wondered what he was doing so she followed him. And when she came to the edge of the village, she saw her son feeding the lion cub and rubbing its belly.

'Andede, she said, you must not do this. This is a lion and lions like to come into our village at night and eat our children. You must kill it Andede. She handed her son a knife.

'Take the cub over to those trees and slit its throat, Andede,' she said. 'And bring me back its heart to show me that you have done what you have been told.

'But Andede and the lion cub were good friends now and he could not do it.

'I cannot kill you lion cub,' he said, 'you are innocent of all blame against my people. You run and be safe. And the cub ran away.

'Andede found a young buck and killed that and took back its heart to present to his mother.

'But six months later, the lion cub came back to the village now fully grown and entered the bedroom of Andede's new-born brother.

'Lion, it is I,' said Andede intervening, 'I saved you as a cub. You must remember me. You must not hurt my brother. The lion took no notice of Andede and grabbed the baby between his jaws and took it away. And Andede was so ashamed of himself he threw himself into the well and drowned.'

'And what does the story tell us about how we should live our lives?'

'I do not know.'

'Think.'

'Kill something when it is weak when you know you will not be able to kill it when it is strong?'

'Yes.'

'That seems cruel.'

'Then go home and cry, Ode.'

45

He looked at the empty bowl of Kola nuts.

'Ode, is there anything more to eat?'

'There is liver and wild onion stew. Would you like a portion of that?'

'Yes. Please. And bring another portion that I might send to the afterlife for my boy. I do not know if he is being looked after properly.'

With purple and greasy lips my master continued with my education.

'It is not the job of the Griot to make their audience comfortable. Any idiot can do that. Any women knows how simple it is to make a man happy.

'And more than that, Ode. The moral of the story of Andede and the Lion cub, is to have the courage to kill something when it is still *innocent*. That is the harder lesson to learn. For one day it will be strong and if it is your enemy, it may destroy you.'

'Griot. I am curious about Andede. He is always drowning and yet he never seems to learn. Or die. He keeps coming back. And that is not true to life.'

I had been a fool to say such a thing to a man who had lost his boy. He began to scream and beat himself around the head. Saying over and over, I cannot live without you. When you arrived, I passed my spirit to your tiny, fragile frame. Everything I ever was, I passed onto you at the moment when you were born, and my gorgeous wife died making your miracle. I gave you everything quite willingly. And then you left me. But only after so many years of happiness and pride.

I sat silently while he composed himself.

'Andede, is what a Griot calls an Everyman,' he said. 'Andede is all of us, with our human strengths and weaknesses. And he makes the same mistakes again and again as we all do. But he never dies. Because he is story.'

'And we are flesh and blood.'

'Of course. As was my boy. There is difference but no confusion.'

'But which is more important?'

'Neither. Flesh cannot live without fiction. And fiction cannot live without the idea of flesh. This is the education you are embarking on.'

Yet I knew without equivocation that he would have given up a lifetime of stories for one hug from his son returned to life for the briefest moment of time.

All games and props of make believe, are rigorously expunged from the lives of boys, when they turn four and begin to train as warriors. And yet there was I with pubes and dreams, being presented with a set of dolls! My first feeling was of offence, but then I had to pause and take stock. It is easy to react, yet much harder to ponder.

'Ode, do you know why I have offered these to you?'

'I think I am not to take these things as simple playthings or baubles. You have not presented me with toys.'

'Exactly, Ode. They are not toys. They are objects in the form of humans. Think of yourself as a God directing their lives and loves, their deeds and failures.'

One stern looking figure held a shield and spear.

'Ahahil was a great warrior, he was an expert at war,' I said placing him before me.

'And tell me his story.'

'Let me think.'

'What is missing?'

'His enemy.'

'Yes.'

'Ahahil had a great enemy,' I said.

'Of course, Ode. Without an enemy, there would be no story.'

'If stories are tales of hatred. The Storyteller and the warrior are very much alike then.'

'Almost, Ode. But it is much more dangerous to be a Storyteller than a warrior!'

He laughed wildly at his own joke.

There was a page in my father's book. A drawing of a western weapon. A small spear held in a taut instrument of, I deduced, bent wood and coiled gut. The idea was I concluded to make the small spear fly. That way a man could be injured at a distance. I had already fashioned a facsimile of this instrument in miniature from a small bone and a whittled twig. I brought it to my master.

'Ahahil had a great enemy,' I said to my master, 'and he killed him with this device.'

The doll of Ahahil held the bent twig. And his enemy lay dead with the bone in his throat.

'Show this to your father,' the Griot said.

Not far from the city lay a valley that was a natural place of returning calls. My Master spoke and his voice travelled as if it had become separate and proud to be on its own. It bounced around the valley and sang back at us some time after he had closed his lips and taken a brand new and silent breath.

'Ode, try. Send your voice beyond you. And each time send it further, until it escapes you. Then learn to do the same with walls and buildings, each valley, each square, each room has its own unique way that it will talk back to you, be in command of that.'

And so I did as I was instructed and my voice became quite huge with practise. And I spoke to my arm, are you not ashamed? Hear how my voice has grown, and yet you still hang there limp. If I were not a coward of pain, I would have you removed.

I stripped, dressed myself in mud, and hid in a bush.

My master had said to me.

'Ode, learn to imitate the animals, their calls, their yammering. Imitation will bring perfection to your tongue.'

I waited for hours before I saw the cat, returning to sleep under its favourite tree.

'This is the sound,' I said to three girls later, 'this is the sound of a cheetah's purr as it sleeps.'

They had never heard a cat so close. They were beguiled.

'How did you get near, Ode? They smell us and run.'

They were happy to laugh at my impression. But they didn't want to go out with me. But it was a pleasant moment in my childhood. And Mkelle patted me on my head.

'Ode,' she said, 'you should wash. You are covered in mud and you smell of big cat piss.'

My Uncle Luxxor had an obsession about crossing into Wollof territory as a scout.

He was frequently injured. And only appeared in our house when he needed repair. My mother would sew him up, my mother would set the sling if he had broken a bone. He never made any mention of his pain. Instead he blabbered excitedly about what he had found.

'Beyond the trees, remember I mentioned a patch of black mangrove, beyond that there is a river. From my calculations it travels from south to north. This is a very important discovery, the water is calm. So it is navigable. I took a Wollof boy that had come to get fresh water and made him talk to me.'

Which of course was not the truth, because our tribes shared no words.

'I got him to draw the shape of the river for me. How far north I pointed, and he drew a great long line.'

Luxxor was my father's elder brother and so he did not question this information, but I could see his face. And so could Luxxor.

'You think he might have been lying? I had already cut one of the tendons in his heel. He knew that I would kill him if I suspected a lie.'

'Luxxor, you killed him anyway,' said my father.

It was not a criticism. It was the way of life. I did not take time to be appalled. I loved my father. I held my uncle in the deepest respect. The Wollof were cunts. I had never heard anything to the contrary.

'Of course. I did not want any of them to know that I had travelled so far into their territory. I had to cover my path. I shall go back there again. It is important work.'

'You will need to heal first,' said my mother.

'Ah, why is flesh so slow?' said Luxxor.

'Uncle,' I said, 'do you never feel pain?'

'Ode, pain is irrelevant. It is only a sensation. You are a great thinker and so you obsess about pain. I am not a thinker. I do not think of my flesh. I think of what lies beyond these lands. Come here Ode.'

My Uncle took a blade from his belt.

'Do not worry; I will not hurt you. Ode, lay your hand in mind.'

'Don't hurt the boy,' my mother said. 'I get tired of you men bleeding all over the place.'

'Ode, when I put the blade to your palm, what are you thinking?'

'That if you press down upon the handle you will cut me and it will hurt.'

'But have I hurt you yet, Ode?'

'No.'

'So you are worrying about hurt before it has even happened to you.'

'Yes. Because I can imagine it.'

'And do you imagine, Ode, that I will hurt my nephew, here and now before my brother and his wife?'

'No, I do not think you will hurt me.'

'Yet you are sacred of something that you know will not happen. Now Ode, you take the knife and rest the tip on my palm.'

I blinked.

'Ode, do what you are told.'

I took the handle and placed the tip of the blade on the ball of this thumb.

'And how are you feeling now?'

'Scared.'

'And yet you are the one holding the knife!'

'Whoever holds the knife I am scared of it.'

'You think me brave, Ode, because I can withstand the knife. I am brave because I do not think of it. I do not even look at it. You can't take your eyes away from its point. You mind is full of imaginary blood. My mind is travelling up a river heading north from a patch of black mangrove.

'Have you finished with your sewing Brother?'

'I have.'

'And Uncle did that not hurt?'

My mother put a mug of brew before him and he raised it to his lips with the arm that had just been closed.

'It hurt very much indeed, Ode. It hurt like putting my hand in a fire and leaving it there. But I chose to ignore it and concentrate on talking with my clever nephew.'

'Show me your new found skills, Ode,' said my father.

We sat in our courtyard. My mother, my brother, three girls who followed my brother around like imprinted birds. It was dark outside and I had a candle at my side. My brother had been offered a goblet of fine cassava wine for the first time and the girls thought it very manly of him as he chucked it down his throat.

My mother smoked, and as always looked as if everything around her was exactly as it should have been. Less a look of happiness, but more an attitude of neat contentedness.

I opened the one book my father owned and settled upon a page that I had studied before with great amusement.

A rabbit pinning down a man and inserting a stick into his eye. A rabbit cutting off a man's head. A rabbit hammering a stake into a man's side.

And so I spun a tale about the killer rabbits and the rhinoceros's attempts to catch them, but none of them could, because even for the rhinoceros the rabbits were too fast.

The story ended with a pot of steaming carrots. And their greed leading them to the rim of the pot and being pushed in, thus making grievous rabbit stew.

'That, was most ridiculous, Ode,' said my brother. 'Is that what they show in their books?'

But everyone else was greatly amused.

'But why were the rabbits so angry with people that they wanted to kill them?' said one of the girls.

'Have you never heard?'

'No one talks to me much about rabbits'

And not having thought that far through the story, I said slyly.

'I will tell you that next time.'

And the girl clapped her hands.

But the next time my father asked me to read from the book, my brother wasn't there. So the girls weren't there either.

'Ode, you have read a picture,' said my father. 'You should learn to read those symbols as well.'

'The Griot says it is not the tradition to learn the writing. I do not want to offend him. But I will not go against your wishes, Father.'

'To ride the rhinoceros has not been our tradition. We must also look to innovation. I shall get you a teacher. You shall learn to read the symbols in this book. Would that give you pleasure, Ode?'

'Yes, Father, it would.'

'And you shall not only tell the stories of our impending conquest, you will write them down as well and they shall stand for all time.'

'Yes, Father, but where shall we get a teacher from?'

'It is about this time of year that the Arab comes to trade. He will teach you.'

'But, Father, he may not want to do so.

'Nothing shall stand in our way now, Ode.'

He would visit us once a year. The Wollof let him pass. The Arab bribed them for safe passage. Later I found his name to be Al-Katib al-eazim. But he was always happy to be called the Arab, in my language. Arab.

A single Arab came for our crystals.

We sat in the courtyard of our dwelling, on soft cushions of giraffe hide stuffed with the feathers of the blue buzzard. Mosaa played the good wife and fed the Arab sweetbreads and fermented wine. Bowls of scented fats burned around the room giving it a luxurious and heady smell.

Mosaa smoked her pipe and was languorous. She wore a gold and green headscarf and string of stones around her neck, looking for all the world, the queen of creation, watching her make-toys go about their business.

My father pointed to his mouth, he stuck his tongue out and wagged it, he pointed far away.

'I speak the languages of the scholars,' said the Arab. 'The Latin and the Levantine. There are many hundreds of local tongues around the world, but I do not bother myself with them. All knowledge is contained in the books that I can already read. So I know everything about the world.'

I did not understand his answer at the time. And only understood it later when we had learned to converse.

My father pointed at the book on his lap. He made a crude writing motion with his hand. He pointed at the Arabs feet. Which caused a moment's consternation. I think he feared us uncivilised. Did we cut away the feet of men who disappointed and disobeyed us?

My father's gesture was meant to convey the idea of stay. Make a home and a life here. You will be safe from your wandering. Help my son to become the man he has always dreamed of being and you will be rewarded with all I have the power to bestow upon you.

'All you can eat, each and every day, a house of your own and three wives. Arab man you are old, end your days in comfort, forget your nightmares of being robbed of your treasures. If you hesitate you must be ignorant of the delicious nature of our food, the charms of our women, the security of our villages. You will die alone on some distant path with your throat cut and your wares handled by thieves.'

The Arab understood almost none of that, but I was so keen to keep him that I performed all of my father's words in dumb-show, including a painfully childish and ill-informed attempt to describe the benefits of having three young wives.

My mother called out and three young women, bare-breasted, came to flank her.

'Father I will study every day,' I said, 'as many hours as the warriors train.'

Again I mimed want I imagined the actions were for reading and writing. The Arab smiled and nodded.

He took an instrument from his satchel and beckoned me to him. He gestured for me to kneel before him. The device was two armed and fierce. He went to measure my head with its prongs. My father pounced, plucked it from the Arab's fingers and threw it to the floor.

Mosaa restrained my father from strangling him.

'Trust him.'

'Why?'

'He is alone among our thousands, he will be dead in an instant if he crosses us.'

The Arab retrieved his device and carefully, carefully in the way that someone who does not want to die by being misunderstood is careful.

He leant towards me and placed each end of cold metal across my temple. He took my measurement and smiled.

Then he looked at the girls and ran his finger down his thick beard.

If I was a young man again! Ah! What joys!

My father dismissed the girls.

They scarpered with as much deference as they could muster.

The Arab pointed as his stomach which was now full, he pointed at his lips which were red with wine. He pointed at his sandals which were old and broken.

I would love to stay in one place and eat and drink and instruct this promising young man.

'Ode, show the man the house with the maze stalks on the lintel. I will send for a woman to be his housekeeper.'

'You are to be scholared in the written word?' said my master the Griot. 'You know how I feel about that. That is the white man's way and not ours. The white man writes only for the rich and powerful. The Griot's story is for all men no matter what their station.'

'It was my father's suggestion, I could not go against that even if I wanted to.'

'And nor can I, and yet it feels to me that I have lost a son twice over.'

I rubbed my tribal scar with the knuckle of my thumb.

'But master if I became a man schooled in the art of both the Griot and the written word, might I not become something new? Our world has changed so very much in the last decade. I would like to be part of that change also.'

There was an immense silence in that man's eyes and I wondered if I was being selfish.

'I cannot go against my father's wishes, but I could prove useless at the task and he might forget …'

'You would fail your father and yourself just to please me, Ode? Such compassion and tenderness of feeling towards me is foolish, Ode. I shall visit my son's grave today.'

We stood on the roof of the house with the maze stalks on the lintel. We had spread out a throw. We had water and wine in flagons. The Arab had his umbrella. A pot of salted groundnuts at hand. We had paper and ink and pens from his own foreign supply. I was excited beyond measure. I praised my father's decision. My mind was dancing on the roof. I saw my Griot Master walking past some streets away and below. And I called to him.

He did not hear me yet I had put much practice into my voice and my projection under his tutelage.

We sat on the throw.

My teacher pointed at the sun and then drew a circle on the page, then to the left of that circle he drew another.

'Yesterday?'

'Hesterno. Fi al'ams.'

And I drew a circle to the right of the first one.

'Cras,' said my teacher, 'ghadaan.'

He began as he would continue, to teach me the sound and script of two different languages at the same time.

I was obsessed, seduced. I was excellent. Words and writing flowed from me. The foreign languages danced on my tongue. Language unfolded in my mind, the structure of it, the rules were as clear as water rising from a well. Almost as if these foreign languages were already inside me, waiting to be brought to the surface.

My mind had been waiting for this moment.

I never forgot a word once I had learned it.

I would work on through the night copying the two very different alphabets, again and again until the muscles in my hands and fingers knew as much of writing as did my mind. My brother and myself shared a room for sleep, but he was away from the house six days of seven, tied to his Beast and in training. On the night that he came home I was not allowed to sleep in my own bed. I did not mind as such. I had my study, and my bedroll sat as comfortable among the papers as it did elsewhere.

I could hear the sounds he made.

I imagined that my parents were proud of their son's rutting grunts. And maybe less aware of the sound of my quill dancing across paper. And even if I stiffened, I knew that I could not wank with the sound of my own brother's fucking, ringing in my ears.

I soon exhausted the ink my teacher had at his disposal and it took us days of collecting and mashing berries and roots until we found an acceptable substitute for Arabican ink.

'It is a pleasant evening, Ode. I am keeping my eye on that star just over there. I have told it not to move and I am hoping that it will be obedient. Ode, does your mother not complain that you spend your evenings with me rather than at home?'

'She does not.'

'She is very understanding.'

We had achieved such ease and fluency. We might ask each other a question in Latin and speak the reply in Arabic. We might change language half way through a sentence, despite the grammatical turmoil, simply because we had a preference for the Latin or Arabic word for the impending subject. My teacher said my ability to learn was extraordinary. That is not how it felt to me. Let me explain. If you were to give a starving man a very large plate of food and he were to fall upon it, his greasy fingers dancing against his lips, you would not say, what an appetite you have! You would say, you were hungry.

'Does each language in the world have a different script like Latin and Arabic does?'

'No,' said my teacher, 'Roman and Arabic scripts are very different as your eye can see and your hand can attest. But many languages in Yurop use the Roman alphabet.'

'So they can all understand each other?'

'No, they do not understand each other at all, Ode! And although they use the same script they speak different languages.'

'Then they are foolish. And if they are foolish they will be easy to conquer. I shall tell my father this.'

'Are you to go with them?'

I did not answer him truthfully.

'In Yurop, I will make myself understood. I have many questions. I want to speak and listen and I want to read their learned texts. My father wants to take their land. My brother wants to take their gold. I want their learning.'

'Yours might be the most fateful appropriation.'

'Yes master, because when you have land you stay put. When you have gold, what can be done but to polish it? But when you have learning, you have power over ignorance.'

'And, Ode, most of this world is infected with the most dreadful ignorance. But be careful, Ode. Do not aim to have dominance over the ignorant themselves. An ignorant man is a hungry man refused bread. It is not his fault he has no wheat.

'Ode, the Latin that I am teaching you it is not the language of the common Yurop man. Only the highly educated and those that they think have been chosen by God can speak it.'

'Then those are the people I shall talk with. My father shall conquer them and I will stand beside him as his voice.'

We had eaten under our own roof. My brother soon to be home. The pot kept warm for him. I sat close to my father with the book. My mother smoked her pipe.

My father stared at an image of black men shacked around the neck and tied in a row by chains.

'What do the words say, Ode?'

'The text says, that although some religious souls may find the trade in human flesh disturbing, they must steel their more tender natures and realise that blacks are not like us. They are closer to animal than human. Their mental capabilities are awful constrained by the pitiful size of their brains. They are violent by nature and must be treated with great discipline or they will pose a terrible danger. If you own a hound, you know that you must leash and muzzle it. You might on occasion let it lounge before your fire, but you would never let it enter your bedroom, nor would you ever leave it unattended with your children.'

'This is how they really see us?'

'It says so in their book.'

'These squiggles, these letters, these words, were invented to spell that message? Ode, maybe it is better that you do not learn this language.'

'Father, you do not mean that. And I am sorry if you think I am contradicting you. But if you are faced with an enemy that has a spear, you do not abjure the spear itself.'

'No Ode. You learn to command the spear. You build it longer, you fashion the tip sharper. You dedicate more hours to controlling its swiftness. I knew it all along. We have always blamed the Wollof, because they like to sell any of us that they capture. But I just thought that was part of our thousand year argument and natural hatred. I had not realised that the Yurop man thought us so degraded. I did not know there was *philosophy* behind that. I thought that those taken had simply been unlucky.'

And then in the next chapter there was an image of heaven.

'And what is this cloudy world?' He asked of me.

'This is where the white folks go. It is a place of perfection for all eternity.'

'And yet we are to be collared and used.'

He went to grab the book from me.

'Father please, I need this. Do not take it from me. Please, with all respect.'

'But it is vile, Ode. Why would I let a child of mine look upon this shit? I was happier when you and I did not understand these words and thoughts at all.'

'Father, if I am to be part of your fight for greatness, I need to understand the contents of this book.'

And my father's anger turned to laughter.

'What is it about you, Ode, that can turn me so easily? I think I am going in one direction and you steer me otherwise with your words and sweet, kind eyes.'

'It is only through love and respect, Father, I have no desire to promote myself.'

'Keep the book, Ode. The collared hounds by the fire will rise when the master is sleeping and feast upon his balls.'

My mother who had been quiet until that time, exploded into giggles. And my father kissed me on the head as my brother entered the room and said.

'Have I missed something?'

We stood on our roof after the sun had just risen from its lair. There was a warrior in waiting in the alley below us. Sentries stood on roofs beyond us, one hundred yards, two hundred, three.

'Just make sure you don't kill anyone.'

'Of course not, Father.'

My father should have tried the bow himself, but I understood why he wanted his son to prove himself.

'Brother, do you need me to show you where to put your fingers? I have studied the illustrations.'

'No Ode. It must come natural to me if I am to find this instrument of worth.'

He released the arrow. The first sentry, flung up his hands, then the second and the third.

'None of them saw it fall,' said my father.

'Warrior, run to the sentries and tell them to double their distance. Go. And to think that was your first shot my son.'

Back in the room I called my study, stood the doll my Griot master had given me. Armed with his tiny bow of twig and arrow made of bone. Copied from a book. And now the real thing. Not made by me. But fashioned under my instruction. A bow string of giraffe gut fashioned by a butcher.

A man who had carved my parent's thrones spent four months working on the wooden bow. A secret between us.

My first mistake, Ode, you extraordinary boy, was to think of making the bow from a single piece of tree. No. There are as many layers of thin cut wood as there are fingers on my well-worn hands woven into this bow. That is the secret. That is where the flexibility comes from. That is the resilience. Not one thing, but many things together. Bonded. Ah but the glue! Inventing the glue nearly killed me. The potions I made! The headaches. The vomiting.

'I want a thousand of these made,' said my father. 'And we shall practice the excellence of this device until we can shoot like breathing.'

'Father, this device is not of my own invention, it is a copy of an illustration in the book. But with the help of a butcher and a carpenter I have brought that illustration to life. I may, if it is not too arrogant to say so, have even improved upon the Yurop design. I think I have done something that will offer our warriors an advantage.'

'You have, Ode, and I am immensely proud and grateful.'

'Then take me with you.'

'Ode, we have spoken of this before.'

'And the answer is always no.'

'Because you cannot defend yourself, Ode. I do not wish to put you in danger. I love you too much for that.'

Shit.

58

Writing, I had a book and a pen. And I found that I also had a passable ability to draw. I did not draw beauty. I drew ideas. Inventions, practical, mechanical things. Some months previous I had devised a way that I myself could shoot a bow and arrow. I had asked my mother to construct for me a harness, three straps of leather that met in a point in the centre of my chest. I showed her the sketch that I had drawn.

'What is this for, Ode?'

'It will help me Mother.

'How?

'I do not want to tell you yet. My idea might be a failure. Can you just trust me for now?'

Although we did not have the technology of smelting metal, my mother and my father had a small collection of bartered trinkets. I attached a piece of iron to the centre of the harness. I named it the finger, because that is what it was a substitute for. I hooked the bowstring to the curling hook and twisted to my left away from my one good arm that held the shaft of the bow. Thus I created great tension in the string. My inverted arm was supple enough to load an arrow and to release it I would turn my torso suddenly to my right, the string would ping from the finger and the arrow would be released.

I could shoot. By rights my aim should have been awful poor, yet it was part of my character to apply myself obsessively to any skill I wished to master. But in this case I had no master, and practiced unseen. If I failed I did not want anyone to know. If I got my Genitive and Locative cases mixed up in my Latin studies no one would have laughed at me. But if I tried to control a bow and failed, I feared there would be much amusement to be had at my expense. So I would wrap the wooden bow and a handful of arrows in a linen sheet and take it out with me into the scrub beyond the city.

I had flung aside the linen sheet and carefully placed the bowstring on the finger when a group of Wollof who had delved deep into our lands for their initiation, came upon me.

They regarded me with mockery and arrogance, these boys who wanted to return home as men by capturing one of us, or killing one of us and taking home a severed limb to prove their handiwork.

They knew immediately that I was my father's son. The cripple armed boy, the only imperfect one of his kind. They would not kill me. They would take me for ransom and demand of my father the giving up of ten of our fine warriors for my one miserable life. And my father would do so. And then rather than being ignored, I would be universally hated by my people. Ten warriors sacrificed for this specimen of myself.

I thought, let them kill me and spare my family the pain and humiliation. Not that I did not love my life. Despite my malformation, despite my loneliness and general rejection, I still clung to each and every day.

Many times I have sat under the dark sky perched on my haunches, and asked myself the inevitable question. Would I have wished things otherwise? Would I have wished myself whole? And although in many respects the answer would be yes. I would have liked two strong arms to hold a girl of my tribe and whisper in her ear. I would have liked friends.

But if I had been born different, I would not have been a more perfect version of myself, I would have been another person entirely, with no knowledge of the original that I knew myself to be.

Can one wish that one had not been born? No. Because only those that have been born can make any wish at all.

I knew I could not defeat them, they were five and healthy. But I thought that if I could hurt just one of them, they would be duty and honour bound to kill me and not carry me away for ransom. So I twisted my torso to the left, keeping my right arm straight out and to the right. My feet firmly square, as the boys pissed themselves laughing at my ungainliness.

The Wollof boys were most amused by my antics, finding me utterly foolish and only when I released the arrow and took one boy right in the middle of his stomach did they desist their mocking laughter.

The boy fell to his knees moaning loudly, the others raised their spears and approached. They would kill me, but I would not bring shame on my family.

I was not scared, Anna.

I did not say you were. And I am not the sort of person to judge you on such feelings. Surely you know that of me.

Of course I do. What I am trying to express was that the feeling was deeper than fear. I almost felt exultant. As if one act could cleanse me of all the disappointment my life had brought to others.

I was never disappointed in you, Ode.

I know. And it gave me such courage and contentment to know that.

So you killed them all. All five of them, with one arm and a strange contraption?

No.

I know you didn't because you have told me this story before. Many times. Do not worry I am not bored by it.

In my confusions and surprise I could not reload. They came for me. I growled the largest voice my training had prepared me for. And they froze.

And then one by one they fell with arrows in their faces. I turned sharply.

'Ode,' my father cried, 'are you hurt?'

The boy with the arrow in his stomach was gurgling his last.

'I killed him, Father.'

'I saw. Myself and your brother were out racing, when we saw you and these scum. You shot him, Ode.'

'I did, Father. I had no choice. They would have taken me for ransom if I had not challenged them.'

'I was wrong, Ode, to say that you cannot defend yourself.'

'But, Father, I failed. You had to come to my rescue.'

'But, Ode, you tried. You with one arm against five trained warriors and yet we did not find you running or pleading. We found you on the attack. And I know, Ode. You did not want to be taken. To have had you released would have cost us many warriors. So you were willing to give your own life. That is bravery of the highest order. Ode, you may come with us on our conquest if you still wish it.'

'It is the greatest wish of my life, Father.'

My brother extended his hand and pulled me up to sit behind him.

'Father, can Ode ride with me?'

'If you both so wish.'

'Ode, you will ride with me,' said my brother. 'I will have a special saddle made and you will ride behind me and I will protect you.'

My family, they took me home. They loved me. I belonged.

We knew in advance the time of year when we would begin. For the last month before our departure, I rode with my brother, getting used to the special saddle our mother had made entirely herself, making sure that I did not in any way impede my brother's facility with his spear and bow. I was not to go into battle armed. I was to go into battle to observe, to remember. I needed to focus on the campaign, not on one individual aiming to harm me.

'Ode, I will protect you.'

We removed the leather helmets and slipped them in the saddlebag. Undid the lasses of our boot-stirrups, dismounted and sat under a tree. Flagons of water were brought to us. A thousand men drank.

'How do you think will it be Brother, our first battle against the Wollof?' I said.

'We kill them all. No argument.'

'Only the warriors should die,' I said. 'The women and children, they are innocent of any injustice we have received from their tribe.'

'Do you know the meaning of life, Ode?'

'It is a question I have often pondered. But never got near to answering.'

'Then you have not put your thoughts in proper order, Ode. It is a simple question to answer. The meaning of life is life itself. To pass on your life spirit to the next generation. If you do not do that, then your people die out, and that is a crime against the countless generations of your tribe that went before you. You must do what must be done in the present, to ensure your tribe's survival in the future. If you are plagued with guilt by the thought, that is your selfishness, because you don't want to feel the burden of guilt.

'Women are mourning widows wailing to their Gods to demand us cursed, and children are snot nosed kids already dreaming of the day they will have their revenge. Old men bring up the young to plot against us.

'We have to kill their hatred. If we kill them all, every last one, there will be no one left to even think of revenge. Their tribe would be gone for all time. The dust would cover their dwellings, the wind would blow away all fragments of their culture.'

I looked at him closely.

'That is what Uncle Luxxor says about it all. And our father agrees. All of our warriors have been instructed in the correct way to see our mission. You should not voice any other opinion on this matter in front of any of them.'

'Brother we will meet many innocents along this quest. Are we to wipe out everyone we come across? History would not take kindly towards us if we did.'

'Our father says we should deal with the Yurops according to their behaviour. Meet respect with respect, disrespect with disrespect, force with force, fear with fear. And the Wollof have never shown us anything but blood-hatred and we shall repay them in kind. Kill them all. No argument, Ode.'

'We are strong. Are we not? We are stronger than our enemies. Therefore we can afford to show compassion.'

I could not bear the idea of killing a woman or a child. Even if it was a logical tactic for the future success of our own people.

'Ode, if you do not have the stomach for this, you must stay behind.'

I did not want to stay behind.

And there I saw the difference. My job as a Griot was to train myself to see the world through the eyes of others than myself. The warrior's training was to see the world through one single lens.

And guilt was an arm tied behind the back, an arrow with no bow. And yet my own infirmity moved me to compassion. But of course I had always wanted to be strong.

There was a fruit that flowered once a year, and when the bud first appeared couples prepared for marriage. No warrior would leave without leaving a wife behind. No man would leave without leaving a child in the belly of his chosen woman. And no wife would send her warrior away without a future generation within her.

'Your mother is strong and while we are gone she shall rule.'

'Father I should have left a child behind.'

'I know, Ode, I am sorry.'

My mother and my father had decided not to have another child after myself, but I wondered if they changed their mind that night. Was a new generation to be left behind to gestate? Might there be the thought of a brother or a sister in her belly.

'Ode, all the men in my life are leaving me. Have you any idea how that might feel?'

'Mother I have known loneliness myself.'

'Yes I know you have, Ode. But what I will feel will be more than loneliness. I will not simply be a woman with no one to love. I will be a woman with all the men she loves far, far away and no hope of listening to them or touching them until they return to me after years of adventure. If they do return, and don't die.'

'We are invincible Mother.'

'Nonsense, no one is invincible. Not even the Gods. I have known your father since I was a girl. He has always been there. I cannot even remember a time when he was not there beside me. I cannot remember a time when I had to wonder who to talk to. Now I will sleep alone. Now I will live in a house of silence. Now I will live in a house with no boys to discipline and wonder at.'

'And you hoped that I would stay.'

And at the thought of it I felt a pang of pride, that I might selflessly abuse my dream to bring comfort to my mother.

'I will stay if you want me to.'

'I wish you to stay as much as I wish you to go.'

'My mind and body will miss you every second that you are away from me, my husband.'

'And I will dream of you each night and lament when I wake up to find that you are not truly at my side.'

'Look after our Boys.'

'They are no less precious to me than they are to you.'

'I know. But I will not be there to look after them and you will.'

'You have my word.'

'I knew I had it before I asked.'

My mother held my father's hand in our main room. I stood in the doorway unseen. Our house was very formal. My father, whose rule over our tribe was absolute. My mother's imperiousness that brooked no contradiction. Yet on that evening, they were simply a husband and a wife. Frail, human, real, stripped of status but beautiful and powerful in their love for each other.

'What if the men see?'

'The men look to your face husband. Not to your hands.'

'They will think that I am scared.'

'They will think no such thing.'

Mosaa released her husband's hand. It shook. My father stared at that part of his own body with revulsion.

'Why has this infliction come back now of all times? It was nearly two years ago that I had my last relapse.'

'Because you are nervous and overwrought. I shall get the medicine.'

'That a fly can so effect a grown man. It is perverse.'

Malaria.

'Husband, we are blessed, we are chosen.'

'Yes, we are elect.'

I slipped quickly down the hall as my mother went to get the medicine. I did not want then to know that I had been watching.

'He cannot see you,' said Irin. 'He has taken to bed.'

'I shall be gone a long time. I owe him many things. I will be brief.'

'He cannot see you.'

'You are aware I presume of the height of my status and the lowness of your own, yet you feel free to command me.'

'The command is my Master's not mine. He has the will, I am just a voice. I beg you not to punish me. With you gone, I will be all my Master has.'

'Irin, I would not dream of punishing you. Surely you know that of me. Tell your master I am deeply in his debt. I will do all I can to honour his teachings and make myself worthy of the time he spent on my education. Tell him also that I will this day, pour a libation upon the grave of his son. And there is one other thing you can do for us all. Remember when I knocked into you and you dropped the water jug.'

She nodded.

'Your master has an earthenware bottle that he keeps beside him. Are you aware of its contents?'

She nodded again.

'Take that bottle from him and as if I were foolishly bumping into you, drop it until it cracks wide open.'

To come across a Caryx, is to come across a Beast writhing even in death, animated by maggots and mantra bugs. When they know they are about to die, they search out the long grass and lay down on their sides. The make no sound in their death throws and die as shy as they had lived.

If a Kikuyo comes across the corpse of a Caryx he will remove the horns with a sharpened flint.

The horns are spiral in form and by cutting away the very tip, the bone can be put to the lips and blown to create a sound that is part plaintive spirit and part angered child.

Since the abundance of giraffe hide, many new instruments had been invented and perfected. Drums that came to a man's waist, with the leather stretched over an earthenware body. An instrument like a small drum but with an outstretched arm of straight wood, strung with dried and woven giraffe gut.

On the day of leaving, our Arkestra sat under a roof of dried leaves.

Troupes of young girls danced a practised piece in wonderful unison, thrusting out their bums most provocatively, their arms outstretched, their hands drawing circles, the bangles on their wrists spinning faster than the eye could follow.

This was not a party. There was no wine made available. We shall not drink before battle, my father had said. We are an army of disciplined warriors, not louts on a rampage.

This was a farewell. This was man and beast off on a great adventure. This was women left behind. This was leaving home.

My father stood to make his speech.

'We go.'

Water drawn from the well. The tiny grains of black fonio thrashed from their husks with mortar and pestle. Cassava pounded with wooden spoons. Naked children trying to run faster that the sun. Boys with wooden swords. Teens with home-made arrows at practice and keeping score. Women with small lips at their breasts. Men sleeping with an unlit pipe.

And then a thunder.

The Wollof raised their chins beneath the blue sky. No, not from above. They studied their feet and the ground between their toes. The thunder was beneath them.

And then a thousand warriors on a thousand beasts descended upon their land and peoples. And in a pre-ordained plan, we split into two columns, not charging at the Wollof but encircling them.

Life is precarious. There is safety in proximity. To be too far from each other is to be open to be taken by another tribe. Wild dogs. Compactness is strength. Except when it is not. And it is not when you are surrounded and there is no one to attack your enemy from behind. Because you have been caught as one, one tribe, one destiny, one fate. Those few scouts that had patrolled the gorge had been taken at a distance by our bow and arrow with hardly a thought.

Did they even know it was us? How could they imagine it? We came from our own direction, from the gorge where it opened into their lands. But our armour favoured us as animal rather than man, and neither beast nor human had ever rode the rhino. The Wollof were faced with something beyond any nightmare that might have plagued them. We were simply not possible. Yet there we were. And all we had to do was move towards the centre of the one vast circle we had made to silence their confused thoughts forever.

For fifteen years we had kept our secret. Now it was released and unstoppable. I watched a boy hardly older than myself, impaled at speed and left hanging with the horn peeping through his shoulder as the Beast ploughed through flesh and bone and trampled underfoot those that had been disrespectful to our tribe.

I studied one young fellow staring at his pulped and ruined leg, still attached to him by flesh and the screaming lines of pain. A rhinoceros paw had disintegrated the bone. Neither their tribe nor ours had the skills of amputation that I was to later discover in Yuropa. Their poor stumbled through their lives, pocked, truncated, bald, without limbs, eyes, noses, ears. We had no truck with such things. If you were not whole, you died. Unless, like me, your father was the Chief Elder of the tribe.

Their dwellings, much less substantial than our own, fell under our paws. Despite the frailty of their homes, women still dragged their youngest inside while the eldest came at us with swords or sticks. The eldest went down, the walls went down, the Wollof were crushed. The insides of their meagre huts offered no more protection than a moment's blindness in the face of our appalling conquest.

And how did I feel? How did I fare? Of course despite the extensive training the warriors had undergone, they were all virgins of a proper fight. Training takes charge of the mind. For me, my training was story. I searched for detail amongst the melee. A scream from a toothless mouth. A corn husk doll held upright with a twig as if it was determined to stand against us. The viscera behind a man's face.

As we approached the centre, the circumference of our might drew tighter and our troops moved in tandem, crushing further those who they had already destroyed, stamping the last cries from the meat into the earth.

My father had decreed there would be no rape. But also no mercy. We did not stop for spoils. The children were to be wiped out. Kill the innocent before they have time to grow up to be your enemy.

Utter rout and then voices behind us.

Speaking the Kikuyo tongue. Members of our tribe that had been taken over the years and enslaved. Those that had not been sold on because they had neither the beauty nor the strength to make them worthy commodities, worth caravanning to the coast. They held their arms above their heads and saluted us.

You have come to save us!

There were strange inflections in their voices, as if tainted by being surrounded by the Wollof tongue.

They spoke to the back of our necks. To the tails of our beasts.

They were poor specimens that had no place in our force. But they could not be allowed to go home to our lands as free men. What of their resentment that we had taken so long to rescue them? I thought of our women, our children and a gang of resentful men roaming our city that felt that they had been let down, abandoned, and all the warriors away on a mission.

Maybe we should have said this Wollof land is now yours, enjoy it. But what would there be to stop them returning home after we had gone?

As I pondered this dilemma, Luxxor was already decapitating them one by one. Killing those that had once been our own. Death at the end of misery. A man enslaved by another tribe, ceased to be a man. And as the taken, no place of prestige in the afterlife.

'What do you think my sons?' said my father, coming up to the side of me and my brother on our Beast. 'We have left not one alive. The name of their tribe will never be heard again. No lips shall ever mouth it. But we shall be talked of forever. We can go wherever we want. No one is going to keep us in our place ever again. At last we are free.'

My tent was erected by the servants and I sat with my paper, my pen and my ink.

I thought of the faces of the women as their children were hacked and pierced. I thought of their unheeded pleadings. I thought of the screams of young girls, who expected to be raped but instead were sliced into pieces or trampled under paw. I thought of the fear in the faces of the Wollof Warriors who had always been so arrogant. I thought of the screams of men. I thought of the old men and women crawling from their blazing huts, their clothes on fire, their old flesh melting.

And then I wrote about our great victory, the skill and bravery of our men. I wrote about how we had destroyed an entire tribe and not lost a single man. The few wounds we had incurred were sewn shut before the ink dried on the page.

I stood before a thousand warriors arranged with great precision in a wide arc. They had been given dispensation to loll. They each had a jug of wine.

My voice carried my message to them all as I was trained to do. I told them the story of what they had just done that day. I reflected their actions back at them. Deeds transmuted into words, polished, abbreviated, heightened. They were heroes who had defeated their greatest enemy. They were magnificent. They were one and all, the greatest army that history had ever known. We would be the envy of the world. And we would take that world as our own. They had completed the first stage of their great conquest with astonishing bravery.

My father stood behind me.

Not one of them laughed at me or told me to fuck off.

I had written the first chapter of our history.

I won't dwell on those tedious weeks we charged pell-mell across the scrub. The beasts beyond eager beneath us, my arsehole swollen in the saddle like a plum. I lost all feelings in my legs.

None of us had ever travelled far.

The Arab pointed where we should go. He knew the route. My brother complained that he thought there should be a quicker and easier way. But he had no idea of where it might be found.

We were no more than one month north of our tribal lands when we were stricken.

Our warriors were hardened man who had endured a lifetime of physical challenge and so despite the vomiting, the thrashing headaches and the copious shitting on grass, they did not pause or falter.

For myself lacking the warriors training, I was wildly sicker than the rest, only the stirrup boots prevented me from falling off in a faint.

Where had this pestilence come from?

We were unprepared. A different tribe of mosquito? A hidden sickness in the wild fruits that we thought we knew by heart?

A curse, a deliberate poisoning by invisible forces bent on our destruction?

We began to suspect the new meats that the rhinoceros were killing for us. What is this animal? The horns are misplaced. I do not recognise this shape of hoof. The eyes are rheumy. Is its flesh forbidden by the Gods? Are we being punished for consuming something sacred?

Warriors who had sat silent while a foot long gash in their bodies was sewn closed, groaned at night. They sniffed suspiciously at the water in the lakes and rivers like worried girls.

At the end of each day the servants would erect the tents and bathe and feed the warriors. And no one noticed that the servants were themselves immune from this ill.

One night vomiting into a bowl I understood. I crawled on my hands and knees to my father's tent. He lay their sweating like a pig.

'Father, I think I know the reason for our illness.'

'Then speak, Ode.'

'It is the dried meat we have been carrying with us. Something has infected it. Curse or bug, I do not know.'

'We are eating fresh meat are we not?'

'Yes when we can, but we are also eating our dried supplies. The servants are not offered to eat the dried meat. They exist on the tubers and roots we find and they are not stricken.'

My father began to laugh.

'What we thought of as a privilege is the cause of our sickness,' he said and rolled over to vomit. 'We shall destroy all the dried meat tomorrow.'

Jettisoning our dried supplies, and eating only fresh and simple fare our army recovered quickly. Yet I fell afoul of some other curse. A fever of the mind. I simply was not strong enough for this adventure. I had not trained. I was a writer, weak and sedentary. The desire of my mind to embark on this conquest was not matched by the strength of my flesh.

I became confused. I struggled to separate geography from hallucination.

I have a memory of an incline that seemed to last for days, snow-capped mountains in the distance, impossibly fast rivers, sudden deserts. All the time I was lashed with a rope to my brother's body to keep me upright. If he complained I never heard of it.

And I have a recollection of the beginning of a long slow cruise on flat barges that had been constructed by threatened, unwilling men of coffee coloured skins and woven hair.

As I recovered, I asked my father how long I had been delirious?

'I do not count the days, Ode, what advantage would that give us? We can't control the days by counting them. They come and go without recourse to our intervention. What do we achieve in their naming?'

'As sabat, Al' ahad, A lith nayn, Ath thu la tha, Al ar ba al, Al kha mis, Al jum ah,' I said by rote.

I raised myself and went from man to man, across the barges to ask what I had missed, what had they seen.

The back of my hands, sickly yellow. The neck of my Beast. The taunting horizon. Piles of my own shit under a bush. Heat haze. Sand in the eyes. Try and make a story out of that, Ode, our Griot.

'Father did I dream it or did we come across a tribe of tiny people?

'That was no dream, Ode.'

'And they were all as tiny as children?'

'Tiny, but ferocious. We lost three men to them, they use a poison at the end of a wooden dart that they blow at people.'

My father mimed it.

'We couldn't even see them before it was too late. They waited for us when we were washing. So we didn't have our armour to protect us. Whatever was in the poison, it made a fool of the dying men, left three of ours naked and screaming. Blood pouring from their noses, shit pouring down their thighs and the others staring at them ashamed. I would have liked to have caught the little runts and roasted them.

'We took the deaths as warning and left their lands in haste. Imagine, Ode, a thousand men and beasts chased away by little people that hardly came to our hips. We captured one of them and kept him as a prize.'

'Is he alive?'

'No, to have kept it alive would have served no purpose. We filleted it, and kept its bones as proof of its stature.'

'And did we come across people who were taller than us?'

'No Ode, that did not happen, it you saw that you were dreaming in your fever.'

'They were as big as houses, they reached down and grabbed us around the waist and bit off our heads. Father, do you think that dreams are prescient?'

In the distance, across the sand, maybe a mile from our place on the river, stood a man of extraordinary height.

'It is much larger than in my dream, Father.'

'It is not moving, so therefore it is either asleep, or dead, or made of stone.'

'If it is a statue, it is either a portrayal of a very important person or it is a real representation of the giants that live around here.'

'Or lived, Ode. Maybe these giants are of the past.'

The figure became clearer as we navigated a bend in the river. He was made of stone and therefore only an effigy, unless of course there were wilder things in this world than we had expected and there were stone men, who breathed and lived in their own material way. They would be quite inviolable, and would surely have conquered the world by now if they had will and motion. And maybe they did own the world and they would stamp us out before our adventure had begun.

'The men are bored, Ode. In the saddle they have purpose and direction but sat upon this endless river their minds are turning to mud.'

Our army, men and beasts, were dispersed over a flotilla of ten wooden rafts. We sat upon the deck under a shade of woven leaf. The rhinoceros lay on their sides. The warriors lay against their bellies, maintaining the symbiotic nature of their bond even in that temporary paralysis.

The air was thick with bugs. The men who had built our rafts had given us a cream to make ourselves less tasty. We stank. It saddened me to lose the touch of my father's familiar sweet smell.

'I know all the old stories, Father, the ones that the Griot taught me, stretching back a thousand generations.'

'The warriors have heard those stories many times before, Ode. Their old history makes them sleepy.'

'But it is our tradition to repeat the adventures of the people. Repetition is the foundation of our culture.'

'Repetition was fine when we had no recourse to dream, when all we had was what we had always had, and we never thought of that ever changing. But now things have changed, Ode, and we need new stories to celebrate that change.'

'But, Father, I have so little experience of life. And I cannot even relate clearly what has happened to us these last two months.'

'Ode, you can you make things up. You have done that before.'

'Imagine a giant carriage, like a cart, but many times larger and more powerful, moving at great speed but lashed to no Beast. Whatever power facilitates its motion is quite invisible.

'It is commanded by a Prince, wonderfully powerful and rich. He sees us on our beasts and he is speechless with admiration and wonder.

'He invites us on board his craft and somehow there is room for all of us, all one thousand. It is almost as if the carriage is larger on the inside than it is on the outside.

'Beautiful dancing girls are commanded to entertain us. We are offered foods we had never eaten of before. Olives, figs, halva, delights.'

'What about our beasts?' interrupted one warrior.

'We leave them behind to graze, the Prince promises that he will return us to them.'

'No one would have the courage to try and steal them, and our beasts would never go with anyone else apart from us. Carry on with your story, Ode.'

'I see no beasts that pull your ground ship, my father asks the Prince. What is the source of its power?

'Come with us and I will show you he says. He takes my father below deck. And there are a thousand pygmies tied to various devices, wheels, pulleys, levers, they are thrashing their little arms and legs and wailing pitifully.

'The movement of their limbs creates the power to ambulate your ship?' My father says.

'No,' laughs the Prince, 'my ship is powered by their *wailing*.'

My audience were amused.

'Good.'

'Those little fuckers took three of us with their poison.'

'They are vile creatures sure,' said the Prince. 'They have neither courage nor honour. We have a medicine that makes us immune to their darts. We round them up and work them till they die, then we go back for more.'

The warriors cheered.

'And more. Another story from our travels. From pathetic small to larger than life. The stone people, we passed one of their kind down river. We all saw him. Remember? He towered over us but we were not fearful. Even faced with a stone giant, a Kikuyo Warrior stands his ground without flinching.

'Five thousand years ago they strode around the land. Their Gods had made them from the rocks that had in turn been made from the stars in the sky that had fallen to earth. But they were vain, they showed no humility to the powerful Gods that had given them life. They gave no prayers, offered no libations or sacrifices.

'They would find a lake and drink it dry in an instant. They could find a herd of a thousand goats and toss them into their mouths like groundnuts. They would have a nap on the trees of a forest that had taken hundreds of years to grow to maturity and flatten every trunk.

'These stone men and stone women when they fucked they caused the earth to heave and split and fields of bright flowers would fall into the cracks, and the

Gods said fuck this, I've had enough of these arseholes, you are ruining everything we have made with our love and tenderness! You show us no respect! You destroy everything and yet you make nothing yourself!

'Yeah and what the fuck are you going to do about it? They said leering and making signs with their stone fingers.

'We are the givers of life and motion, said the Gods. And we shall take that away from you. But we shall not dull your consciousness. You will not be able to move, to eat, to make love, to wander. You will live a fixed life, rooted to one spot but with your minds still alive to fully understand the punishment we are to inflict on you. And one day each one hundred years we will give you back your motion, and you can spend that day running, gambling, fucking, but that one fine day will be marred because you will know that at the end of that day another one hundred years of immobility faces you and with you fully conscious.'

I told each story ten times, once on each barge. And any part that didn't fascinate my listeners on first telling, I would change before the next session. I would add details, divertissements, subplots, I would insert sex and death wherever I could. I would insert the Kikuyo, always brave and fearless and essential into the plot. What had started off as ten minute tales slowly turned to one hour epics and the warriors knew that they had had been part of the creation and they thought themselves very smart indeed.

We came across a caravan and tethered the barges.

Twenty-two Arab traders.

'Luxxor, Ode, come with me.'

'What about me, Father?' Said my brother.

'You, Son, are in complete charge of our army, whilst I go and parley with these foreigners. But you can join us if you wish.'

'No, Father, I have an important job to do here. My place is with our troops.'

We cantered towards them. Myself perched behind my father for the first and only time. They stood high on their long legged beasts. We sat low upon the stocky rhino.

'You ride the rhino?' Said the trader.

'And you ride the Camel?' Said my father through my translation.

'We should race,' said Luxxor. 'It would be sport.'

'The men could use some entertainment.'

74

'Then, Brother, we shall show these Arabs what speed we have at our disposal. But first let us talk of trade. Do you have weapons for sale?'

'One hundred of the finest scimitars. Freshly forged. Worth a fortune. But do you have a fortune to pay for them? You look strong, well prepared and disciplined. But do you have money?'

'Diamonds from the Sub-Sahara.'

'Then I see no reason for us not to be the best of friends, and for this day to end with great joy on all sides. But let us race first. Sport and then business. What a time we shall have.'

A race is usually run from one fixed point to another. Yet here the land was flat and featureless. Dry, sandy soil and scrub grass.

Luxxor commanded our thousand to stand side by side, one arm's reach apart to make one long straight line. The race would begin at the first warrior and at the one thousandth.

The starting signal would be … me.

'Ode, you have a voice that carries. You will tell them when to start.'

'But in which language, Father?'

'In no language, just yell.'

At full tilt the camel and the rhino were an even match. And I thought, don't let Luxxor loose. If he is shamed in front of his men he would be enraged and unpredictable.

The trader was as hardened and proud as my uncle. Two proud men racing against each other, can easily turn from a sport into a grudge.

Towards the finish it looked as if the trader had the advantage and then at the last moment the camel slowed and Luxxor urged his Beast to find that last spurt of energy and thankfully he won.

'At one point towards the finish I thought you were going to win,' I said.

'I was.'

'Then what happened?'

'I reined in my Beast.'

'Why?'

'For the sake of profit. If you beat a man in competition before a deal he will haggle and be belligerent. If however you let him win you can raise the price of your merchandise and he will happily pay, even thinking he has taken advantage of you again. Maybe I should not have told you that boy.'

'Under no circumstances would I tell my uncle that you let him win.'

The sun was setting. The moon looked at itself in the river.

'I have used a sword before,' said Luxxor. 'Each day at sunrise there will be instruction before we ride for the day.

'Ode, go and tell the servants we will need one hundred belts made to hold our new acquisitions. We have brought enough leather with us, but they must work fast as soon as there is light. Take one sword to show them, so they know what is needed to keep them safe at our sides.'

He hung there. From a tree. Blood red. I did not know his name. He had been sent forward as a scout and we had caught up with him now. His beast had been left to rot. The horn sawed away.

I turned my back.

'Kill me Luxxor,' said the warrior. 'Please and quickly. You know me, I have taken many wounds without as much as a sigh, but this is beyond any torment I could have ever imagined.'

'Why did they do this to you?'

'They wanted to see if I was the same colour inside, so they removed my skin.'

'If we find them we will ask them the same question,' said Luxxor. 'Goodbye Brother, reside in peace with the spirits. Your courage will be remembered by the tribe for time immemorial.'

Luxxor silenced him with a single blow.

'This torture,' said my father, 'it is something we shall learn from. It will not go unanswered.'

My father raised his nose.

'That smell? What do you think it is, Ode?'

'I think it might be the sea.'

My Teacher came to us and bowed before my father and pointed towards the horizon.

'Ode, tell your father I have brought him and his men safely to the Northern shore of the continent. I have a sister that lived not far from this place. I wish to find if she still lives. It was a joy to educate you, Ode. I hope to see you again upon your return.'

Shopkeepers frantically grabbed their oranges and figs, fled indoors and pulled down the shutters. Women on balconies stepped backwards quietly into the shadows of their rooms. Grown men simply turned and fled into the tight-staired alleyways that roamed through the city. Or forced themselves into the gaps between decrepit and unwanted things.

Some braver boys ran along beside us.

Can we ride? Can we ride!

I translated for my father who told the warriors that any child that wished to ride with us could do so. A number of our men leant down and grabbed a child by the arm and swung him up to sit before him upon the rhino's neck.

By the time we arrived at the harbour we had maybe a hundred boys riding with us. We were in our full armour, but with our helmets removed they could see that we were tall humans and proud and smiling black men.

The harbour. Shouting, grunting, hauling, swearing. Sweat pouring from half naked bodies, most of them black. But not well fed bodies, not muscular, but full of sinew. Bodies worked to the last of their strength. The black men that hauled the freight both to and fro the ships and quayside refused to look at us. We are abject, you magnificent, we are not brothers.

There was no way to save them, if we had forced their freedom with our power, they were far from home and would starve here. No one would take pity on them. And we could not take them with us.

'Dismount the children,' my father ordered. 'Let no one think we have taken them.'

The warriors picked the kids up and slung them carefully to the ground. Each child complained, but their faces betrayed the thrill they had just experienced. To ride such beasts. To be held by such men.

And then the sea. So many boats of so many shapes and sizes at its edge. I wondered if there was a book of drawings of these various designs that I might study.

'We have reached the end of the world,' my brother said.

'No, this is the body of water that separates us from Yurop.'

'Oh I know that, Ode. I mean I *know* that. But it is not what it feels like. It feels like this is the edge of the world. And I fear this water hates us. Man was meant to live on land, as birds perch in trees or glide the air.'

'That is why men have designed boats so that we can cross it.'

'I know. I am just saying the sea wants us dead. It does not want us anywhere near it.'

'Brother there is nothing to fear.'

'Ode, there is everything to fear. Do not misunderstand me. I am not scared. I am in awe and it is wonderful. Father taught me to be forever confident. Yet this water makes me feel a new emotion.'

I asked who owned the most of the ships at harbour and was given a name and address that meant nothing to me. A boy volunteered to show us if he could ride again.

Ten of us went off to find the merchant leaving the majority of our force at the quayside. Timid vendors approached them with baskets of fruit, small fried fish on sticks, sticky cakes.

He was tall, slightly more so than myself, but shorter than both my father and my brother.

'Ode, tell him we wish to speak to the man of the house. This merchant.'

His tribal marks were two diagonals on each cheek.

'The master of this house does not do business with black strangers.'

'You are a black man yourself, do you have no pride in your own skin?'

'I will have no skin at all if I let you past the gates.'

'Your life stands in the way of our plans. You forfeit that or change your mind.'

'My life does not have variety. I am not blessed with choice. My bed is poor and lonely, my food meagre. But I still have my life to love. Will you take even that from me?'

'Then let us pass. You cannot stop us. We ask this as a formality. If you stand in our way, we shall crush you. So please stand aside.'

'It is my job to say no to the uninvited. It is my only worth and commodity.'

'My uncle is getting bored.'

The man raised his sword above my head. His life ended moments into the swing and I had to move quickly aside to avoid the blade that fell from his hands.

'Is that gate unlocked, Ode?'

I tried it with my hand. The lock held but with a certain sway.

'The metal is closed, but I think the foundations weak.'

We strolled into a hallway with a white tile floor and wine red walls. At the end a double door led out into a courtyard. Luscious green. Rainbow petals. Talking water.

Birds flittered. A man appeared, walking down the stairs. He was in Arab dress.

'You have forced your way into my house uninvited,' he said. 'You show me no respect. You have not left your shoes at the door. But then what should I expect from black-skins.'

He laughed.

'And here am I talking to savages as if they understood a word.'

'I understand every word,' I said in Arabic.

His eyebrows raised.

'And what are you? A black-skin that speaks the language of the educated man. A trained monkey perhaps. Maybe you talk in the town square and people throw you small coins. Or oranges.'

'I understand everything you have just said, but choose not to translate your disrespectful words to my father who stands here. He is the Chief Elder of our tribe and used to great respect.'

'Well he will get none from me.'

'My father would happily cut out your tongue if he understood your meaning.'

'What is he saying, Ode?'

'He is annoyed that we have not taken off our shoes, Father.'

'He will be more annoyed when I press the sole of my foot onto his face.'

'Tell your blacky father that he can go fuck himself,' the Arab said. 'I will not have savages cross my threshold unless they are on their knees. You think you have me at a disadvantage? I watched you kill my guards in the street. I watched your beasts break down my gate. I watched you as you strolled up to my front door showing your teeth. I could smell your stink from the floor above. I have already sent a servant out the back way to call for reinforcements.'

'Such a prospect does not fill us with fear.'

A small head appeared on the balcony above.

'Nasir, what did I tell you? Go back inside your room and lock the door. Do not disobey me again.'

'But, Father, I have never seen blacks like these before. They are magnificent. The ones we put on ships are so broken, so unhappy and I don't know why anyone would want to buy them. But these are fine men, Father. We should welcome them. They are strong and tall and have you seen the beasts they ride?'

'Nassir, be quiet and do what I have told you.'

'Sir,' said the boy to my father.

'Don't address a nigger as sir,' said the Arab, 'it demeans you. These men are not to be addressed as sir in my house.'

'Sir,' said the boy again. 'Can I see one of your beasts up close?'

He started down the stairs and his father commanded him to stop. The boy, his son, Nasir, paused, full of expectation.

The Arab calculated the distance between three armed warriors and his son's sweet neck.

This boy was almost my age and he had strolled into mortal danger. This was no abstraction. No adventure. My father wanted something from the man and had been presented with the leverage he needed. I wished the boy had climbed out of a back window, run through the back garden and escaped into the twists and turns of the city's coiled streets.

'Father shall I tell him, that we shall not hurt the boy.'

'Silence your scruples, Ode,' my father said. 'This man is a slaver and his son will one day inherit the profit that has been made from bartering black people like ourselves.'

'Father,' I said, 'we mustn't. For the love I bear you, Father, please. He is only a child, think of him as your own.'

'What makes him different from any of the Wollof boys we killed?'

'This one has culture and learning, I believe.'

My brother looked at me appalled. Luxxor turned his head.

'You are right, Ode, we shall not hurt the boy, but it might be to our advantage to let his father think we might. He has a low regard for us and thinks we have no scruples. We shall let him continue to think like that for now. Why should we bother to illuminate him if he wishes to judge us ill?'

'Boy,' said the Arab to myself. 'You have not yet translated my insults to your father, have you?'

'I have no desire to see you hurt or bereaved. You have a fine boy. Let him still be with you when we are gone. Turn your injured pride to false welcome.'

'Your father has already read my brow.'

'Then change it fast.'

And just like an Arab changing the conditions of a deal, he burst out laughing, made welcoming gestures, grandiloquently fawned, invited us into a room. There were sumptuous sofas. A low table was bedecked with dried seeds and flowers in ceramic bowls of delicate decoration.

And upon one wall hung a full-length mirror.

We knew ourselves by our reputations. Those warriors who were successful in the hunt, in combat, knew that they were brave because they were told they were. Their victories were reflected in the blood they saw on their hands.

The handsome men and pretty girls amongst us found themselves celebrated with pouts, smirks, winks, hands on hips, crotch grabs, a quick show of tit. If you were desirable, you knew it, you didn't need to seek a stream and stare at your wobbling reflection.

And there stood the mirror.

I had this hideous idea that my father or my brother might turn on the reflected image of themselves and not knowing who they were faced with, might challenge the others to combat.

The Arab would think them fools.

So I had to talk them down.

'Father on that wall, there is a large looking glass. Although we do not possess such things because we know our worth and have no need of them, you might like to look at yourself for a moment. The glass is like the stillest water. A looking glass is a vain thing, not worthy of a warrior's attention maybe, but it is here and so are we and to waste a moment …'

My father took not notice. My brother turned to the looking glass, caught himself for a moment, snorted.

'That is not me, I am taller.'

The Arab, with much obsequiousness sat us down, commanded food to be brought and let Luxxor take his son outside, beyond the sanctuary of his front door, out into the street to have a closer look at the warrior rhinoceros.

Food arrived held aloft on a silver tray by an African woman of the most sublime beauty.

'She is a slave?' my father said.

'I bought her, but I did not sell her. I bought her from a black man.'

She had three scars in each cheek.

'Do you know her tribe?'

'I do not.'

The food was placed upon the table. Another servant, black also, but male, no less beautiful, arrived with decanters of sweet wine.

'My God forbids me wine,' the Arab said, 'but I keep the very best of it for guests. Such is our hospitality, I hope you will not defile it.'

And so we began our negotiations.

'Firstly,' my father said, 'you must send another servant to cancel your call for reinforcements.'

'It never happened, it was a lie. You took me by surprise. You are here for a reason. What is it that you want from me? Speak plainly and I shall treat you as I would any other businessman. As you might imagine, this is not the first time I have been threatened. A man as rich as myself experiences many conflicts in life. Sometimes I think it might be easier to live a more modest life and then I look around at the splendour of my house and I know that I could never bear to live otherwise.'

'You own ships. We have diamonds. Do you have ships for sale?'

'Everything is for sale. So show me the merchandise.'

And my father did so. Removing a soft leather wallet from the inside of his armour, opening it with great care, unfastening the woven bind and proudly displaying the rough-cut stones upon the table.

His hand shook very slightly as he helped himself to halva.

The Arab's face changed not one bit. I would rather my father had tossed the stones across the table with complete disregard for their worth. These things you find of so much worth, our children find them on the ground and use them in stupid childish games.

'We know you are enamoured of these shiny stones, we have them in abundance.'

Untrue. But a lie full of future promise. That which we offered the Arab had taken fifteen years of backbreaking, dangerous exploration to accrue.

'We have heard that northern men kill each other for these stones. This is an example of our riches. I wager you have never seen anything like it in your life.'

'And what do you want with ships? You wish to sail? I thought that Afrikas like to stay at home in the dust. Give them a mango and they are happy to spend the rest of the day under a tree. What makes you different?'

Speaking for myself and in no way translating my father's reply I gave voice to my own thoughts.

'We are very different. We are chosen. We are inevitable. Years from now you will tell others of this meeting with my father and you will tell that story with all humility and awe. My father is a great man. He will be remembered for all time. You will not. I am a writer and I will only put you in my story to show your foolishness.'

'Why should I fucking talk to you nigger boy!'

'Because if you are not polite to us, Luxxor, my uncle will cut your son's throat.'

The Arab, swallowed. My own threat appalled me. I did not want that boy to be harmed.

'Please merchant, do not put your handsome son in danger. All of the girls in the city will curse you if he dies.'

'You are an intelligent boy, Ode, let us get on with this. You want my ships, let me count your stones.'

The Arab took a nut from a bowl and studied it as if it quite unique, then he put out his tongue to bring the brain shaped nut in between this teeth, before rifling through the diamonds as if they were as common place as grains of rice.

'Where do you intend to sail to? You have made it to here, after no doubt a long journey from some place I've never heard of.'

'Yurop.'

'And can you or any of your troops command a sea going vessel?'

'We will learn.'

'It is not that easy. You cannot go to sea and just learn from scratch. You will need pilots and crew. That will increase your costs. Had you thought of that?'

'The Arab says we will need a crew, Father.'

'One per ship, no more than that, we will do the rest ourselves. Why does the man keep grinning like that?'

'My father says he doesn't like your grinning.'

'Tell him I don't like him in my house.'

'I could. When we first left our homeland, we conquered our old enemy. I estimated that they numbered at four thousand or more. We left not one of them alive. I think I shall advise my father to put the diamonds back into his purse. We shall burn your house down with you in it and simply take your ships from harbour by force. When my father has finished taking a sip from his goblet I shall tell him what I recommend. It is considered impolite in my culture to talk of serious things when one is eating or drinking.'

'Okay, Ode, stop. Tell me why do you intend to travel to Yurop?'

'We intend to take it.'

And here the Arab laughed aloud and my brother took great offence, took to his feet, scowled, and fondled the handle of his blade.

'Sit down, Son,' said my father. 'Let Ode do this.'

'I don't like it.'

'Nor do I. If he doesn't behave we shall kill him together.'

'Father,' I said, 'the Arab is simply laughing at a joke he has made. It is not worthy of translation, it lacks wit, he means no offence.'

And my brother sat down again, shrugged and refilled his goblet.

'And that is why you are here, in my house? You want me to help you sail to Yurop?'

'We do.'

'What do you hope to find there?'

'Our destiny.'

'You will not be welcome. They will not be happy to see your black faces.'

'You saw our beasts.'

'There are unique, I have never heard or seen such a thing. Yours must be only a handful of such creatures on this globe.'

'Those you have seen are just ten of our one thousand.'

'You have a thousand of such beasts? Holy fuck! What has God allowed to happen to this world? Are you lying to me?'

'I can take you to the harbour to convince your eyes.'

'And you wish to unleash a thousand beasts upon the Kristan Yurop?'

'My father says that we will take everything they own and make it ours, and become that which our spirits and storytellers have always said we should be.'

'I will not do a thing for you,' the Arab said, 'whatever you threaten me with until my son is back beside me.'

'Father,' said the boy appearing at the doorway to the room.

Luxxor had his arm around the young man's shoulder.

'They let me sit astride. They say they have another thousand.'

'Did they hurt or threaten you?'

'No, Father, they did not. These are fine and beautiful warriors and I wish that I could join them in their adventure.'

'I will rent you five ships for these shiny baubles. But they will not be enough to carry you across the Meditana, you will need at least ten. I will lease you another five in return for a percentage of your plunder. I shall send men with you to protect my interests. They shall journey with you.'

I translated this for my family.

'I don't like it,' said my father, 'but I don't care. If this Arab's men annoy me for an instant I shall kill them and that will be the end of that debate. Agree to his terms and lets us get this done. These glass stones mean nothing to us, but crossing the water is our destiny.'

'I'd like to see Yurop fall,' said the Arab. 'That heathen continent.'

'But we are heathen also in your eyes.'

'My enemy's enemy can be my friend. And why not help the heathen to destroy the heathen? I could send my people to convert those you leave behind alive after combat. I am sure that after they have seen you and your fearful beasts they will think their God has left them and will be looking for another. I will make the arrangements. Let my servant show you to my broken door and to my smashed gate.'

The tall black that had served us food ushered us along the hallway.

'Ode, does this slave man share a common tongue with you?'

In the service of an Arab I thought he might, which I quickly ascertained to be so.

'Shall I give you your freedom,' said my father, 'as a gift and apology for disturbing your peace.'

'And what should I do with such a gift sir?'

'Grab it with both hands and be grateful. Go home to your people, they will rejoice at the sight of your return.'

'My tribe lives far from here. I will have to walk for many months. I have no map. I will have to travel through the lands of tribes hostile to mine. No one will feed me or provide me with water. And if I am lucky enough to make it home, my family will not know me. I have been here half my life.'

'You have been a slave half your life. What sort of man are you that does not accept the gift of freedom? No man at all.'

'I have a woman here. The food that she cooks at the master's instruction, we eat also. We have our own room. There is a small garden at the rear of the house where we are allowed to walk. This house is guarded. This house was safe until you arrived.'

'You never leave this house and its gardens?'

'No. We are property. We might be stolen.'

And in disgust my father spat in the man's face.

'You treat me with less respect than my master,' the servant said.

'How dare you speak to my father like that?' said my brother unsheathing his blade. 'Father shall I teach this nigger some manners.'

'No Son, we shall leave this house without bloodshed if we can. For fuck's sake slave, wipe my spit from your cheek and show some pride.'

'It is a fine drawing Nassir. Quite exceptional.'

'But I never should have done it. The world is God's creation, not ours. We must not presume to copy him.'

We stood in the courtyard. Nassir fed a parrot from small black seeds that he held in his palm.

'I am sure your God gave you the talent to draw like this. So how could he complain?'

It was the middle of the day with the sun high and no shadow. There were flat breads, fava beans and felafel, hummus, kofta, sausages and liver, on a small table under an umbrella.

'How did you tame them, Ode? Did your God give you the power or the blessing to do that.'

'One day the rhinoceros came to my father, and knelt before him.'

He took the drawing from my hand and went to tear it into pieces.

'Stop,' I said. 'You should treasure a fine piece of work like that.'

'No, it is too dangerous to keep. My father would not be pleased with me if he found it in my possession. No, Ode, you have it. You keep it safe for me.'

'But do you not want to keep a memory of the warrior beasts that have so impressed and excited you?'

He laughed and pointed at his head with a finger.

'You think I could ever forget a sight like that. Ode, there is something I want to show you down at the harbour.'

'Your father would not allow you to leave the house alone.'

'I would be with you.'

'Your father might find that an even worse option'

'My father is busy readying the ships for your voyage.'

'Nassir how old are you?'

'I will be twelve next year.'

Not that much younger than myself. His affection and respect made me feel like an older brother. I thought of my mother's possible pregnancy back home.

'Ode, you will be gone in days. My father does not allow me friends. Let us spend a few hours together before you go.'

'You will be seen wandering through the streets with me.'

'Please,' said Nassir. 'I never get to do what I want.'

'See. These are made from the finest iron on earth. They are like your steeds, except they never move and cannot breath. But no, they do breath, they breath fire and smoke, and the noise they make!'

'I have seen pictures in a book my father owns. This is a cannon.'

'We have twelve, all pointed out to sea. We can take out any invading fleet at a distance of one to one half mile.'

'So the elevation is not fixed?'

'It can be adjusted. But it takes ten men many minutes to do so.'

We had attracted attention. Three boys.

'Your family has a new nigger Nassir.'

'This is not a nigger, this is my friend.'

'I don't much like the look of this one. It is deformed. What made you buy it? You should take it back and ask for a refund.'

'Fuck you,' I said turning on them. 'I am the son of the Chief Elder of my tribe. And you are nothing but dirty little cunts.'

One of them produced a knife.

'You will bleed for speaking such words to us nigger boy.'

Nassir, twelve, the shortest by far amongst us all, stepped forward.

'If you intend to hurt my friend, you will have to kill me first.'

The boys scoffed, but they knew his father. Their fathers knew his father.

'Nassir, shall we put it about that we found you with his big black thing in your mouth?'

'After I tell my father that you pulled a knife on me, no one will come anywhere near you to hear a fucking thing.'

'Nassir I didn't pull the knife on *you*. You don't have to be like this. We are all friends. You came to my sister's wedding last year man.'

'Come Ode, we must return home, but please walk two paces behind me.'

'Your slave cannot enter the library.'

'They know me here, but this man is new,' Nassir said to me in a whisper.

He thought for a moment and put his arm through mine and said.

'When I was young, I contracted a disease, and it made the muscles of my left leg very weak. Afterwards I could not walk un-aided. This man is my stick. I cannot go anywhere without him. I fall over otherwise.'

'I am sorry to hear about your disease. I have a niece. She uses a chair that has wheels on the side. You are well dressed and must have learning to want to come into the library. So I assume your father must be of some import. Tell him about the chair with wheels.'

'I will sir.'

'Now, it must be silent, it must keep its eyes to the floor, it must not get into anyone's path. Is that clear?'

'Yes sir.'

And so we walked through an atrium, passed grooved columns and into a room with walls as high as a waterfall.

'How do you reach the books at the top?'

'You use a ladder.'

'And do you read the book at the top of the ladder or can you bring it down?'

'Sorry,' said Nassir, 'it was all I could think of. I am sorry that I called you my stick.'

'I have been called worse things than that.'

'Yes,' said Nassir, 'we all have, but not by someone who is our friend.'

It was there that I found the book I was looking for. A set of illustrations of the different types of sea going vessels. The shape of the bow, the arrangement of oars, the position of the sails. And with the paper and pens we had brought in preparation, Nassir and myself spent the day copying the illustrations. Our styles of drawing were different but complimentary and we left the library with our own condensed version of the book.

'I have an idea,' said Nassir.

We found a stall that sold needle and thread and Nassir showed me how to bind the sheaves of paper together. We used his drawing of the rhino as the cover.

The wasted, black men, with their hair falling, spines bent out of shape, ten of their number to make a full mouth of teeth, loaded our ships with supplies under the noon heat with the gulls spinning above.

'When we return, Father, we should do something for these men.'

'Ode, by the time we return these wretches will be dead.'

We had been offered slaves to mount the oars, but my father declined.

'My men are stronger than the poor souls who you think you own,' he told the Arab. 'Let the slaves row your own vessel, if your own men are not up to the task.'

The Galley ships sat low on the water. Tents had been erected between the rows of benches to house the rhinoceros. Not to protect them from any bad weather that we might meet, but to protect them from the sight of the sea. We had no idea what effect the sight of water would have on them. On the river we had always seen the land. On this journey the horizon would be liquid in all directions.

Mphuno took his place safely under canvas, the others dutifully followed suit until they were all aboard, one hundred each on ten vessels.

Nassir came to me and I shook his hand.

'There is a man I want you and your father to meet. I wish we had had the time to be proper friends, Ode. But you must go and see the world and I must go to my room and study. That boy who pulled a knife on you, his father runs a textile business. But not anymore. I have seen to it.'

He winked at me and then he was gone, slipping through the pilled nets and coils of rope. A magpie hopped on a barrel, inclined its head and cawed as a beggar took his bow to his rebab and began to sing for food.

The man approached and began to talk at us without introduction.

'There is much talk of your enterprise.'

The man had a leather case, which he put upon the ground. Kneeling on his haunches he opened the lid, took out a device about the size of a boy's chest, and handed it to my father.

'What does it do?' said my father.

'It is an instrument for measuring distance.'

'And what use is that to me?'

My father held it in his hand and turned it over and over upon itself. It had the shine of dull amber. There were notches ground into a half circle of metal, a tube with a glass end.

He passed it to my brother for inspection.

'You look through the lens and take the measure of a man, or a man on horse, heights you already know. From that you can calculate the distance between yourself and that man.'

'Why,' said my brother interrupting, 'why do things that are faraway look smaller? Is it a trick, a trick of the mind?'

'If things that were far away did not look smaller,' the man said. 'I think we would all go insane.'

'But what is to be gained by the use of this instrument?' said my father.

'Knowing the exact distance between yourself and your enemy can be the difference between victory and defeat.'

'We prefer to fight close, for then we possess the true might of our beasts.'

'The Yurops have cannons and the long bow. They can kill you without even getting near.'

'Ode, what do you think? You had studied something of the numbers.'

'I believe it would be useful, Father.'

'And would you be able to understand and work this contraption.'

'I believe so.'

'Then we will take it. Son, pass the device to Ode.'

'Can't I have it?'

'Son, we must let Ode master this thing. You already have your Beast, your blade, your spear. Do not look jealous or with covet. Smooth your brow. Ode, ask the man what he wants in return.'

'Nothing.'

'Then this device comes cheap,' said my father.

'No, it comes at great expense. My brother was killed by a Yuropan. I have long wished for some form of revenge. If I can help you in any way, I will have served his memory. Here, take this device it will help you in your war. But do this for me, find a Yuropan of high standing and cut his hands away from his wrists as he still breathes.'

I spent the next two hours before our departure studying the device until I understood it perfectly.

'Ode, did you not hear me?'

'Sorry, Father, I was …'

'It is time to leave. Your brother is being sick and we haven't even yet moved out to sea.'

'He thinks the sea wants to kill us.'

Nassir's father stood upon the dock with his son by his side. The father had a pipe, the son had something wrapped in paper. Something sweet I imagined from his grin. A dog waited to lick the paper after it was tossed aside.

Skinny black men, poorly dressed, hollow-eyed, they untied the ropes that bound us to the quayside. Moments later and although no more than a few feet from the wooden quay, I keenly felt that we had left the solidity of land for the capricious waters. Water for our tribe had always been the life giver. But it came to us like a promise. Like a tease. This much and no more. Are you still thirsty? How long do you think it will be before it will rain again? How far is it to the next stream? Can you walk that far and still have the energy to return?

And here we were about to travel across the surface of the life giver, knowing from all reports that the sea itself was a conduit, to be skimmed across, but also a merciless killer.

Our vessel had two rows of twenty-four benches across the deck and twenty-four oars each side. Forty-eight oars in total, two men per oar, ninety-six of our warriors readying themselves for the journey. The tents that covered the rhinoceros, stood between them long ways. A bench without oars at the front. I sat there with my brother, father, Luxxor.

We were one hundred men per boat, the distance from this port in Northern Afrik to our destination in Southern Yurop, estimated as four hundred miles. Rowing ten hours each day at an average speed of two miles an hour we would make the journey in twenty days. But we had sails also, and any favourable winds that we could cleave to our cause would speed our journey considerably.

The sea was calm, the sky blue and with no hint of adventure.

We disembarked with my father's compromise. We took ten vessels. The eleventh bore one hundred men employed by the Arab to move in our wake. To convert those we left alive and to take their cut of the spoils. I had noticed them loading nets to provide themselves with fresh fish on their journey. We did not possess the skills of fishing. We had in our turn brought goats to slaughter and to roast.

Luxxor beat the skin of a drum to keep our men in unison and we moved slowly, almost painfully away from the edge of our own continent.

Nassir waved.

I raised a hand in return. And watched them all get smaller as they grew further away.

I focused the lens on Nassir's father, I knew him to be of standard height for his people. And thus I could calculate the increasing distance between ourselves and the shore, and by a simple calculation ascertain our speed out to sea.

'Do you think you will find it useful, Ode?'

And then in the lens I saw something I had not expected to see. Nassir, in obvious and deep distress, beating his father about the chest. Had his father admonished him for showing me the cannon, for being with me in public without permission?

The cannon.

The dog was barking.

'Father, ships are at their most vulnerable at a certain distance out to sea. The cannon ball has a limited range. But there is a danger zone of some margin.'

'Do you think the Arab intends to sink us? I think not, he will become rich from his investment in our venture.'

We had insulted him, entered his house un-invited and even suggested that we might hurt his son. It seemed to me perfectly reasonable that he would sacrifice both part of his fleet and the promise of bounty to regain his pride. And of course he had his reputation to defend. Others must have heard how easily he had capitulated to a bunch of hated black men, unnaturally riding into town on the back of our grey, leathery beasts.

We were one mile out at my estimation.

'Father,' I said. 'We may be in danger.'

But such advice came too late. The cannons fired. One of our ten ships took the first hit, splitting the mast. I turned the lens of my measuring device upon their plight. One warrior stood stock still with wood through the centre of his stomach. Another was open mouthed and screaming. A second volley overshot very slightly and sent up a barrage of salt water.

The rhinoceros squirmed under the surface of the canvas. What of this situation could they possibly understand?

'Nets.' I said. 'Father, I saw them loading nets. They were enormous, thick and strong. They seek to sink us, Father. The rhinoceros can swim and we cannot. They do not care about us, or their fleet. They wish to take the rhinoceros for themselves. That is the great prize they desire. Not the gold of Yurop, not the souls of Kristans.'

'Our beasts are loyal to us, to me, they came first to me, they would not ally themselves with Arabs.'

Another vessel was struck. A glancing blow that shattered part of the gunwale. Pieces of men were flung wide and spotted pink patches stained the blue Mediteran sea.

'We can outrun the range of these cannons if we can survive the ...'

The first vessel struck was listing to the side.

'We are vulnerable between a distance of one and one and a half miles. We will have another one half mile of this bombardment.'

'What are you saying, Ode?'

At that moment I knew that I needed to trust myself in a way that I had never done before. I had always found it easier, to feel sorry for myself, to almost celebrate my uselessness, and there was my father asking of me for such advice as might save or ruin a thousand men and beasts.

'We have to turn about and sail back to the inner limit of their range,' I said. 'That way their cannon balls will fall uselessly into the sea *behind* us.'

'Back to shore,' my father ordered, 'turn about.'

And the command was hollered from ship to ship and the oar strokes reversed.

'They may reposition the cannons to get us at close range,' said Luxxor.

'Yes they may. But how long will that take?' said my father. 'We will outrun them by running towards them, not by fleeing.'

'Father I hope this works.'

'Ode, you made calculations, you made an informed plan. It is all a warrior can do.'

I was a warrior now in my father's eyes?

'If we all die today it will not be your fault, Ode. Bravery does not always lead to victory.'

'We will not all die today,' I said with false conviction.

'I agree with you, Ode. I feel no sense of death upon us.'

My brother was staring at me. I gave him a twisted smile. His face was blank. I didn't know if he was proud of me, or angry that my father had asked me for advice and not him.

The first vessel to be struck split in two along the length and Kikuyo and rhinoceros plunged into the water as the ship full of the Arabs men came close with their nets.

Nine of our ships rowed backwards towards the quay as the fire flew over our heads.

We slammed into the wooden quayside and those timid, broken blacks rushed to take our ropes and last them to the posts, even as they were beaten with long, fat sticks wielded by ranting officers of the port.

Our warriors had already mounted and laced themselves into their stirrups. Our servants flung back the canvas and nine hundred poured ashore in one tumescent rage.

There was no plan, no direction, just nine hundred pissed off, Kikuyo, still alive and on un-stoppable, armoured, horned, beasts. Saliva poured from their black lips. Every one of our warriors was helmeted and his face unseen.

Those humans at the port wondered what they had unleashed. Did we just try and kill these Motherfuckers? What were we thinking of? Were we born fools? Or did they put something in the water to confuse our minds?

We rampaged at will, men were crushed. A fire started and began to tear through the wooden toll and custom huts on the quayside.

There was a small market, selling vegetables, live chickens in woven baskets, bowls of nuts and figs. Old men sold their wares.

The Italian painters had, as I was later to discover, found a way to paint a flat surface such that it looked to be real in all dimensions. The market had been rounded, solid, breathing. We left it flat as a bloodied tapestry.

The screams of the dying mingled with the hollers of our tribe incensed and outraged beyond reason. The black dockers, cowered behind bales and casks, and prayed that they would not be hurt by those of their own colour.

Ten soldiers awakened from a tavern, stumbled down towards us at the quayside, saw us, shat themselves in their pants and began to fire small round balls of lead that simply bounced away from the leather armour my mother had designed for us all. Realising their weakness they turned and ran and bumped into their master who began screaming and slashing at the air above their heads with a scimitar.

Some youths threw bricks and stones at us from behind the safety of a stone wall. They shrieked with laughter and hollered foul words at the cunting niggas. The shit thick black bastards. They weren't worth killing, but one of the stones hit Luxxor on the forehead, which although it hardly hurt him at all, it infuriated him. And that was the end of them. Asked in the afterlife how they had come to die, they each said that they had done so with great bravery.

Gawpers leant from windows and watched as if this were entertainment. They had never expected to see such a scene. They would tell their grandchildren they were there that day, and probably insert themselves into the action in some brave or compassionate act.

There was a child alone upon the ground below. I couldn't just stand there and watch. I ran across the quayside dodging between the giraffe men and their rhino beasts. I got a small wound to my shoulder.

Show me, show me!

It is fully healed now. Anyhow, I got to the child and took it into my arms and made it back to the house.

They gawped. And although they had no clear evil intent against us, they had stood there with their children happy enough to watch our intended destruction.

I clung behind my brother as my father ordered twenty warriors to take the cannons that stood above us. We could see the men trying to turn them from the sea to point at the quay, a thing they had not been designed to do.

The cannoneers lost their heads amongst swift blows and their shocked decapitations were stuffed into the barrels.

And then it was done with no more might left to meet us.

I could hear the locking of doors and shutters of the houses throughout the town. They hid their young in basements. They feverously held onto kitchen knives and hatchets. Women stuffed their hair in caps, found blacking in their pots and smeared their cheeks and chins. Borrowed their husband's pantaloons and stuffed onions into the crotch and practiced lowering their voices.

In the silence that followed our warriors itched for spoils, for redress, for brutal intercourse. But my father called a halt.

'We sail again. We have men and beasts still in the water. Let us move with all speed.'

'Shall we not raze the town?' asked Luxxor. 'They would have cheered to see us drown.'

'No, not this time.'

And I was glad. Not for the people, but for all those books that lined the walls of the library. And then looking around at a place I did not expect to see again for a long time, there among the carnage lay Nassir. The dog licking at the candy on his lips.

'Brother let me dismount I want to go to the boy.'

'Ode, it is too late to save him. Father says we are to get back on the ships.'

'Brother halt the Beast and let me dismount.'

I was later to discover, in Yuropan stories, the notion of a character's dying words, in which in the last few moments before death, there was just enough time to whisper profound and loving sentiments, to console the person they are about to leave behind.

But the boy was dead. His poor and youthful body quite limp. I wanted him to say to me that he had enjoyed our brief and tentative friendship. Strangely and against all normal feeling, I wanted him to say that one day he might have grown to love me as a brother. That he was sorry for his father's duplicity.

But had he known? Was that why he had shown me the cannon and told me of its range? Did he know and wanted to help, but could of course not betray his father. But then why the anger, why did he hit out at his father, a thing he had surely not done before. Why show that great disrespect if not suddenly shocked by his father's intentions?

His father lay a few yards away, his left leg crushed, white bone peeping through the flesh.

And Nassir, now faceless and limp. I picked him up and took him to his father.

I lay the body of his son upon him.

'Did your son know?'

He could not for pain of injury reply.

'He showed me the cannon yesterday, he told me their range. If he had not done so, we would all have drowned. If he had not done so we would not have reversed and brought this down upon you.

'Your plan to destroy us and take our beasts has led to this. If you survive your wounds you will no doubt blame us for his death. But *you* are the murderer of your own son. And that will be the first thought in your head each and every day for the rest of your life.'

Back at sea, we picked up those warriors whose ship had been sunk. We found them clinging to the shattered remains of their craft. The water was calm and the men stoic. We lost eleven in all. Eleven out of the one hundred men that had been aboard. Eleven out of a thousand. That is how we had to think. Eleven out of a thousand. Not eleven men, with wives and families and hopes and dreams and their own personal thoughts now extinguished.

'It could have been so much worse,' my father said.

Eleven men lost out of a thousand, my brother chalked that up as a victory.

Our nine vessels surrounded the other that contained the Arab's men. The rhinoceros were in the nets still in the water.

'Not one of our magnificent beasts shall drown today,' my father called. 'And not one of these men shall ever see land again. We shall take this vessel as our own and we shall again have a full complement of ships.'

Of the one hundred men on our ship, fifty boarded the Arab's vessel. The Arabs lay down their weapons and went to the knees with their hands joined in supplication.

The rhino were dredged up on board, a feat for even our strength. They were shocked and quiet, their eyes puffy with the salted water that they had no previous experience of. They crawled under canvas and lay on their sides.

The Arab's men, we cut them slowly one by one, so that the next and the next and the next knew what awaited them.

I had never myself experienced great pain, but I wondered if sometimes the threat of it, the wild workings of the imagination, were worse than the shocked reality.

It appalled me, I could not look, I stuck my fingers in my ears. I was ashamed. I thought, Father, how can we do this?

My brother asked Luxxor for the hammer and brought it down on the blade.

Then he rushed to the edge of the vessel and threw up over the side.

'I'll do it again,' he cried. 'It was not the sight of blood that had made me sick, it's the lurching of the sea, and the smell of these deceitful bastards that has turned my loyal stomach. Next, I shall release the hammer for the next, the next and next.'

'I want to do it, Father. In revenge for Nassir.'

'But, Ode, you will not be able to.'

'I know I will not be able to, but I want to.'

Luxxor took charge.

'They are so terrified,' I said.

'They will not live long. Their terror will soon be forgotten. Ode, these Arabs intended to kill us all, all one thousand of us, the hope of our race. They must die in agony. It cannot be otherwise. If you have to close your eyes do it so that the others cannot see. If you have to weep cover your face with your hand is if you find the sun too bright.'

'I can watch, Father.'

I thought to myself, I have to watch, I have to study. How can a storyteller be someone who closes their eyes?

A string was tied around the Arab's wrists, the wrists forced upon a slab of wood. What took my attention was the crunching sounds of the bones as the metal split them apart. I thought of the neck of a goat prepared for table.

I thought to myself, I must remember this sound, it is particular. Better that than to remember the sound of the man's piteous wailing, the names he called us all.

Addressing one wailing Levantine I asked.

'Do you know the boy Nassir and his father, the merchant who lives near the square?'

'I have served the merchant for many years,' said the man through his screaming teeth.

'I hold you responsible for that child's death.'

We kept them on their knees to shake and scream for an hour before we tossed them overboard to die.

We left one alive. It is a good tactic. In a massacre, there is sometimes value in leaving one alive.

Luxxor stripped him, tied him to the helm and held his mouth open with a piece of wood. He de-boned a pair of severed hands from the pile, pierced and roasted the meat over coals, and fed the Arab parts of his own countryman. He writhed like a snake against it, but we closed his nose and we closed his jaw and when he vomited Luxxor pushed back his head until the reflux shot back down his throat.

Sea birds dive bombed the decks, taking hands in their claws and at each grasp, the Arab shrieked as if his own hands were being taken up into the sky.

'You always leave one,' said my father, 'unless they are Wollof scum. Sometimes one can be worth more than a hundred. When they are the last one left alive. It helps them to focus. We need his help and I will promise him his life if he complies. Or his death if he refuses me.

'Go to him. Tell him, Ode. Use all your skills and wiles. Leave him in no doubt that a long interview with Luxxor and his knife would be the cruellest death we have yet to conceive. Here take him wine.'

'Father they do not drink wine. It is against their beliefs.'

'Then take him wine but no water.'

'You will pilot us.'

'I will not.'

'Arab, you know the way, and we do not.'

'I will not help you.'

'How much pain can you bear?'

'My God will favour me. What awaits me will recompense me for any worldly hurt that you may inflict.'

'You are a brave man to stand by your principles and be willing to endure the torture my father has put aside for you.'

I put the flagon to his lips, but he spat out what little he had drunk.

'Fuck you black skin, if you think to gain my trust. You cut the hands from ninety nine of my people and then drowned them, I will not speak to any of you barbarians.'

'It is not the tradition of my tribe to cut hands. We got that idea from one of yours. You wish to protect the Yuropans? Because they are your friends. So you will not help us conquer them. Because the Yuropan race and Arab race have lived peaceably and with mutual respect.'

'You are an ignorant fool if you think that.'

'I may be young but you should not judge me a fool.'

'Even if I were to pilot you to Napoli, you'd kill me the minute we arrived.'

'Do you have a knowledge of maps?'

'I could find a fart in a sandstorm black skin.'

'Then you could be useful for a long time. You would have a safe and happy time to look forward to.'

'As a slave? Doing the bidding of barbarians just to save my wretched skin. I would be truly damned in the afterlife for such a sin.'

'You would not be a slave as such. You would be indentured, yes, but you could still find much to enjoy. You would eat well and sleep well. Certain trinkets could be yours for a lifetime. There is no reason why you might not choose a mistress from our conquests. Someone much younger and prettier than you deserve.'

'There will be time for that after death.'

'Yes, but if your paradise does exist why do you fight for life so? Why not kill all children at birth and offer them eternal bliss rather than pains, disappointment and degradation.'

'God does not allow it.'

'And yet you love him?'

'Speak to your father.'

I looked across the water and admired the dark blue of its nature and the sky above that seemed to me to be its sister.

'Father, with respect, please release him. And let him wash. And might I suggest that we give him something to eat that will not defile him. Give him free range of the ship, and tell our warriors not to spit on him.'

The Arab ate and scowled, but I knew he would do what we asked. No man who'd rather die than be coerced had his sort of appetite.

'We have never seen these animals? What are they called?'

'Ode, I do not wish to talk to you.'

I understood the game. His pride, my boyhood.

'I like to talk,' I said, 'I like to learn.'

'Go talk to someone else, go learn from someone else.'

'My teacher was an Arab, I miss my talks with him.'

'I shall be no substitute for your tame scholar. We are not all so easily bought.'

'Then you are not thinking clearly, I am the son of the Chief Elder. Having the comfort of my good word would be a benefit for you in the coming times.'

'I am already ruined. You forced me to eat the flesh of my own kind. To drink wine. My chances of paradise are ruined. My life on earth is an insult to my soul. I have nothing to live for and yet cannot die. You have no idea of the hurt you have caused me.'

'You had a plan to kill us all, and that plan failed. Do you feel wrongly treated?'

'You should have cut my hands off and drowned me like the rest.'

'That can be done now, if that is your wish.'

I stood quickly and turned and the Arab lunged for my arm.

'No Ode, please, did you see the men's faces as they were cut, did you hear the sounds they made, and I was to be the last, after bearing witness to ninety nine butcheries. Know this, Ode, that when you forced me to eat human flesh, I was grateful. Although you dammed me by the taste of that meat, I counted my blessings that you did not put my wrists to the blade. If my life is now intolerable, I crave it. I cannot part with it. I am not a brave man, Ode, but then I never said I was. The man with the broad shoulders, that stands next to your father …'

'My uncle Luxxor.'

'There is something about him. I watched him as he butchered my fellows and I thought, if the same were to be done to him, he would spit in the face of the man who had brought down the hammer, and walk away without his hands as if he had done nothing more than pricked his little finger with the end of a needle.'

'My Uncle has conquered pain.'

Seabirds reeled above us.

'Shearwaters, this time of day is a good time of day for squid. They come out here to feed and then return to their nests on the Southern shores of Yurop.'

'And those animals we saw a few minutes ago?'

'Dolphins,' said the Arab.

'I liked them. They made me smile. They looked like children playing in a stream.'

'They gambol, just as you did when you were a child.'

'I did not gambol much.'

'The other children did not play with you because of your deformed arm.'

'They are fish?'

'No.'

'They are mammal then. And that is why they come to the surface to drink the air.'

'You are clever for a black boy.'

'I am clever full stop. You don't need to comment on my skin to comment on my mind.'

At that the Arab rose and removed his shirt.

'Look at my back, Ode, between the shoulder blades.'

His skin was coffee rather than the ebony of my own, but between the shoulder blades he was as white as foam on water.

'I did not gambol much as a child myself. The other children said I had a white infidel on my back.'

'Put your shirt back on before my father sees you exposing yourself to me.'

He did so quickly, like a boy caught pissing up a wall by his aunt.

'Are there many other animals we shall encounter in Yurop that we have never seen?'

'The horse is the finest and no doubt you have seen those. Their goats are the same as ours. They have cows which are stupid and sheep as we do, but their ones look like clouds. And, Ode, look into the sky, the darkness of the sky.'

'A storm getting ready for a fight.'

'You have seen storms before.'

'We see them rarely but when they come they are fierce. The wind threatens to destroy the trees, the animals become frantic. The loose earth makes clouds of dust to choke us.'

'But the earth itself does not move, does it, Ode?'

'No.'

'But now, Ode, we are at sea, when the storm hits, the sea churns. If you have never experienced such a thing you will be surprised by it. So will your beasts. If you have any way to do so, you should calm them. For if they go berserk they will not only be a danger to themselves.'

'You are advising me Arab?'

'I am trying not to die, Ode. It is not very graceful of me to say so. I am not proud of my fear of death. If your beasts are untamed by this storm, this craft will sink for sure. You are carrying a strange cargo and you are not prepared. Tie everything down, the oars to the gunwale, the beasts to the metal rings that run the length of the bow, tie yourselves to the beasts, tie everything to the ship and tie yourselves to each other.

'Know this, Ode, I will work as your father's map reader and orienteer, I will not cheat you, I will not deceive you, I will in every regard be as honest as I can, but know this also, that although I will not work against you, I shall each day pray for your utter destruction. But not this day. For if you drown, I will drown also.'

'Father there is a storm at sea approaching.'

'That I can clearly see, Ode.'

'I pointed that out half an hour ago,' said my brother. 'I have no fear of it.'

'It may unsettle the beasts. What if they were to go berserk?'

'They have endured storms before.'

'Yes, Father, but not at sea. It will be a new experience for them.'

'It will be a new experience for us,' said my brother. 'We shall face it.'

'And how should we calm them, Ode?'

I passed the Arab's words along to my father.

'I do not like to be advised by this man.'

'He advises us out of selfishness, Father, he has no care for us. He simply doesn't want to die.'

'Only a fool refuses good council even from his enemies.'

And so my father commanded that all the oars be stowed and tethered and that each warrior should join his Beast under canvas and embrace the animal that they had known since their earliest boyhood.

There were many coils of rope aboard. A series of metal rings ran the length of the bow under canvas and we slipped the ropes under the saddles of the beasts as the light above us died and the vessel began to heave. Then each warrior tied himself to his Beast. The animals that the warriors had known without absolute intimacy since the age of human four. If they were to be washed overboard they would go together. Each warrior massaged the withers of the Beast through their leather armour and cooed and hummed. And in compassion forgot all fear for themselves.

'If we die today,' shouted my father from the stern and over the noise of the increasing wind, 'we die as one.'

I slipped a length of rope around my waist and tied myself to Mphuno. My brother was I assumed with father or my uncle.

And when the storm hit, the wind took the canvas and it flew like a dark bird into an even darker sky. The clouds broke above us and we lay bare headed under a raging waterfall and the sea beneath us heaved and spat, and our vessel began a wild listing.

Our beasts waved their heads and snorted. And the warriors tried to cover their eyes with their hands.

The rhinoceros is a quiet animal. They keep their own council, their small eyes let in little light. But they made a noise that hour that no one had ever heard before and would never hear again.

And man and Beast puked over each other's snouts, and man and Beast shared foul breath as the wooden structures beneath us bucked like a first mounted gazelle.

My father approached me on his hands and knees, vomit on his chin.

'Ode, where is your brother?'

'Father I thought he was with you.'

'I thought he was with you, Ode.'

'Let me find him.'

'No, I should go.'

'Father stay with the men, your leadership will comfort them. I shall return in a minute do not worry about me.'

I unleashed myself from Mphuno.

I found my brother stood at the prow of the ship.

'Father commands you to join us. It is not safe to be standing here like this.'

The Arab had tied himself to the mast.

'You have never seen such a thing as this!' He said. 'I was born in a storm such as this. My mother spat me out on a sea such as this. Let this storm take me back to where I began. Drown these fucking niggers and take me to paradise my saviour. Merciful lord, the foul meat and wine was forced upon me, I committed no crime intentionally.'

'Brother what are you doing?' I said. 'Why are you not lashed to the ship and to all of us?'

I went to him and put my arms around his waist. Even with us both precarious in wind, and stood on saturated planks, and even with the heaving I felt safer with my brother's body pressed to mine. He turned his head and hollered in my face: 'I told you, Ode, the sea wants to kill us. And what do you do when faced with an enemy? You do not hide. You challenge it to battle.'

'Brave words, Brother, but join me and Father, join the men.'

A bank of water hit us against the side and the vessel lurched upwards to almost forty-five degrees, the salted spray slapped my face and my eyes closed involuntarily. I fell backwards and involuntarily released my grip.

'Come Brother, come and join us,' I shouted wiping salt from my vision.

He simply wasn't there before me.

I rushed to the side of the boat and there at sea was an arm.

I stripped myself of my leather armour in frantic haste.

'Can you swim, Ode?' The Arab shouted at me from the mast.

'I cannot, nor can my father.'

'Then if you jump in to save your brother you will die also.'

'Then I shall die also, I cannot leave my brother alone.'

'Ode, if you give me your soul I will save your brother. My God may forgive me if I can bring a convert to his house.'

'No Arab, I must do this myself.'

I did not swim towards my brother. I was simply swept to him. I grabbed his waving hand with my one good arm.

'Brother we must remove your armour. It is weighing you down.'

I did not know if he heard me, but I fumbled with the fastenings with my withered arm which found an inner strength from desperation and desire.

Now my brother understood and rising and falling with the waves and spitting out salted water and working blinded by the spray, together we removed the leather from his body.

And two naked brothers at sea, neither of whom could swim, lashed by salt water. My brother embraced me and shouted in my ear.

'Ode, we die together.'

And then through the squall I could see curved black shapes moving in circles around us. And despite the roaring sky and the fucking wind, a shoal of dolphin closed ranks around us and held us buoyant.

The sky cracked above us, one last ferocious hurrah and it was spent. The water calmed, we blinked our tender eyes. And the sun appeared so fast from a sky that had been impenetrable minutes before that.

And then they were gone, arcing out of the water and then cutting back through the surface.

We stood naked on the deck in our embrace. For a Kikuyo, nakedness before other men is of no regard. Only later in Yurop did I find that for a man to see another man's body was an outrage.

'I thought I had lost you both,' said our father putting his hands on our shoulders.

'Ode saved me.'

'And the dolphins saved us both.'

'What are Dolphins, Ode?'

'They are animals that live in the sea.'

'Ode the storyteller invents animals that live in water, when it is his own bravery that saved his brother.'

'Father ...'

'Enough.'

I noticed that the foremast was gone.

'The Arab?'

'He is no longer on board.'

'He had tied himself to the mast.'

'We have lost our scout.'

And then I heard the cawing above us.

'No, Father. We have other scouts to help us,' I said pointing upwards. 'The Sheerwater, it comes out here to feed on squid and then returns to its nests on the Southern shore of Yurop. We follow the birds.'

We were met with canon on the quayside. Mounted to destroy us at close quarters. Only ten of our men stood visible on each deck. Our feet planted firmly on the planks. The bulk of our force were under canvas, with heads down and shoulders hunched.

I could hear the breathing of their hundred beasts, could hear their hooves scraping at the deck.

They snuffled at the foreign smells.

And on the fat stones of harbour, dogs raised their noses and brayed.

We stood in our armour. We held our helmets in our hands so that they could see the colour of our faces.

'We wish to land,' my father said.

And I in the voice of the storyteller, translated.

My words were met with a moment's simple silence. Followed by gabble and chatter. Fear and amusement. I did not know their language, but what they said was clear. Where had we come from? What the fuck were we doing here? Black skins did not come to Yurop! They might be *brought*. But they did not *come* of their own volition.

A soldier fired a warning shot over our heads.

And not one of us flinched.

So the soldier, un-manned began ranting and waving. A woman on a balcony laughed at him and threw some old soup into the street near his feet.

A fat man began to push his way through the crowd, in his wake limped a tall skinny official in a purple hat with a feather nestled in the band.

'Did one of you niggers speak in the tongue of the learned?' Said the fat man arriving before us out of breath, with drool on his chin. 'What in God's name is this abomination?'

My father spoke through me. And I burst with pride. I used the volume of my voice my Griot had trained me in, and the depth of language accrued from my studies from my Teacher.

A young woman leaden down with pails blew a kiss at me.

'We have read of this continent. Will you honour us with safe landing?'

The fat man translated that to the skinny man, who then informed the crowd.

And every white person laughed, except the woman on the balcony who simply spat into mid-air. The soldier who had fired above our heads smiled at her, but she huffed and turned her back.

'I am the major of this town,' said the tall skinny man through the translation of the short fat man. 'Our dogs are not happy with the smell of you. Where are your masters? Have you killed them at sea and thrown their bodies overboard, you will be taken and punished if that is so.'

'We have no masters, we are free men.'

'Free men or not you have no business here, do not disembark. Go back where you came from.'

'Have we travelled a long way, spent many long and arduous months in transit to be visited with such disrespect. It is not acceptable. Would you like to be spoken to like this if you had made so much effort to come to our lands.'

'We have made many attempts to travel to the coast of your lands. And when we arrive you try and kill us.'

'That is because the men you send are thieves.'

'And what are you?'

'We are conquerors.'

'You will fail. Our cannons stand against you and over a hundred good men, fully armed, stand beside me. How many are you even? I can see no more than a handful on each vessel.'

Under canvas the beasts were scuffing at the wood.

'And what is that smell, that noise coming from your vessels? What abominations do you think to bring to this place?'

They seemed unhealthy, paunched, or withdrawn into themselves. Their skins were shocking, pocked and marked and no tribal scars to give them prestige.

'Turn your ships around,' said the major, 'or we will sink you and blow you black skinned bastards into pulp.'

'Are we to charge,' asked Luxxor of my father.

'We shall stroll onto this continent. Let the white faces shit themselves slowly.'

We had already lashed our vessels to the cleats. The servants primed the ramps and settled them on the quayside. The white people strained to see. We were no danger. We were entertainment. Something to talk about in the taverns later. Did you see those fools, they thought they could just turn up on our shores and be welcome. I missed it all. I was hammering at my forge. What did they look like?

'You are fools to even think of doing this,' said the major. 'Why do you wish to provoke your own death? We gave you fair warning. You will regret your deafness and your pride. You will die here and be forgotten by tomorrow. Tell your Gods to expect you.'

The soldiers raised their rifles. Squinted. Stood firm.

And slowly as a needle through parted flesh, the servants pulled back the canvas and revealed our might. Our troops strolled into the weak foreign sun of this particular day in two by two formation from all ten ships.

Is that their skin, a costume? Are they dressed as animals? Is this a circus?

Are those horse? They are the wrong shape entirely?

I have never seen blacks like this. Their backs are straight.

These are not from Afrik, this is an army sent from hell. I told you those stinking priests were angering God with their gluttony.

You touch a young boy's arsehole too many times and you open the gates to the devil.

Twenty, forty, sixty, eighty, my mind is sore from counting. There are more of these bastards than I have bottles of wine in my cellar.

The madman that sits in his own shit by the water trough said that one day something like this would happen. A million creatures from the underworld would come to blacken our sky and take away our sun.

The major exclaimed fire, and a cannon ball ripped into the deck of the ship next to ours and a million flying splinters peppered the air, and our forces took it and survived it, with the triple skins of their armour and the thick skins of the pachyderm.

'And charge,' ordered my father, and our heavy beasts exploded in their limbs.

My father led with Luxxor at his side. Myself behind my brother, my arms around his waist. Behind us one thousand beasts and men, Behind me! Mounted, bright warriors, angered by cannon, sparked by gun fire, one thousand beasts and men in forward flight, the soldiers went down in wails and disbelief, their bones crushed inside their popping skins.

New boats, still unfinished, were crushed and turned to splinters. We had travelled for many months and here was our release and I wailed with triumph when my brother, in my embrace, cut away the head of a soldier that had foolishly clambered back to his feet.

The woman with the soup and spitting, looked down upon us from her window and began to clap her hands in joy. Our Beast barged a cart of apples sidewards, slamming an old man against a wall. I heard his chest crack and whispered a small apology. We did not come to hurt you old man, be happy in your heaven.

A young child dropped its breaches, shat into his cupped hand and threw it at a soldier. A statue of a general upon a horse toppled and crushed a blind man.

We left the streets behind us besmirched with human muck and headed along the main thoroughfare of town. Short fat men in drab clothes threw themselves into doorways. Some men ran before us, thinking that surely they could outstretch these low, fat, thick beasts, not knowing for an instant that a rhinoceros can, when charged to do so, moves as fast as an Afrik cat. And we took their heads.

Only with the tallest and most elaborate building in our clear sight did we rein in. We knew that we had reached their sacred place.

A priest came from a door within a door, clutching a large silver cross and wiping sweat from his eyes. Skittering down the stone stairs, he lost his footing, and fell headlong onto his Khrist.

'We haven't come here to hurt you,' I said.

'What? You speak in Latin. Is this a test? A test from God. Or Satan. Yes, you have been sent by Satan,' he stumbled to his feet. 'To divert me from my path. This is a sacred place, heathen shall not enter.'

'Should we honour what you hold sacred, or should we burn it down?' My father said through me.

And although all I did was translate, I felt the words pour through me as if they were mine. I am a crippled man, but the might and compassion of my father resonates through me and me alone. You will listen to me.

'We are looking for shelter.'

'You cannot enter the House of the Lord.'

'Has no black man ever come through those great doors of yours?'

'Not that I know of. But if he came in peace, with his head bowed and asked for the favour of the lord, I would grant it.'

'I do not believe you for one moment. You would turn your back on him and send him away. Listen to my father. We seek sanctuary. We need to eat and rest, we need somewhere where the soldiers will not aim their cannon, a place where our men will not be set on fire while they are sleeping. We will rest here and your church will stand. If we offend you, take the offence. Digest it, then pray for it to be forgotten. Your church will stand for a thousand years after we have gone.

A small crowd of townsfolk appeared from the roads that led to the square. They held white handkerchiefs and carried baskets.

The men were olive skinned, hairy around the jaw, short and squat. We as always kept our faces clean, shaved our head to avoid infestation, we were leaner and a good head taller. Their women in particular were disappointing. Unlike our women folk back home, our tall and graceful females.

Crowds of children tumbled over each other's necks and shoulders to see the mighty beauty of the beasts.

My father dismounted, removed his leather helmet and stared at the church doors. They were vast and decorated with skulls wearing crowns and papal hats.

'What do you think, Ode? We are in Yurop. We have taken this town with no loss to our own. We stand before their sacred place.'

It began to rain and the townsfolk scurried forwards with their baskets of food. Warriors dismounted to inspect them. Loaves of bread. Cheeses, cold cuts of meat. These small offerings, the townsfolk bartered for their lives. A bottle of red wine, I offer you barbarian, you do not need to drink my blood.

The blood was pumping in my temples, it had been a thrill to charge, but what had we overcome? This was the beginning of my story, the mighty adventure that would be told for a thousand years. The black man landed in Yurop and was met by a rabble. They had neither skill nor pride, they were weaklings that fell over and wailed. The women fat and tiny, their men shed tears. We took their house of God with hardly a threat. And now they wanted to feed us!

A great adventure must have great deeds, and great deeds must arise from the defeat of implacable enemies. One has to be cornered, outnumbered and then through skill and wit and bravery, overcome everything in your path. What man wades through a thin stream and hails himself a hero at the other bank? Any mountain that be climbed in a day does not deserve its name.

No.

That day we had to use every ounce of our reserves, for although at first we could see nothing to withstand us, what lay in waiting was something so monstrous that it would challenge us to our core and show the might of the Kikuyo even in the times of greatest dread.

The great gateway to the Yurop lands was protected by a one-eyed colossus that they kept chained in a cave.

Under the white man's assault, only one of us had fallen, the victim of a cowardly axe blow from behind when the warrior was trying to save a Mother and her swaddling child from a charging horse mounted by one of her own.

The cowardly townsfolk smuggled away the victim's body before we could retrieve it. And they took it to the monster and pressed the black flesh of our fallen comrade to the foul spilling, pitted nose of their freak.

Smell them out and kill them, bite through their necks as we know you like to do. Crush the skulls with your back teeth for snacks. We are about to unchain you, go feast.

The ogre crushed two of our beasts, his feet breaking through their backs and he stumbled on with them attached as if they were shoes. His fat hands swooped down and plucked the riders from their beasts, he brought them to his mouth and chewed through their armour.

It fell to my father to face him, this one-eyed ogre the size of a house. He had already fallen upon us and eaten fifty of our men. The rhinoceros repeatedly gouged his legs, but their horns were blunted by the iron leg braces that he wore.

'Remember, Ode,' my father shouted to me, 'when we left the north of our continent, we ran *towards* the cannon.'

My father wove the end of a shipping chain round his waist. And he ran towards the legs of the monstrosity pulling the chain behind him and dodging the swinging fists of the leviathan, he ran circles around the villain's ankle, then taunted him and ran back towards the quayside.

And as the ogre came for him with outstretched arm, his tangled ankle held him back and he fell with a mighty crash into a crowd of those that had released and commanded him. And then my father was upon the ogre's neck slicing open the veins that bleed the most. And the blood poured across the quayside and drained into the water and as we cheered we heard behind us a flapping sound as if from giant leathery wings.

In the square my father still held his bow, arrow armed and ready. My father who could move quicker than a cat, whose hearing was so acute, heard the sound of a shutter being opened, above and behind him, and spun around to raise his bow as the muzzle of a musket appeared at an upstairs window. And my father should have released his arrow, but I noticed the quiver in the hand that held the bow, he could not steady it, and I thought of my mother holding that hand the night before we left. The time that he had been ill two years before, the disease you get from a fly, that shrinks into periods of remission, but never truly leaves.

This lack of control on my father's part must have lasted no more than a half second, but half of that short time was all the marksman needed to bend his finger.

And my father fell with a hole in his exposed neck. Luxxor flung himself upon the body in great protection before another shot rang out and caught Luxxor in the shoulder. My brother was already running to the door of the building.

A thousand men, a thousand beasts, the townsfolk, froze. A moment. It was unsupportable that my father had been hurt. The warriors could not be without their leader. The white men and women with their offerings of food, died within themselves, if this man had been killed there would be no hope of their reprieve.

A white man, hoping to find some favour in this awful moment, began shouting in his own tongue and pointing to a high window. There, still visible stood the end of a rifle, and I imagined I saw a drop of rain fall upon the heated barrel and instantly turn to steam.

Luxxor inspected my father's flesh.

'There is no pulse or remedy.'

My father had planned this adventure for fifteen years.

We were not invincible.

The townsfolk understanding the irreversible nature of the deed that had been committed by one of their own, reversed and began to stampede into the darkened, sodden alleys.

'No one leaves this square,' Luxxor hollered.

And the warriors dismounted, their beasts would have been a disadvantage in these narrow streets, and with their long, strong legs they herded back the whites and flung them back into the square.

On your knees and stay silent until we say otherwise.

Alone upon the saddle of the Beast, beyond horror or dismay, I gazed upon my father's body on the ground.

In a panic of the mind I wished to be gone from this place, this sight, these feelings and be returned to home. I wished to be wandering my village, my head filled with stories of adventure. Could I rewrite or un-imagine my father's death.

Could I, by force of words alone reverse or undo this tragedy. Could I transmute words into a pulse, a breath?

Minutes before I had my father slaughtering an Ogre many times his size. Now he lay on the ground. Shrinking. As if the doors to the afterlife were low and tight and he had to accommodate.

Why was I not holding his dead hand and weeping as Luxxor was now clearly doing? I was glued to my saddle, my ankles on the stirrups.

My brother dragged a man out into the street. He was well dressed. My brother held the two rifles he had taken from him. My mind, unable to focus on my grief, wondered for a moment while the man had two muskets. Muskets take time to load, so he had carried two already primed. To be able to fire two shots in quick in succession he needed two weapons side by side. The death of my father had been planned. Any soldier might fall in the field. But the death of my father had been planned. As the assassin primed his weapons he dreamt of puncturing my father's skin. He thought in great detail about putting a hole in my father's flesh. He for-heard the gurgle in my father's throat.

Some days before our arrival at the port in Afrik, we had come across a train of peasants wailing. I had asked a camel herder why they acted like that. The Mother has died, he replied, this is the way they show their grief. Imagine a sack of stones, so heavy you can hardly bear them. You either take one stone out each day for the rest of your life or you empty the sack upon your head in one moment of pain and grief.

The white folks gawped. A young girl gathered her mother's skirts.

'Coward, to shoot from behind and above,' I said in the Latin, and the murderer seemed to understand.

'Tell him, Ode, that his death shall be extraordinary.'

'Where is your wife?'

'I have no wife?'

'Nor child?'

'No, I am a bachelor. Untethered.'

'Brother,' I said, 'cut away the finger that he used to shoot our father.'

'Ode, he must suffer much more than that.'

'Oh, he shall. But I have a thought. May I pursue it Brother?'

My brother took the man's arm and prepared a blade.

But I did not watch.

I was not squeamish. I knew where to look. The crowd.

And as the man screamed, one woman gasped more than the rest and the girl beside her screamed.

'Daddy no, please don't hurt my daddy.'

'And now we have your wife and child,' I said. 'And can you imagine what we shall have to do to them to punish you for *your* offence.'

'They had nothing to do with this. You have me already, do what you want to me. But do not hurt my wife and child. Do not prove yourselves to be the brutes this crowd would accuse you of being.'

'You ask this favour of me?'

'As one educated man to another, I do. Any man that can speak the language of philosophy, must have some moral compass by which to orientate themselves.'

'And how have you earned my favour? By killing my father?'

The man fell to his knees and vomited. His daughter cried his name. Above and behind, flames erupted from the window and the glass shattered. A cat with a half tail walked through the square oblivious between the feet and hooves. The blood, the dung.

'This is the body of a heathen. It has no right to be here in this place of worship.'

'This is the body of my father, the Chief Elder of our tribe, commander of a thousand men, the one chosen by nature to command a thousand beasts. My dead father here is as close as you will ever get to divinity. You should kneel.'

'Before a dead nigger in a consecrated church? Your father stains the reputation of this house.'

I looked to Luxxor.

'I know. Ode, I may not understand the language you are sharing, but I can read this man's face. This man's disrespect is obvious to all. Warrior, go outside and command someone to bring us four long nails.'

The warrior looked confused.

'If you don't know the words, mime it,' said Luxxor.

'My cousin has sent for nails,' I told the priest.

We sat hard bummed in the pews.

'We are without our father,' my brother said.

'We are without our leader,' said Luxxor.

'We are an army decapitated,' I said.

'But we are not without purpose,' said Luxxor, 'we are not without hope. We are poised on the verge of our great adventure. All we have to do is take the next step forward.'

'But in which direction Uncle?'

Behind us in the rows sat a thousand men, silent as leaves. The priest stood sweating at the lectern.

The succession of our leadership should have fallen to Luxxor, my father's second in command. But the bloodline pointed to my brother.

Bloodline, Ode? I thought Luxxor was your uncle.

I have always called him uncle to honour his closeness to my father. But he was not family. Anna, Kristans call their God their Father do they not? And you are not related.

And then the great door of the church opened with a grating whine, but no man stood there. Instead, Mphuno.

'We should not have left him outside,' I said. 'We should have brought him in with us. He must be grieving also.'

'Ode, I thought to leave him with his own for comfort. Am I to know how beasts grieve?'

The Beast let the door close behind him. His shoulders moved and his great thick skin rippled very slightly.

'Come,' said Luxxor.

Each row of warriors stood to their full height as we passed.

We knelt upon the cold stone floor.

Mphuno surveyed us one by one. The Beast was to be our arbiter.

I knew beyond any doubt that it would not select myself. It was unthinkable. And yet of course the unthinkable has that habit of scurrying across the width of our imaginations. And I thought, no not me. Not even a Beast would be so stupid as to choose me.

Mphuno made a small movement towards me. His tiny eyes, his fat lips, the speckled horn. I flinched.

'Are you scared, Ode?'

'No Brother, but it is father's Beast. I thought that it might blame us for his demise.'

I never understood those leathered faces that betrayed no expression. Many times I had tried to see inside their minds and wondered about the nature of their thoughts. Had the storm been the world's reaction to the change in their behaviour, or had the unsettled elements turned the minds of the beasts.

It is the story that my father was the chosen one. But could this have happened to any child of our tribe? What had I lost, a father or a Prophet?

We had the one mantra. We are chosen. We shall make history. Father was our Prophet. What now? And what had the rhinoceros ever wanted? Was it glory? Certainly not revenge. But there was no one to ask. Certainly, not the beasts themselves. With my father dead, everything was out of balance. And as I struggled for understanding, I tried pushed away the rawness of my grief. Better to wail than to analyse. But we cast ourselves in the mould we spend a lifetime, making.

Is it possible that what we saw as destiny was merely a series of accidents that presented themselves in such a way that we found meaning and order within their pattern and unfolding.

'Beast,' I said, 'I know your worth and esteem, your courage and your wisdom. You shall be a cornerstone of my Story. The greatest of the beasts of all time and repute. I will search the learned libraries of the continent for the finest words to celebrate your bravery.'

And as if understanding and accepting my compliments, as if telling me the Story had to be written as it had been planned, and that he was satisfied that his place, was to be secure within the Legend, he turned to Luxxor next.

'You know my skills. I shall not fail my warriors or your beasts.'

Then Mphuno, chief amongst the beasts, the bearer of my father, knelt before my brother, huffed.

'It has chosen you,' said Luxxor satisfied that things were in their right place.

'Yes, and I am honoured. But am I not too young to be the leader of our tribe?'

'You are your father's son, said Luxxor. 'The warriors will respect the lineage of blood. No one will go against you unless they want the visitation of my wrath. It is done.'

My brother tried to get to his feet, wiping his eyes.

'I must not let the men see my weakness. How can I lead them with girlish tears in my eyes.'

'Stay. To cry for the death of your father, is not a sign of weakness, it is a sign of strength. Each man here wants to cry, but feels that he lacks permission.'

And my brother walked very slowly along the aisle until he arrived at the nave. The Priest scarpered and hid in a shady alcove. My brother turned to his men and ran his long fingers across his eyes and displayed his grief.

And then the men before him began to cry. A thousand tears multiplied.

Luxxor strode towards my brother and took a position a few stone steps below.

'Ysoun, my brother by love and respect over blood, and my Master also, father to Ode and Baaku, husband to Mosaa, son of Adebe, Chief Elder and commander in the field to every one of you, is elevated to the Afterlife. But you still reside upon the unsubtle ground. And your duty now is to honour his death and to bring to life his vision of conquest. His vision of the glory of our tribe. I call upon all of you here…'

And then he began to name them, all one thousand of the warriors. Mbasu, Ngege, Arunde, Akelele. Each man took notice as their own name tumbled from Luxxor's lips. And they felt proud, singled out, special, but also part of a greater whole.

'And to you all, I say this. Know that our Chief Elder, even in death, honours you all, and has taken your names to the spirit world where you will be revered and welcomed when it is your time. You will be awaited. You are amongst the greatest men that have ever lived upon this world.'

It was enough. The warriors stamped their feet in unison, wept again and embraced each other.

The warriors searched the surrounding houses for furniture to make a pyre. One man had tied himself to an ornate chair. They cut him free before they added the wood to the pile. His roasting flesh would have tainted the solemnity.

My father's body was rested upon the broken. Luxxor set the fire.

Our traditional burial service was cremation followed by liquor and dancing. Men drank and danced, they swigged and wiggled until stupefied and then fell to earth to be dragged home by their ankles by the no less grieving wives. Cremation because our dry, thin soil, made an easy grave to dig, but a body easy to be exhumed thereafter and gnawed upon by dogs.

The last I would see of my father's body.

My mind being learned, practical, I struggled to imagine the location and dimensions of the Afterlife. I had never asked, what of the first man to die? Was he there alone? Did he pray for the death of those he loved the most, so that they may join him? And when they arrived was he ashamed to have wanted to hasten their departure from their earthly flesh?

Then, of course, there were countless millions eagerly awaiting the arrival of my father. My father had led a thousand warriors to the gates of Yurop. He would be celebrated beyond all others.

Mphuno watched the flames with his tiny eyes. Blank and rhinone. We knew he could make decisions. But where were his thoughts? The warriors had lived side by side with the beasts for the majority of their lives, and yet not one of them had any understanding of their minds. The beasts were mighty. They were loyal. But they were opaque.

Mphuno went to our Beast and they stood snout to snout. Whatever passed between them I could not see the language of.

'Ode, should I ride Mphuno now?' said my brother taking my arm.

My father's face was flame.

'He cannot be without a rider? But then do I abandon my own Beast who I have known since the age of four. Ode, I do not know what is required of me. Ode, could you ride our Beast alone?'

Only the Chief Elder's Beast was named. We watched as our own walked towards the pyre. Into the fire.

'No,' cried my brother. 'No!'

'Brother, he has gone to be Father's Beast in the afterlife.'

'Why did Mphuno not put himself into the pyre?'

'Brother he has yet to finish his pursuit. He lives on in respect to our father. We shall ride him.'

After the wood and flesh were reduced to ashes there was no drinking. No dancing. Not this time. The death was too severe. The warriors and beasts curled upon the flagstone floor of the square and tried to sleep.

I found no comfort in the thought of a world after death. I could not believe it, because I could not visualise it. There was no depiction, no description. Just the faith in its existence.

'That was a good plan, Ode. Now we have his wife and child. We will find the parents also, any brothers or sisters. His entire family shall be hung in the square. It is a quite popular form of entertainment here so I have been told.'

'Brother, we shall not hurt this woman and this child.'

'And why not?'

'Brother we fight those who wish to fight us. We fight those that resist our plans. Father would not be proud of us if saw us punishing the innocent. He would not want that child to scream in payment for her father's actions.'

'But it was your plan to reveal them? What do you suggest we do?'

'I shall tell him stories that will torture him from all sanity.'

'Stories, Ode?'

In Yurop they liked to keep those they wished to punish in the dark. Back in my lands we tied criminals to a tree under the full light of the sun. They could not shield their eyes against the mighty star, as any common man might do, because we removed their eyelids. A strange punishment that caused very little pain upon execution but great discomfort forever more. And we used rope, where they used chains. Rope bit, chains chaffed. It is always the ankles and the wrists that commanded attention.

I stared at him. This man. This killer of my father. Bound in his chains in the cellar of an inn. Bloodied about the face, his lips fat. The open wound of his missing finger.

'What have you done to my wife and child?'

'You ask me that as if it were my duty to tell you.'

My aim was to tell him tales of the foul violation of his wife and child. To remind him again and again that this was the consequence of his murdering my father.

I had told Nassir's father that he was the murderer of his son, and I would tell this man that he was the violator of his own family.

'Every disgrace that is being visited upon them is the result of your actions and yours alone.'

'I did what I did because you were invading us. How many of my people did you kill?'

And so I steeled myself to tell him a brutal tale, to pain him beyond measure.

But the words would not come. As all Griots know, words are the translations of the pictures of the mind. And I could not bring myself to picture a violated girl child. To be able to tell a story of terrible foulness, I would have to imagine things I could not bear to imagine.

My attempts to torture him would be torture for myself.

I could record violence, because it unfolded before me without my encouragement. I wrote of pain, but my words did not cause the hurt. I baulked at the invention of harm. A sensitivity that would have made my brother scoff.

And then it struck me that I was a fool. I did not have to do the imagining. I would let the killer of my father do that himself. I would not tell him story. I would let him imagine it for himself. I would let him be his own torturer.

And so I said.

'I will not hurt you. I will leave you here to ponder the unendurable pains and degradations that your beloveds are currently suffering, especially your child. It is a truly pitiful sight and sound. She is calling for her father to save her and we have told her, that all the truly terrible things that are being done to her are *because* of you.'

'No,' he said, 'please make this stop. Is there anything I can do to save them? I do not care of the cost to myself. Whatever hideous torture you can envisage, I will bear it if you save my wife and child, for they are beautiful and blameless.'

And then another thought occurred to me. At first I fought it back like tears, and then I looked at the man who had taken my father. They say I am the clever one. But I shall hurt you more than any trained soldier might do. I shall hurt you with lies and I will tell it as if it were true. I am trained for this.

'If you wish to end their suffering I will have them killed on your request. In death they will find peace.'

'You want me to ask you to kill my own wife and child?

'I want you to beg for it. It would after all be a mercy. I can hardly imagine that they will survive this ordeal.'

He flailed about in his chains.

'I cannot do such a thing. It is unnatural. The Lord would punish me for such a request.'

'Who do you love more your family or your lord?'

'The Lord is my shepherd, but I am the shepherd of my family. The question that you ask cannot be answered.'

'Your lord is nothing and is powerless to save your family from harm. But you can. You can save them. You can be the shepherd that you wish to be. I will let you think upon these things. I will come to you again tomorrow. Think of your child's flesh, think of her violation and I will ask you again tomorrow if you want me to order her swiftly sent to a place of peace. I know nothing of the character of your wife, but your daughter is still a child and will surely go to heaven.'

'Ode, come with me.'

Luxxor took me to a back room of the Town Hall. The door had been smashed through.

'Look, Ode.'

Guns.

'Ode, I cannot figure their number.'

'Maybe two hundred,' I said.

And looking around I found barrels of red powder, wooden crates of small metal balls, boxes of cotton pads.

'Ode, have you learned how to use a gun in any of your studies?'

'The shot goes into the barrel of the gun. The powder explodes and shoots the shot out of the barrel.'

'Whereabouts in the gun does the powder go?'

'I do not know.'

'Do you put it in the barrel before the shot? Or is there a special compartment?'

'Uncle I do not know!'

'Then find out. Experiment. Solve the puzzle.'

'Uncle I am too distraught with grief to do so. How could I concentrate in the task?'

'And what is your grief for?'

'What is it for? I am grieving for my father, what else?'

'Your father is in the Afterlife celebrated as a mighty warrior. The first ever Kikuyo to tread on Yurop soil.'

'Where he died!'

'Where he was killed! Shot from behind. There is no blame on your father.'

'I never said there was.'

'Your grief is for yourself. It does not help your father, it does not help you, and it does not help our campaign.'

'Uncle do you not feel my father's passing?'

'My heart is broken. But like a wound you have to bear it and wait for it to heal. Tears and sighs, fainting and mopping your brow will not help. Courage and time are our only medicines. Now focus your mind on the mechanical. Let that be your task. Your father was shot by a gun such as one of these. If we can learn to shoot we will kill these white men in their thousands with their own weapons.

'Ode, with your father gone, it falls to me to order you to do things that will benefit us all. Yet I would rather not command you against your wish. I would rather ask you, and for you to comply.'

'Yes Uncle.'

He left me to my studies.

I pulled back the hammer and dry fired the gun by pulling the trigger. It was easy enough to determine that these were the working parts. The hammer held a section of flint that struck against a moving metal plate, creating sparks. At the base of that plate sat a pan. So I concluded that the sparks set fire to any powder that was in that compartment.

So I filled the pan with powder.

I put a metal ball inside the barrel and pushed it to the base with the rod.

I put on my leather helmet, raised the gun and fired at the wall. There was a flash in the pan but the bullet did not fire.

On closer inspection I noticed that there was a small borehole between the pan and the barrel. One explosion lead to another? I poured powder into the barrel. Assuming that the cotton pads had some role to play I forced one of those in before using the rod to push in the metal ball. Then I filled the pan and cocked the hammer. But I did not want to shoot at the wall. I wanted to kill something.

I took the gun out into the town square. A snot nosed kid was sat on the cobbles adjusting the rags he wore in place of shoes. I pointed the gun at him. He didn't seem to care. A dog appeared from an alley. I swung to have him in my sights. The dog scarpered.

Luxxor appeared behind me.

'You want to shoot something?'

'But I can't.'

'Is the gun properly loaded?'

'I think so.'

'Then shoot me.'

'Uncle?'

'An experiment. To test the strength of our armour. If I am unhurt then we will know of our strength. If I am killed then I shall be with my brother tonight.'

'Uncle I cannot.'

'Ode, you will do as you are told. We have already spoken of this. Now I will stand at one end of the square and you will fire at me from the other end.'

'But I have no skill. I will miss wildly.'

'That instrument you use for measuring distance, do you not point it at the thing you want to see. Do the same with the rifle.'

And so I knelt and rested the gun on my withered arm and looking along the length of the barrel aimed at my Uncle in full armour. And pulled the trigger.

There was the sound of breaking glass. I had shot out a window.

'Ode, reload. I will stand here, still.'

I shot the cobbles. I shot a wall. I shot out another window. I scared a bird.

'Uncle …'

'No, Ode. You do not give up.'

I tried again.

Fuck.

Luxxor clutched his chest.

'Shit. That hurt. Well done, Ode. That fucking hurt.'

Luxxor opened his armour and stared at his chest.

'No blood, Ode. I will have a fucking great bruise in the morning. But no blood. I am not dead. Their guns do not penetrate the armour your mother designed for us all.'

He looked up into the sky.

'Brother of mine, we will have to wait a little longer before we see each other again.'

I brought the murderer his wife and child.

'They are unharmed?'

'And so shall you be.'

'Ode, what are you doing?'

'Punishing this man, Brother.'

'And how?'

'This man called me earlier this morning and begged me to kill his wife and child. It is a thing he will never forget.'

'Sometimes, Ode, you are a fool. You leave this man alive and he will think he has outwitted you. He will rejoice when you are gone. He kills our father and is rewarded. It cannot be. We will not discuss this further.'

Three warriors entered the cellar. My brother nodded to them.

'Ode, come.'

I stood my ground.

'Ode, do you want me to drag you up the stairs. I will do so if you force me to, do not think I won't.'

We hardly had to command our plunder. They gave us everything they had with no thought of breakfast and beyond. Hungry sprogs were slapped across the head by their Mothers and told to suck their thumbs.

Olives, oils and cubed cheeses in salted water were delivered to us in glass and earthenware vessels. Pickled vegetables. Air dried pig thighs. Trinkets and little Khrists on chains. Coins and fine lace. One dried bird in a glass dome.

The treasures of the church were confiscated. The priest watched as we loaded, silver, gold, glass, upon a series of simple horse driven carts. He didn't remonstrate, instead he muttered to himself.

'Holy God on high smite these devils where they stand. Send down bolts of lightning to extinguish them, pestilence to plague them, let their foul black skins erupt in boils. Then send them hell bound. Even there they will not be welcome. What would the devil want with these barbarians? Send them to hell and anger hell for the sending.'

And then in a panic he began clawing at the air above his head.

'Lord,' he cried aloud. 'I cannot hear you. And lord I have heard you since I was a child. Have you turned against me? I should not be letting them plunder your house. But I do not know what to do. They are so many. How do I fight them Lord?'

'Brother, who will man the carts?'

'The men who own them.'

'They will not want to come with us. It might be a disadvantage to have a troop of souls travelling behind us that wish us ill. They will surely spend their time being slow, to slow us down. They will surely do all in their power to sabotage us in our mission.'

'No Ode, they won't, for the men shall bring their wives and children with them. A strong man is made weak by the presence of his family. You taught me that lesson, Ode.'

When the warriors dragged a wooden Khrist on a cross down the church steps, the priest stopped his muttering and ran at them with his fists, for which he received a blow, toppled over, and cracked his knees on the cobblestones.

The Khrist was loaded into a cart next to a women breastfeeding her child. The man who held the reins, made no comment and just stared north.

It would have made more sense to leave this bounty here and collect it on our return. But my brother wanted this gold and silver, this Khrist, he wanted it here and now, it was his first booty. And what did it matter to carry it a thousand miles, when you had someone else to do the carrying?

We were to leave.

A hammer echoed around the square. Metal upon metal, the resistance of wood, high-pitched screams.

The priest was nailing his left hand to the wooden door of the church with a hammer held in his right.

At the end of a line of simple rustic carts, led by simple, slow, ponderous horses, sat a carriage. Fine, decorated, enclosed. The equines before it alert and startled. A man in livery upon the seat. Bald with a great white beard. The reins in his hand.

A woman's voice within, loudly complained in the local tongue.

'Fichy y bastardy!'

'Brother, who are we taking with us?'

'A special guest. I have taken the Mayor's daughter hostage to ensure the safety of our fleet at harbour. I do not want to leave men behind to guard the boats. Luxxor agrees with me. Any men ordered to stand guard here while we push through Yurop would feel sorely used. They might turn against us.'

'If our father had asked a man to stand in one spot without moving for a thousand years, he would have been happy to do so.'

'Then I will have to learn to command the same respect my father found so easily.'

'So, Brother, you have abducted one of their women? I do not like it. I do not think Father would have done that.'

'Ode, do not question me on matters of tactics. Myself and Luxxor have agreed this is the best course of action. You are here to record, not make suggestions. Can you think of any other plan to preserve the safety of our fleet in enemy territory?'

One woman among a thousand warriors. In my imagination, I could see her, small and slight. She had already given up any hope of rescue. Her father gave her up after all. She was desperately looking for something to kill herself with.

And ta-da, I enter the story.

What is ta-da?

It is a sort of exclamation, you put your hands in the air and cry out ta-da!

'If we have taken her,' I said, 'put her in my charge. I will protect her.'

'Brother Ode, you have not yet even set eyes upon her. What if she is hideous?'

'Does she have to be beautiful to deserve my protection?'

'I have seen her. She does not appeal to me. Her lips are as thin as leaves.'

He turned around in the saddle and we embraced as brothers. His two strong arms around my shoulder. My one good arm around the small of his back. The other lying limp.

'She is yours, Ode, protect her as you wish.'

'Brother, I will need your help. Please, make it known that anyone who hurts or offends her, hurts and offends me, and by definition yourself.'

The bearded man in livery sat upon the box, leather reins in his hands and chuckled to himself as I approached.

As I opened the carriage I was met with phlegm. I blinked. Making the natural assumption that a woman would not be educated in the learned languages of Latin or the Levantine, I could not express that I had no intention of hurting her.

She stared at me in disgust, and then made a mime, with her mouth open and two fingers pointing at her lips, to indicate, I presumed, that the very thought of me made her want to retch.

The sight of her, even in her righteous anger, even having spat on me, had a remarkable effect on my heart. Her neck was very long and quite white, even though she came from a country with clear wide skies and a bouncing orange sun. I assumed that because she came from a wealthy family she did not have to spend time labouring in the fields.

Her dress was decorated with fauna, blooms and blossoms. Dark hued and yet exquisite. And I myself, was be-decked in my soft and leather armour. Mauve and black and magenta dots swirled around my body in Mandalas and Archimedean spirals.

The helmet that I wore in battle rested in my hands.

Her dress reached the floor of the carriage and was so voluminous that it was hard to judge the shape of her that hid within it. But that which I could see, her slender arms, that pale neck, that gorgeous face of hers with the dark brows like

126

Arabic script quite beguiled me. The upper part of her cheeks were decorated with small indents. A white version, I assumed at the time, of the tribal marks that we Africans wore with such pride.

Only later did I find out that she was not proud of these scars. Rather than being part of her identity, she saw them as a curse.

At this point of pondering she spat at me again, her gob landing on my nose. And I laughed. I could see no other option.

'Pulchra femina,' I said with no hope of being understood.

Her face twisted awfully and she began to scream.

'The nigger finds me beautiful, and he knows how to say it! What devil's work is this. Is he possessed?'

My brother appeared behind me laughing.

'The pale women is all yours,' he said.

The men were not without company.

We called them carriages. They were simple farmers carts, but clean enough and decorated inside with any garish things the girls could beg, steal or borrow.

They had been with us since the beginning. They flocked to us. Not the same individuals, not the very same curtained carts. But interchangeable in their type. When they saw us camped for the night they would park at a respectful distance and light oils lamps which they hung on high poles. There would be ten to twenty of these woman and Luxxor would say who could visit and who would have to wait their turn for another day.

They were of all ages, heights and weights, rouged and sometimes bewigged.

By all accounts they enjoyed themselves as much as the men. The most magnificent men they had ever parted their legs for. Who by some tradition they were unfamiliar with would leave a piece of token jewellery over and above the standard charge.

These were our warrior's companions.

I of course refused. Not out of squeamishness. I did not want to be relieved. I wanted to be loved. I did not want to pay someone to ignore my disadvantage. I wanted someone, who through love, saw me as whole.

Did our black skins retain something that the white skins had lost over time and distance? Or was white the proper realm for man, and our blackness some form of stain. What I was certain of was that the white skins found us quite appalling. They stared at us with open revulsion, in many cases seeing our darkness as a possible manifestation of the devil in their religion. Whereas, in general we studied their white skins and felt rather sorry for them in their pallor. If our blackness made them want to foam at the mouth and cut the hearts from our chests, their whiteness struck us as something rather blank and desperate for decoration.

And later I came across an unusual word, a word that I struggled to fully comprehend the meaning of.

Palimpsestos. Palim meaning again. Psestos meaning rubbed smooth. Its meaning seemed to me that it referred to writing that had been written over other writing. And I wondered how often that happened that there needed to be a word for it. But maybe our black skin was palimpsestos? The stories of our troubles written over and over again on the surface of our skin, until you could not see the words for the weight of our experience.

And the whites were blank skinned because they had no story.

Except in the case of Anna. But her story was written not upon her skin, but in the depth of her eyes.

The town stood on a low hill. The road to it withering. We met no resistance. The town was deserted. Yet the market stalls were still full. Meats, cheeses, fruit and vegetables. Still fresh. The streets were tight and stepped, winding and with no apparent plan.

'Shit,' said my brother. 'They have just run away. What sport is that? Every single Motherfucker and their children has just run away.'

A number of us dismounted and strolled around the town.

We found an old lady with twisted legs.

She gabbled at us and smoked her pipe.

'One old lady, that is all there is to fight? They are mocking us. Right, let them run. But we will leave them nothing to return to. Take everything of worth and load it on the carts.'

'Brother would it not be better to keep the town intact. To keep it as our own. Our conquest.'

'But then we would have to leave men behind to enforce that. I cannot ask such thing of any of our warriors. To spend weeks, months, a year sat in some crappy town waiting to see if white soldiers arrive, when we are fighting in glory?'

'Soldiers may arrive in ships to the south and retake the towns behind us.'

'And if white soldiers did appear, what could our abandoned warriors do. Fight them on their own? Try and get a message to us? And how?'

'I had not thought it through, Brother. I had no need to do so. I expected to simply do what our father asked us to do without question.'

'Yet you question me?'

'No Brother, I will not question you. But you must let me speak my mind. Even Father let me do that. He said that it was the thing that I did best. To see what I see and speak of it clearly is my destiny, as yours is to conquer after the fall of our father.'

'Then let us not argue, but think, Ode, what will there be to retake after we have conquered a town? They will find nothing to encourage or sustain them. We will burn the buildings, loot the churches and the cellars, destroy the fledgling crops in the fields, poison the wells.'

'But how can we say we have *taken* a town if we have destroyed it?'

'We take the *memory* of the place from them. They will never forget what we have done. If we merely bash in a few doors, steal some candlesticks and loaves of bread, kill a few peasants then what? They will have forgotten about us when we are a few miles up the road. That is hardly the stuff of legend. You should know that.'

We plundered each and every house, but there was nothing of any value. Earthenware is not worth its weight to carry and so like spoilt children we simply smashed it on the stones floors. What art there was, was awful amateur daubings in wonky handmade frames.

The chapel had no gold. No silver. The villagers had taken it all in their flight.

Upon the walls was a reverse shadow of a cross. A shape upon the stonework that was lighter than the rest of the wall. They had taken their prophet with them.

We gathered straw from the stables and piled up wooden furniture and cloth. And set the place alight. And watched the smoke.

'And Brother, what have we achieved?'

'What have we achieved? I have led us over fifty miles into mainland Yurop. The whites run in fear before us. And we have yet to lose a single man.'

'We lost our father.'

'For fucks sake, Ode, stating the obvious does not make you insightful or give you the moral high ground. I know we lost our father. I was there. That is why we are continuing with our conquest. For him. For his sake. For his vision.

129

In his memory. If I had known you were going to be like this I would never have convinced Father to bring you along.'

'Brother, I am the Griot, the storyteller. What could I say about today that would make the story worth telling? These people, they were poor, simple folks, with no one to protect them. There was no gallant army for you to defeat. No cannon to dodge. These people had no argument with us at all. And yet we have just destroyed everything they had and for what?'

'Yeah, well. Fuck them.'

I had found a leather bound ledger in the Town Hall, a record of those who had lived in the town for the last one hundred years. I took it to study later.

That night in my tent by candlelight, name, name of spouse, children, occupation.

Farmers of olives, tomatoes, artichokes. Blacksmith, Carpenter, Butcher, Apothecary.

And then a name and a title. Patronum. Patron. Not the Major or the Chief of Police. But Patron. Someone who gave donations to the church to maintain its magnificence, and always made sure that everyone knew. A man who organised a spring banquet each year. All food and drink from his purse, a present for the common people.

The Occupation. Slave Trader [Retired].

No date of death registered. He was still alive. He had run with the rest.

I went to my brother's tent.

'Brother that old woman with the bent legs. The one they left behind. Did we leave her in the fire to die?'

'No Ode, a couple of my men carried her to an orchard outside of town. They left her under an olive tree. I don't think she even noticed.'

'Brother, there is something I want to show you in this ledger.'

Her horse drawn carriage had come to a halt, but still rocked wildly on its suspension. Her driver gone. No doubt enjoying his stipend of cheap wine and sausage under a tree somewhere, bottle half full, crumbs of pork in his beard. Eyes lolling. Happy.

But from inside the carriage, a commotion. Screams and wailing. The sound of fists and boots going at the interior. She was not being hurt. Not by one of us.

I understood. Her carriage, her luxury, was also her cell. Her elevation, her submission. Her comfort, a manacle.

I carefully opened the door. She did not scream this time.

Her face was red and swollen. Her brow was ridged, her knuckles blue, her nails cracked. The tips of her boots had lost their polish and their pride.

I showed her my open hands, my palms. I am not armed. I carry no knife. Look at the softness of my flesh, these are not the hands of a warrior. You do not need to fear my strength.

I smiled.

'My name is Ode.'

'Lucky you,' she said.

To our left stood a forest. The sky was grey above us. Despite our leather helmets, tiny bugs flew through the eyeholes and settled in the corner of our eyes. Or headed towards our lips. We had to keep our mouths shut or they would charge down our throats.

Mphuno suddenly dug in his paws, and in respect and with due obedience, all those behind him follow suit.

'They have smelled something in the woods.'

Horse and riders burst from the gloom and trunks, and charged us on our flank. The first wave blew into long brass instruments they had mounted on the skulls of their animals. The human lips vibrated at the mouthpiece and the horses salivated at their champs.

If this sound was meant to scare or subdue the rhinoceros, it failed. The white armies did not know us. They could not read us. We were the unknown. We were the bogeyman of the dark continent, made real in statuesque black.

Our beasts charged the first wave of horse and rider without even receiving our instruction. And gouging them, and unsaddling the soldiers they beat the bodies of the white men with their stony paws.

The first wave had failed, but the sound of a thousand screaming men fell upon us. Wave after wave of horse came bristling through the bark.

'We can take them,' said my brother. 'These horse can be ridden, but they are no danger in themselves. The white man has domesticated a drone. We have control of fast moving killer beasts.'

'We can,' said Luxxor, 'but it might be costly. Let us show that they can send an army against us and we do not lose a single man. Our beasts have learned something of the water this adventure.'

'I will follow your advice Uncle.'

'Into the river,' shouted Luxxor. 'And dive on my command. If a horse's head goes under water it will quickly drown. Pull them under from beneath.'

One thousand of us crashed into the water, followed by the white men on their steeds.

'Now!'

The rhinoceros plunged below the surface. We the warriors, held our breaths and kept our eyes wide until we could see the horse's legs above us.

In the swirling water my brother tied a fast, wet, knot into his leather rope, and on the third try lassoed a horse's leg and tightening the other end around the neck of the rhinoceros spurred the Beast into lower water.

Above us the horse thrashed and drank water in place of air, and quickly drowned. Their riders struggled to extract themselves from their drowning horses. And as we rose again we sliced away their dancing legs before they could break the surface.

And we surfaced with breaking lungs to see a mass of drowning horses, cursing, flailing legless riders. Their only options to die right there and then in the blood stained water, or by miracle to survive and have the miserable life of a begging amputee.

Our army were already singing when a hundred men appeared on the bank, armed with arrow. We sailed towards them, our feet lashed to the stirrup, the rhinoceros's legs swimming under us as dogs do. Our leather armour, now soaked right through and quite impervious to their soft metal, weak, sapling, arrows.

Run from the fight and your enemies will chase your back and kill you from behind. But run towards the fight and your enemy will turn and flee!

We pressed them so hard into the earth that their burial needed no spade.

'Let me look at your face, Ode,' said my brother as he turned to me and shook me by the shoulders. 'Look at that great big fucking smile across your gob. Adventure for me and tales for you to tell. Shit, Ode, look.'

'I am looking,' I said.

Two white soldiers sat side by side upon the box and drove the horses down a lane away from us. The wheels humping the uneven ground. The old man with the beard sat with his back against a tree. A flagon of wine in his hand.

'They are not moving fast,' I said, 'we can easily outrun them.'

'Ah, Ode, to the rescue of his maiden,' laughed my brother. 'Shall we get her back, Ode?'

We rode at speed and overtook and simply cut across their path. The two horses by now knew Mphuno, we had marched together side by side for many weeks. They blew air at each other through their nostrils.

The two white soldiers jumped from the box and fled, and we couldn't be bothered to chase them.

I opened the door to check on Anna's condition. She kicked it shut and swore at me. She was fine.

Our entire army was seated. I knew they have been commanded to listen, but I wanted them to offer their attention willingly. I had prepared my script in Latin, and now translated my words freestyle into the tongue of my Kikuyo audience.

I recounted the details of our last battle, the reverberation of my voice filling the valley.

'We drowned a thousand of their horse and rider. We were impervious to their arrows. We buried our foe under the weight of our beasts.

'You brave warriors! You upstanding men! Fearless enemy of the whites. Black skinned revengers. Men of such height and physical prowess, that the white men weep. And weep again when they catch their reflection in the water or see their weak shadow upon the ground.'

They were listening to me. Ode, who as a boy, no one had wanted to play with.

'This story and all others that I will tell in time, are of *your* exploits. You are the heroes of my tales. Under the leadership of my brother and your Chief Elder.'

My brother joined me in front of the men and put his arm around my shoulder as the warriors screamed with pride.

This is why I brought you here, said my father from the Afterlife. And I have heard every word.

'Ode,' said my brother squeezing my shoulder, 'your words give the men more strength than a leg of lamb.'

At the very back of the crowd sat Anna's carriage. I knew she would not understand my words spoken in Kikuyo, but I hoped she might appreciate the power of my voice. I hoped that she had pulled the curtain back a very tiny bit and seen one thousand men giving me their complete attention and respect.

I couldn't sleep. I wondered if the events of the day had caused her more anguish than might have been her daily fare. Had we saved her or thwarted her?

And so at some late hour I stood there in the night staring at the silhouette of the carriage. There was a light breeze ticking through the dark leaves. The popping sounds of small fish rising to the surface of the water. Some young cicada practising their rhythm. Frogs locked in disagreement with each other.

A figure appeared from the carriage door under the face of the moon. It was not her. She had been visited by a guest, a jailor, a paramour?

I walked towards him as brave as I could muster.

'You are a stranger here,' I said, 'hiding amongst a thousand men that will cut you without pause.'

He did not understand me. He pointed a pistol at my chest.

From inside the carriage the woman's voice gabbled and lamented. I imagined her meaning. He had a gun to my breast! I am not to blame for bringing him amongst you!

'You are a spy,' I said. 'No doubt looking for our weaknesses. And you came to us hiding in the carriage. That was clever. We didn't look inside the carriage because the lady kicked the door. Yet how could you have known we would take the carriage? You did it in plain sight, attracting us. You were too easy to catch, because you wanted us to take the carriage back into our own camp.'

The man rolled the barrel left to right across my ribcage.

'Our hearts are in the same place as yours,' I said.

He didn't understand a word of what I said and strangely I was not afraid. The curtain that covered the window in the carriage was pulled back. The glass caught the moon. A smudge of face was visible. I always longed to see it clearer and for longer.

What was she thinking? She had thought this man had come to rescue her, when in fact he had used her as bait and she was now recaptured.

And what could she see of me? My height. The weakness of my left arm hidden. Moonbathed. This man had a pistol to my chest and I was smiling and unafraid.

134

But unsure what to do next. I had to be decisive or my strength would quickly turn to weakness. My greatest power was language and memory. But we had no tongue to share. Yet I spoke anyway.

'If you kill me with that thing, everyone will hear.'

Then suddenly his mouth fell open, the gun slid down my chest, and slid to the ground, as did he moments later. I was confused beyond all understanding and almost missed the flurry of skirt that flapped away from me, and the crisp slamming of the carriage door.

Ten of our number crept into the hamlet quite undetected. The streets were empty, the stench foul.

There was some sort of commotion before us. We moved quietly. We wanted to see what they did when they did not know we were there watching. We had heard their screams and seen the running of their backs many times before.

My brother had posed beside me enough times in the last few weeks as I spoke of routs and adventures. I was aware of the repetition, the lack of spectacle.

The villagers sat on the stones of the square. Jars lay about. The foulest smell pervaded. They had come together to watch a show of some kind.

At the foot of the church stairs sat a horse cart. The flat bed had been curtained on three sides. The rear painted with a scenery of mountains and a lake. A boy with stubble sat upon a chair. He wore a dress and a wig of long yellow tresses. Beside him stood a man in a purple robe. He had a crown upon his head. He declaimed long and loud and the object of his affections, played with her hair and looked forlorn. Although the king spoke the common tongue of which I was unfamiliar, his style and clarity showed him to a professional speaker for the public. He was of great height, large chested. He had physique and eloquence. And the painting behind him was of such exquisite colour and detail that it made quite an impression upon me.

Although the audience were clearly drunk and had little time for the love affairs of princesses and kings, they listened. How often did such a spectacle, modest as it was, ever come to town? I imagined most of the troubadours took one whiff of this place and headed off across the ploughed fields to avoid it.

'This crowd of fools will jump to it when they see us,' my brother said.

The king tried to kiss the boy, but she refused him, and rather than respond with a girlish slap to the cheek, she punched the poor king upon the chin. The king reeled and clutched his face.

The crowd roared.

The object of his desire jumped to his feet and jumped from the cart and began to run around the square emitting girlish squeals with the timbre of a barrel-chested lout. The king followed at a gallop.

The audience clapped and jeered at the race. And not knowing their words, it was hard for me to tell whose side they were on. Catch that bitch and spank her! Or. Don't let that old fart get yer girl!

A race around the square by two men in costumes. It was the best thing they had seen for months. Even better than the eloquent protestations of love from an elderly king to a young girl played by a brutish boy. The king stepped on his own robes, crashed onto the flagstones, slammed his nose and came up again with blood streaming into his beard. The torn robe fell from him revealing a bare chest pocked with red blotches. The audience roared at his nakedness and taking his cue from that, the fair maiden, pulled up her skirt, pulled down her britches and wiggled her hairy arse at the crowd, who became quite overcome with the wit of such a gesture, until by a trick of the low afternoon sun, light crept into the tight alleyway where we had been basking in shadow, and revealed us in waiting.

All laughter stopped. The delicious virgin, thinking that he had commanded the audience's undivided attention reversed himself and pulled down the front of his britches to display his tackle. But no, they were looking beyond him and he turned to see what could possibly have upstaged the grand appearance of his naked cock.

And there we were and no denying it.

The king grabbed his robes with the one hand and covered himself as best he could. With his other arm he introduced our presence as if we were part of his show. Confused beyond measure the audience bit their lips. Were we this pretend king's real entourage? Had they drunk so much they were seeing visions? Had he conjured us by magic? They had laughed at him when he had fallen face down onto the flagstones. Was he offended? Might he now turn them into frogs, might he cause giant pustules to appear on their private parts, might the skeletons climb from their graves and dance upon the church steps? Were we to be feared or marvelled at? After all what *could* we be? Some local farmers with soot on their faces. Sat upon ponies strangely attired.

The king displayed and ushered us, as if only *he* knew who we really were.

'Do you speak the learned tongue?' I said in my storyteller's voice.

'I do,' said the king.

I awaited his comments on my ability. He made no such comment. Faced with such fearsomeness, he had come to a sensible decision.

'Are you from this town?'

'Sir, I am from nowhere. I am a travelling player, I move from town to town to tell my stories in the hope of the offer of small coins. I am alone and have to employ local louts to play the part of the princess. I have to pay part of my wage to some moron in a wig. Me who has played before kings and queens! What a fall from grace.'

'And have you done well today?'

'Here? No, this place is a shithole. And God does it stink.'

'We had noticed that.'

'Might I suggest that we repair to the local tavern to continue this conversation,' said the king.

'We are comfortable where we are,' said my brother through my translation.

'As am I. I was thinking only of your comfort. Now about this fucking pong. This is the town of the horse. Everyone in town works with the horse. People come from around and sell their horses when they are knackered and on the point of death. The butchers get to work, meat sausage, blood sausage, offal pies. Craftsmen boil the bones and ligaments to make glue. And the tanners cure the leather, and that is the foulest and most pungent job of all.'

'My mother is the finest of leather makers. Her work never makes this foul stench.'

'A woman's farts never smell, is that not what a gentlemen says?'

My brother looked murderous. The king knuckled himself in the forehead and fell to his knees.

'Forgive me I did not mean to suggest that your illustrious Mother ever broke wind. You are a marvellous sight. For a man of imagination,' he tapped his head with a finger, 'you are an inspiration. Already I am thinking of a play that will celebrate your exploits. What are the names of your beasts?'

'They are the rhinoceros.'

'The horse has been with the white man for many thousands of years. And when they are knackered they boil them down. Do you do the same to your rhinoceros?'

'We do not. They are our partners. A warrior bonds with his Beast at the age of four and never leaves his side. We give them the same burials we give ourselves.'

'Do you intend to take this village,' he said, 'have you come to conquer?'

'No, we intend to leave. I imagine anything we took with us would have the linger of this terrible smell. Better to leave that behind. We have supplies, we have dreams and ambitions enough to succour us.'

'Can I come with you?' said the king. 'I could entertain.'

'The painting on you cart. Did you do that.'

'It is another one of my humble skills, yes.'

'Brother, we are taking him with us.'

'We are?'

I had no knowledge of the horse.

The bearded man had died in the night. Beside him too flagons of dark, red wine.

My brother had given me charge of the woman. And now charge of the carriage and the two horses that pulled it.

I had no idea how to make them work.

They had reins, leather straps that connected my fingers to their jaws. I did not know what to do. I didn't want to hurt them with my incompetence. What would the woman think of me if I caused them stupid harm?

I commanded them in my best Griot voice, in both Latin and Levant.

They would not move.

The woman giggled inside the carriage.

The men filed past me smiling, their powerful beasts between their thighs under their complete command. I sat on the box and I could not get the buggers to move. Inside the carriage the woman was still giggling.

'I know you,' I said to the animals. 'You have my respect. You draw the ploughs, pull the carts and carriages, the flat bottom boats and rafts that sail the river. You carry the humans on your backs to war and harvest, funeral and matrimony. You haul the bricks and stones needed to make the grander buildings of their cities. Without you the white man would be nothing. So I must credit you with fortitude and intelligence, but I still do not know how to make you move.'

And then I heard the carriage door open and the woman climbed up beside me. 'Give me the reins.'

I did so.

'The other night you saved my life.'

'Yes, I know.'

'Why did you do that?'

'Let me show you how to control the horses.'

'I am Ode.'

'Oh I know *your* name. I have heard it spoken a hundred times within my hearing.'

'You saved my life and you are very beautiful.'

'I know,' she said very casually. 'Don't start getting ideas. I was not put in this world for you to start thinking about me at night.'

But I caught the flick of her eyelids. And I thought, surely I cannot be the first man to have praised you. Not with your beauty.

Like the Arabs of the desert we had our own caravan. The townsfolk from the harbour, those that we had spared, those with families to love and protect, trundled in our wake carrying our booty, much of which had been plundered from their own town. Quiet, docile men sat behind the reins and followed our conquest at their own speed. Their children, for sport and exercise, ran along beside, before falling into their mother's laps.

I rode Anna's carriage in the middle of the train, tactically the safest place in any column.

Peter's carriage trailed the rear. By some clever design, his stage also became his home. The picture panels could be reversed to make the carriage walls, so that the image of nature was on the outside, almost a sort of camouflage. His bedroll and his racks of clothes and a small portable reed organ, stacked under the carriage during a performance, somehow fitted into the interior. I often wondered if Peter himself, a tall, broad man with large hands and gestures, did not somehow have to find a way to fold himself in half to just sleep in there at night.

The elderly horses that drew his cart, had plumes of peacock feathers sewn into leather skull caps and bells upon their knees.

Dressed as a king, sometimes as a queen with long blonde wig, Peter would recite from the Greeks and sing bawdy tavern songs, that, on their parents' advise kept the children away from him. He had a store of wine under the box on which he perched. A flagon sat beside him at all times. And to keep his hands firmly on the reins, he had a tube of waxed paper running from the wine to his lips.

Anna spent her days and nights alone in the carriage. Hidden and safe. And I sat upon the box and drove the horses as she had instructed me to do.

My brother had told me to bind the door each night to stop her escaping in the dark.

In the morning I would unleash her. And she would fling the hinged door at my face. I had to throw myself backwards each time, to avoid have my nose quite smashed. I never learned.

Whenever we could, we encamped by water. The rhinoceros needed to drink and bathe.

Anna went to any river, or a lake when water was nearby. She had brought clothes with her in a chest of wood. Each day she appeared changed. Decked in rich and fabulous costumes of great design. She changed her clothes before bathing, not after. Each day as she left her carriage, she wanted me to see her in her finery, if only on her brief visit to water.

And each day I followed her. And each day she knew I was there behind her. And each day I came a little closer, but never ever close enough to touch.

I followed her to a stone cold lake, flat and sky blue. Small white birds with arrow like skulls, dived the water and came back up to the air with small glimmering fish, the heads and tails still swaggering in the grip of their beaks.

I was now very near.

She removed her heavy brocaded dress and let it fall. A white undergarment ran from the back of her neck, dipped in at the waist and bellowed out to her knees.

She stretched her back painfully.

This is what she did each day. And each day I got a little closer. That day I could see the stitching of her undergarment.

'Are you looking at me?'

'No, I'm just watching out for you. To make sure you are safe.'

I hardly sounded convincing.

She stepped into the lake and began to swim away from me. I wanted to join her. But it was clear you needed two strong arms. I did not want to make a fool of myself in front of her.

What if she had to save me?

I could strip, and charge into the lake and be out of my depth. And she would have to save me. In my failure she would have to reach out to me.

Or watch me die.

Then she was there before me, back on land. Up close, her wet clothes revealed her to be slighter than I had imagined.

'I am so bored each day that I want to scream. Can we talk you and I. Can we have conversations?'

'I would like nothing more.'

'No Ode, that is not true. There are things that you would like much more from me.'

I played with my fingers.

'I thought only educated men and priests spoke Latin. Not women.'

'Because women are stupid? Stupid little brains in their pretty skulls?'

'They say the same thing about blacks, except they don't find our skulls pretty.'

She smiled.

'Your father taught you?' I said.

She snorted.

'Hardly. Not my father, my uncle. And how do you, a black skinned warrior, talk the language of a dead empire?'

'I was taught. By an Arab.'

'Ode, I wish to change the subject of our conversation. There is something on my mind. My carriage is too cramped for me. I can neither stand nor stretch out on my side to rest. My body cannot find comfort. So my days are as unpleasant as the nights. My only relief is when I am allowed out to bathe. And even then I have you watching after me and making sure I don't escape.'

'That is not why I follow you.'

'Really? Then why, Ode? Why this fascination with my movements? Unless you are in love with me.'

'You want me to be in love with you?'

'Hardly, and why should I care? What do you take me for, Ode? And even if you said you did, how could I believe it? Your dark skin, I can't even tell when you are blushing.'

'What is blushing?'

'Well if you don't know, I can't tell you.'

'Do you want me to allocate you a tent?'

'I would not feel safe. Too many men, too many wolves. And I fear the men more than the wolves. Wolves have no imagination. Do you sleep alone?'

I was embarrassed to say it to her face.

'I do. As befits my status.'

'Then I will share your tent, but not your bed. It will be nice to have someone to talk to at night.'

'Do you not fear me?'

'Ode, you have had many chances over the last few weeks to throw me to the ground, and you have not done so. I hope you will continue to exhibit the same restraint in future. And my carriage should stand close by. That will be my private changing room. This is as naked as you will ever see me.'

She picked up her dress and crept into it, with her underwear still wet.

'Ode, you may think that I am not talking to you with due respect.'

She smiled and rolled her eyes, mocking her own shrewishness.

'Ode, if I sound strong, know this, this is an act on my part. We have a phrase in our country. My stomach is full of butterflies.'

'I do not know that phrase. But I like it and I shall use it myself one day.'

'No Ode, you must not. To have a stomach full of butterflies is to be terribly scared and weak and you must never let your brother think that of you.'

'I think that if they could bring themselves to admit it,' my brother said, 'we must look like Gods to them. And who do they revere? Their pale, thin Khrist with a woman's hair, hanging there nailed to wood by the very humans he had come to earth to save.'

We had eaten goat legs and turnips roasted in ash. Our servant had taken Anna her portion to her carriage.

I made a meal of stretching.

'Are you keen to get to sleep, Ode?'

I shrugged.

'All of this, Ode, should be ours. These lush fields and flowing rivers. The fish in the water, the deer on the woods, the fruit in the trees. I love our homeland, Ode. It is the place of all our spirits, alive and dead. But fucking hell, Ode, we have lived with dust for too long. Soil, Ode, that is what we need. We have our sun, we have our pride, if we could only take this soil home, Ode. What do you think it is made from?'

'It is made from the same stuff as grows in it.'

'Grass grows on stuff made of dead grass? Trees grow on land made good from dead trees?'

'Yes.'

'I am sure you are right, Ode, you have read the books. But I think the white man must be lying about that fact. If trees and grass grow on soil made of their dead ancestors how did the first ones grow?'

'How did the first man and woman make a child?'

'God made the first men and women, you know that, Ode. After that it was up to man to populate the earth. The Gods give you beginnings. Man has to tell the rest of story. What is the word the Khristans use for their perfect place?'

'Aden.'

'I can't pronounce that, Ode,' he said laughing. 'This place is the word you just said, and it should be ours, because we are superior to these ugly whites. They fall before us so easily. They cry so loud. Do you disagree, Ode?'

'I do not.'

I did not include Anna in that description. I didn't much care about the rest of them.

'Ode, you are writing the story of this adventure, do you write down the things we say to each other? When we are like this?'

'I do.'

'Ode, when you write my words, am I clever, or do I sound stupid?'

'I never let you sound stupid.'

'So you make me smarter than I am?'

'Maybe a little.'

'Then do so, on and on. You have permission and encouragement. Ode, that woman is approaching your tent.'

'She is to share it with me.'

I expected him to laugh, to make some childish comment.

'She says she is alone and bored and craves someone to talk to.'

Still he did not mock me.

'The nights can be lonely, Ode,' he said. 'I know this as keenly as you do. I may be married, Ode. But by the time we got used to each other I had to leave.'

We sat opposite each other with our bedrolls laid flat on the hard ground. A short fat candle sat in a gold dish between us. Our faces moved in the light. We had both been drinking wine.

'Good night, Anna,' I said. 'I hope that you sleep well and that I shall prove to be worthy of your trust.'

'And I hope to prove myself worthy of yours. What if this is all a terrible plan of mine, Ode, and I shall wait until you are asleep ...'

'And escape into the night?'

'No not that, Ode! There was never any need to lash me into my carriage. No. What if I wait till you are asleep and cut your throat for you!'

I grabbed my own throat, and gasped.

Anna laughed at the mockery of my own death. The candle-light danced across her open mouth and I wanted to put my lips to hers.

I had noticed that her teeth were not good. I went outside to find a fire and asked for a bowl of hot water. Back under cover I took some salt from my bag and stirred it in.

I lay the bowl between us and handed her a small strip of giraffe leather. I showed her how to wet the end of the leather strip and to rub it against the teeth. And we knelt like each other's mirror as we cleaned our mouths.

'My Uncle taught me Latin,' she said, her mouth refreshed. 'He thought the world was changing. He was wrong. Least until you black men landed.'

'We have hardly made the world a better place for you.'

'No. I studied Latin and the scriptures. But no priests would ever engage with me. I was not to be heard. I wanted to study astronomy at the university but they wouldn't take me. My uncle was the only person I could ever talk to of serious things. But he was much older than my father and passed away when I was still quite young.'

'Anna, I cannot talk to you of your Gods and stars.'

'Then tell me the story of theses fearful rhinoceros of yours. Is this just the first wave of yours, or are there many thousands more of you both to come? Swarming from your continent, armed and mounted on the beasts we cannot stop. Hell bent on our destruction.'

'To my knowledge there is only us, our tribe. The first rhinoceros that crossed over the river that separated man and Beast ...'

'You say the river? Is that a metaphor?'

'Yes. Exactly. The first rhinoceros that crossed over knelt before my father when he was just a child.'

'And you have inherited his greatness.'

I looked at her to perceive if she were mocking me. I thought that she was not.

'I have never seen you with a weapon, Ode. All the others are married to their blades. But not you.'

'I have no skills in that regard.'

'Yet you can speak Latin. Can you read as well, can you write?'

'Yes.'

'Amongst a thousand violent men, one handsome scholar who is willing to be my friend.'

Again I looked for signs of mockery and did not find it.

'It is the tradition of our tribe that one man should play the part of the Griot. His job is to recall the struggles of our people and memorise the stories of our resistance and pass these stories down the generations. So that our proud history is never lost, or broken.'

'And you are that?'

'I am both a Griot, and a memoriser. I shall remember everything that I have ever witnessed. And against our tradition, I shall also write that down, so that it can be read by those that will never hear me speak.'

'And am I to be remembered in your story, Ode? I think I would like that.'

I did not know how to answer.

'So, Ode, if you are witness to the exploits of your army, you must mostly write of death and slaughter? And not of love.'

'I write of honour and conquest. I write of the story of our tribe. The world has ignored us for too many generations. This world is vast and rich. It is not right that we were given such a small corner of this globe and told to stay put, be grateful for what you have. You must know this, we are not greedy. We are angry. If we are ever perceived as being violent it is because we are fighting for our very existence.'

She gave me a short smile and did not contradict me.

'Ode, I am sleepy now. Do you mind if we don't talk any more tonight.'

'Of course not, Anna. Get some rest. These days are hard on us all.'

Trying to sleep that night I thought, I swear I will not lie with you until you want me to.

I knew that I had fine seed. I had had it across my palm for many years. I never had any problem getting hard. If I were to make her pregnant, would that make her safer in this life and in this history? Or would a child half white and half black anger my brother. Would it have to be removed, unborn.

She *was* older than me. But that was neither a fetish nor a concern.

So what was it that I saw in her?

When I first saw you, Ode, I hated you. Because you were part of the tragedy that had befallen me. Yet I was always struck by your great beauty and your tenderness. It seemed to me almost impossible at that time that you could find me as beautiful as you did. And I so trusted you. I always knew that you would rather die than see me hurt. And I would still have loved you even if we had never been allowed to touch. Your presence. Your conversation. Your respect. All those things turned me. What you saw in me was someone who wanted you as much as you wanted me. Lover, companion, sounding board. Just the being there. The world was always grander with you simply standing beside me.

Peter stood in his caravan of costumes. He had his face in a small mirror.

'Come in, Ode.'

'It is not possible.'

'Ah! I am too low? Only a pretend king. Where you are a real Afrik Prince.'

'Peter, be advised. You must think before you speak to me like that.'

'Am I to be admonished by a boy?'

I put a bottle of wine before him on the floor of his carriage.

'This is better than you are used to.'

'And you presume to know what I am used to. You presume to understand my tastes.'

He took a draft.

'Fuck me, Ode, where did you get this! This is superb!'

'I stole it from an actor who did not know how to control his tongue.'

'Sorry. Excuse my exuberance.'

'You are, remember, in the presence of a Prince.'

'And you, sir, in the presence of an artist.'

'I meant to say that I cannot come into your carriage because there is no room for my tall frame. All I can do is lean in. You have many costumes.'

'I once had many more.'

There were racks of men's trousers and waistcoats. Women's dresses.

'I haven't played the female roles since I was a teenage boy,' he said stroking the hem of one. 'Back when I was still beautiful. Now I only play the king. A king with no land to command. No courtiers. No swain to please me.'

'I want to learn about this Yurop storytelling that you call the play. I am a Griot.'

'I have not heard of that.'

'It is a very highly regarded position within my culture. You may think of myself as a combination of both writer and actor.'

'Yet so young.'

'The Play.'

'Yes. Oh the Greeks would weep to see what has happened to their art. The problem is the *audiences*. The common man is thick as shit. In the houses of the rich, I was treated as the kings that I impersonated. Yet now I am forced to play the provinces and hamlets. The common man is known as the salt of the earth, Ode. Yet do you know what happens when you salt the earth, the soil? Salt poisons the earth! And nothing will grow where it is sown.'

'My warrior brothers are uneducated men, yet they are the finest men I have ever known. And the whites with all their education fall before us.'

'I am a saddened man, Ode. Don't let me offend your men. They are so gorgeous.'

'They are handsome and fearless. Do not use words that would better suit a woman.'

'There is a white woman with you. I must meet. She must be petrified. A white face, even one as ravaged by the pursuit of art and the passage of time as mine, will I am sure, be a comfort to her.'

'I can comfort her sufficiently myself.'

'Can you, Ode? Yes of course. You are young and handsome. But tell her if she needs the comfort of a white to talk to, she may visit me at any time. I will not touch her. I have many stories to tell that might amuse her.'

At that moment I regretted bringing him to join us. Yet I had an idea that I needed him to help me with.

'That picture that you have behind you on the cart.'

'A backdrop, we call it, or scenery.'

'It was very finely painted I thought. Could you paint one of our warriors sat upon a rhino?'

'You want me to paint a rhino and his mount?'

'I want you to draw and paint one hundred. I can help. I cannot initiate, but I can copy well enough.'

'Is that how come you speak the language of the educated whites? Are you merely copying what we say?'

'I was taught to fully understand Latin and Levant. I am not performing a trick.'

'I heard tell that the blacks are un-educatable.'

It occurred to me that he was not deliberately testing my patience with his rudeness. But that in addressing me, a black, the usual rules of politeness did not hold sway. If my brother had been privy to this exchange, he would have killed Peter on the spot and forgotten it a moment later. For my part I took notes as it were.

'Then what you have been told was clearly wrong,' I said with disdain, imagining my brother's hand upon the knife, and projecting that image with the power of my imagination, the timbre of my voice, the gaze of my eye.

Peter bowed his head very slightly.

'Yes. And what size are these characters to be?'

'The same size as life.'

'And where are we to find a length of cloth wide enough.'

'We have many things in the carts.'

'Ah plunder, the joys of conquest. This is for the play?'

'Yes.'

'You write the plays yourself Sir Griot?'

'I recount our adventures and tell the warriors how brave and magnificent they are. It is an evening's entertainment. I weave stories around their exploits. But I think a big picture behind me would help.'

'And what do they do?'

'They get drunk and cheer.'

'Ah. At least they cheer, that is something.'

We had bolts of thick canvas in one of the carts. I got the servants to sew them into one very long stretch of cloth. We found an old barn. We shooed out the cattle and I asked for the place to be swept, and for the cloth to be nailed to the wooden wall.

'This will take time, Ode.'

'The vision is not to be studied at close hand. We do not need to obsess about detail. Rather capture the energy of our warriors at speed. Can you do that for me to copy?'

Peter knew how to make his own paints from bark, berries, blood, and egg yolks. The lines from his brush vibrated with a starling energy, an outline in blood-black, that represented our power and of course, the nature of Peter's desire. He drew that which he longed to caress. I, myself, had once tried to write a fantasy of a sexual encounter with Naima. But my tumbling and inaccurate phrases, full of lust and acute embarrassment offered no pleasure. If we had acted as I described, what contortions and disappointment would have ensued!

'You study and copy that, Ode. I need to pee.'

My studies had led me to being quite expert at holding an image in my mind. I stood before Peter's work for five minutes of concentration until I knew it as if it were my own creation.

I dipped the brush and began. Peter returned from his pee, flushed about the face, fumbled amidst his supplies to find wine and began to create more warriors. As did I. Peter with lust, and myself with pride. My emotions being more refined, but my brush moving slower.

'Ode, you wish to turn the exploits of your army into a play, and here you have beside you an actor expert in the classics. Who is the hero of most of your tales?'

'My brother, for he commands and leads us.'

'You tell the story but you have no actors.'

'No, just me and my brother in pose.'

'Does he move about the stage? Do his movements and comportment reflect the inner conflict and turmoil of his mind?'

'Not to a great extent, no.'

'Now, there are two problems here. But neither insurmountable. Your warriors will not understand either my common tongue or the Latin. And I cannot speak the language of your tribe. So I shall speak in my language and you shall translate from the side. Secondly I will need to black my face.'

'Why?'

'Because your brother is the main character of the stories. Which is right and good. The main character in the play should always be a most powerful man. So I shall have to black up to play your brother.'

I needed Peter to paint half of an army and so I did not tell him that if he went on stage pretending to be my brother, you would be dead in a minute.

I heard the sound of her cartwheels and went outside to meet her. She held the reins.

'What are you doing, Ode? Is it interesting?'

'Very.'

'You are not hurting someone in there are you?'

'No, of course not.'

'Good. I couldn't hear any screaming, so I thought that maybe you weren't.'

She took the offer of my hand to help her down from the box.

'Ode, your hands are dirty.'

'Come see.'

'This is impressive. Peter how are you?'

'Madame.'

He took her hand kissed the back of it and bowed.

'You two keep drawing. I will find a rag and put in some colour, some shading, some brown and orange for the colours of you giraffe armour, some greys and white highlights for the beasts.'

'You have done this before?'

'My father thought it very pretty to be able to draw and paint. He would buy me flowers from the market and set them in a bowl by the window. I would rather have been out horse riding or practising archery. This is for the play.'

'Yes.'

'It is a shame,' said Anna, 'that we do not also have musical accompaniment.'

'But I could play the portable organ,' said Peter excitedly. 'I have one on my carriage. Before my entrance. I could make music for the prologue. If only I could sing. But alas no more. Time has ravaged me. In my day I was known to be as full of voice as Marcelo Anoulette.'

'I heard him sing once.'

'You never!'

At one point, Anna and Peter fell into the common tongue.

'Hey,' I said, 'I can't understand you.'

'Sorry Ode, it's just that I haven't been able to speak in my mother tongue for weeks. You get to speak in your mother tongue every day.'

'Sorry, Anna. Continue.'

'What the fuck is this, Ode?'

'It is what is called scenery. The next time I tell the story of our bravery I am going to have this put up behind us.'

'You and Peter did this.'

'Anna helped.'

'It's fucking extraordinary.'

'And I have another idea, Brother. If my story has scenery, then it becomes what is known as a play. And plays have actors.'

'I am not having that queer acting in any play that celebrates our victories.'

'Forget that for a moment. I want you to be the main actor. Brother, rather than just pose, I want you to move a little. Act things out. I will speak your words, but I would like to see you in motion and I would be overjoyed to see your feelings written on your face.'

'Me, Ode? No. How could I?'

'You are the hero of the warriors, and nothing is beyond you, Brother. Every eye should be on you and I should be nothing more than a voice inside the heads of our audience. And with this scenery behind us, the play will seem as real.'

'Have you told him?' said Peter breathless beside me. 'Have you told him I am to play his person on the stage.'

'No, my brother is to play himself.'

'But you said …'

'I said nothing to make you think you were to play my brother, you took that on yourself.'

'So what am I now? Nothing more than a scene painter! A low craftsman. Me?'

'You get fed and you are not dead,' said Anna sharply. 'I would not speak to Ode like that. Especially with his brother stood beside him.'

'Don't I have any part at all? After I have contributed so much!'

'I have been thinking. Yes, you shall represent the White Man of Yurop. You shall be the image of your race and a voice for your people who suffer at our hands.'

'Am I simply to be the victim?'

'Was it not good enough for the Greeks?'

'They were able to express great feelings of depth and conflict yes.'

'Then give dignity to those who lose. Anyone can play a winner. If you are the professional you say you are, then you should rise to the challenge of representing the soul of the oppressed. You can give voice to the suffering of your people.'

'I am not happy with you, Ode. Not happy at all.'

'Help me to improve the play? Let me learn from your great experience. That must surely be a pleasure for you.'

'Shit. Okay, look. You want my advice. You have a backdrop now. I will provide the music, but something very important will still be missing. You put your brother before the crowd, yet you cannot bear to show his weaknesses.'

'It would be unforgiveable to suggest a weakness in our Chief Elder. To me and my Tribe, he is inviolable.'

'And your army win every battle they fight?'

'Yes we are trained from a very early age. We have unstoppable beasts under our command.'

'So there is no tension in the story. From what you have told me, your plays are recitations. They lack conflict and therefore they lack drama.'

'My work is a celebration of that which the warriors have already experienced. It is not my role to make them question themselves. I can tell you this with absolute certainty, every single armed man in our army, despite the fact that they long for their wives, and long to see their new born children and hold them to their chest, and wish their scars were more superficial and their bed more secure and comfortable each night, every one of them, the One Thousand is beyond proud of what they have achieved.'

'Let me propose to you an idea, Ode. You could write me as a character that challenges your brother. I know I couldn't be a character with any status. Maybe I am his prisoner. But he comes to me each day, because there are many things on his mind. And gradually we begin to trust each other. And he trusts me because I challenge him when everyone else around just agrees with everything he says.'

'I don't think that will work at all.'

'And you know better than me?'

'If you challenge my brother he will stab you.'

Anna took me to a tailors and selected the very best. A high collared shirt in black with three pearl buttons at the neck. A black waistcoat and trousers that reached my ankles, both decorated with a repeated motif in white. Black leather boots.

'With your height and colour, you look gorgeous.'

She tried a hat with a feather on my head.

'No you don't need that.'

And then she chose some dresses for herself. And I swooned and cooed as she tried them on. The owner of the shop stood behind his desk both hands on his chest. Parts of his city were already in flames, but the destruction had yet to reach the central square.

And then we left.

'Anna, is it strange for you to leave a shop without paying?'

'I have never paid for a thing. Where I grew up, people knew my father. They simply put it on his bill. I have never held money in my life.'

'Back home we don't have money. We have trust and barter.'

I went to one of the carts and chose three fine rolls of Arabian silk. I took them back to the shop. The man still stood behind his desk with his hands to his chest. I put them on the counter before him.

He said not a word. But already the flames were flickering in the mirror behind him.

We were encamped in a glade surrounded by rolling hills with clear views on all sides. The evening was still warm. A cloud of birds flew above us, their collective shape wildly oscillating, turning itself inside out, breaking apart and then coming together again.

The day's fight had been without glory, no loss, but no challenge. We left with some cheese and some hams. We killed three soldiers who stood against us. Two who were decrepit, and one who had no hair on his chin.

Sometimes I thought, can we not just pass through and leave them alone. But my brother insisted that a conquest was a conquest. We could not start making exceptions. And I thought why not? Why not pick your targets and leave the weak and poor alone.

For the play that night, we were to revisit the story of our great victory some weeks ago, when we had taken on their full might, drowned their horses, and killed them all.

We erected the backdrop on poles and disguised it with branches pulled from the trees.

The audience arrived. The warriors had divested themselves of their armour, and dressed in the Yuropan clothing they had selected along the way.

Behind them all stood Anna's carriage. Her curtain shut.

I wrote a short declamatory about the day of the change. The choosing of my father. Our training and our journey North through our own continent. His death on Yuropan soil. The passing of his power to my brother. I read it to Anna and she thought it very fine. She said that she had heard Peter's music for the event and thought it appropriate. I had never spoke over music before. I had no idea how it would work. So I took Anna at her word. If she were happy so would I be also.

It would have to be short or my brother would be impatient. Brother, I am not taking the stage from you. I am setting the stage *for* you. No great man appears in the first moments of a play or celebration. My words are to increase the audience's desire for your entrance. Ode, are they not already expectant? Brother, do not be difficult. I do this only to enhance you. I need enhancing now do I, Ode? Then he burst out laughing.

I spoke my Prologue with Peter's pipe organ, strangely lilting beneath my voice. His music was not heroic. It was rather elegiac, as if everything were already finished rather than just begun. After my last words, my brother took to the stage at great speed, gurning and giggling.

He was met with a wave of applause.

'Keep the polog, Ode,' he said. 'I like it. It makes the men impatient for my entrance.'

He was not wearing his armour. Instead he was bedecked in fur and gold brocade. He raised his sword above his head and charged at a group of men in the front row, who all fell over backwards.

And with his sword so raised my brother began to laugh and the warriors righted themselves and joined in the laughter, although with an obvious undercurrent of embarrassment.

'Who does not fear us,' I cried?

In the confusion, no one replied. My brother stomped back to centre stage with his back to the audience and then he swung round at speed.

'Who does not fear us!' I cried again?

'Everyone fears us!' The warriors shouted back at me, a deafening blow of a thousand voices.

'Do you remember when horse and riders burst from the gloom of a forest, and charged us on our flank?'

'We remember!'

'Do you remember the brass horns mounted on the skulls of their horses. The sound they made to scare us?'

'We remember!'

'Did they succeed in scaring us?'

'No!'

My brother raised his sword high in the air as ten servants rushed upon the stage and removed the branches to reveal our scenery.

There was a gasp from the audience. Look, it is us!

'Our beasts charged the first wave of horse and rider. They gouged the animals in the belly, unsaddled the soldiers and beat them with their stony paws.'

My brother quite overwhelmed, mimed his own Beast beating in the skulls of the enemy.

The audience roared and beat their fists upon their knees.

'Then a thousand came to challenge our One Thousand and we led them into the water, dived beneath the surface, caught their legs with rope and pulled them down to drown and hacked away the dangling legs of their white riders.

'And then, as they floated dead in a river of their own blood, we chased the last of them through the forest. One of them, a Prince, a gaudy popinjay, a man used to fine clothes and wines, used to being waited on, sitting before the fire.'

Peter sauntered onto the stage area. He was wearing his best princely clothes. An elaborate ring adorned each finger and both thumbs. He wore a long scarlet robe.

'And my brother grabbed him by the collar and threw him hard upon the ground.'

Which my brother, performed with all dramatic commitment.

And then I spoke Peter's words for him in the language of my people, as he spoke for himself in the learned Latin, the audience did not understand.

'I am my people. Look upon me and see my race. Look upon my anguish and know the anguish of a continent.'

It was not hard to write. I simply thought of how I felt about myself and my own people, and put those words into a white man's mouth.

'Our leader raised his sword.'

My brother raised his sword to behead Peter and the audience began chanting.

Kill. Kill. Kill.

And I thought, my brother really might.

So I hollered.

'But our great leader took compassion on the Prince. What honour is there to strike man on his knees? Bravery is shown when the adversary is proud and strong. A weak effeminate man on his knees is no challenge for a warrior.'

But I knew my brother was itching to so something.

'My brother, our Chief Elder took out his proud member and pissed upon the man's upturned face.'

And my brother in his role performed that deed.

Someone threw a bone that they had been chewing on.

Hey mutt, chew on that.

Then someone threw an apple core.

And then anything and everything that came to hand was pelted down on Peter. Sods of earth, stones, bones, half eaten morsels. And the warriors tried out every foul word in our language.

And Peter crawled from the stage area on his hands and knees, to his mark behind the cloth, and when no longer in view, he was scripted to scream. And a canvas head, a milliner's prop, decorated to vaguely resemble Peter's bonce was flung over the scenery to land upon the stage to much cheering. I stepped forward.

'Before we end tonight, the ending of our Play, I wish for you to look again, at the drawing upon the cloth. For that is a drawing of you, your might, your pride, your valour.

'And my brother, Chief Elder of the Kikuyo Warriors stood before his troops.'

My brother did so and stood with his feet wide apart, the tip of his sword on the ground and both hands on the pommel.

'Think for a moment in silence about all that you have sacrificed and all that you have achieved.'

A respectful quiet descended upon us all. Everything fell before us, but we had not been without our losses. I thought of my father, the greatest loss of all.

The only sound to put a stain upon the respect was the sound of Peter cussing.

'Cunts! You have no idea of my worth. To you I am merely a toy that you have picked up for your own amusement. You will regret this. There are still powerful men in this province that respect me. Mark, Ode, one day one of those powerful men will come for me. And he will have an army behind him. And you will not survive that day.'

I poured her a glass of wine. We had three candles burning in the tent.

'Peter asked me if I would like to see the costume he had worn when he first played the female role. I felt sorry for him after your brother urinated in his face and all your boys threw shit at him on the stage and so I agreed. My acceptance of his offer pleased him greatly. There is hardly room for two inside but he ushered me in. Which one am I to admire? I said. There are so many. But he did not answer. Instead he slammed the door on me and turned the lock. Not funny I said. I do not like being locked inside a room. I have not done anything wrong.

'There was the sway of the carriage as Peter climbed upon the box, the lash of the reins and we began to move.

'Peter, I called, stop now and turn around.

'He made no comment.

'Peter think for a moment. Ode has taken it upon himself to be my friend and guardian. He will kill you for this. Literarily kill you. He will find you and kill you. Still no reply. Do you not understand I said, do you not understand the word I have said three times in a row now?

'Then I thought, hang on, his carriage turns into his stage. It comes apart. I pushed a rack of costumes aside and felt into the corner of the space where the rear side and the back panel meet. My fingers found two bolts and four rings.'

'You pulled out the bolts.'

'I pulled out the bolts, and the wall began to wobble. Pushing myself through the dusty clothes, I began to sneeze. Really loudly and at last he spoke.

'You alright back there?

'It's dusty. I sneeze when there is too much dust.

'Do you know why I am taking you away? He says. No I do not know why you are taking me away because you have not told me. All I know is I am being taken against my will.

'I am performing my latest role he says. The rescuer of damsels in distress.

'So I say, do you know where we are going? And of course he has no idea. It's before midday and he has already got a least one bottle of red wine inside his gut. He is not even really doing this. It's an act. He is in a story. But he doesn't know the next chapter let alone the ending. He's just whipping the horses and thinking of himself as a hero, an adventurer.

'I don't want to be rescued by this arsehole. Where is he going to take me? He won't be able to defend me if we get waylaid. I'll get raped by the roadside and he will be waving his arms and speechifying. My fingers are feeling for the other two bolts which I presume are at the other corner of the carriage. You are going to regret this mother-fucker I shout. I get the bolts in my grasp, wrench them out of their sockets. I kick the back panel with all my might. Bang, the whole side falls away. I grab hold of the rack and push. Whoosh, all of Peter's clothes are now sprawled across the dusty road. I grab hold of his make-up table, that goes out too. I get hold of his pipe organ, but I just can't do it. It is too beautiful and delicate.

'The carriage stops abruptly. I am stood revealed on the bed of the cart, embracing a miniature pipe organ and Peter is running down the road to his scattered costumes, crying, Juliette, Hermione, Fair Grace, Aubronne, Master Luigi. Each of his costumes have names, named presumably after the character he played when he first wore them. It is quite touching. But at the same time I am pleased that I have brought him this much distress. I wanted to punish him. But it is hard to hate him, Ode. He's such a sad man. Just look at him closely and try and peel away the years, the fat and the folding skin, he was I believe once quite handsome and had his pick of other handsome men.'

'That is not something I wish to hear about. He is an unnatural.'

'He is not unnatural to himself. No more so than you are unnatural to yourself.'

'What? You are comparing me with Peter. Peter is perverted. I have a birth defect. Peter will pay for what he has done.'

'I suppose he will,' she said slightly.

And I could not read her face at all.

'You took Anna.'

'Your people are dirt, Ode. Mannerless brutes. I wanted to save her from you.'

'Shall I translate that for my people?'

'No. God no. Ode. They will cut my throat. Can you untie me?'

'No, not until tomorrow.'

'I can't spend a night tied to a fucking tree. My back hurts. It is excruciating.'

'Anna is my friend and you tried to take her from me. If you had done a similar thing to my brother he would have had both your hands cut off. So stop whinging about your back.'

'I am I presume no longer to appear in the play.'

'On the contrary.'

I asked two servants to bring his costumes and the portable reed organ and place them before him on the ground.

'That is everything I own, Ode.'

'Anna told me that your costumes have names.'

'That is because they are dear to me.'

'That is what I concluded. And Anna is dear to me and you tried to take her from me.'

'Ode, I was angry and drunk. Man to man let us not argue over a woman. Oh dear, Ode, don't do this. Don't destroy my friends. Look take an ear or a finger. Anything. The Organ was built by my father. He lived his life on the road, he taught me everything I know. When I play it I feel his breath on my neck.'

'I have a new costume for you to wear. Wear this on stage without complaint and I will spare your friends.'

I still let Peter play the organ for the Prologue. Because it pleased me to do so.

The backdrop was resplendent and still novel enough to draw breath. After some recounting of our brave exploits, I went for crudity.

'And the enemy shat themselves!' I cried.

The warriors roared and waved their hands. Peter staggered out onto the stage, his costume a peasants smock, be-fouled with a mixture Anna had made for him from herbs and mud. Even in his dun robe, a figure of Yuropan decay and dread, he attempted to give his character gravitas, but I undermined him with my words.

'Thin brown shits pours down their legs, their stench is foul,' I said. 'They know they are about to die and they have shit themselves like babes. And like babes also, they sob.'

And Peter fell to his knees and wailed in abject fear and disgrace.

'So the white man was always a be-shitted bawling child, and we walk tall amongst them, taking their lives, rounding them up.'

And the show unfolded in that fashion, no struggle, no fear, no reversal of fortunes. Because we were always mighty, and the white man always abject.

And then Peter crawled from the stage. Like a dog. And behind his curtain he screamed the scream of the quick and bloody dead. And a servant threw the head upon the stage.

That night as we lay down on our separate bedrolls she said.

'There is something I must do.'

And she came to me on her hands and knees and leaned over my face and gave me the quickest and lightest of kisses.

I had yet to blow out the candle and we could see each other clearly.

And I just lay there. Thinking, ah this is a kiss. It is such a simple thing, a mere brushing of the lips. Yet why has the universe changed within me?

But I did not reach out for her and bring her to me. Fear held me back, yes. Concern that whatever I did would be inadequate, yes. Fear, even that she was teasing me. Yes. All those things. But the saddest part was my inability to act. To simply respond at a physical level. Anna had kissed me and all I could do was *think* about it!

And so she slunk back to her covers.

'I thought you liked me. I must have been wrong. I must have been fooling myself. When you said nice things to me you were just being polite and now I have made a fool of myself. Ode, I am so sorry that you are not attracted to me. I know I am not an attractive women. But I am a women. And you are the most gorgeous man ever. You will no doubt fall in love with some other girl, and I will want to kill her.'

And then she began to cry and I wanted to leap from my bed and embrace her. But I couldn't. I thought of the girls back in my homeland and how they would never consider me. Those girls had taught me my failure. I was educated in disappointment by their brows.

There together, so near, under the same canvas ceiling, under the same sky and moon.

And what a fool I was for all of my education and my wit.

I sat beside her in the carriage. The roof was low for my frame and the fabric worried at my skull. She showed me her embroidery. Not of flowers or birds, but of the back of a hand, with the flesh peeled back and the bones and muscles and veins clearly drawn.

I could smell fire in the distance. Someone was screaming. I had taught myself not to listen, and watching Anna, I realised that she had done the same.

'Ode, all these lands you conquer, what are you to do with them?

I could not answer with clear conviction.

'You kill the people, rape the land, plunder the churches and then move on to the next. What is the plan, Ode? What was it that your father envisioned?'

'Be careful not to accuse my father.'

'I would not do that, Ode. I am asking the question because I would like to know. What was your father's vision? You see, Ode, Khristans have an excuse for their rampages. We say we are doing it in the name of God. But you have no God like ours and yet you still rampage. So men must love to rampage, and if our God is only an excuse for us, then we have simply made him up to justify our urges. Every act of violence I witness makes me love him less.'

'And do you feel the same about me?'

'I think you and your brother want revenge on the world. But the world never abused your people, Ode. You just lived in a shitty place and were very poor. The greatest crime that has ever been committed against your tribe, was that you were ignored. Ode, if you are victorious what will you do with victory? What can you even do with gold? Polish it and look at your own reflection in its surface?'

I looked at her delicate fingers, the needle that pulled the thread through the detail of her embroidery.

'Ode, I have to keep busy, to stop from going mad.'

'Does the swagger and bump of your carriage not make it hard to be so delicate?'

'I do not sew when we are in transit. I sew when my carriage is at rest and your men are putting others of my race to the slaughter.'

My brother kills. I write. Anna sews.

'Would you like me to teach you the Arab script, it is beautiful like your embroidery.'

'There was a man I knew, he lived not far from my house and I would sneak out sometimes late in the evening. He had a telescope mounted on the roof and he would let me view the skies. My father would not have approved. The man with the telescope was very ugly and had no wife. In return for letting me view the stars I had to lift my skirts and let him view my legs. Un-ladylike I know. Don't flinch like that, Ode. I was safe with him. He never touched me. Just stared at my legs and played in his pocket.

'Now I spend the day waiting for you, Ode. And there are no other women to talk to. It is hard for a woman to live without others of her sex. There is no one to comb my hair. It is a thing that women do for each other. You see it in the street. The boys are fighting with sticks. The girls comb each other's hair. It could not be otherwise. Any child who did different would be severely punished. Can you imagine boys combing each other's hair?'

She looked at me with my head rubbing the ceiling.

'Ode, are your people born bald?'

'We shave our heads from an early age.'

'Could you let it grow, Ode? Just so I could see what it looks like on you.'

I laughed.

'I had never thought of it. No adults of our tribe grow their hair. Unless they go mad, as some do. Mad and talking to the stones and the sky and never washing and not shaving their heads.'

'Then go mad for me, Ode.'

She smiled at me. Her teeth were now whiter than when I had first known her. My hair grew wide and wild.

'I love your smell, Ode. There was a man that my father wanted me to marry. I couldn't stand the stink of him. And yet I didn't know what it was until one time when I was ill and taken to my bed and our doctor visited when the stinking man was there. His fists was filled with fragrant flowers to heal me and make me sneeze. And after he was gone, I said to my doctor, what is that smell? He grimaced. Gangrene, he said. The man's feet are rotting in his boots. And I called for my father and said to him, Father, why do want me to marry a man who's feet are about to fall off? Of course he didn't reply, because my father is all politics and strangely, Ode, a single white woman captured and held captive by a thousand black warriors and in your care, I feel safer than I ever did at the dining table with my own father.

'Everyone I have ever met has bored me, Ode. Bored me so completely, that I wanted to scream. And I have often thought this, that the imaginary conversations I have in my head are usually so much more interesting than the shit that other people talk about. Even if they are your family, or you pretend that they are your friends. And so I would rather listen to the voices in my own head. But it is different with you, Ode. I could talk to you forever and listen to you forever, and I would never ever again have to make words in my head just to stop from going insane with boredom.'

I had noticed it before, but not thought too much about it. One cart manned by a husband and wife from the port where we had landed many weeks before, parked their cart at some distance from the others at the end of the day. While the others cleaved together for comfort in their distress. Often foolishly I thought to go and talk to them and try and explain our mission. Personally I would not have dragged them along. These were simple, common people. I had no animosity against them. But they weren't harmed. They might have even been safer with us than at home, where following our departure all manner of things might be happening. Our arrival had triggered a war. With us they could be certain to be fed, they would be protected by our warriors and in maybe not much more than a year or so they would be home again. We hadn't broken families apart, they travelled with their children. They all spoke the same language and dialect. We gave them wine at the end of the day.

The husband and wife that drove the particular cart that had attracted my attention, wore kerchiefs across their mouths at all times. I assumed that they had some disease or ailment that could be passed on by breath and they chose not to infect others. I genuinely hoped that they would get well soon.

They had gone down to the river to wash.

I strolled over to their cart. As I approached with curiosity I was hit by the most foul stench. I twisted to the side and almost vomited. But from my position I could clearly see that indeed the bed of the cart was quite empty. Why were we pulling an empty cart and what was the source of the foul stench?

My name is Ode, I am a Griot. A storyteller. And no storyteller can ever walk away from a curiosity.

Ode, I do not like this. I too smelled that smell. Move onto another part of the story. Tell me again of the times you watched me washing myself in the lake.

As I approached the cart the husband came running towards me. He began blabbering at me. I waved him away with the back of my hand.

The stench was overwhelming. There were some small yellow flowers growing among the grass at my feet. I picked a handful and pressed them into my nostrils. I put on my leather helmet. The stench was still in the air, but bearable now.

I stared at the empty bed of the cart. At the rear end was a brass ring and what looked like very small trap door.

Oh don't open it, Ode.

You know I must.

I put my finger inside the ring and lifted the trap. And there below me, I saw a mouth. The lips moved. But I could hear no sound. I called the husband over and indicated that I wanted the planks of the cart raised. He shook his head. I had

163

no time for negotiation so I took my flintlock from its sling and pointed the barrel at his head. He nodded manically and went to the front of the cart to rummage through a box. He returned with a metal bar with flattened ends and began to prise apart the planks.

And there he was, lying on his back, his hands shackled at his sides, the man who had killed my father, nailed between the original cart bed and a false one. Like a coffin. Yet alive. The trapdoor had obviously been fitted to feed him and pour water into his mouth so that he could not die.

'Ode, what the fuck are you doing?'

I tuned quickly to face him. He must have been watching me. Hoping the stench would deter me from investigating.

'Brother why did you not tell me about this torture?'

'Because you would have been compassionate. And I had to make sure he suffered for what he did. What justice is there in this world, if we do not torment our enemies? You were going to let him go, Ode! How could you even have thought of such a thing! So it fell to me to do the right thing. So don't judge me.'

'Brother, this is not the right thing.'

'It fucking is, Ode.'

'It demeans *us*.'

And with my flintlock still in my hand I put the barrel to the man's forehead and fired. The first man I ever killed. The murderer of my father. And I did it to spare him more torment.

'Fuck, Ode, I did not give you permission to do this.'

'And I did not give you permission to do what you have done. So we are equal. What you don't understand brother is that I had broken him. I had taken him to a place where he begged me to kill his wife and child. I had broken him, yet left him sane. You have driven him out of his mind to a point where he can no longer comprehend his torture.'

He lay there with his head opened. His wife on his left, his daughter on his right lying alongside him. Utterly rotten and crawling with maggots.

'We shall unleash the horses and burn the cart, Ode. The stench will infect anything we try and carry upon that.'

'And what are the husband and wife to do?'

'They can join any of the other carts or make their way home. Why would I care either way? Tell them that.'

'I do not speak the common language.'

'Of course you don't, Ode, of course you don't. Don't you dare challenge me again or poke your nose into my business.'

With more of the enemy routed and more plunder in our hands and bellies, it was my time to present the story of our army's great victories over the last week.

The warriors sat in half circles emanating from my position. Some sat on the stone floor, others on wooden benches, others on the roofs of carts. The scenery was nailed to the stonework of the town's fortified wall.

My brother took his best position and I stood to the side prepared to voice the eloquence that did not come to him as natural.

His strong arms bulged with tales of bravery, my withered arm hung limp at my side.

'You know the things I am about to tell you will be true, because the deeds I will relate are yours. If I am to praise your bravery, you will know it to be true in your hearts. If I describe the enemy, you will already know them, because you faced them, and you beat them down. If I describe a town, you will know it from the taking, from the plunder. When I talk of leaving for our next adventure, you will know of this also, how many times have you looked back over your shoulder and watched the flames?

'And you are mighty and you are proud, and you will still be fighting after you are dead. Because the story of your actions here today, this last week, next week will be told for a thousand years.'

In that scripted moment, on cue, they all hollered back at my brother, back at my words.

'Or more.'

'When first we espied this town, we noted the strength of its walls. We knew the day would be hard won. We knew the day would be glorious. Fire rained down from the sky and did we turn and run from the danger. No we did not, we ran towards the danger ...'

In an extemporisation on our scheme, a carriage appeared over the cobbles. The vehicle came to rest beside me. The horses snorted. I knew them. They didn't hate me any longer. We had got used to each other's smell. The carriage door came open and a women fell out. Fell out as if she had been kicked from behind. I knew instantly that it was not Anna.

I went to raise her and offered a hand.

'Might I help you, madam?'

But she was already raising herself on her knees. She stood carefully and the audience began to laugh. I moved so that I could see her face. And despite her long and flowing locks, she possessed a full beard.

For it was Peter.

And then my brother descended, grabbed Peter round the waist, bent him over, lifted his skirts, and pretended to mount him from behind.

The audience, our warriors, stamped their feet and wept. Warriors love to hear tell tales of their worth. But even more, they love to see a man pretend to fuck another man, when he is wearing a woman's skirt and wig.

My brother released him, kicked Peter's arse and sent him tumbling to his knees with a crack.

I spat and walked away from my vocation.

'Ode, did you see how they laughed? I had their undivided attention.'

'You sought to mock me.'

'Mock you how, Ode? Shit.'

'I was speaking of great bravery. I was being lyrical about victory. I was elevating you. I had worked hard in composing my words. And you just turned the whole thing into a farce. What respect of my craft did you show me Brother? Would I disrespect your skills in battle? No, never, and you know that. And yet you cannot show me the same consideration.'

'It was just a little thing I thought might spice up our celebration. Don't be sensitive.'

'You mocked me. And you did that because I questioned you about what you had done to our father's killer.'

'And why would I do that Brother? Ode, we are very different, in temperament and skill, but I think of you not just as my brother, but as my twin.'

'How can we be twins when we were born apart in time?'

'By all the rules of nature, we cannot be. I am trying to find a way to speak my heart. But Ode, was that not funny? Our men have suffered hardships this day. Many are still bleeding. Brother, I would not have insulted you in the way that you think. Come, Ode. The men are staring.'

The river curved around a hill with a large castle sat atop. Turreted like those I'd seen in the northern part of our continent. I was sat with Anna at the reins. The halted horses bristling in the harness.

'Look, Ode, see how beautiful that castle is. Hear the sound of the river as it tinkles. The birdsong. Look at the sky and try and find a cloud.'

'It is a beautiful day, Anna.'

'And now your army can do what is does best, destroying everything before it. Smash the castle. Pollute the river with the bodies of the people who live there. Let's have screaming in place of singing. Your men can darken this perfect sky with smoke.'

'And I should write about birdsong and tinkling water?'

'At least no one would die if you did.'

There was a thiripp sound followed by a chorus of wood splitting thuds that struck the side of our carriage.

Luxxor, with his shoulder on fire came alongside us and hoisted us onto his rhinoceros's back. The horses bolted with their burning burden behind them in the straps.

'Come, let me take you amongst the trees for shelter.'

'Ode,' said Anna, 'I have never been aboard one of these beasts.'

'My father was the first ever human to ride one. The first time I tried I fell off.'

We reached the edge of a forest.

'Tell Anna to dismount,' said Luxxor. 'I will take you to your brother.'

'No,' I said, 'I will not leave Anna here, alone and unattended. I will not leave her here prey to any passing man. I am sorry but today I will not be able to witness your great deeds and turn them into story. Luxxor your shoulder is still on fire.'

'Unlike your brother I do not need your words to celebrate my strength.'

Then he turned his Beast towards the fight and the rain of torch lit arrows.

Anna took my hand.

'Thank you for not leaving me here alone, Ode.'

She pressed me against a tree.

'Ode, let's do here under these leaves and branches what is natural between a handsome man and a wicked woman.'

I let her study the weakness of my arm. The way the bones didn't lie straight, the feeble muscle. That part of myself that I had always been so ashamed of, was now tended by my lover with such tenderness. She put the fingers to her mouth.

'If I hadn't been the son of the Chief Elder, they would have taken me by the ankles and smashed my brains out against a tree.'

I saw tears pop into her eyes.

'No, Ode. Please?'

'The doctor that delivered me was appalled. He approached my father in great fear. He had nursed my mother through the last weeks of her pregnancy. He had made her potions to calm her and to lessen her pains. And then I appeared. And I was imperfect. He had failed. And my father had lost face. Does my deformity not offend you?'

'No, because it is nothing. Ode, I have been abducted by a thousand black skinned men, the like of which I never seen or dreamed of. The horrors that I imagined at the time, the visions that made me bite my knuckles and wished myself dead, never came to pass because of your decency. What you see as a defect is nothing compared to the lack in the men that my father would have had me marry. And one thing I think you will have no idea of, Ode, is your face. The most beautiful part of any man is his face. And, Ode, you are beautiful. Your brother is stronger, but he is ugly.'

I had never thought of my brother as anything less than perfect.

'My brother is desired by all the women in our land.'

'Because your women celebrate power. I would rather celebrate beauty. Are your women as beautiful as me?'

'No one is as beautiful as you, Anna.'

And I believed that to be the total truth. I loved the way her hair grew low on her brow. In respect, I will not describe her body, but it enraptured me.

We were as beautiful as we told each other that we were.

Why had it taken a white skinned woman to love me? Or was she in pretence. Was this a play to bemuse me? Were her caresses part of some plan for escape or retribution?

If I was a fool, it was me that made me so, not her.

I put such thoughts aside and held her. And we breathed in rhythm. And I knew that for all my brother's power he would never have this feeling. Any women that lay with him, would always be about to poison his wine, let her real lover into the room at night to cut his throat. Leave him for his conqueror. And me in my slightness and deformity, I felt that I was truly loved. I wanted to take her away from our ongoing campaign, to take her from all conflict and bloodshed.

We acted with all naturalness. We complimented each other. She led me to sweetness. Unclothed, the odour of her body overwhelmed me.

I spent the battle in Anna's sweet arms. And as we adjusted our clothing, four white children, a boy and two girls, one girl with a baby in her arm rushed up to Anna. Her eyes darted between the two of us. She clearly could not understand that Anna's face showed no pain to be with a man such as me. I wanted to tell the child that she had nothing to fear from me. That I would rather hug her than harm her. But then I also knew that one of my warriors had probably already killed her father, and that if her mother wasn't with her, she was most likely already dead, or wishing to so be. And later I would have to write a poem of celebration of our achievements that day. And I would not be able to mention Anna and her flesh.

The girl offered the baby to Anna but she shook her head. The girl held the babe as if it were a turnip and she didn't like turnips at all, but accepted that turnips were after all a reality of life.

Then they ran off.

'Ode, that was only four. There must have been so many more alive today. What happened to the other children, Ode?'

'They have run into the woods. You have seen this yourself, Anna.'

'Show me, Ode. Use your device to sweep the area. Show me the other children running.'

Her brow furrowed. Her dark brown eyes clouded and she pursed her lower lip.

'Don't bother.'

The truth of course was that I didn't know what had happened to the other children, that day or any of the days before. The truth was I didn't want to know. The truth was I was scared to know the truth. I had accepted the death of the Wollof children as a brutal necessity and not thought further.

'The next time there is a battle, I will show you how we release all the children. I will show you how we let them run.'

'And do they laugh? Or scream?'

'We do not make them scream.'

'But, Ode, your warriors will have killed their parents.'

Later walking through the burned arch of the castle I was approached by my brother.

'Where were you?'

'I was protecting …'

'I know where you were. Luxxor told me.'

'Then why did you ask?'

'I mean why? Why were you not at your post?'

'The arrows. They struck Anna's carriage. Luxxor took us to safety. Should I have left Anna lone in the forest?'

'Anna's safety is hardly my concern. You should have been at your post. If you fail me again I shall have this woman sent away.'

Brother no.

'Fuck it. Ode, your face. Your eyes. Do not let the others see you like this. I will not take this woman from you. She likes you, and that has not always been the ways with girls has it, Ode? I am not insensitive, but you must join us in battle, even though you do not fight. The men will turn against you if you stay with a woman while they are fighting for their lives.'

'It will not happen again.'

'Talk to the warriors, and make up tonight's story from what they tell you. I was thinking. Could there be a moment when some of the warriors join us on the stage? It is just an idea. I am not interfering in your business. The stage is big and there is only you and I to fill it. They might be honoured. I do not know, Ode. I have a thousand men to keep happy. They must tire of whores and wine.'

'Brother do we kill all the children?'

'Ode, have you not used your eyes? It is your job to document our conquest.'

'I pay attention on the warriors. I do not watch the women and children.'

'Ode, most times, the people send their children out into woods, to hide. Those that are told to stay are treated as potential enemies. Ode, I began my life as a warrior at the age of four.'

'Give us our directions, Ode.'

I had made the choice myself. One warrior was injured. I wanted to show the reality of our situation. Everyone apart from myself had been injured at some time. His presence on the stage would touch them all.

'How did it happen? In your own words.'

'They appeared from the ground beneath us. They had dug ditches and covered them with twigs and leaves. They were armed with pikes and hatchets. They went for the legs and soft bellies of the Beast. Mine died this day and that is a greater pain than the wound in my shoulder.'

He was waiting his turn for his wound to be sewn closed. He did not complain. 'A well placed pike penetrated my armour. I know your mother designed our protection, so I do not wish to speak ill of it.'

'No offence will be taken. Tell me your true experience as you see it.'

'It happens. No protection is complete. I was on the floor. My enemy stood over me and put all his body weight upon his weapon. I could not defend myself. The blade forced its way through my armour, I could feel the battle between steel and leather, only slowly did the giraffe skin tear, it had no choice such was the force behind the pike. The metal tip sliced my flesh and ploughed through my shoulder. I heard myself gasp, I did. I was not a coward, I did not cry, but I gasped, the body must react. And then the blade came through me on the other side and dug a hole into the earth.'

The others nodded.

'The death of one's Beast is a hard blow for a warrior.'

There were a few moments of silence and reflection.

'What are our directions, Ode?'

'They are simple enough. You enter when I say five brave warriors appeared shouting death to all that try and stand in our way. Stand still. Look strong and fearless. I shall be your voice, I shall tell of your manliness. You will be admired and spoken of. There will come a time when the only story told around the world, will be the story of your bravery.'

'Do we speak?'

'If you want.'

'What should we say?'

'Death to all that try and stand in our way.'

'We can remember that.'

They all made ferocious faces.

'With respect, not like that. You are showing strength. But what does it feel like? What are your thoughts when facing the enemy?'

'Not one of us is scared.'

'Not for a moment was I about to suggest that you were. I have the deepest respect for you all. You know that of me.'

'I sometimes think of my new wife. We were only together for two weeks before I had to go. So I think of my enemy, the more scared you are of me, the quicker I shall kill you, and the quicker the killing is done, the sooner I go home.'

'I want to see if I have a son. I think that my wife may have been pregnant when I left.'

I looked at them with a new-found respect.

'Look out above the heads of the crowd. Swing you swords when I say the warriors swung their swords. And rather than make ferocious faces, think of your wives and children, think of home. Think of why you are fighting.'

'That is well said, Ode. You may be lame of the arm, but your mind and soul are well made.'

And later in my tent, in the Latin script, I wrote a version of what had unfolded that day. The warrior had talked of his wound with pride, and I who hated pain, had to find the words to portray feelings quite alien to my own.

With the pike through my flesh, I was pinned to the earth. I thought not of dying, but of living. My assailant stood above me. I held my sword aloft to protect myself. I could not remove the pike without putting away my sword.

I lay there completely open to attack. I thought of the turbulent history of our people, the poverty we had endured, the disrespect we had …

No, no, no. That would not do. There could be no mention of weakness.

I thought of the proud history of our people. I would not be defeated. Still holding my sword to defend myself against the many weak slashes of the enemy…

No not weak.

Powerful …

No again. That celebrates the enemy.

Still holding my sword to defend myself against the cowardly blows of my enemy. I put my left hand upon the ground and began to raise myself, the pike head still firmly in the ground, the shaft still within me, the wood scraping against the bloody wound, until I was before him. He looked appalled. He let go the shaft. I put my sword under his ribs and with a circular motion carved his heart into his guts.

In victory I saw the shadow of my dead Mother, her hands clasped in praise of all my actions. Behind her stood my grandmother, similarly supplicant. And in front of my mother stood my wife, and before her in her place stood my daughter. All lost in admiration.

There will be a time when there is nothing left to conquer, when all the white men are in the ground, and these damaged bones of mine will find rest. I shall be with you. I will tell you tales of the past. And I no longer will have to shed my blood to create the destiny that we all deserve.

Anna let me read to her.

'You will read those lines, Ode.'

'Yes, I will speak them, but I want them to be a truthful expression of how the men feel. The warriors so far, only have to say, death to all that try and stand in our way.'

'Ode, your blacks are always invincible and us whites abject.'

'In my stories yes. But between you and me, Anna, it is different is it not?'

She did not answer.

'Anna, do you miss your home?'

'Ode, if you were to command some magical, winged Beast, to fly us across all the lands you have conquered, and take me home right now, my father would not want me back.'

'He would love to see his beloved daughter surely.'

'No. He would want to see me married. But no man of my country would marry a woman that has been, for so long, and un-chaperoned, in the company of blacks.'

'You would have had such a happy life if you hadn't been taken, Anna.'

In compassion I want her free. In love, I wanted her enslaved.

'Back home, I have heard what the women say about love. But their words in no way describe how I feel about you.'

On our stage, my brother made much of his muscles and his waving. I coated him in my fine words.

Then the five warriors took their turn, charged into their space, yelled their moments of glory and stood there brandishing. And then they looked out at the audience, a moment's pause, a moment's pose, and let their faces clearly show, the loneliness and pain they had endured and how it had harassed their spirit and their heart.

A deep silence descended on the men. They had read the unspoken thoughts.

The next evening after a brief skirmish, quickly sketched, a few white dead, for us a small prize of some lamb and spades.

And for the umpteenth time, Peter, robed but besmirched in the fake shit I had devised, crawled across the cobbles of the stage in lamentation of his fate.

Cursing the weakness of the white man and wailing how could such fine black men ever be defeated?

My brother chased him from the scene.

And when he was hidden from view, there was the usual scream. And the usual head flying head.

But this time this was not our usual milliner's prop flung upon the stage. This was a lump of flesh and blood.

And I thought, my brother has killed my actor. I wondered what Peter had done to aggrieve my brother so badly, that he had decapitated Peter on the spot. And despite my clear and present gaze upon this thing, it took me a moment to notice the glaring detail of the beard. For there was none. This head was shaved at the jaw. Peter could hardly have had time to shave himself before his decapitation.

And despite being quite appalled by this head before me, I began to giggle. My brother ran back onto the stage and picked it up by the hair and threw it into the audience who took up the game.

Smiling hugely my brother put his arm around my shoulders, but there was bitterness in his voice.

'Did I surprise you Brother?'

'For a moment I thought you had killed my actor.'

'I found a man hiding in a beer barrel. I hate it when they hide. If you are not a man you have no right to live as one. Ode, this is the second time you have given the warriors upon that stage a line to learn.'

'Five warriors and one line between them, Brother.'

'Yet I the Chief Elder and your brother do not have a single line to myself at all.'

'You can voice any of the lines I write, I am not greedy.'

'No Ode, I don't have time to learn them, I have too many responsibilities. No, it may simply be better if we no longer encourage the warriors to take part in the play. It is a distraction.'

'But Ode, it is not amusing at all. The man whose head was used for sport, he was loved by someone no doubt. Tonight someone is weeping for him.'

We had a bottle of wine between us and it was hardly full anymore. There was a wind going and our tent flickered above us.

'Everyone thought it very funny.'

'And you should have been the exception.'

'My brother and I have a thousand men to appease and entertain.'

'And only one woman to appal.'

'It is not right for you to tell me what is right and wrong.'

'Because I am a woman? Because I am your hostage? Because I am your property? Because your pride is more important to you that your decency?'

'No, because it is not for you to make me a better man.'

'But I think it is, Ode, because I love you.'

'You have never told me that before. And how can I know you mean it?'

'Well I cannot prove that by bedding you. Any woman might do that, for her safety. Ode, the only way that I can prove my love for you is to be unkind. By criticising you, I put my very life in danger. And why would I do that if I did not love you?'

'I would never hurt you.'

'You would hardly need to. An unkind word about me to your brother? The next day you would find me hanging from a tree. Or worse. Ode, this situation that I find myself in, it is not an inconvenience. I feel each day and every day, that I am on the verge of the most terrible death.'

I was silent. Sick inside myself, and silent.

'You are not my hostage.'

'I am your brother's hostage. And he has simply loaned me to you. He could change his mind at any moment.'

'I will not allow that to happen,' I said.

'I want to believe that.'

'But you find it hard. After all I am not a warrior. How could I ever fight for your life? I am a one armed cripple against a thousand men.'

'But you would die trying wouldn't you, Ode?'

'What choice would I have? If I did not, you would be so disappointed. And then we would have another argument.'

'Ode, if you think this is an argument, you do not know me at all.'

Anna was attempting humour. I was not responsive.

'The head was hairless at the face?'

'Yes, as I said.'

'As if Peter had crawled off stage and somehow shaved in the instant before his death.'

She smiled at me and laughed lightly.

'It is funny. It is cruel and I don't approve. But it is funny.'

'How many do you count them, Ode?'

'I can only estimate. Say. Two hundred cannon, maybe four hundred on the wooden lance, maybe three hundred at bow, there will be horse and rider behind. There will be as many of them as there are of us.'

'They have mustered their best to wish this day the end of us, Ode,' said my brother. 'They are certain of their victory. But we shall disappoint them. We are as both man and Beast, so much mightier than they. So much finer. We shall take them head on.'

'That is what they want you to do,' said Luxxor.

'And should we disappoint?'

'That is why they have brought their cannons in force.'

'We have met the cannon before.'

'There were only two at the port. Ode has counted two hundred.'

'Numbers are irrelevant. We know how to sidestep the cannon fire. Ode, you suggested to Father that we should to go *towards* the enemy, if we wanted to defeat them. And that is what we will do again. What matter if two hundred cannon balls sail over our heads rather than two?'

'These cannons are larger than the ones we encountered at the harbour,' I said. 'I cannot guess their range. Nassir *told* me of the range of the cannons at the harbour. Here I have no one to give me that information. And without it we may charge right into their volleys and be exterminated.'

'Then do not guess, Ode. Calculate.'

'All I can do with my device, is estimate how far away the enemy stands. I will not know their range until they fire.'

'Then throw that fucking thing away, Ode. It is useless.'

'I need two pieces of information to make a calculation. It cannot be done with one. Two and two make four, but two on its own is no sum.'

'So we charge whatever, take whatever losses we must and crush them completely.'

'But we cannot replenish our losses,' said Luxxor 'We are an army on the move with no reinforcements in our wake. There are no soldiers here that we can take on as mercenaries. The whites won't fight on our side. We are alone, and far from our lands.'

'They will not fire upon us until we are in range,' I said. 'And we won't know their range until they fire upon us.'

'We could send fifty poor souls out as bait. But I will not command that. I will not treat any of our men like that.'

'And furthermore we do not know how quickly they can reload.'

'So what do you suggest, Ode?

'We charge, but when they fire we turn and run.'

'What cowardice, they will jeer at us!'

'Then we charge again immediately after.'

'I do not want our men to act the part of cowards.'

'A good warrior takes all advantage,' said Luxxor. 'We should listen to the boy if his idea has any value.'

I was just about to protest that I was only a year younger than my brother when I realised that labelling me as the boy, my brother became the man. If you cannot convince a man by logic, appeal to his vanity.

'And even if we do run, can the rhino outrun the cannon ball?'

'No.'

'Then your plan is useless, Ode! Brother, you are of little use this day. You are beginning to vex me. Shit! Motherfucker. What do we do?'

'In forward charge we are compact,' said Luxxor, 'like the head of a spear sharpened to a deadly point, like a hammer with all of the power concentrated in the head. In reverse we could scatter.'

'It would look like utter disarray and lack of control.'

'Spread out we are a harder target to strike,' said Luxxor, 'there will be space between us.'

'The men will feel used and enfeebled. I know them they would rather die with honour than live …'

'It is not just their life that I am trying to secure,' Luxxor said. 'I know the men better than anyone. What the men want more than life is victory, and if we are cut to pieces before we even get within fighting distance of the enemy, there will be neither victory nor honour, and we will have failed this day. And if they take that failure to the afterlife who will lavish praise upon them? I feel my brother's eyes upon me, upon us all this day.'

'Ode, your woman wants you, let me and Luxxor discuss this further.'

I turned to see Anna standing there, her eyes fixed upon me. She smiled and made a motion with her brows. I was loathe to leave the conversation, and felt belittled. I am talking to the men. What do you want?

I went to her muttering. She took my arm and led me to safe distance.

'Ode, I do not speak your language but an argument has its own recognisable melody. And it seems to me that you might be discussing the cannon, because I think you could crush those foot soldiers with all ease. And so I think that it is the cannon that is the cause of your concerns.'

'I do not know their range. I do not know at what point we are most vulnerable'

'No Ode, I very much doubt you do know their range. But *they* do. They need to know at what point to fire so as to be most effective. The problem is the same for both of you. You wish to avoid the danger zone. They want you to get caught in it. So they will have measured and marked that themselves. See that copse of trees over there, Ode. Use your device to scan it closer.'

'You have become a tactician, Anna?'

'No Ode, I remain a woman with a brain.'

'What am I looking for?'

'A man, Ode. Your device has a simple telescope. Find him if you can. I shall tell you what to look for. A man dressed like the leaves and bark. A dun coloured man in hiding. He should be holding a flag. The flag will be of a different colour to everything around it. Clean white maybe, vermillion, scarlet.'

I scanned the copse through the lens of the measuring device. I could see a family of deer. I studied a thousand leaves with one eye at the lens and the other closed. Then I noticed, he was stood incredibly still. He was staring right at me. But of course he had no lens, and I was just a tiny figure amongst a thousand trees.

'There is a man there, but he could be anybody.'

'Show me, Ode. Yes. That is the forward scout.'

'How can you tell? How do you know these things?'

'My father had a great library. I was not invited to many parties. Why would such a filthy man be hiding at the edge of the woods with a clean white sheet if he did not have a job to do?'

'If we are wrong many men could die.'

'If your men cannot die, Ode, they should not embark on conquest. That man, he will signal the moment you are vulnerable. They will fire and you will ride into a hail of cannon balls. You are strong and skilful, your beasts quite extraordinary as we all know, but you are not Gods and you are not immortal. This is the point at which they think to defeat you forever. They will leave you unburied to be eaten by the worms and ravens, by the hogs and wild dogs. And you, Ode, who want to remember everything and write it down for all time, you, Ode, and your people will be erased from history forever. If anyone ever mentions what they saw, a thousand black men on the backs of the rhinoceros, they will be treated as village fools, drunks, delusionary.'

We charged in close formation at full pelt, and the moment the dun man raised his sheet, I slapped my brother on his back and he ordered the short retreat. Our beasts dug in their toes and wrenched themselves about. Five seconds later the gunpowder cracked. The beasts hauled a mighty reverse fanning out to left and right as the cannon rained down upon us. If it looked like cowardice to the eyes of the enemy so be it. We knew that the enemy would soon know our true might.

A warrior to my immediate left was unseated by a sea of mud that erupted in front of him, seconds later he was on his feet but acted as if blinded. Another warrior took the iron between his shoulder blades and came apart. The Beast beneath him collapsed to its knees. With my master dead I shall never graze again. I will join him soon enough in death.

We halted our retreat.

'How many have we lost?'

'Maybe as many as fifty, Brother.

'Shit.

'If we hadn't retreated,' said Luxxor, 'it would have been many more.'

Twenty seconds.

'Brother order the charge again.'

'We go!'

We knew their range, because they knew their range and had sent a man out to mark it. But that was not all the information that we needed. The dun man had already given that away. What we needed to know was how long it took them to reload. If the dun man raised his flag when we were aligned with him, we would reverse again. And have to consider an alternative plan.

'Again,' cried my brother. 'Spread out as much as possible, don't ride too deep.'

Twenty three seconds.

We turned and sped to the line, I swivelled in my saddle and studied the dun man and as we came to the line he was to mark, he had not yet raised his flag.

Since the last volley I had been counting inside my head. Thirty-four, thirty-five, thirty-six.

We passed him and he had still not given the signal. For he knew the reload time and what point was there in signalling a volley when he knew the weapons were not yet armed.

I slapped my brother on both shoulders and he screamed a command that was passed down the line.

We commanded our beasts to charge at the full limit of their nature and when the cannons blew most of those metal balls flew over our heads.

Forty-seven seconds.

They could fire again. Forty-seven seconds. But they would need to adjust the angle of the barrels. And I had no idea how long that might take. But if we were to be fired upon at closer range, the destruction would be devastating.

The rhino now at the limit of their speed were like rocks rolling down a mountain, they could not decelerate or desist.

We came upon the lance-men with all velocity and mass, and too many of us were skewered though the throat and chest. The lance-men did not have to force their blades into our softness. We were travelling so fast, all the enemy had to do was hold firm, with the base of their weapon pressed to the earth and let our own speed be the cause of our own piercing demise.

Many men were lost in this fashion and the rhino slowed and presented its strength in stillness.

Some soldiers sought to kill our mates from under us and pressed the weapon's point to the breast plates of our beasts. But the rhino just moved slowly towards the men that aimed to hurt them. If the blades managed to spilt the giraffe skin and then their own thick hide, they showed no discomfort. The lance poles were pushed back through the lance-men's grip, bending the wood as the dull end sat firm upon the hard soil. Then the lances split and the fore-length of the lance entered their chests and saw light again on the other side of their spines.

The rhinoceros hoofed the eyes from the sockets of these whites beneath them, they found out the tender elbow joints and knees. And they all went down under us with feeble, remorseful complaint.

Wave after wave of thin arrow failed to pierce our triple bonded armour.

But the third time they fired, their cannons were turned towards the mêlée. They shot into the fight. Black and white men were torn apart. In their desperation they were willing to kill their own if that meant defeating us.

'Forty-seven seconds,' I shouted.

'Kill the cannon bearers,' hollered my brother.

We were on them in one, two, three, four, five, six, seven, eight, nine. And with their heads flown the cannons stilled. But of course we left one alive, always leave one alive. Luxxor went to him pointed at the cannon and taking a knife from his belt ran the blade flattened across the back of his hand. Twenty warriors quickly dismounted and made a circle as the white man showed them how to prime the weapon. They understood after the first demonstration, two each ran to a cannon and prepared. Out of interest I wondered how long it might take them, for it would be their first time. Forty-five seconds. But of course they had been warriors and free men since birth and these cannoneers were probably farmers before they were conscripted to die by their lords. The white men had been sent out into the field in jerkins, the leather hats of blacksmiths. Their leaders cared nothing for their lives. They stood above them. While our warriors were the definition of our tribe and race. And my brother and Luxxor, the two men most deserving of respect lead from the front, the armour no more protective than that which the men wore. Their swords and flintlocks no more special than the men bore.

We moved swiftly to the trees and behind us the newly educated warriors turned the captured cannons on those Yurop men still vainly holding to their lances, or brandishing their blades. They simply pounded them into fodder.

Forty-five seconds and again.

Now soup.

And there before us stood the horses. And between them and us, stood hogs and men with flaming torches.

What contest would this be? Their tusks, our horns, their fire, our armour. The conquest seemed in our favour. With great slowness they lowered their torches to the backs of the hogs and their pitch soaked fur burst into fire and they were set towards us.

Their screaming was intended to enrage and fear our beasts. But the rhinoceros has ears that can swivel and they turned their ears towards our comforting, commanding voices.

Run them down, skewer them, we told them softly. Send the rest back the way they came.

The hogs, their skin alight, their blood boiling in their skins, bore down upon our horned beasts.

It is not natural for a rhino to rear, yet it can do it for a short time. We did not command it. It might have been a natural response to being charged by flaming hogs or it might have been a tactic of theirs devised to make them look so tall. Either way they reared and the warriors strapped into their stirrups held fast.

'Make noise,' called Luxxor, 'make noise!'

A very few of us carried a caryx horn, we had not had cause to use them before. The rest of us, a thousand no more, but eight hundred at least surely, screamed and ranted at the limits of our lungs and caryx horns wailed and the hogs stupefied with pain, dug in their hooves, reversed in utter bewilderment and headed back towards the horses and their riders reeling among the trunks.

Their horses hoofed in circles and bucked as our rhino fell back upon their two front legs. The whites, simply perched on the saddle with open stirrups, had insufficient purchase. Many were de-horsed.

And we fell upon the unseated men and hacked them into butcher's cuts.

Those that fled still mounted, we chased them down.

We left not one cannoneer, archer, lance-man, cavalryman alive.

Those men sitting beside a fire, with a glass of mead or port, those men who had reached into their purses, fat with taxes derived from the poor, who had given orders and then sat down to dinner, would never receive a report.

There would be no bodies to bury.

If you stood up to our army, you simply disappeared from the face of the earth. What you sent to hurt us never returned to you. And you are next.

Luxxor's face was torn from eyebrow to chin in the shape of a crescent moon. His servant worked him with needle and thread, pausing to let his master force fierce red wine between his lips.

'Those of you that can be repaired,' he said, 'clench your teeth and hold your tongue. I do not want to hear from anyone who cannot bear their pain. And with heavy heart I say those who are hurt beyond repair, make yourself known or let your servant do that for you. I shall send you on myself with all honour and with dignity.'

And those that could be repaired with the time and facilities of an army on the move, were helped by their comrades to safe ground, tent erected, bodies washed by servants, wounds sewn warrior to warrior. Slings and splints applied when the damage was not too grievous.

And those that were too badly hurt too become well again in our circumstances, were sent to the afterlife by Luxxor himself. He knelt beside each one, kissed them on each cheek.

'It will not be many years before I see you again. Enjoy the next world as you enjoyed this one. Tell them all of our exploits and how we are making magnificent the name of our tribe. Also, Brother, know this, your wife will not begrudge you the taking of a second wife from those girls who died unmarried. That is until she arrives. Goodbye and bless you, Brother, it was an honour to ride beside you.'

Of those fallen dead in battle, their brother's cremated them, each and every one. Of those assisted to the Afterlife by Luxxor, it fell to him and my brother to tenderly pyre them all. And if it took them all night as it did by the light of flaming torches, then it took them all night.

My brother came into my tent at sunrise.

'You awake, Ode?'

'If I have slept badly, I know that you have not slept at all.'

'Is Anna asleep?'

'Yes.'

'It is nice to be awake in the presence of a sleeping woman. You have had more nights with yours than I had with mine.'

'I am not unhappy, Brother. But I am not proud either.'

'So much death, Ode. How will we ever find the glory to excuse it?'

'Not a single man we lost, would have wanted any other life or death.'

'But I think they would have liked more time on this earth. Why are we fighting for soil and sod if we are happy to leave it all behind?'

'But is the Afterlife not the better place to be?'

'All our teachings say so. But, Ode, the flesh is experience. The Afterlife is faith. Is flesh not more wonderful than faith?'

My brother stood there bloodied. Knackered. Hardly able to open his mouth.

'You have worked long and hard this night, Brother. Get some sleep. Have some wine and just let yourself collapse.'

'You were brave today, Ode. It was such a bloody battle, and I never heard any complaint from you sat behind me.'

'I am too busy watching and trying to remember every detail to think of myself.'

'And I am too busy thinking about winning to think of myself. In their eyes today was meant to be the last of us, Ode. But we destroyed their plan. They sent their best numbers against and lost completely. Those few that survived will run back home with tales of our invincibility. Two hundred lost is a heavy number to bear. And it would have been worse without your calculations. You did well today, Brother.'

The next night, after that bloody and costly battle, we did not erect the scenery or use the warriors or Peter as low comedy.

Just a few words, Ode, no drama or high jinxes tonight.

My brother stood at the centre of a semi-circle of candles. His audience were full of hog and fermented grape. My brother rose himself to his full height upon the stage, a patch of earth designated sacred and I raised my voice to match him.

Actor and voice, separate but one.

'From the tit Yurops have been taught that we were lower creatures, incapable of their prowess. How was it possible that we should best them, and their saviour would not send bolts from the sky to burn out the eyes in our dark heads?

'We were the impossible. And yet we were real. We were the unthinkable. And yet they fell before us.

'We are history, myth and dream in one. The greater our victories become, the more their faith will crumble.

'We shall take them. We shall take their lands and we shall take their faith. And their mighty churches shall be used for nothing more that storing grain. When they look at us, they will see a tribe so glorious it destroyed their God.'

I paused. There was silence. My brother's face was serious. He turned to me and made a patting motion with his hands to his mouth. Asking me to be silent. He spoke for the first time in the play.

'And shall we take this land? Shall it be ours? Can they withstand us? Can they match our strength?'

The warrior's bones were fat with ache. So many men had had their flesh recently sewn whole again. Some wore my mother's slings and knew that they were to carry a useless limb for at least a month or more. But their bellies were stuffed with meat and wine. They were happy in their own way.

'And shall we take this land?' he said again.

My brother swung his sword in one great arc. The warriors rose carefully and raised their swords.

'Can they withstand us?'

No.

'Can they match our strength?'

No.

'Then history shall be ours for eternity. And when the learned books are opened, the stories will begin with once upon a time there was a tribe called the Kikuyo. And they were mighty.'

My brother was content with his first speech, but exhausted.

At Anna's suggestion we let her sing to us all.

You must let Peter accompany me.

Just this once.

We were in general unfamiliar with Yurop music. For Kikuyo, singing is performed by large groups and always with the accompaniment of many interlocking drum rhythms.

But Anna sang with only the plaintive voice of the pipe organ to accompany her. She sang in her common tongue that not one of us understood the words of.

Her songs were sad, full of longing and remembrance. And we were sad. And we had lost so many men. And our faith in the Afterlife never really made that loss any happier.

And for that evening, with her fine voice, she was the wife of all of them, caressing her man back to sleep after he had awoken from a nightmare.

'What do you believe in, Ode?'

I had my arms around her and her back to my chest.

'Apart from you? I believe that we are made from the material of the universe. We come from the earth, the stars, the sun, the water and the wind and are gestated in the wombs of our mothers. Our lives are but a short period of flesh. And when we die the material of our bodies must be returned.'

'But that is not what your tribe believe, Ode.'

'No, that is I what I believe. The traditional belief, to which the warriors adhere, is that there is an Afterlife which is a mirror version of the corporeal world where brave actions are celebrated everlasting.'

'And that does not appeal to you, Ode?'

'I have not been a warrior in this life, and so I do not know if in the next world I will be deemed worthy of praise. I have made a place for myself here, on earth, in the flesh. I am the storyteller. But the Afterlife may be more traditional. I have broken my bonds here. I do not wish to return to being shackled after death.'

'What happens to the women who die?'

'Women go there to be their warrior's wives. Farmers farm, servants serve.'

'So the order of the world is unchanged? In my Khristan heaven, women still have to do what they are told. Ode, your body was fashioned from the material of the world and yet somehow your arm was made incomplete. Sorry I am not being insensitive, or maybe I am. I am just trying to understand how you see yourself and the world around you.'

'If someone is born with a defect it is said that an evil spirit interfered at the time of your making. Or that your mother committed a sin that was passed on to the child. Now not only would my mother never have slept with another man, she loved my father too much for that. But her status would have excluded her from such a thing. Why would she have had relations with another man, when she was the wife of the Chief Elder? And no man would have touched her for the same reason.

'At the time of my birth things had changed, because of the rhinoceros, but for thousands of years before that, life was very difficult. A man or woman could only survive by working to their very limit of endurance. If a child was born that could not contribute because it has been poorly made …'

'No Ode, I will not hear of it. You are not poorly made. Don't say that. Your arm does not reduce your beauty.'

'A child that could not work would be a burden to the other members of their family.'

'Then the family works a little harder to compensate.'

'But they are already working as hard as they can. You cannot work harder than you can work. It is like demanding a man is two inches taller than he really is. A burden can destroy an entire family.'

'And if you hadn't been the son of the Chief Elder you would have been killed at birth.'

'Yes, but my father saw something in me that no one else could see. But he did not know what it was at the time. If I had been born complete I would have trained as a warrior. So my defect was to assure my destiny as the storyteller. There was no evil spirit at work, no infidelity on the part of my mother. But it took a long time for me to realise that, and for many years I detested my deformity. Before I realised that I was *meant* to be born this way. So that I could document the history of my people. But if all time and history resides already in the Afterlife, what use will they have for me there? I am special in my own way, but only maybe in the flesh.'

'If your afterlife will not offer you the respect you desire, maybe I could try and sneak you into mine.'

'I don't think I want to go to your Khristan heaven.'

'Nor do I, it will be full of men that will refuse to talk to me of learned things. I shall have to spend an eternity being told to be quiet and ladylike. Fuck that, Ode.'

We sat on the top of a hill with a spread of wine, bread, meat and cheese before us. Our servant sat at some distance with his back against a tree and a flagon of cider and a pie in his mitts. He looked as if he had just been invited into heaven after having had a secret shit outside the gates.

Not far from us a mountain stream chuckled.

Anna liked to sit near water.

'Water sings, Ode. And it is never out of tune. It babbles but it never complains. It speaks, consistently of the same concerns, but never repeats itself.'

She had her chin on her knees. And looked down into the valley. I touched her lightly on her sleeve. She turned her lovely face to mine.

'I have never seen a city so grand. Or a face so beautiful.'

'It is the capital of this province,' said Anna. 'I recognise the skyline from a painting we have in our museum.'

'It is wonderful to eat like this, Anna.'

'It is called a picnic, Ode.'

'This is picnic,' I said looking at the wedge of cheese in my fingers.

'No Ode, that is gorgonzola. Picnic means al fresco, eating outside, en plein air.'

'What are you two talking about now, Ode?' said my brother approaching.

'We are talking about eating cheese outdoors.'

'I don't like the stuff indoors or out. It stinks. Why do Yurops eat something that has already gone rotten?'

He squatted beside us and took a slice of bread and pork.

'Your beasts will not be able to breach the walls,' said Anna, looking over at the city.'

'What of the gates? They will be made of wood surely.'

'They will pour boiling oil upon you from above as you try to breach them. You and your beasts will burn despite your armour and your thick skins.'

'We could lay siege, let them rot inside,' I said.

'But how long might that take, Ode? I prefer a swift victory and along to the next adventure. I don't want to be sat outside a wall for months on end staring at my feet or your arse. They will have soil inside to grow their veg. They will have sheep to eat.'

Anna laughed.

'Anna, could you enter the city and find out how well it is defended? You are white, they would not be suspicious of you.'

'Am I to be part of your campaign? Am I to help?'

'You told Ode to look out for the man with the flag.'

'Brother, I did not tell you that it was her advice.'

'No, I figured that for myself. And then you sang to the men. You sang to them when all the excitement of battle was gone, and all they were left with was the physical pain of their wounds and their grief at the loss of the fallen. Ode, have you asked Anna to marry you yet?'

'No, Brother, I have not.'

'Then you are a fool.'

'My accent is different from theirs,' said Anna. 'Our cities and our provinces have been at war many times. And I am a woman. Who would talk to me apart from other women at market? And how would they know anything about military matters?'

'Brother,' I scalded. 'We are not putting Anna in danger.'

'We put ourselves in danger every day. We feed her, protect her, she sleeps comfortably in your tent. She travels in an enclosed carriage.'

'I will do it,' she said.

'No Anna, you will not.'

'I will if I chose. Or am I your prisoner, your hostage, to command?'

It was my brother's turn to laugh.

'No Anna. You are yourself.'

'Then I will do it. I have never been asked to do something so exciting and dangerous.'

'I will come with you.'

'A black man will not be safe there.'

'I shall be your slave. Mute. Eyes to the ground. I shall walk behind you at all times.'

'Tell your brother to look through his treasures. I want gold and silver, baubles and coins. I shall enter the city free and rich.'

'Now, Brother, please leave us to our picnic. Go into the woods and kill something if you are bored.'

'I do not like this, Ode. It is not right for you to walk behind me.'

We had driven in by carriage and found a place to feed and water the horses. The horse-man did not like the sight of me, and I wanted to slap him when he tried to flirt with Anna.

'You now have power over me, Anna. One scream from you and I would be taken away and flogged.'

'Shall I do that, Ode? Shall I?'

She danced with the teasing of it.

'You would be free, if you did.'

'No Ode, I would not be free, I would be lost.'

We talked Latin in the presence of sausages, wines and cheeses.

'My brother intends to fight whatever the size of the garrison here. He only wants to know the number so as to appear thoughtful and mature, to show that he is thinking tactically.'

'A thousand warriors.'

'No longer that number.'

'The Thousand warriors and beasts at the beck and call of one young man. How old are you both, Ode? I can never tell. And I have known you for so long and not asked before. I did not wish to offend. Your skin is as smooth as the finest leather. Your voice is the richest, warmest tone I have ever heard from a man, young or old. You are so tall it hurts my neck to look you in the face.'

'My brother is sixteen in Yuropan years.'

'Sixteen? And he is your older brother?'

'Yes.'

'Shit, so I am having an adventure with a boy. Ode, stop fucking walking behind me.'

'I am your servant remember. Should I walk in front?'

I am your slave, you are my mistress. I said that to myself. It moved me.

'No.'

'How old are *you*, Anna? Not that I care.'

'In Yurop it is considered impolite to ask that of a woman.'

'Sorry.'

'The great Alexander of Macedonia was only sixteen when he began to conquer the world. He used elephants, like you use the rhinoceros.'

'Did you watch them, Anna?'

She burst out laughing.

'You asked me how old I was. If I had seen Alexander's elephants I'd be nearly two thousand years old by now.'

'What happened to him?'

'He conquered half the world and then went mad. He became convinced he was a God, and told his soldiers to kneel before him. They did not like that. Ode, look, a soldier, come.'

Anna put her hands together and curtsied before him, giggled, flew back her head and wiggled her hair. My manhood raised and I had to place my hands in front. The soldier, being older and more disciplined than myself ignored her.

She spoke fast in her own tongue. The soldier stared straight ahead.

'Schiavo,' she called at me curtly.

I stepped forward, still ridiculously erect in the soft pants that were my disguise. I gave Anna the shoulder bag I carried. She looked around for great effect. Open the flap and let the soldier look inside. He swore in surprise. Looked at her disbelievingly, whispered something, and let Anna hand him the goblet, only then with it in his hand and the information we wanted past his lips, did he realise he had nowhere to hide his bribe.

We did not stay to watch him resolve his dilemma.

'The garrison has two thousand men. And you, Ode, you seem to have the most enormous erection. Come lets us get our carriage.'

'Hey,' said a voice, 'I have seen that woman before. She runs with the black conquerors. They destroyed my brother's town and left nothing alive or standing. Grab and hang that bitch and the nigger too.'

'Do you trust my legs, Anna?'

I grabbed her around the waist, slung her over my shoulder and ran for the carriage. Pausing briefly to untie the reins I flung her in the back of the carriage, took to the box and urged the horses to the gate. The gate was in front of us, the man who had recognised Anna behind us. All we had to do was move faster than the man behind us, nobody at the gate would know what was going on. But then turning back to see the extent of our advantage, I saw a red flag speedily hoisted to the apex of a pole. It didn't take me long to realise that this was a clear sign. Do not open the gates to anyone.

'You do not want to do this,' I said.

The guard not knowing my Latin shrugged his shoulders.

A posh man and a priest came to visit me.

'Where is Anna?'

'The white women you were with? She is somewhere else. You wished it to appear as if she were your mistress and you her slave. But you are not a slave are you? You are part of the Nigga army. And Anna is someone you captured along the way and forced to be your whore. It is uncertain what will happen to her. There are two quite contradictory opinions. One that the nuns should take pity on her and try and bring her back to the love of God after her terrible ordeal. The other is that she is in league with you and your army and as such she should be tortured to confession and then executed in the town square by breaking on the wheel.'

'I suggest you release us both. My brother will be here soon to get me. Anything you do to harm me will be revisited upon you and your people a thousand fold. If you hurt Anna, I will personally torture you beyond all the limits of forbearance.'

'Now there are some people here who think that torture is the quickest way to the truth,' said the posh man through the priest. 'Personally I am not of that opinion. When you crush a man's fingers he will say anything to halt the pain. So that which he says is not necessarily going to be the truth. And the truth is what I want from you. I don't know your name, can we at least start with that simple information?'

'My name is Ode.'

'Ode.'

'No, that is not how you pronounce it. In my tongue it is said with two syllables not one.'

'O-dey.'

'That is better.'

'I never expected to have my language corrected by a black. But then every new experience helps us to improve ourselves, does it not?

'My name is Commissioner Albini. I, want to know everything there is to know about your army. Your strengths and intentions. You, on the other hand will not want to tell me that information, because you will think that to do so would be to betray your comrades and friends. And that is of course where the trouble lies. So let me put this simply.'

At that point two guards brought Anna into my cell.

'Ode!'

'Shh. Anna. Don't speak.'

'Now Ode,' said Albini. 'It would of course be very easy at this point to get one of my men to bring me a heated poker and put out this woman's eyes. Or put a knife to her throat to prove my intention of getting you to speak. But that would be so crude, would it not? A black that can speak the Latin is something I never thought to come across. There must be something special about you. It happens sometimes amongst the whites. A man is born with a mind that runs so much faster than the minds of all the others around him. Such a man usually has the choice of two fates. One, he is hailed a genius and finds a profound position of employ at a university or under the patronage of a rich and powerful man. Or, he is perceived as a threat to our values and understanding and is burned to death.

'So let me assume that you are a very special black, who has managed to learn the tongue of our education. And if that is true then I should offer you a certain respect and not hurt this woman, just to very crudely prove a point.

'So I will tell you this. There is clearly a door behind my back and before your eyes. And beyond that door stands a corridor. To the left of that corridor stands a jailor. He is a crude man with a very ugly wife and a son that is a stone cold moron. He has this strange fetish for capturing cats and setting their tails on fire. It is a thing that he takes very seriously indeed.

'There is nothing that Anna could say that would in any way make him sensitive to her plight. Nothing that she could *do* that would in any way make

192

him act with compassion. As a man he is quite lost to all hope. Yet, and I have seen this with my own eyes, he believes the lord loves him and that what he does, despicable as it is, in some way serves a higher purpose. He truly believes that he is combating Sataan and that Sataan has infiltrated the bodies and minds of those that are handed over to him. And in so torturing them he is not perversely attempting to hurt their frail bodies but the presence of the devil within them. I have seen him weep in church. Not because he is stricken with guilt, but because he believes he is appreciated by the Lord.

'On the other hand, or should I say the other foot, because Anna will soon be walking through that door behind me. The other alternative is to go to the right. At that at end of the corridor stands the sister of a nunnery. She is not an easy woman. But she will absolutely not hurt your friend. They will hardly light a pipe and sit before a warming fire and drink a glass of port whilst talking about the attractions of well-built men. But Anna will not be hurt. Now or ever.'

I don't think that Anna heard a word of this. Her mind had become quite stupefied with fear.

'Let her walk to the right and I will truthfully answer all questions you ask of me.'

'You have been hurt before maybe and know the extent of it?'

'I have never been tortured.'

'Your left arm.'

'I was born like that. Let Anna walk to the right and I will tell you everything you want to know about our campaign.'

They took her away and …

And so I began with the starving boy and his meal of rhino shit. I spoke to Albini about the extent and depth of our training. The precision of our armour. The skill of our warriors. The mission of our adventure. And none of this was a betrayal. This was story. I entertained him greatly, but he got no military advantage from my tale.

'You will be defeated,' I said. 'If you see any worth in that foreknowledge I am happy to provide it.'

'You are an arrogant and mocking man, Ode.'

'No, I am the storyteller that seeks the truth.'

'We have woods around us,' my brother said. I was not there. These things happened without me. 'We could build a structure. A wooden shield, like a roof, that would protect us from the oil.'

'The trees are mighty here,' said Luxxor. 'We have three axes only and they would be blunt before we felled one tree, let alone split it into planks.'

'Then what do you suggest?'

'We destroy the smaller towns that surround the city, cut off all goods going in and out. Starve them until they open the gates.'

'I do not want to siege. We have a thousand men and beasts eager for glory. I will not disappoint them.'

'Our father waited for fifteen years before we began our quest,' I said, even though I was not there. 'He did not lack patience.'

'But he is dead and now I am the chosen one and must act in the way that I see fit.'

'How do we protect ourselves from burning oil?' said Luxxor. 'They will pour it straight upon our heads. I think it is a cowardly way to fight, of course, but these people are desperate and weak. But still we must protect the men as best we can.'

'Brother,' I said. 'I have an idea.'

'Speak, Ode,' said Luxxor. 'You have some of the natural intelligence of your father.'

Of course I was not able to speak. I was in a cell, wondering if Albini was true to his word about the treatment of Anna.

'We are used to sitting upon our beasts,' I said to my brother. 'Let us reverse the order of natural things as has been our destiny so far. We travel under the belly of our beasts. We ride them from below and are thus protected from the flame.'

'Might our warriors not find that demeaning? To be found clinging to a rhinoceros's tit like a babe.'

'If you were to tell them that they were hiding, clinging to the belly of Beast, they might think so. But if you were to tell them that they were being cunning in the art of war, if you were to tell them they were to outwit the white man ...'

'Write me some words, Ode, that I might get that right when I speak to them of my plan. But still the burning oil rains down on the rhinoceros's back. Thick skinned as they are, I'm not sure they could bear it for long.'

'So we give them a shield for their backs.'

'Like a shield of wood? But we are poor of axe.'

'Yes Brother, but I have another idea for the materials.'

'Ode, do you insist on being strange?'

'I insist on making our adventures a story that will be told for a thousand years.'

'Only a thousand, Ode? Why not forever?'

And so we rounded up livestock from the surrounding fields. Calves, sheep and goats. We bound them in combinations and hauled them onto the back of the rhinoceros. A back plate of still living flesh, with moos and bleats and the strange, childlike chat of the goats.

And with a hundred of our thousand we began our charge upon the gate. The first wave, just ten pairs, men clinging to the belly of the beasts, were stunned by the weight of wood before them as they strove to crack it open. The oil rained down and the white men's animals screamed to be so used and to be hurt by their masters and husbands. A second wave, with our warriors below and chanting, made a split and retired throwing the burning livestock from the back of their beasts.

The third wave caused a crack in the heavy gate. Each of our rhinoceros weighs near five thousand pounds. Twenty five times the weight of a warrior. And we were twenty rhinoceros in flank, headbutting the wood and moving aside for the next wave to widen the damage.

And then the gate spilt wide open. The heavy timber collapsing on itself, the men above shrieking and pouring oil on their own livestock unable to get to us or the skins of our beasts.

And we were through.

The mass of calf, sheep and goat, were untied and discarded. They roasted as they still complained of death, cooked as they still lived. Filthy whites came from alleys and doorways, and rushed the meat. Whole families of foulness where the children were as ugly as their parents. The limbs of the animals came away easily from the bodies, the people feasted on the blackened chunks as the conflict raged about them and the full extent of our army poured through the gates.

Archers on the ramparts, swarmed us with arrows.

'Stand your ground, let them rain down,' my brother said. 'Let us show them their arrows are of no concern to us.'

And so we sat as volley after volley of those metal tipped sticks came upon us. They slid off our well-oiled armour.

'We have shown them how useless they are,' screamed Luxxor. 'Now kill them.'

On foot our warriors took the ramparts and dispatched the coward's heads and tossed them into the pots they had used for boiling oil. Threw their bodies over the stone wall, out of the city. The dogs could have them, and the worms. Fat happy dogs, good manure in the earth for the next run of weeds.

Just inside the walls, the houses were poor hovels and the white men pinched and bent. Ragged women came to us and displayed their saggy paps. Men threw themselves on the ground, children tried to sing.

It was not our order or our intention to harm the civilians. We did not wish to inherit a ghost town, nor did we wish to deal with many thousand rotting bodies. We were to stay here a while and we did not wish to pollute the air that we should have to breath ourselves.

The streets at the periphery were tight and winding. We were met with soldiers armed with lance and sword. They did not have recourse to horse or to canon, both of which would have been a burden in this cramped conflict.

The windows behind which the city folk lived were not slammed shut, instead people leant from them and watched. They did not throw things down on us. We did not have to advance through a cloud of cabbage and shit, plant pots and old soup.

Clothes hung on strings between the houses, they waved like flags at our advance.

As I was to find out later the soldiers of the garrison were not from the city or the surrounding villages, they were paid mercenaries from another province. The logic being that they would have no great love for the people of the city and would not protest at quelling any home grown riot or insurrection. So in their fight they did not have the support of the people, and they were not defending their own.

But they were soldiers and did what they were paid to do. In this instance to die. Because they fell before our hooves, they watched parts of themselves fly, taken by our scimitars.

Streets led to compact squares, at each square stood a statue or a fountain. Shops and restaurants abandoned, city folk all at their upstairs windows, watching, peeling oranges or drinking clear white spirit.

After maybe a mile of such confinement, oh our battered knees, our scraped elbows, we entered a grand boulevard and were presented with a phalanx of armed men, well disciplined, massed, determined and they thought impassable.

You will get no further than this you band of black shits.

But this show of force did not deter us or contain us. Quite the opposite, it released us, and we simply charged, scabbarding our swords, holstering our flintlocks.

Our speed and weight was all that we needed. We did not defeat them, we trampled them. We put them under our feet and squashed the goodness from their bodies.

Further along, before us, more men. More determination. Two hundred men convinced that *they* would not let us pass even if that other useless lot down the way had succumbed so easily.

The soldiers were brave enough in the face of us. But their bullets could not pierce our armour and they never had a chance to show their swordsmanship. You can cut a large tree that stands still before you, but you cannot cut a rock rolling down a mountain side.

We left them with no eyes to survey their damage. No jaws to blabber that they had been ill-informed by their commanders. No swirling ear to hear the sound of our victory.

And so we ploughed, the hovels had become houses, and the houses had become villas, and the villas became mansions, and the mansions eventually gave way to the palace.

There were guards with pikes and muskets outside the palace dressed in silly clothes.

They were not mercenaries from out of town. They were the private army of the holy man. They would not desert under any circumstance. In their minds they would rot in hell for doing so. Their fear of hell made them fearless in this life. They stood their immobile. Stony faced. I think it was simply beyond their comprehension that we would try to enter the palace. Such a thing had never happened in all the city's history. In fact the soldiers had hardly ever killed anyone at all. They were symbolic. Their presence was all the deterrent the holy man thought he needed. Soldiers trained by God.

But they did not know us.

'Men,' shouted Luxxor, 'those that have the flintlocks, come to the front and load with deliberation. Do not hurry.'

Seeing this, the soldiers took their guns from their shoulders and took aim.

A number of them frowned, we were still loading and they were already pointing, why were we not in more hurry?

Their captain ordered them to fire and they did so with a calm accuracy.

All we did was dip our heads to save our eyes.

The shots were well taken. Our men received many bruises. A couple were concussed and slumped upon their beasts.

'Now,' said Luxxor.

Our shooting was not so accurate, but our one hundred shots felled twenty-five of them. The others, maybe four times as many, began to reload in haste.

'Men,' cried Luxxor, 'reload fast this time.'

The men in the foolish clothes were primed ahead of us and shot again. We sustained more bruising, more lack of consciousness among a very few. One of our men did die. The bullet hit his throat and although the armour did not tear, his wind pipe collapsed within.

Then we released another volley. And this strange war of attrition continued with the foreign men dreaming of heaven, and our warriors knowing that even if they did die that day, there was a place of beauty awaiting them, until there was just the one palace soldier and so many of our guns pointing at his one single figure.

Impressed by his bravery Luxxor dismounted, walked up the stairs to the last man and offered him his hand. The man turned his gun on my Uncle's chest. At that range the bullet would have penetrated the armour. So Luxxor lunged forward, grabbed the rifle by the barrel, wrenched it from the man's grip and tossed it aside. The man went for his sword and Luxxor slapped it aside, moved towards the man's chest, grabbed his elbow and twisted. The sword fell. Luxxor turned his back and walked away.

'Just shoot him,' he ordered.

My brother found me in my cell and held me with his two strong arms. I had never seen him cry before. And I don't believe he cried later. When he really should have and I could not.

'It is all my fault,' he said.

'But you have come to my rescue. And I knew you would.'

'Shall I kill this man? He has hurt you.'

Two warriors had Albini by the neck.

'No, Brother, I have told him all about our army, our history and our strengths.'

'Then he cannot be allowed to live, for he will tell others.'

'Brother, I want him to tell the others. I want him to tell everyone. He thought I was giving away our deepest secrets. I was not. I was showing him that we are invincible. Let him go, let him run. Let him tell the others what faces them. Albini, were you true to your word? Is Anna at the nunnery?'

'I did not lie.'

'Where is it?'

'To the east of the city.'

'Show me in person and after that I will let you run. The jailor who would have hurt Anna if I had not complied, is he here in this building now?'

'He would not have left. He lives among these walls.'

'Can you call his name? Will he hear from where we are?'

Albini called and the man appeared, he showed no fear in the face of so many black Sataans.

'Brother, I want this man shredded.'

I have been candid in my story. But I shall not tell you how myself and Anna were reunited. I will not tell you what we said to each other. We found a simple tavern where they were pleased to serve us. There were no other customers there. And the management no doubt thought that if we sat there our army might not burn their business to the ground. We ate very well and were very silent. And quite happy even though we did not laugh much.

I joined my brother at the palace leaving Anna in a grand mansion we had sequestered as our own. Oddly, there were no occupants to evict. No staff either. I went from room to room to make sure there was no concealed danger to threaten Anna. In the library a book sat still open on the desk. In the kitchen, four pheasants had been plucked but not cooked.

Five warriors came up to me.

'Ode, we will stand guard over her while you go about your business. Two shall stand at the front door. The others will position themselves about any room she decides to sit in.'

I was surprised.

'Ask her if she will sing again for us.'

We moved under a series of paintings. They showed great skill, but no variety. Men chosen by God to rule. I had a notion to scrawl smiles upon all their faces. True belief and great power makes men so dull.

'Brother can we have these paintings taken down and loaded onto a cart?'

'Are we to loot these monstrosities? Who on earth could we sell these sad men to?'

'I have an idea.'

'Oh fuck, Ode has another idea. Okay.'

A ridiculously dressed man came out to see us. Bewildered he looked across our faces.

I stepped forward.

'I speak the Latin.'

'There is something wrong with your arm.'

'And there is something wrong with your manners.'

'How dare you challenge me?'

'I challenge you because we have taken your palace. I can have you taken from your comfort here and whipped out in the streets. I mention it in passing.'

He looked at us again.'

'You have come to see his holiness?'

'Yes.'

'Today is not a good day.'

'It is never a good day to lose your palace to an invading army.'

'He is unwell and taken to bed.'

'Then mop his brow, prop him up on his pillows, and tell him to get ready to welcome us.'

'Do your men understand what we are saying?' said the man in purple and plumes.

'Not one apart from me.'

'The nature of his holiness's malady is delicate. He is not in full command of his person and is less than fragrant.'

'We shall be back tomorrow. I wish your master a speedy recovery.'

I turned away.

'Brother we shall come back tomorrow.'

'You have let this man put us off. What is wrong with today?'

'His holiness has the shits.'

We returned the next day. They should have stopped us. A man of such power should not have had his room invaded so easily. Yet we held the palace in all of its resplendent emptiness. My brother, terrifying Luxxor, ten warriors, none under six foot, dressed in animal skin armour, sabres at our sides. The last guards banged their heads against the wooden panelling of the hallway and tried to wake themselves from this nightmare. We entered the chamber without the strange Yuropan habit of knocking.

There were more flowers in the room than I have seen in a hundred meadows. Bowls of spices and fragrant herbs sat about feeling quite useless. The smell of his shit still commanded the room.

His holiness reclined with a curled lip. He wore a cap upon his head. The rest of him lay hidden under the covers. The last circle of his guards threw themselves at us. We tossed them to the floor.

'Your holiness, I speak the Latin. Apologies for this interruption to your malady. My brother and his army have taken your city.'

'You have taken nothing.'

'We have taken all and walked uninvited into your chamber.'

'I am all powerful.'

'You are old and ill.'

'I am the voice of God on earth. All his power flows through me. You will be punished by God's will for this insult. This day shall be the last of your days. You have consigned yourselves to Hell everlasting.'

'We have no belief in your vision of hell. It does not concern us.'

'We were told of your barbarism,' said the old man. 'But, I did not expect the Latin from you Afrik. You may be black as the darkness of hell but maybe there is some light to be found in you.'

'You have gold and it shall be ours by right of conquest. You strove to defeat us but were defeated yourself. So you must pay. It is the natural order of things'

'There is nothing natural here. No, you shall not have your booty. The gold belongs to God. You have not defeated him! You shall not have it.'

'Why? I doubt that God has much use for it.'

'Ah. You wish to be philosophical? Here in Yurop we advise our flock that Heaven is a place of everlasting abundance. After all, the world is so hard and people have so little.'

'If they have so little, why not sell your gold challises and crosses and feed them?'

'Oh I have heard that tired argument before. How long might the money last to feed a city from the selling of a few gold trinkets? A few days, no more. And then we are back to penury. And we have nothing to admire. The presence of gold is a visible promise of the glory of Heaven. Gold is God's promise made real. And I will not let any of your black hands touch it.'

'You will suffer for your obstinacy.'

'Know this, I have taken a potion. There is a red flower that can sometimes be found. My physicians have learned how to dry its seeds and stems and preserve it in a suspension. I took a draft after breakfast. The Universe is inside my mind and God holds my hand at this very moment. You have broken into my chambers but you have no hold on me. I am beyond any physical threat you may concoct. I am too far into bliss to feel any harm. You cannot threaten my family for I have none. You killed a hundred of my special guards and are now trying to threaten an old man. Yet you have nothing to show for either offence. For I will not tell you where the gold is and you cannot make me do so. And I am not leaving my chambers. I was placed here by God and only God can move me. You have achieved nothing by coming here today. Leave empty handed and with my curse. For cursed you will be, all of you. And what matter if it falls upon me too, I am already dying.'

We went along the corridors from office to office and each was empty. One large room had a large globe on a leather topped table. On a sideboard sat a glass decanter full of amber liquor and crystal cut glasses.

Mr brother poured two drinks. The neck of the decanter slamming on the rims.

'This isn't the usual shit, Ode.'

'It is delightful, Brother.'

My brother picked up the globe and spun the world with his finger.

'Do you know what this is, Ode?

'It is a model of the world.'

'Our world is a ball?'

'The Arabs have believed so for many generations.'

'You and your Arabs, Ode. So I hold the world in my hands!'

'Only a model of it.'

'Is that not where we all start? Every lover starts with a picture in his mind, and his thing in his hand.'

'Brother we have taken this city. How long shall we stay?'

We had billeted both warriors and beasts in the mansions that surrounded the palace. It had been Luxxor's idea. He didn't want to stay in a palace and he didn't want his men to do so either. My brother did, but he didn't want to appear grand and mighty over the others. So he didn't.

'It is not to my liking. A life in this place would make us fat and weak. We have fought against all odds. Should we be destroyed by luxury? But we will find that gold before we leave. So, Ode, their holy man is old, addled, addicted to potions and shits himself. Ode, do you know why he is still alive? His God is so disgusted with him he doesn't want him near. He's like, I don't want that old git up here shitting all over my paradise.

'Brother will there *ever* be a point where we stop? Will we ever be satiated by this dream?'

'Who wants to stop?'

'You want to conquer the world forever?'

'Ode, correct me if I have misunderstood this. We left our lands and headed north to the sea and we have been heading north ever since.'

'Not always directly north Brother, but north in general, yes.'

He ran his finger along the orb to illustrate his words and fix his mind in order.

'If we continue moving north and the world is a globe, at some point we reach the top and start going south and then south turns to north again and we might arrive at our own lands from the opposite direction to that of our leaving. Ode, can you imagine that? To leave in front and to reappear behind, and to have seen and conquered the world and bring back abundance and untold treasure. And to have travelled but never had to repeat one's journey. Never having had to go back the same way, to have moved forward always and still return home?'

There was a commotion outside and I went to the window.

'Brother.'

He came and leant against me.

'What a stinking bunch of shits, Ode. What rabble'

'Brother those paintings of the popes. I gave them to the very poor who live just inside the gates.'

'What the fuck did you do that for?

'I thought it was funny. To take the most precious things in the palace and give them to the stinking poor. Just think how offended his holiness of squits will be when he finds out!'

'Yeah, Ode, I like that. That's cool, that's funny. But that doesn't explain why they are here.'

'Brother, they have never been here in the centre of the city in their lives. They have never been allowed to do so. The soldiers never let them leave the area where they live. Then I give them those paintings and they realised, the soldiers and the holy man are no longer in charge. We are.'

'And what do you think they want from us.'

'Everything.'

'I will get some of the lads to raid the kitchen and take them out some food.'

'Brother, why not let them into the banqueting hall and make the cooks feed them?'

'That would be sport, Ode. Should we drag him down here to watch?'

'I think his presence might spoil their appetite.'

They stuffed their faces. They poured the wines and brandies down their throats. They licked the rims of the glasses. They licked the plates so clean they could have been put back on show.

And if they were damned to hell for evermore for their gluttony in this sacred place, they hardly seemed to care. After all they were only doing what the holy man and his men did every day.

We watched them because of their foulness, we gloated in their greed and poverty. We felt superior. Anna stood with us to command the kitchen. My brother had his sword unsheathed to deal with any riot or revolt.

One man, his face ravaged, came up to Anna and went down on his knees before her with his hands together in supplication.

'He is taking food home to his family,' she said. 'His son is unwell and needs feeding up. In all compassion we should do this for them each day, but in all honesty, I find their stench makes me sick. I am not used to such uncleanliness. I am going to bathe now. Also I am going to burn this dress.'

They left with furniture, great heavy wooden chairs that they could hardly lift. They left with glass and crockery. They left with crisp, white table clothes. They tried to take the tables but they were too immense even for a concerted rabble.

And they also left without taking their stench with them.

When they had gone my brother turned the key of the lock of the banqueting room.

'We are not short of fine rooms. Let us leave that one to itself.'

To have a day without fighting.

To have a day without being witness to death.

To have a day were you don't even look to find your clothing until the sun is spent.

To spend a day within each other's perfume.

To have a day where the world outside could burn to the ground and you would not have to give it a second thought.

To have a day with Anna alone.

To find such absolute pleasure, and have no need to dream of the world getting better by the application of some philosophy.

Our thoughts and conversations drifted, we had no need of resolutions, no need of a fixed point to centre our thoughts around. All was flesh and sensation.

During parts of that day we found we had no need to talk at all. A perfect stupefaction, helped no doubt by the Madeira.

She let me comb her hair even though I showed little natural skill at that. She let me suck her thumbs, which she found very funny and dubbed them her two little hand pricks. I did not know there was so much sensation there, she said.

Anna and I, we were full of each other.

'Ode, you are carrying some extra luggage and I have a special little cubby hole where you can keep it safe.'

She sat upon me and we made one lovely Beast. Then I rolled her under me.

'The ceiling, Ode, have you ever seen anything like it?'

'You should be looking at my handsome face. Not the ceiling.'

'I am doing both at the same time. I am imagining your face as part of the painting.'

I rolled her to her side such that I could still be in her and yet we could both look at the ceiling at the same time.

'When you paint on a ceiling, how come the paint doesn't just fall off and land in our eyes?'

'I imagine it often does. Now, Ode, please, do not slow down. You are meant to be fucking me. Don't disappoint.'

'I am doing my best.'

'I'm joking. You never do disappoint me, Ode.'

'I must do sometimes.'

'Oh shit, Ode, just roll me on my belly and ride me to the top of the hill.'

Anna again regarded the paintings upon the ceiling and was beguiled.

'I never thought to see this. To have been under this and under you at the same time. It is beyond any dream I might have had in the cloistered life of my father's house. Ode, and you surely know this, that when the sun is at the highest of the day, there is little shadow on the ground.'

Anna took an apple from the bowl, bit into it and winced.

'Are you alright?'

'One of my teeth has become a little sensitive.'

'Here,' I said holding out my hand.

I took the apple from her and divided it with a knife.

'Thank you, Ode. As I was saying, our house stood in a square and my day room looked out upon the piazza. The shadows hid under the tops of tables, under the skirts and shoes of the passers-by, busy with their days. They hid under awnings where people stuffed their common faces with cheeses and hams and toasted bread. Dogs carried their shadows under their bellies and wagged their tails and shat in corners and pissed on shoes. There was a naked man at the centre of the square carved in marble. He had his own little shadow beneath his balls.

'And every day that I saw the shadows hiding, I thought oh God, oh fuck, it will be so many hours before it is dark and even when it is dark it will be many hours before I will be able to sleep and even after a night of sleep, I will awake to another day just like this one, another day of nothing. Boredom and shadows and nothing to fill my searching mind.'

She had finished her apple and started picking at the grapes.

'Do you like grapes, Ode?'

'I like their sweetness.'

'A grape is a fine enough thing in itself, but I have always thought that it's destiny is to be turned into wine. Standing on the balcony of my day room, watching the shadows grow, a glass of wine would make the clocks move faster. My father didn't approve, so I would have to send a servant out in secret and I never had any money of my own and so I had to steal coins from his desk. And yet he never seemed to notice my theft and my servant never got caught shopping for me. So I think he turned a blind eye to the flaunting of his own instruction. He must have known how unhappy I was. Maybe he wanted to help me, after all I was all that was left of his family. My mother had died in childbirth when I was four, the child she had carried was stillborn. He must have known what I longed for, because despite the rule that women did not study and learn, books would appear as if by magic, learned books, books full of facts and theories, yet it was an unspoken rule, that my father should never catch me actually reading them. I learned about the world with the door locked, in the same manner that I rubbed myself under my skirt. Ode, don't make that face. I am sure that back in your homeland the women do the same.'

I had never thought of it. Even holding myself, I had never thought that women might have their own way of finding release when they felt so unpopular and yet were bursting with such wild passions. Oh to be so full of love and yet to be ignored! Whatever God or spirit invented love and desire, and then ugliness, was the world's first and most experienced torturer.

'Let me tell you of the details of this ceiling. You see I know all about this art, and yet I have never seen these paintings before this day. Is that not the wonder of books, Ode? That you can know so much about something you have never physically witnessed, or something that happened before you were born. You know who that is of course. At the centre.'

'No.'

'Adam and Eve. The first humans.'

'Ah,' I said. 'But that is wrong, they are both white.'

'If our parts were the other way around, Ode, would we switch our genders? I mean, men could still have their larger bodies and the hair that grows on the chests and face, and they could still speak in deeper voices and they wouldn't have tits, but instead of an outty they had an inny, would they still be men? And if women kept their lighter voices, and their hairless cheeks, their ample bosoms, their long lashes and their fair brows, but also had a big cock. Would they still be a woman?'

'I don't want a woman who has a big cock,' I said.

'No Ode, I understand that, No, what I meant is that you and me here right now, right now would it matter if I was inside you rather than you were inside me?'

'I do not know.'

'You are probably not used to women who speak to you about such things.'

I nearly said that I was not used to women talking to me at all. But being as how Anna was already thinking about whether she might like to penetrate me, I thought better of it.

'Anna,' I said. 'Speak to me about anything you wish and speak for as long as you wish, I will always listen, because it is a privilege to know that you trust me with your thoughts. It is what I have always wanted in my life.'

She was happy with that, she put her tongue inside my mouth and with great gusto began to bounce upon my lap.

And above us, Eve said to Adam, those two in that bed, they are having way more fun than *we* ever did. Yes, said Adam, but I could never quite get over the fact that you were made from one of my ribs, so it always felt that I was fucking something that was part of myself. And Eve said, Adam you were so boring in bed that day, I had to eat a forbidden apple just to stay awake.

I felt that I had only just fallen asleep in our curtained cot when Anna cried out beside me. I put my hand on her shoulder. She came awake choking. I quickly felt for her chin and put my cupped hands before her mouth as she gagged onto my palms. I wiped her spit on my chest and stumbled for the candle and the fire.

Her face came alive with the flicker of the wick.

'Sorry, Ode.'

'What is there to be sorry for?'

'I woke you.'

'Asleep I was alone, awake I am with the woman that I love.'

'For fucks sake, Ode, you cannot always be this nice! It is unnatural. Ode, don't give me that face, I am teasing you.'

'You were dreaming.'

'Yes Ode, but not some weird fantasy. I was remembering. Asleep, but remembering real things. Real things in a bad dream.'

'Well you have caused me the inconvenience of waking me from my slumber, you may as well tell me the details.'

'Ode, I can see the whites of your teeth. Close your lips, you are blinding me. I was dreaming of the day your ship arrived in port and you killed so many of us and you took so many of our things, and your brother took me and I expected to die, or worse. For days I had a dagger with me in the carriage, I would hold it to my wrist.'

'Your dream, tell me about your dream.'

'We lived on the first and second floor of a town house. My father was the Mayor as you know and our house should have been grander, but it wasn't. Some political crap that I could never bother to fully understand. We still had more

208

rooms than a village full of peasants. We could wash and shit in private. I could throw my underwear on the floor and it would find its own way to a bucket of suds and a line in the sunshine.

'And in the dream, I was in my bedroom. You had invaded. I had thrown up on my dress in fear. There was a loud banging on the door below. I thought it was one of your warriors. I thought fuck I am dead. Or I am going to be fucked and then dealt the card of death. I had a hidden cupboard in my bedroom. The door looked like part of the wall, there was no handle to reveal it. You simply pushed in the right place and the door opened as if by magic. There was a handle on the inside and just as I was closing the door I heard my father talking to another man.'

'Did you hear what he said?'

'He said, I am going to kill that black bastard.'

'And did he?'

'I have no idea. I heard a shot and more shit. I had a bottle of rose in my mitt, I wasn't even aware that I had it, but I did. I sat on the floor and got drunk. More drunk.'

'There was a shot and a black man died,' I said.

'I will not say that I am happy about that, but your forces invaded our land. It is only right and decent that we should protect ourselves. Did you know that man that was shot.'

'The man he shot was my father.'

I left the room with Anna making animal noises behind me, smacking her forehead with her knuckles.

Anna had not let the man into her house. She had not known who was to be killed. She had not even known me at the time. She was utterly without blame. Yet still I was furious. And even if that made no sense, the conscious acknowledgement of the facts did nothing to make my breathing easier or to reduce my anger.

I consoled myself on the roof, asking the moon what I should do next.

Go back down and talk to her you arsehole.

My beloved was very white. There was white sweat on her forehead. Her hair was messed. There was a dark pool upon her pillow. She had slit a wrist. I screamed for my servant.

'Apply a tourniquet.'

I ran along the corridor, disembodied heads on plinths grimaced in the candle-light, the nervous speed of my journey down the echoing stairs to the front door.

Out in the street at late evening, Peter was pulling a cart.

He looked at me with disgust.

'Wonderful costumes, but will I ever get to wear them on the stage? No, because you have me dressed in rags and covered me in fake shit.'

'Shut up,' I said. 'Anna has cut a wrist, stay with her while I get Luxxor.'

I knocked frantically on the door of the mansion opposite.

A servant answered.

'Luxxor, is he in?'

'Yes but he is quite drunk I'm afraid.'

Even drunk Luxxor was the best surgeon we had.

I stripped her and washed her down. I put her under covers.

'I am so sorry, Ode. Do you hate me?'

'It wasn't your house, Anna, it was next door.'

'But no, Ode, it really was our house, I heard the knocking, I know my father's voice.'

'No Anna, you are confused. The knocking was next door. Your neighbour's voice was identical to that of your father's. You heard what you heard, but you came to the wrong conclusion. I shall blame you only for being foolish and inaccurate in your memory. That can be forgiven easily enough. Can it not? But the truth shall remain a secret. My brother must not hear of this, for he will come for your execution. And I will have to stand between you both, and if that happens I will lose the two people I love the most.'

Anna was asleep. I lay beside her. The wound had not been deep, and Luxxor was sobered by the challenge of sewing up a woman's flesh. Mgebe, the oldest warrior amongst us had assisted and I had yet to thank either of them for their help and compassion.

Let us leave this city, just you and I. Let us be sneak-thieves stealing our own privacy. Anna, I love the colours of this continent. They are a joy. I have never seen such greens before and in such abundance. And then dotted amongst the verdant and the shades of bark and soil, are the bluebell blues and ruddy faced, blood, red blooms.

The rivers that criss-cross your lands are as beautiful as your own face when you are scowling and smiling in tempo. And as you once said to me, the rivers sing. And they are so pure, so clear. There is no disease. You can just stuff your lips into the flow and drink with all the pleasure that you wish.

Anna, you and I could live in the woods, amongst the trees and animals. They would not be disturbed by my withered arm. They would not judge a black man in love with a white woman. The trees would feel safe from me. I could not wield an axe. I would not tell them that you could.

Anna, I love you with all my heart.

'Is she asleep? I thought, I'd visit.'

'Thank you for your concern and for looking after her. I didn't want to leave her alone.'

'I want a new role in the play,' said Peter.

'You are well cast as you are.'

'No more rags. No more fake shit.'

'I am in no mood for this. I am worried that Anna might fall foul of a fever after her ordeal.'

'Yes. I sat with her while I waited for you and Luxxor. She sounded quite delirious and wouldn't stop talking.'

I understood. It is the nature of a secret to be revealed.

'I shall speak to your brother. I will bargain this information for my release. And I shall ask for Anna to be handed over to me. And if you want to do that thing in your fucking play, where the white man grovels on the stage covered in shit. You can play that part yourself, chalk your face and cover yourself in dun.'

'How will he understand? In what language that he knows will you betray us?'

'I can draw,' said Peter. 'I will draw the whole story, picture after picture like a play that is made of tableaux vivant. I will leave him in little doubt as to what happened. That this woman gave shelter and advantage to the man that killed your father.'

'It was not her fault.'

'Do I not know your brother? Will he be concerned by such niceties? I will bring down upon you, Ode, every hurt you have brought down upon me. I shall repay you tenfold. Night after night to have me covered in shit and spat upon!'

211

My brother had employed an artist. He came with a sketchbook and pen and ink. He sat on a portable stool. He was smug and had a fat nose. The window of the room was open. The smell of smoke filtered through.

'He is very famous,' said my brother.

'I do not have much time for this,' said Luxxor.

'Will you not indulge me?'

'I am always at your service. You will find no fault in me.'

'Then let that always be our way.'

My brother stood at the front of our trinity. Bare-chested, armour-thighed, a sword of enormous size that he had plundered from a northern giant held in both fists. Luxxor in full armour, his face hidden by the helmet, stood behind him and to his right side. I further back again, and to the left, sat at a study table, armed with paper and pen. I wore a quizzical, ponderous expression worthy of a poet searching for words.

We posed like that for about fifteen minutes. My wrist started to cramp from holding the pen in the same position. Luxxor huffed and my brother kept his expression of invincibility quite still. I imagine. I was of course, seated and behind him and could not see his face.

'Upon our return,' said Luxxor as if desperate to fill the boredom, 'are we to spread wealth and favour among the other tribes of our continent? Are we to bring the black man together as one? One nation with power and under law. Or is it only our tribe that is destined for history and power? Do we go home and conquer them also?'

'When we return,' said my brother, 'we shall unite the black men of our lands.'

'We should get Ode to teach a few others of the Kikuyo to read and write,' said Luxxor. 'That way we can expand our power over greater distance.'

'We should teach them to obey.'

He stamped his foot upon the stone floor and laughed. He turned to face me, and the great painter huffed.

'Ode, my brother, do not judge me ill for my humour. Are you forever to be my conscience? Do not fret, either of you. I will share the spoils of Yurop with all black men that show their worth and due respect to our tribe.'

'I can't stand here like this any longer, said Luxxor. 'This is not an occupation for a man like me. At least let me walk around the town for a while to get the blood back in my veins. I should be supervising the soldiers.'

'What is there to supervise? Some white men are rioting, and no one knows why. Not even themselves I expect. They have set fire to a few houses. Who cares? Leave them to it if they want to destroy their own homes. They are not coming anywhere near us are they?'

But Luxxor did not heed his command. He went to the man and roughly pulled the pad from his hands.

'This is not proper work for a man.'

Then Luxxor burst out laughing.

'This man is a fool. He had drawn me no bigger than a squirrel. I am twice this man's height and yet he draws me no bigger than a thing that eats nuts.'

'Uncle, what he is doing, is sketching. You know when you draw a simple map in the dust. And you say there is this river here and this mountain here …'

'And the map is smaller than the land you are mapping. Ode, I am not a fool.'

'No. Sorry.'

'Tell him, that I must be my real size in the painting or he will suffer for the insult. I am going to see the men.'

'Ode, can a person be removed from a drawing?'

'Easily enough I believe.'

'Tell this fool to erase Luxxor from his book and to make sure he does not creep back into the final painting.'

'Brother he is from the north.'

'And I give a shit where he is from?'

'He doesn't speak Latin. He speaks a Germanic dialect that I am unfamiliar with.'

'Fuck's sake, Ode. Why is it always left to me to get things done.'

My brother grabbed the sketchbook from the artist's hands, tore out the page, scrunched it up and threw it into a corner.

He then went back to his pose and the artist began again on a fresh sheet.

We had not thought to set up roadblocks to contain the movements of the populus. There was a grand square between us and the palace, and Luxxor had his men charging in great circles. The sight would have been enough to make any white man run for his life.

Yet a number of hardy merchants came to visit us each day in the area where we were billeted.

'Let us go outside. I can hear the market arriving. Let me tie your laces, Ode.'

I had never told her that my brother had to lace me into the stirrup boots upon our Beast. An ingenious knot that I could untie with a single wrench.

Most of the traders were darker skinned than the locals, they arrived in horse drawn carts, stocked with fruits and meats and bread and vegetables. A cart arrived with a cargo of large limbed women, ruby about the face and clearly and visibly armed with long sharp knives.

'Ode, do not flinch, they have come to offer their services as cooks. It is a custom for them to display their blades. It is a sign of their status and their skill.'

'Anna, might they not try and kill us in the night.'

Anna had her damaged arm in mine, she wore the lace gloves that decorated the wrist but left the fingers quite free.

I thought of her blood on the bedlinen.

She wore a pocket belt stuffed with bright coins. She wanted to buy the supplies herself. We moved amongst the wares, like husband and wife, like home-builders. We moved amongst the whites and I did not have to walk two paces behind. Anna did not have to be concerned with being called a whore.

'It is fun to buy things with money,' she said. 'Who did we loot this from?'

'The head of the church and the once most powerful man in this land.'

'Well I am sure he can afford it.'

We had found gold coins at the palace, a cask that had either been forgotten in the rush to leave, or was deemed too heavy to carry, or even not sufficiently valuable in comparison with that they did take. And I wondered what treasures lay under the bed of his Holiness. Or had his most trusted men taken that too and left him on his deathbed in penury. He had said he was too sick to travel, or maybe he was just too unpopular to be taken. Had there been a shift in power? With the city taken had the white men fought amongst themselves? And why had their God not helped the holy man? Their soldiers in the field prayed to God for victory and lost. Our warriors fought to find a place in the Afterlife where, for eternity they would be what they had been in life, warriors. Yet I, would return to the Universe and my story would be told forever.

'Is this not a fine leg of cured ham, Ode?'

'Then pay for it what it is worth.'

'Shh, Ode, I am trying to haggle.'

'We do not need to haggle. We have hundreds of these coins.'

'Maybe we do not need to. But I want to. Because it will be fun. At least for me. I must learn how to negotiate in this world.'

We had a visitor. A man from the University. We had met him between the cheese and hams. He seemed to know me.

'My name is Salvatorea Archembaldo. I have come to talk to you, if you will honour me with the privilege.'

I invited him to enter my house and told my servant to bring tea.

We sat him on a fine chair. Anna and myself opposite on a soft cushioned sofa that sat two quite comfortably. Anna wore one of her best dresses. I wore my black shirt and pantaloons. My feet bare in leather sandals.

'Are there parts of the city still functioning?' I said. 'We don't venture from our houses here. We have no desire to kill any more of your people unless they provoke us.'

'The very poor are still very poor, although a number of them seem to have acquired some rather fine furnishings and paintings so I am told. Some are rioting. They are saying that now it is the time for revolution. The men who held power no longer seem to be around. Where are they might I ask? Do you have them in the cells?'

'When we entered these mansions they were already gone. The palace is deserted apart from his holiness.'

'So they are maybe right to think of this as a good time for revolution. There are no soldiers visible.'

'We killed many when we took the city. Since then no, we have not seen one. Everyone with might or power has deserted. And the only whites left behind are the poor, the trouble makers and the scholars.'

'We are not popular with the administration,' said Salvatorea Archembaldo.

'Always asking questions?' said Anna.

It was the first time she had spoken.

'Yes madam always asking questions. Your Latin is a fine as your husband's.'

I nearly blurted out that we were not married and then wondered why we weren't.

'We do have this annoying habit of questioning the Holy Book,' said the scholar, 'and it makes them so angry. Especially when we can prove that we are right. And we are always hungry for more knowledge. Ode, Sir, we know very little of Afrik. You could educate us, Ode. We could offer you a teaching post at the city university. After all, you own the city now, there could hardly be any resistance.'

'And if we did not own the city,' I said, 'you would not let me through the gates to even clean your stinking toilets in return for a handful of food.'

'Would it not give you pleasure to instruct us?'

There was a silver pot of tea stood on the table before us, there was sugar in a silver bowl and silver tongs. Anna did not pour the tea, and I had never done such a thing, and so it fell to our visitor to do that for himself. The cups were very delicate and almost translucent.

The professor took a large map from a leather satchel.

'May I spread this on the table?'

'Of course.'

He moved the tray to a side table.

Afrik. There were named cities along the Northern Coast, and sections of the East and West. The rest was quite blank.

'The northern blacks speak Arabic but beyond the desert are lands we are so ignorant of. I have never met a black man from the interior with whom I have been able to converse. The traders say that blacks are too slow to understand and learn, but you are proof that they are wrong.'

Salvatorea Archembaldo took his cup of tea from the small table beside him.

'You do not document your languages in written form and so it is hard for our scholars to study them. Yet you are fluent in both tongue and pen, proof, Ode, that the black man can be the equal of a Yuropan. Imagine what you could do for your people by teaching. Imagine the impression you would make.'

'This man is looking to make a fool of us, Ode,' said Anna.

'I can assure you that nothing was further from my mind.'

'This is a trap, Ode.'

'There is no trap,' said the professor loudly and with a snort. 'Might your wife like to take a walk in the gardens while we talk without interruption.'

'Anna, this could be an opportunity for us to be together and to be free of this killing. Can we be truly sure it is a trap?'

'Yes, Ode. This offer solves all our problems. Therefore it is too perfect. And therefore it is a trap.'

'What do you really want from me?' I asked the scholar.

'Nothing beyond what I have already stated.'

'You want me to fill in the gaps on this map?'

'I think that would be to the advantage of us all.'

I leant over the map on the table.

'Let me describe to you our geography. Here at this point,' I said with my finger stabbing the paper, 'has always been my favourite place to have a shit.'

Beside me, Anna burst out laughing and dropped her tea cup. It shattered on the floor. I looked closely at the face of Professeori Salvatorea Archembaldo.

'And right here, in my estimation, is a waterfall. It is beautiful, if you ever get the chance to visit, you should do so. Here, to the left is a swamp. You should never go there. The mosquitoes will eat your flesh. And here is the corridor, through the dessert from the coast to the gold fields. You do not even have to mine. The gold sits on the surface of the earth. You do not even have to pick it up yourself. You can get niggers to do that for you in exchange for any simple button you might find on any one of your shirts. And from that gold you can fashion fine rings like the one my wife bears on her index finger.'

'Is this the truth, Ode?'

'Gather a hundred men, command a fleet, be an adventurer, there is great wealth at the end of my words. I would be most honoured to teach at your university.'

'Then it is decided.'

I was met by a hunchback who led me to the lecture hall. There was a table with a decanter of wine and a glass. The glass was not clean. There was a smear around the lip, a small collection of dust in the bowl.

Anna sat among the pews chewing her lips.

'It is clever,' she said shaking her head. 'We cannot punish those who don't turn up.'

'I wanted to be listened to,' I said. 'I mean I really did. My own vanity has led met to this. It is only proper that I should be rebuked. This way I will have learned something.'

'The place you pointed out in the map. Is that where the mines are?'

'Afrik tribes know little of geography beyond their own lands. It is not because we are stupid or lack ambition. But our lands are sacred to us and so we tend to dismiss the lands of others.'

'We have tempted him,' Anna said. 'Let's convince him. Let him make it his life's work to prepare for an expedition to a place where you simply placed your finger. Let us ruin him, Ode.'

'Yes. But not before we have looked into their library here.'

'When I get home to my country I am going to teach those members of my tribe who wish it, to read and write. I am glad that no one turned up to my lecture. I might have been tempted to teach the whites and forget my duty.'

'Ode, when you go back to your tribe, you will have to leave me behind. I will not be able to come with you. If you fulfil your dream, we will have to part.'

Before Salvatorea Archembaldo I had called her my wife.

'You will be with me, Anna, no one will speak against you.'

'You haven't even asked me if I want to. You are just assuming.'

'I did not pause to think that you might not feel the same.'

'Don't be sorry for yourself, Ode. I do not want to be parted from you. But a white woman will not be welcomed in your land.'

'Then I will stay here.'

'And what of your dream to educate your people?'

'They will have to come to me. I shall build a university here for the education of my tribe. I will take this library as my own and the lecture theatre also.'

'Tribe, Ode? Not race?'

'The tribes do not get on. There is much fighting between them. The tribes all speak different languages. There is little in the way of negotiation.'

'It is the same among the whites, and yet when a language is shared there is less conflict. It is much easier to kill a man when you don't know their word for peace. So, Ode, teach them all Latin. Then they will have two tongues. The language of their race, which will support their traditions, and the learned language so that they can speak to each other.'

'But, Anna, none of the tribes will show any interest in learning the tongue of the whites. For generations they have captured, sold and belittled us.'

Anna bit her lip.

'Then, Ode, collect different words from the many tribes and invent a new language yourself. One that will serve them all.'

I am to invent a language!

'Yes, Anna. If you say so. Anna, it would need a written form. I could adapt the Latin alphabet to our needs. The original is simple enough. I learned it in three weeks.'

'You learned to read in three weeks?'

'I worked very hard at it, Anna. I stayed up late. I did not have friends to distract me with their entertainments. Each tribe will need their own scribes.

Someone like me. I will go to them. I will address them. I will stand before them. I will start with a joke. I will say, give me your worst farmers, give me your least able warriors. They will frown and fidget. I will then explain to them, that I too, took to neither the sword nor the plough, with ease or special grace.

'Those of you whose backs break too easily, I will say. Those of you that stab yourself in the foot with your own spear. The spirits have made you this way with a *purpose*.

'You are the bright minds awaiting illumination. You are as chosen as the kings and warriors you revere. I have come to you with the gift of script.

'Let us create a modern tongue that belongs to us and us alone. The tongue of the black skinned man, the tongue of this land that stretches around us further than we have knowledge of.'

With my Arab teacher we had begun with signs and pointing. Hand. Sun. Me. You. Today. Yesterday. Tomorrow. How would I explain the creation of a future language with such crude devices? It was a difficulty but not impossible. I began to obsess about my laces.

'They are well tied, Ode. Ode, let us read. It always make you happy.'

'Am I not happy?'

'Ode, this book of science says the world is much older than that preached by scripture. I knew the fucking priests were wrong. I never liked a thing they taught me.'

'But your holy book, Anna, it was written by your God.'

'God did not write the bible.'

'Oh I thought he had. I mean I thought he and his son had written it.'

'No, it was written by his followers, ordinary mortals. They wrote things down long after they had happened.'

'They must have had good memories.'

'Or they just made shit up.'

And then below us in the square, we heard the sound of a barrel organ. We took to the window. Below us stood a minstrel with a feather cap. He spun the wheel and the music floated upwards through the open window of the library and we took each other in each other's arms and danced.

And after she sobbed against my chest.

'You are sad?'

'No I am happy. But happiness scares me, Ode.'

'Anna, will you marry me?'

'Ode, I have always said that you must not finish inside me. You may have my hand, my mouth, my breast but not the inside of my womb.'

'Because you think that I might give you an imperfect child like myself.'

'No Ode, no. I had never thought that way at all. No, I simply did not want to bring a new life into this world. Ever since I was taken, I have thought, there is no future for me. Ode might be able to imagine one, with his pen. But my mind, however searching it may be, cannot picture a perfect end to my history.'

'And now you have changed your mind?'

'You have big balls, Ode. You are full of seed. Would it not be a shame to waste it all?'

'Would it not be deformed?'

'How could anything that we make together be anything less than perfect, Ode?'

We decided that we should marry that very evening. If she were my wife there could be no thought of us being parted. Neither of us wanted the presence of an emissary of the Khristan figurehead. My own tribe's traditions required the attendance and participation of an entire village. I could not ask the warriors to attend.

'Who will witness our union?'

'Luxxor.'

'Is your brother not to attend?'

'No.'

'Then we are doing this behind his back.'

'We are.'

'But Ode, he said, did he not, not long ago, that you were a fool for not asking me to marry you.'

'My brother is fickle. And when I marry you, you will become part of his family and he will be duty bound to protect your life and honour.'

'And he may not want to do that for a white woman.'

'He may, he may not. But if he forbids me, that will be the end of the story. He will never change his mind. And I will never be able to ask again.'

'You don't *have* to do what he says.'

'I don't have to. But to go against his wishes would mean tearing what is left of my family in two.'

'What you are saying of your brother I recognise in my father. Will Luxxor not feel that he is disrespecting your brother?'

I did not tell Anna about the painting session and how when the finished work came back three days later Luxxor was not in the picture. He did not even want to be in the picture, but he resented being removed.

'I asked him to sew your wound. Which he did. For Luxxor that is a personal connection and an honour. Each and every day, he visits every warrior in our army whose wounds he has personally sewn shut, and asks after their health. If they are struggling, he will personally attend them.'

We had taken wine and meat for the barrel organ man and Anna told him where and when he was needed and how much he could expect to be given in recompense. He did not complain.

'Luxxor it is good of you to come with us. I hope you will not upset your nephew by doing this.'

'How is your wrist?'

'It itches, but I can feel it healing.'

'Enjoy yourself tonight. I shall come round in the morning and change your dressing again.'

'Thank you.'

'There is no need to thank me. I do not leave jobs half done. Ode, what is the Latin for "I am glad you are alive"?'

'Ego gaudeo, quod vivens te.'

'Ego gaudeo, quod vivens te, Anna.'

She turned to him and burst into tears.

He looked at us both.

'Was my pronunciation that bad?'

And then he threw back his head and laughed.

'See, Ode, I have remembered it. These languages of yours are not so difficult after all. You will teach me one phrase every day from now on. Tomorrow you shall teach me, "I am thirsty, where is your wine?"'

'Sum siccus, ubi est vinum.'

'Tomorrow's lesson today already. And friend?'

'Amica.'

'Ego gaudeo, quod vivens te, amica. Sum siccus, ubi est vinum.'

We were surrounded by row after row of empty seats, arches and columns.

'This was a theatre?'

'Yes. Of sorts.'

'All those seats. The plays they wrote then must have been very good. I shall try and find some in the library.'

Luxxor stood there very stiffly. In honour of this great occasion he had dressed himself in the finest clothes he could find in the closet of the mansion he had commandeered.

We faced each other, took each other's hands.

We were about to recite our texts.

But then we heard a noise of many thousand feet upon the stone steps outside.

An invading army had sneaked into the city under the cover of night. We would be the first people they would find. A black man with a white girl, holding hands. No dungeon would be too deep for us, no method of torture too perverse.

I thought to ask Luxxor to kill us both there on the spot before they got their hands upon us. We would both be material again. Two bubbles in the same stream rushing between rocks. The tips of two leaves in the same vast forest. An ovum and stamen not so very far apart that a waiting bee could not bring us back together.

Luxxor moved his robes apart and from a belt removed a scimitar.

'Whose feet are those, Ode?' said Anna. 'What are we hearing? Has your brother sent the warriors to stop us?'

'Why would he need so many feet?'

'Their breathing, Ode, listen to their breathing. It is the sound of your beasts.'

And as if taking their cue from Anna's words, they appeared from the shadows and the arches, and a thousand pairs of eyes looked upon us.

'Ode, have they come to kill us?'

There kept their distance. They showed respect.

'Anna, they have come to give us their blessing. I had never imagined such a thing possible. The rhinoceros chose my father's destiny, then the destiny of my brother. And now they have chosen mine.'

'We should finish our vows before them. They will not understand the words, but they might enjoy the tenderness to be found in our voices.'

'We are born as if halved

And if we were not

Why would we strive?

We are born hungry and sow the fields

We are born cold and build a house

We are born to die and so we make new life between us

You are my soil, my harvest, my nourishment

My impregnable walls, my roof, the window from which I can watch the world in safety.

You are the other half of me that has been waiting to be found.'

Peter knocked on my door and was let in by my servant.

Anna and I were sat in a room made of glass that looked out onto a beautiful garden.

He joined us dressed like a king. By which I don't mean that he was dressed in a fabulous way. I mean that he was dressed as if he were a king. But a fake crown. Fake rings. Fake king.

'You have had time to think, Ode?'

'Yes I have,' I said not looking up from my book. 'Do you like our garden?'

'It is very pretty.'

'Would you like to spend some time there, helping the flowers to bloom and flourish.'

'I would yes. That would be most appealing to a man of my sensitivity.'

'Shall I show you around? Anna, will you join us?'

'Yes but only with my veil, the sun is too bright.'

'With your veil, Anna, you can never see a thing, even that which is right before your eyes.'

'Then I shall take your arm and you can guide me. And I shall not have to look at anything that doesn't please me.'

Earlier that day I had asked a warrior for three heads. Note, I said emphatically, from three men already dead. Do not kill anyone to do me this favour. They do not have to be in good condition, but I would like them to have beards if that is possible.'

'I can do that for you, Ode. No problem. How is Anna?'

'She is doing well thank you soldier.'

'We knew she was sad because of the way she sang to us that night.'

I had asked the warrior to plant them in the garden by the back wall.

'It is a joke I want to play on my brother,' I explained.

'You should do it at night,' said the warrior, 'in candlelight. Your brother will shit his pants, no offence, Ode.'

'No offence taken soldier. Is there anything I can do for you?'

'You figured out all that shit with the cannons, you saved many of our lives. We don't understand you, Ode. You are still strange to us. But we owe you our gratitude.'

Anna took my arm and we strolled into the garden, past many luscious blooms, to the newly turned bed at the back wall.

'You wish to be a king, Peter. But I might have a better role for you. Anna?'

'Yes, Ode.'

'What is the word I am searching for?'

'Compost.'

We were in bed. It was the middle of the night. The knock on the door had woken me. Now they were in our room. My brother was drunk, behind him Peter could hardly stand. The candle that he held waiting to be dropped. I had left the curtains open. The moon was nearly full.

My brother went round to Anna's side of the bed, grabbed her by the hair and pulled her from the soft covers to the floor. I scrambled after them both and put myself between them.

'Ode, even the love I bear for you cannot stop my hand this time. This woman assisted in the killing of our father, the leader of our tribe. It must be answered.'

'That is not true, Brother.'

'Anna herself told Peter what she had done, and Peter drew it for me so I would understand. Her father let the murderer into his house as Anna watched from the top of the stairs. Do you remember, Ode? There were two shots. One a moment after the first. Luxxor took the bullet in his shoulder. That is because there were two rifles. Anna held the second rifle while the first shot was taken.'

My brother reached down and grabbed Anna's ankle as if to pull her towards him through my legs. It was a crude and clumsy move fuelled by anger and wine.

'Let her go Brother, or I will throw myself at you with all I have. It may not be much, but it will have my full commitment.

'She must pay for her deeds. You say no? Do you wish to turn the world upside down?'

Behind me, Anna struggled to her feet and pressed herself into my back.

'I did not see the man enter and certainly did not hold the other gun for him,' she said.

'I know.'

'I had no idea,' said my brother, 'that the murderer operated from the house where Anna and her father lived. If I had known, things would have been very different from the start.'

'Your brother didn't take me from my house, Ode. He took me from the town hall. My father was sat at his desk. I had just taken him his lunch. Your brother did not even give me to time to say goodbye. I was told to send my servant for my carriage and my clothes. I was told to follow on pain of death.'

'I was grieving for my father, lashing out.'

'Your brother has an excuse for everything, Ode, don't translate that.'

'If he had tried to defend or protect you, I would have killed him on the spot, but he did not even try.'

'But Brother, you informed him that we were taking his daughter hostage to ensure the safety of our fleet? And that we would return her.'

'No Ode. I did not. I just wanted to take his daughter away from him, as my father had been taken from me. If I had known they had offered their house to the murderer, I would have cut his daughter's throat before his eyes.'

'You are talking of my wife. Are you listening? Anna is my wife now.'

'Just being in bed with her, does not make her your wife. That just makes her your whore.'

'Brother, Anna and myself are married. She is part of our family now'

'Married? When?'

'Last night.'

'By what God or ceremony?'

'By a ceremony of our own creation.'

'And who presided over this ceremony and made it binding?'

'Luxxor.'

'And how drunk was he?'

'Less drunk than you are now.'

'No, you are not married at all. Anna has no claim to be part of our family just because you both held hands and made cooing noises at each other while your drunk Uncle tried to stay awake.'

'Brother listen, our marriage was consecrated in the presence of the beasts.'

I told him as quickly as I could …

'Brother the same beasts that chose our father, that chose to pass the honour of Chief Elder onto you after his death. Those beasts accepted Anna as my wife.'

Peter hovered smiling. He could not understand our words, but he revelled in seeing two brothers at each other's throats, delighted in Anna's utter misery.

'I wish I had never known her complicity. I would have preferred ignorance of this betrayal. How long have you both kept this from me?'

'No more than a day.'

'Would you have told me if that shitface had not blabbed?'

'I would not. My wife's secrets are not for even you my brother to share. And she did not know herself until the day before. Not until I mentioned the circumstances of our father's death. A thing I had not talked of before. Her father had let a solider into his house. She had no idea of the target then or even after.

'Anna tried to kill herself when she realised that her father had given help to the murderer. That is the depth of respect she has for our family. I asked Peter to sit with her whilst I went to Luxxor to ask him to sew her. She told him things as she bled, and then he tried to twist her words against us all. She is utterly innocent. But that man is not.'

Peter jolted at my pointing.

'You plotted for the death of my wife, for your own selfish gain and you have lost.'

'You were going to bury me in the fucking garden.'

'That was to scare you. You were blackmailing us. Brother, if you do not accept that the rhino chose to honour our marriage, if you do not allow them that … then you will have to accept that our father was *not* chosen by the beasts at all. It was simply coincidence. And you will have to accept that you were not chosen to succeed our father by them either.

'And if Father was not chosen by the wisdom of the beasts, then all this journey is fluke and farce. If we are not chosen, if none of us are, none of our tribe, then we are just common raiders, and as history can prove such forces never win. They begin well and then fall apart.

'And Brother, why do you want to believe this man. Why were you taken in so easily by a man you despise. A man practised in the art of dissembling. Why did you want to hurt me?'

My brother sat upon the bed.

'Tell Anna I am sorry. I am sorry for my actions tonight and I am sorry that you felt you could not invite me to your wedding.'

My brother turned on Peter.

'You come between brothers for you own advancement. You besmirch the reputation of a female of my family.'

'But what I told you is the truth, the truth from her own lips.'

'I don't give a flying fuck about the truth you fat queer. I care about family, honour, brotherhood. What is the truth? Everyone has their own and they are not always the same.'

'Your brother has gone behind your back to marry this woman.'

'And that was your fault.'

'How.'

'He was protecting her, and your fucking prattle and threats made him see me as his enemy. I missed my brother's wedding because of you. Cunt!'

And strangely in this argument, I of course had to translate each line of theirs so as they screamed at each other I took turns screaming at myself as Anna held my arm and wept.

My brother punched Peter very hard in the face. His head slammed against the wall, he slid to the floor, he dropped the candle, my brother stamped upon the flame and we were left with only the moon. My brother dragged Peter from the room by his feet.

'Don't kill him brother I have not finished with him yet.'

'You want to hurt him more? He shouted as Peter's head hit each step on the way down from the first floor to the front door.'

'Please.'

'Then I will make sure he survives this night.'

Unlike the Yuropan art that I was to find on that continent, which prided itself on landscapes, scenes from the holy book, portraits of the rich, Kikuyo art is almost exclusively decorative. The line is not a representation of the world, it does not have to bend its will to looking like a nose, a mountain or the feather in an angel's wing. The line is a celebration of itself. The line dances, takes itself for a walk, turns back on itself for the pleasure of revisiting its beginnings.

The line belongs to its own nature.

Mgebe the oldest of our warriors and the man who had sat beside Luxxor and sterilised and threaded the needle, who had passed my Uncle the bandages and brought Anna flowers the next day, and been so good as to care about her welfare, was very skilled at decoration. He had taken Anna's carriage, covered the wooden body in gold-leaf, and painted upon the shimmer a thousand Mandalas and Archimedean spirals.

It waited for us outside our front door.

'Are we to travel far Mgebe? Anna was sick this morning.'

'I am sorry to hear that about her, Ode. No, we are to travel only a very short distance. But we shall travel in great luxury. And we hope to make her very happy this day.'

'Anna, take my hand we are going on a very short journey.'

Indeed the journey was only to the square before the palace, which took us no more than a few minutes.

We were parked in the centre of the square.

'Ode, please disembark.'

There were two soft and carved chairs placed for us to sit ourselves in the centre of the square. The carriage was led away. It was nearly dark and no torches lit.

'The square is quite deserted Mgebe. Are we in for a surprise? It is two days since we were married. I never expected any fuss.'

'You cannot tell a man that he is in for a surprise and then expect him to be surprised when the surprise appears.'

'I cannot argue with that.'

There was a sudden explosion of rhythm and noise, and from each side street poured the warriors all in full armour upon their beasts. They marched into the square and lined up on three sides.

The rhythmic patterns of our drums are as complex as the weaving in a Yuropan tapestry. And of our Thousand, there were maybe one hundred warriors upon the drum.

'This is not like music at all,' said Anna, 'it is more like wonderful thunder, a caressing storm.'

Servants ran into the squares with wooden posts that stood on wooden legs. They stood them in a circle at some distance from with us. I rose and went to study one in the fading light. Attached by a nail, sat a paper tube coiled into a spiral.

'Ode, come back.'

'What on earth are they, Anna?'

'You *are* in for a surprise.'

A servant came out of the palace with a candle.

'How did it suddenly get so dark?'

As many as fifty servants were there. They all had candles and the first flame was passed along and multiplied. The music stopped.

'This evening,' cried Luxxor, 'we wish to honour the marriage of Ode and Anna. It is an unusual thing to do, and all the more worthy of celebration because of that. No Kikuyo has ever married a white woman. It is not against our laws. But no white woman has ever visited our tribal lands and so there was never any need to forbid it.'

Laughter.

'Ode, we never thought to see you married, to a woman. We all expected you to be betrothed to a book and father to a series of little pens.'

Another wave of laughter followed that.

'Ode, we have benefited greatly from your presence amongst us. Your clear thinking has saved lives. Your skills with language had eased our troubles many times.'

He raised his hand and the drumming began again and the servants put the candle flames to the ends of the paper coils.

Over the sound of drumming and the wild spirals of pluming fire, Anna hollered into my ear.

'Oh Ode, I hope I am not to be presented with gifts. I need no more decoration than the ring you bought for me as our wedding present. I do not want fancy clothes at all. I wish to wear the same clothes that I brought with me, for many of them were made for me by my mother before she passed away.'

'I am sorry. You never speak of her.'

'She began to exhibit what my father called strange behaviour. I thought she was just learning to be herself. He had her sequestered in a nunnery. She didn't last long.'

And then two warriors appeared carrying a chest and placed it before her.

And despite her protestations she did her best to smile before the troops. She gave them her widest smile. Put her hands together and bowed.

'Sing, Anna,' I said.

'Are you sure?'

'It is how you have their hearts.'

'I only know sad songs.'

'Those are the ones they like. When you sing they have visions of home, they see the faces of their wives and children.'

'Really?'

And so, Anna sang and received her due applause.

'I will have to open the chest now won't I, Ode?'

'And smile in gratitude, whatever it may be.'

'Here goes.'

Anna opened the chest.

'Fuck,' she said. 'I don't believe it!'

We stood on the roof of our mansion and Anna put her eye to the lens.

'You say you did not tell them. So how did they know?'

'My brother,' I said. 'He is the only human being that I ever told you used to show your legs to an old man for the chance to see the stars.'

'Well you should not have told him that. But I am glad you did. Ode, I do not want to offend you, but could I do this for a while on my own? I want to cheat on you with the universe for a while. Ode, before you go. I meant to ask at the time but I didn't want you to find me ungrateful. This ring you gave me as a sign that we are betrothed. Did you take it from someone who treasured it?'

'I did not.'

'Did you buy it with plundered money? For I fear it is very expensive.'

'No. I would not give you something stolen as a sign of my love for you. My brother, Luxxor and myself, we all have a small pocket sewn into the inside of our armour. Each of us carries a small pouch of uncut diamonds for emergencies or special occasions.'

'Ode.'

Anna rolled over and put her hand on my chest.

'I spent hours watching the sky and then adjusting the lens I thought to have a closer look at the city, but of course the city was dark. And then, with no real intention I decided to look beyond the city walls. Ode, I saw fires. You know what that means?'

'They want their city back.'

'I don't care. I've had enough of this place. Let us move on.'

'I will speak to my brother in the morning.'

The man was dressed in red, the mud stains on his robes quite fresh. He carried a bag that looked to me to have been made from a decorative curtain. He had appeared waving a white flag on the end of a long branch, while we looked down on him from the second floor of the palace. My brother had wanted him garrotted. I said let us hear what he has to say.

'Come inside and take a glass of brandy with myself and my brother.'

'Do you drink from glasses?'

'No,' I said. 'It is the tradition of my tribe to pour our liquor into an earthenware pot and then go down on our elbows and our knees and lap at it like dogs.'

He looked at me with neither disgust nor humour.

'Come upstairs,' I said. 'The brandy was in the cellar and therefore rather chill. I have decanted it to bring it back to room temperature.'

He nodded at me with no committal and ascended the stairs two steps behind me.

We sat at the table. My brother wore a long silk robe with his chest exposed and a large ruby on a woman's necklace. I imagine that the white man dressed in purple, silently said his prayers. He held his bag tight on his lap.

'My name is Ode,' I said. 'I am a storyteller of the Kikuyo tribe. And my brother here is the commander of a thousand fine warriors and beasts. We call ourselves the One Thousand for that defines our might. If you have business to discuss with us, then do so with humility.'

'Here is a story for you Kikuyo,' said the man sniffing at his brandy. 'We want you to know it. There is disease outside the city.'

'We have seen the fires.'

'How?'

'Did you not know? Blacks can see for miles.'

'I did not know that.'

'We are physically superior to you in many ways. Now you say that there is disease abroad. And you wish to warn us? What purpose would that serve you?'

'The presence of this disease is no accident. A small island to the north of our continent was blighted by a plague. The sick found themselves no longer welcome in their own country. Great plague ships landed at our western coast. At first we thought to destroy them in the water but then we saw advantage. We have brought the infected to the outside walls of the city.'

'Logistically that must have presented many problems.'

'They are led and commanded by the Brothers of the Plague.'

'They cannot have found much welcome on their journey here.'

'The same could be said of you. There are now fifty thousand dying men and women surrounding you.'

'And why have they let themselves be led here?'

'Because of the promise of a cure.'

'Is there a cure?'

'I am not at liberty to discuss that.'

'And are you immune yourself?'

'I am blessed by God. The sick wait at the gates to be ushered in. They will touch you if they can, if they cannot do that, they will breath on you, if they can't get close enough for that, no matter, they will disease the air. They will rub their bodies across the walls of the houses. They will spit upon the roads. They will lick and kiss any food or drink they find. They will burrow into cellars and vomit on the barrels. They will piss in the river and the wells. This has been ordered.'

'By who?'

'By the rich and powerful. Who else? By good Khristans appalled at your presence here.'

The man delved into his bag and produced two large glass jars. He placed them next to the decanter. Human flesh floated in amber liquid.

'Pay attention to this head Kikuyo. Note the pustules upon the skin. Agonising and hideous. Imagine your lover's disgust at such a sight. And then to die of it with no one willing to hold you in your last hours for fear of contagion. And see these hands. Look at the swollen joints, knuckles the size of eyes. I have brought these preserved specimens with me to prove the true terror of this plague. I give them to you for your consideration.'

'What sort of offering is this?'

'Ode of the Kikuyo, every murderer and thief in the prisons of Yurop have been rounded up and brought into the presence of the infected, so that they are now infected also. The Brothers of the Plague, they are religious men, a faction of our church. They believe this disease is a gift from God to defeat you, they relish it. Men are volunteering in their thousands to take the disease upon their bodies. To defeat you.

'Now. I have the mandate to make a deal with you and your army. Retreat to the southern boot of the continent and we will make a border three hundred miles south of here. Stay there behind that border and our fight is over.'

A sanctuary for Anna and myself. A return to the land where she was born. We could build a life there. We could be safe. The land would be ours, and it would be our law and our customs that would prevail. And no one could make comment on the difference of our skins, or the weight of my withered arm. I would make sure that it was unlawful to do so.

'We will rebuild our cities and leave you in peace. You are only a thousand men. There will be abundance there for so few. If you wish to send home for your families to join you, we will provide them with safe passage.'

'Safe passage!' My brother lost his composure. 'When you look at me do you see a fool! All of my people, all the warriors in waiting and those retired, our wives and children. All the Kikuyo on a boat. Safe passage? You would sell the lot of us, or sink us out to sea! And my warriors, all men, alone. Our race would die out. We would become extinct as we once nearly did, before nature favoured us and showed that the Kikuyo were not destined for extinction but for glory.'

'I can assure you that they would be safe.'

The man took to his feet, quickly realised his mistake and sat back down so profoundly that I heard the small of his back crack against the wooden back of the chair.

'I can assure you that this promise comes from the highest church dignitaries and the most powerful men in the land. This is your last conquest. You will die here or head south to a place of safety that we have provided for you.'

'Have I not just spoken?'

'You will be safe. That is what I have been authorised to tell you.'

'What is to stop us carrying on with our journey North?'

'The ring of plague that surrounds you.'

'We will break through that ring at such speed and with such might that this plague of yours will be as nothing to us. We will be too fast for your contagion to follow.'

'Beyond the ring, to the North, there are more of these poor souls waiting, ready and willing to infect you. The next thirty miles north from here are betrothed to the plague. Sick flesh, foul bedding, tainted water. You will have to move through that with great danger to yourself. You will be destroyed or fatally defeated. For after that those very few of you that do survive this disease will encounter a thousand men at lance and pike, dug in to a ditch that lasts the length of fifty miles.'

'We shall burn the villages that promise the plague. We shall hoof and trample the bearers of your lance and pike. You will not present any impediment to our ambition and resolve. Tonight we shall drink and tomorrow we shall continue on our quest and you sir will turn and run before I put a dagger through your voice box.'

'And also I wonder are you even to be believed,' I said speaking for myself. 'You said that if we did not abandon the city, you would allow the infected entry to these walls and kill us all by infection. This plague you threaten us with will kill your own. The rich of this city will die due to their own badly conceived plan.'

'The rich are already gone. You must have noticed that.'

Of course, I had.

'They have been leaving at night ever since you arrived. In small groups so as not to attract attention. Under every palace, villa, place of worship and of commerce there are stairs that lead down into the earth to underground catacombs and tunnels that lead in their turn to a place beyond the city walls. Merchants and clergy in the sewers, fat hands full of jewellery and gold. Their wives holding their children, their mistresses adjusting their breasts and complaining that their shoes are too delicate for such a journey and really when can we sit down and have something to eat?

'When they come out into the light they find themselves upon the bank of a fine flowing river that meanders through a valley. And from there it is an arduous but bearable climb to safety in the mountains. Even there they have great vineyards, orchards perching on the hills in terraces, peasants to tend them, goats to slaughter, fresh water from the springs. They don't care about the people left here in this city. They are expendable.

'They will wait for you all to die of the plague and then send in poor sods like me with a rag stuffed into our mouths to reduce you to ashes and sweep away the dust. The city will be raised, the poor hovels will turn to smoke, but the grand stone buildings will stand. Our city will be thrice purified. The poor, the plagued, and the blacks. So why not take my offer and leave.'

'Why offer us an escape route at all? You surely want us dead.'

I returned to my tribal tongue.

'Brother, our men are physically superior to this weakling lot. They are not certain that the plague that lays them so low, will be as effective against us.'

'They threaten us with something they are not sure will even work?'

My brother studied the dismembered head floating in its preservative, and with a sideways slash of his hand knocked it from the table. Inevitably it shattered.

'Ode, tell this man to kiss the dead man's lips or I shall put his own head in a jar.'

My brother had given the general order for mobilisation, be ready to leave on my command. We were heading North again.

There was no market that day. No sign of the white traders. The city silent. Then we all heard the distant sound of the south gate that we had destroyed and indifferently repaired being shattered.

'Ode, I did not expect them so soon. But this will not affect us. There is time for us to leave. The men should be ready by now.'

'Brother come with me a moment.'

'I rushed up to the roof, and focused the telescope on the south gate where thousands of raged souls passed through. The north gate, the east gate, the west gate. All open.

'Brother they are coming at us from all directions.'

And so my brother and Luxxor ran from mansion to mansion, knocking wildly on the doors and giving instruction. Lock the door, close the blinds. Help the beasts up the stairs to the first floor. Have your belongings packed, be dressed in your full armour, have your sword at your side, if you have a rifle load it now. Await further instructions.

From all sides they slunk, filling the streets with their moaning. Men with cowls walking slowly and chanting song. The Brothers of the Plague. Women and children clutching crucifixes.

'Anna?'

'Yes.'

'Close the windows and shutters.'

They took up residence in the palace square and in the avenues that faced the mansions. We were encircled by a ring of white death.

They knew that before them lay a slow and painful death and after that paradise. And they wanted us to join them, but not in paradise.

'Anna!'

Anna came down from the roof with her telescope under her arm.

'You were outside?'

'I was on the roof.'

'But the roof is outside.'

'I was nowhere near those poor creatures.'

'We have no idea how virulent this disease is, how it is passed from one person to another. It may even travel on the breeze. You should not have gone up on the roof.'

'We are to leave at the first opportunity are we not? And I was not about to leave this fine instrument behind.'

She placed the telescope very carefully in its case and rubbed her arm.

'Hungry?'

'Not very.'

'I will get us some bread and cheese.'

'Let your servant do that.'

'He is hiding under the stairs and won't come out.'

I came back with a tray of sliced bread, cheese, some ham and jug of wine. Anna took the tray from me, dropped it and fell back unconscious upon the bed.

I moved her so that I could pull back the covers. I undid the buttons of her dress and tucked her into bed in her underclothes.

'Anna, you should not have gone onto the roof.'

Putting the telescope away she had rubbed her arm. The left or right? The left, I pulled back the covers to study it. There was a small red mark. An insect bite. An insect like a mosquito had drunk the blood of one of the infected, then bitten Anna. The plague was not passed from one human to another by touch or proximity, breath or infected water. The carrier was an insect and the medium was blood. And the closer you were to the sick, the more likely that the insect that bit you had bit someone around you.

I lit a fire in the hearth and heated the end of a poker. I would burn the mark on her arm and incinerated as much of the poison as I could. I was hardly in my element. I wished that Luxxor had been there. But he was across the road and the road was sick.

This mosquito was not the Afrik variant that I was sure. The symptoms of malaria looked nothing like the swollen remains in those glass jars. But might the same protection be afforded. Back in our village when we went to the lake for water, we covered our bodies in goat fat. That repelled the insects. It was a barrier between us.

I pulled back the cover, turned Anna's arm upwards and took the poker from the fire.

In the morning she stank of sweat and piss. She could not be raised. I rolled her from one side of the bed to the other and removed that half of the sheet and then rolled her back.

Did everyone die of this disease? Were there exceptions? Was there a gradient of illness, were some sicker than others? It struck me that the poor souls outside were probably from the very poorest sections of society. Those whose diets were meagre. Those who were already weak every day of their lives. Those that easily succumbed. Anna for her part had always eaten well.

But she could not take food now and I had to force the brandy water between her lips. If she were to weaken, the disease would have a greater hold on her and she would weaken further.

'Ode?'

She was awake, her voice feeble and shaky.

'I have the fucking disease haven't I?'

'You have, but I think you are strong enough to fight it.'

'I was on the roof, the sick people were down in the street. How did I get infected?'

'You have an insect bite on your arm.'

'Yes I felt that at the time. I slapped my arm and killed it.'

'They bite because they want your blood, then they bite someone else and the disease is passed on. Anna, I read that Yurop doctors sometimes bleed their patients. If the disease is in your bloodstream would it help if I bled you?'

'Don't be a fool, Ode. Bleeding is the idea of fools. Taking away some of my blood will make me weaker and then the disease will take more hold of me.'

'That is what I thought. But I thought to ask anyway. Should I get you a doctor?'

'Where from, Ode? Do we have one hiding under the bed?'

'There are doctors at the palace.'

'Well that might be so. But how are you going to get to the palace when the streets and the square are full of the diseased?'

'I might be able to protect myself from being bitten.'

'And you are sure of this?'

'No.'

'Then whatever your idea is, don't try it.'

She began to shiver. I put an extra blanket on the bed. Her cheeks were enflamed.

'Ode, now I am too hot.'

'I dabbed her brow with water from a bowl.'

'Anna, could you eat something?'

'Maybe a little something if I tried.'

I went back to the kitchen. I passed the cupboard under the stairs. The servant was still behind the door.

I knelt down.

'The disease is carried by an insect not unlike our own mosquitoes back home. You are safe in there. Nothing can bite you. But you will also be safe I think in any other part of the house. All the windows are closed, all the doors.'

'I'm not coming out till it is all over.'

'Okay I am going to bring you a plate of food, a jug of water and a bucket to... well a bowl in case you need one. I will leave it just outside the door and when you hear that I have gone, you open the door very quickly, pull everything inside and close the door again. Do you understand me?'

'Ode, can you get me the bowl, I am going to be sick again.'

She was. Her vomit black and red.

'Now go away. I will infect you.'

'It is passed by insects we have already discussed that.'

'Yes but what if it is also passed just by being near someone, or by coming into contact with the sweat on their bodies.'

'Anna, you have been in bed now for two days now and I have been at your side and am showing no sign of being ill. Anna, you collapsed within a few minutes of being bitten. Anyway I am not leaving you under any circumstances.'

'What if I get well again, but you die from caring for me?'

'Let us not waste our energy on something that will never happen.'

'So I am not going to die?'

'I am not going to leave you.'

I knelt beside her as she slept. I couldn't rest. I had pictured her vomiting in her sleep and choking. In reality there was nothing left inside her that could have caused such harm. But I remained vigilant.

I poured brandy on my hands and rubbed and intertwined my fingers. I poured brandy on a cloth and patted her brow. I poured brandy down my throat.

I looked at the burn I had made on her arm. It wept liquid and red.

But I knew, that there was nothing I could do if her condition worsened. I had no skill. My tribe, me people, knew only the one procedure. The sewing of flesh wounds.

I opened the door naked and approached them. They gabbled at me. They showed me cupped hands, pleading for food. I held my sword in such a way to make it clear I would slice anyone who tried to touch me. I stood amongst them naked, covered from head to toe in lard.

Was I to be bitten? I studied my arms and watched in terrified wonder as one of the little bastards landed on my arm. Are you going to bite? Almost immediately, it flew away again.

I went upstairs to see Anna. Her eyes were open.

'Ode, you are naked and you stink like a dead animal.'

'They don't bite you if you're wearing fat.'

'And you tried this out?'

'I conducted an experiment.'

'And if it had failed?'

'It didn't fail.'

'Yes. But you didn't know that at the time.'

'I do now.'

I stripped her and covered her body in the lard from the kitchen. I dressed her in the heaviest clothes I could find in the wardrobe. Thick woollen socks that reached the knees. Voluminous knickers that reached her knees from the other direction. A long sleeved dress, leather gloves.

I tore a sheet into straps and wrapped it around her neck and mouth. Put a cap on her head.

'Do we have to do this, Ode? I am feeling tired.'

'We can't risk you getting a second bite.'

I added more of the fat to the surface of my skin. Then I wrapped another strip of cloth, around my mouth and neck. Put a bedcap on my shaven head. A strange thing, to wear a cap at night. I had found it in a drawer when I had ransacked the room for medicines.

Despite her malady, Anna ventured: 'I wish I had the energy to laugh at the sight of you, Ode.'

Then I put on my armour and my helmet and my gloves. A sword in my scabbard and a flintlock in a holster. The area around my eyes was the only flesh exposed. As in battle.

I had taken a large sheet folded it in half, tied a knot in each end.

'Crawl into this.'

'How shall I walk?'

'I shall carry you.'

'No, I can walk, Ode.'

'Anna you are weak, you will slow me down. Once I am outside I have to move as fast as I can. So no arguments please.'

I heard rapid footstep behind me and turned to see Mgebe running at me full tilt.

'I saw you.'

'Have you been bitten? By a mosquito?'

He was in full armour but with none of the extra precautions I had taken.

'No I don't think so.'

'Then come, come fast.'

'Ode, your arm. I mean your arms, they are not as strong as mine.'

He took Anna from me and we continued to race for the palace doors. The infected dived out of our way. Are we already dead? Are these devils? There must be some mistake. I was a God-fearing person in my life.

The doors were locked this time. Not to keep us out, because they knew our rhinos would simply smash down the door again, and these fabulous ornate doors had been a present from the king of Spain! But to keep out the infected.

Mgebe took his pistol from his holster and pumped a bullet into the lock.

Still the door didn't open.

'I will have to reload. Take Anna.'

Mgebe swiftly primed his gun again. I could feel the interest of the mob behind me. I could feel them encroaching.

The second bullet tore the lock and we were in.

I closed the doors behind us. But there was no way to secure it.

'Mgebe come with me to the kitchen, then I will tell you what we are to do.'

I lay Anna down on the table, still invisible in her cotton cocoon. I pulled back the fabric for a moment, all I could see of her was her eyes.

'We are in the palace, Anna. So far everything has gone to plan.'

'Then why were you shooting?'

'The door had been locked. But we are in now. I don't have time to talk, sorry.'

Mgebe spread the sickly white fat across his groin, his bum, his thighs and legs. While I spread it across his chest, his back, he finished his own arms and face.

'Now put your armour back on. Sorry if it sounds like I am giving you orders.'

'That is no problem, Ode. You are trying to save my life.'

'And you mine.'

'I heard the shooting. You cannot see him now, he is not well.'

'Doctor, the city is ours and we can do as we wish.'

The hallway was lined with marble benches and I lay Anna down upon the cold stone. I pulled back the sheet.

'Anna, how are you doing?

'Great,' she said from within her shroud. 'I feel as good as I expect I look.'

'Whatever that package is,' said the doctor, 'take it with you.'

'That package as you call it is my wife. She is sick and you are a doctor. I am asking you for your help.'

'I am beholden only to his Grace, no other human being is my concern.'

I removed my helmet and undid the cloth around my mouth.

'The disease is spread by blood and body fluid. Help this woman or I shall kiss you.'

Mgebe lunged forward, grabbed the doctor by his collar and swung him around to face him.

'I am infected also. One drop of my spit in your mouth you will become as sick as me.'

'Is there no depth to which you will not sink?'

'Go, get your medicine.'

I unwrapped Anna's mouth leaving the rest of her face still to be discovered. Her body still enwrapped. Her hands still gloved. The doctor returned with a black leather bag. He took a bottle from his bag, poured some of the liquid onto a linen cloth, and brought the cloth to his own mouth.

'You are not the patient,' I said. 'You are wasting time.'

He produced another amber coloured bottle with a cork stopper. He poured a spoon full of the liquid and handed it to me.

'It is a tincture of many plants and herbs of a healing nature,' he said. 'Make sure she takes it all.'

'And will it cure her?'

'I am afraid not, but it might give her a few more days.'

'Days? More time for her to suffer and more time for me to lament.'

'I am not God.'

'No but his Holiness inside has the ear of God so I have heard tell.

'You are not even a believer.'

'No but she is. She is one of his children, even if she does not always obey him. Take me to him.'

'You shall not enter his chamber.'

'You cannot stop me. Better that I enter with your introduction.'

'An interruption would displease him.'

'If you will not help me, my friend will kill you.'

No. In all my violent posturing, I had used the threat of others.

'Doctor I will not try and infect you. I shall take my friend's sword,' I made a gesture, 'and I shall take your head. You will be in your heaven shortly and your God will be pleased that you gave your life for his holiness. He will of course be less pleased that your death was both cowardly and that the giving of your blood in no way helped God's emissary on earth. And if his holiness does not help me, I shall kill him too. And all three of you can fight it out amongst the clouds. I wish to save the life of the woman I love, the person I love most on this earth. And there is nothing I would not do.'

'We have some medicine,' he said. 'Maybe his holiness might spare a spoonful. I will be damned for this I am sure.'

'At least you will get to live first.'

'The woman can't come in, not into his Grace's presence. Not with the plague. Be reasonable.'

'I will stay with her,' said Mgebe. 'Ode, hurry, we do not have time to talk about it.'

The doctor opened the door with the tips of his fingers. The stench of illness and candlelight filled the room.

'Is this an angel come to take me home?'

'No your Grace, it is a nigger in armour.'

I espied the blue glass bottle on his bedside table. The silver spoon beside it.

'Have we met before?'

I lied and said that we had not met before, and it was a great honour and pleasure to be invited into his presence.

'I don't remember inviting you into my chamber. Common people are not allowed in here, you know.'

'Your doctor said that I was to see you.'

'That obsequious cunt. What business is it of his I ask?'

'My wife is dying and he was convinced that you would take pity on her and try and save her life by interceding with your God.'

There was a blue bottle on his bedside table. A silver spoon.

'That medicine ...'

'That is a very special medicine, blessed in chapel, blessed by God. It is a thousand gold coins by the bottle and not for the likes of you.'

'Your Grace, you are weak and I am strong. Would you like me to carry you on my back?'

'Carry me where?'

'Out among your people. They are clamouring to see you. Desperate for a touch of your healing hands.'

'I am not going out *there*.'

'You might if I decided to take you.'

He looked at me and then looked at his own frail hands.

'I feel sorry for you son, and sorry for your wife. Let me see what I can do. I will offer you one half spoonful of this blessed curative, let me pour it into this glass for you. There that is the proscribed dose.'

'Doctor will one half spoonful be enough to cure my wife?'

Although he did his best to hide it, his face quite clearly showed that, no, one half spoonful was not enough to elicit a cure.

'I cannot give you more,' said his Grace.

I strode across the room and grabbed the bottle. The doctor tried to intervene but I pushed him to the ground and the doctor in his wisdom decided to stay there for a while.

'In the name of God most high, I command you to put that bottle back this instant.'

'I am not a believer, so your God cannot command me to do a thing.'

'What have I done to deserve this my father? A black comes into my chambers and talks to me this way. Strike him down Lord. The world has been turned on his head. You must in your infinite wisdom put this world back on its feet. Where are my fucking guards?'

'The guards were killed days ago,' said the doctor from the floor.

I left them to their blather.

Mgebe held Anna's gloved hands.

'Wife,' I asked, 'how stands your faith?'

'I have railed against it often enough. But like all weak humans, when I fear I am near death, I begin to question my questioning.'

'I am holding medicine given to me by his Holiness. It is blessed by God. I do not know how much to give you right now, but take some before we have to go outdoors and walk through the sick again.'

She could not see me through her wrappings. I raised her to my chest and put the bottle to her lips. She drank of it. I waited. I had no idea of the medicine's true effects. For all I knew, the holy man's illness was a result of this potion. Rather than trying to cure him, his doctor was in the process of slowly poisoning him to death. Anna began to choke. I let her breathe. I was squeezing her too tightly.

'Do you want to vomit?'

'No, Ode.'

'Then take another small sip.'

'Listen, Ode,' said Mgebe.

A gang of the sick appeared before us at the end of the corridor. I slipped the medicine bottle into my pocket.

'Anna, are you strong enough to talk to them?'

'I shall have to be. What do I say?'

'Tell them his Grace has many bottles of the cure for them in his chambers. All they have to do is ask for his blessing.'

'Ode, let me try and walk, I'm sick of being carried like a corpse.'

She extricated herself from the sheet, and took my arm to support herself.

The mob approached us with trepidation. We were two very tall men dressed in the skins of an animal that they had never encountered. We held a swaying women bundled like a washing basket.

'The cure is waiting for you all, by God's grace. It is waiting and bottled for you, in his Holiness's chamber,' said Anna as loud as she could manage.

The mob ran right past us, crashing into the double doors as we hurried down the steps.

Outside the mass of death awaited the sight of us.

'His holiness has found a cure,' Anna cried. 'You are saved!'

The mob raised themselves with terrible effort. Some cast aside their sticks for walking, and promptly fell sideways. Others flung away their bandages and ran towards the palace. They flew around us like we were stone and they a tainted stream.

'Mgebe. Go to Luxxor as I shall go to my brother. Tell them and tell them to tell the men. The plague is carried by a mosquito. Cover your flesh in all places with fat from the kitchen. Wrap cloth around your face so there is no part of your face unprotected. Wear your full armour and gloves. We are leaving by the north gate.'

'I shall act with all swiftness.'

'Anna, I shall get the carriage.'

'The telescope, Ode. Do we have time to load it into the carriage?'

'You will watch the stars for many years my love.'

We left in all commotions and although my brother commanded all those men and women of the south to haul our bounty in their carts, they lagged behind our swift charge to the north gate and I imagine executed their own charge towards the blackened arch of the south gate, leaving the contagion to riot in the palace, and beginning their long voyage home.

We headed North. We had lost our plundered silk, our chalices, our stolen gee-gaws, our casks of things that none of us Kikuyo knew the nature of. We lost the wines and meads, the fabulous hanging hams. My brother was not concerned. Enough, Ode, there are greater riches to the North. We have hardly begun on this adventure.

The roads were clear. No toiling in the fields.

Each village that we came across had a sign stumped at its outskirts.

Crude boards attached to a stake.

Peste.

And each village was stone quiet.

Had they died before they had achieved their aim of infecting us? Had their plan misfired and they had killed their own?

Peste.

'Plague, illness.'

'Ode, we shall have to go around, across the fields. The rhino will stamp the ground flat for your wheels.'

It started to rain.

'Let's move before the fields turn into mud.'

I thought of Anna in her carriage beneath me, still ill. The wheels would sink into the mud and I would have to whip the horses.

Peter someway behind us, jumped down from the box of his carriage and ran alongside our train. Any one of our warriors could have shot him with an arrow, or leant down and taken his head with a blade, yet no one saw the honour in it and my brother had yet to command it.

And Peter ran past the sign and towards the collection of low houses.

'He knows we cannot go after him,' said my brother. 'And he knows that we would never take him back even if he begged.'

'He will die,' I said.

'You of all people should rejoice in that, Ode.'

'The nights are getting colder, Ode. Or is it me? Maybe I am not fully recovered.'

'The nights are getting colder. Anna if you are cold let me get you another blanket.'

'You are my blanket, Ode. Snuggle. Enwrap me.'

The thousand men at lance and pike, we were warned about, dug in to a ditch that was to last the length of fifty miles. Either they didn't exist, or they had died waiting for us.

'What are your thoughts, Ode?'

'My love for you.'

'Yes. Let us think of that. And not this fucking campaign. Your beasts are becoming sluggish. The warriors, their backs are not as straight as I remember them. I am glad that we are no longer finding people to kill and rob and maim. But where are they? Those people that I do not want your brother to butcher.

246

Where is everyone? Where is everybody? Ode, have they fucked up massively, and by importing this plague to defeat you, consigned themselves to oblivion?'

There was a small town ahead.

The sign of Peste. Yet also a small hill of offered plunder.

'They are dying, yet strong enough to make an offering.'

'Brother. It is not an offering, it is a temptation.'

Sacks stuffed with loaves of bread. A pile of fat cheeses in their wax. Sides of salted lamb. Baskets full of fruit. Crates of wine.

'The food is diseased?'

'We shall never know. We are hungry and they tempt us with something we cannot dare to try.'

'The plague is passed by blood, Ode, is it not?'

'I am no physician, Brother, but how hard is it to prick a finger and let a drop fall into the dough or the neck of a bottle.'

'Ode, it is Autumn and we are hungry. The fields are not ripe. Our supplies are low. We need someone to taste this food for us and determine whether it is healthy or infected. Shit I wish we had not let Peter go. He could have been our taster. I would not let a warrior risk his life for such a thing. I will not demean a servant either.'

Then we heard the sound of a young women's argument from down the road. This was not the moan of disease. That was the sound of life.

'Ode, come.'

My brother grabbed a loaf of bread and a shank of lamb.

'The owner of that voice shall try the food for us. If she lives we shall eat, if she dies, she dies as part of her own people's plan to defeat us.'

A few minutes down the road, before the small town, we found a large house sat behind high walls. There was a gate twice the height of a Yurop man. Made of metal bars that reminded me of a phalanx of spears.

The gate was locked.

We pressed our faces against the cold metal, like children waiting for their mother to cook a pie.

There stood the strangest birds. Extravagantly plumed. Large bodied, yet graceful on their slender legs. They had an air of comfortable arrogance. A suggestion that flying, was for them an unbearable chore. Better to wander an impeccable garden and cry.

A young woman, finely dressed, was arguing with her father.

'I have been shut inside for three days now! I must get some air.'

'But daughter, it is dangerous outside. We knew days ago the black army were approaching. They might already be here. Be sensible.'

'I'll be sensible when I am old and fat. Look I am only a few yards from the house. If I hear anything I will run indoors.

'How shall we defend ourselves against them anyway?' said the girl. 'By simply locking the door and hiding inside!'

'Ode, do you know what they are saying?'

'No, but I can guess. The girl is head strong, she is sick of being cooped up.'

My brother was already climbing the metal gate.

'Brother what the fuck!'

My brother was already over, the girl shrieked, she looked frantically at the glass doors and realising, I would imagine, that my brother could easily intercept her before she could get indoors, she ran in the opposite direction and out of my line of sight.

The mother came from the house with a knife. The father with a poker.

They too disappeared from view and all I could hear were the shrieks of the birds.

We walked back to the men.

'We stay here today and tonight. I shall give the troops a day of rest. The food is good. I shall tell the men to eat. The girl. She said she had never seen anything like me.'

'In what language Brother?'

'In the language of her eyes. I shall take her as my wife. She is quite willing. She is so bored of home and longs for adventure.'

'And how did she convey to you her state of mind?'

'With frowns and pointing. She is very pretty. Her body is good. A man could be happy. She will travel with us. She will keep me warm in my tent at night. She can travel with Anna in the carriage. You will have two women to escort. We shall all be happy. We shall marry tomorrow.'

'And how was that discussed?'

'In our performances, Ode, I am been gaining skills in the language of gesture. But I will need Anna to go visit her and explain the details.'

The bread was fresh, the cheese pungent and hearty, the fatty lamb soft. The wine thick and heady.

A good half of the One Thousand were asleep with their bellies full.

Anna, was teaching Luxxor and Mgebe a few phrases in Latin, as they ate. They had to pause between mouthfuls to both instruct and practice the pronunciation. Anna was very comfortable with them. They were the eldest men amongst us.

I felt a pang of jealousy, embarrassed by my youth.

'Brother, have you not considered that you are already married?'

'That is back home. This girl shall be my Yurop wife.'

'And when we are finished with Yurop?'

He shrugged.

'She can go back home I guess.'

'Ode, I called the family through the gates,' said Anna. 'I did not even know the girl's name, because your brother does not know her name. She came out with her mother and father, they came and stopped about a yard from the gate.

'Are you a friend of the black man?' said the girl.

'I am married to his brother.

'Then I pity you. Before you were married to his brother did that black man rape you?

'No, he did not.

'Then you are lucky.

'He wants to marry you tomorrow. There is to be a ceremony in the garden.

'I would rather die.

'I noticed the lace on her right wrist. I have done that three times to myself in my past. I said.

'I am a doctor, said the father.

'I know this is vile, I said to them. But I fear that if you do not comply, things could be harder still for you and your family. Ode, what shame. What shameful behaviour. I felt as if *I* were threatening the girl myself. I felt complicit. Fuck I was complicit. How easy it is to become part of something you detest.

'What else is he capable of?' said the father. 'I heard that his army destroyed the walled city.

'We did not destroy it, we took it.

'Then who burned it to the stone roots?

249

'I cannot say for certain but the black army did not burn it. I Know. I was there. That was the authorities. They wanted to rid the city of all traces of the plague.

'And what will happen here if my daughter does not agree to marry this black brute?

'I wanted to tell them to flee, but your brother already had warriors watching the house.

'Honestly, you will all die and the town will be razed and all killed. I do not want to convince you to do this despicable thing. But let me return with an answer of yes for now and spend the rest of this day thinking of a way we might avert this tragedy.

'Girl, I said.

'Annette.

'Do not cut yourself again. It does not help.'

'Ode, I want you to write a play that myself and her can perform before the ceremony.'

'Her? Does she not have a name Brother?'

'Of course she has a name. All females have a name. I want to write a story about how we met and fell instantly in love. It will be touching, as she will be beautiful and I shall be heroic in my love. And you might add something like there were three, or maybe five, armed guards hiding in the bower and they jumped out and tried to force us apart, but I dispatched them. Something like that, if we could find the actors to do it.'

'Brother I cannot write this nonsense that you ask of me. Anna has spoken to her.'

'Good, then we all understand each other.'

'You raped her, Brother. Do not pretend otherwise.'

'Ode, do not talk to your elder brother in that way. What would Father say if he heard you talking to me like this?'

'Brother it is because of the love and respect I have for you and Father, that I must speak to you the truth.'

'I want a story of how a black man from the heart of Afrik earned the love of a high born white.'

'You didn't earn her love you forced yourself upon her.'

'And did you not force yourself upon Anna the first time before she learned to love you?'

'No, Brother, I am not like you!'

'Brother be silent or you will push me beyond the limits of my restraint.'

'And you will both live a happy life together? Brother, she tried to kill herself after you spoiled her.'

'That is one version, but you will write me a better story than that and I want the family to attend.'

'That would be a cruelty with no reason for it.'

'Their presence will give credibility to our version and the girl shall play herself in the role.'

'She will refuse surely.'

'Her compliance will ensure the safety of her family.'

'I cannot tell her to do this. And even if I could, I do not speak her language.'

'But Anna does. You can tell Anna what to say, and she can speak to the girl again'

'Ode, I shall not do this and you shall not tell me to. The first time was vile enough. And now this? You are to write the play and I am to instruct the girl in her lines? She has to pretend to fall in love the man who be-spoiled her. And you are to write the words? I know that it is your job to elevate your brother, to make him into the hero that his heart desires to be. But Ode, this time you must refuse.'

'I have to write the play. My father brought me here as the storyteller. That is my function. Me refusing to write would be like a warrior refusing to fight.'

'Then write the truth, Ode. Write the truth about what happened to that girl. Put that in your play.'

'And shame my brother? In front of his men? It is unthinkable. And I know you are not seriously suggesting I do that.'

Anna swept back the covers and slid away from me. She flung a robe around her shoulders and the breeze nearly extinguished the candle at our bedside.

'Write this farce for your brother if you must. It will entertain the common soldiers. But somehow write the truth as well. You are a Griot as well as a scribe of the play. It is the job of the Griot to remember. That is what you told me, Ode. Even if you write the farce, you must *remember* the truth.'

'I could never tell it.'

'Speak the truth first. Find a listener later. If you are only interested in being heard, you will always be a liar. Write it down. So there is a record.'

'Who could read it?'

'We shall read it together.'

'My brother would be very angry if he found me writing against him. I have seen him holding precious objects that we have looted from a church and tossing them aside. Bounty has begun to bore him, but when he talks of the adventure, Ode, he says to me, do you really think it will come true, that my name will be known a thousand years from now? That children of the future will get sticks and play fight the battles that I fought and won.'

'Ode, your brother cannot read.'

'Come back to our bed, Anna.'

'Ode, I know you are sensitive about not being man enough because of your withered arm, and so I hate to say this. But if you persist in this, you will cease to be the man I took you for, and hoped you would always remain. Tonight I shall sleep in the carriage. As I did before I loved you.'

'This is the script and these her lines.'

She took the paper from me reluctantly.

'Aren't you going to read it?'

'I don't have to. I know it is going to be full of shit.'

'It is the best I could do.'

'I do not want to do this, Ode, it goes against everything inside me. But if I do, at least that way she will have some understanding of her terrible fate. I may be able to console her in some way, rather than having your brother explain in dumb show So I will do this for her, certainly not for your brother and I am sorry to say this, not for you.'

'You are disappointed in me?'

'No Ode, I am appalled by you. Yet you carried me on your back to the palace of his Holiness to seek my cure, moving through many hundreds of the sick. How many wives could boast that their husband showed such love and bravery? Ode, so high above all expectation and now so low beyond all yearning of my heart.'

'You make me strong, my brother weakens me.'

'Then cut the ties.'

'To do so, would to be to cut the ties to my tribe.'

'When I cut myself from God, I had nothing to replace him with. My mother was dead, my father never showed me the love I craved. I had no suitors, no siblings. Yet I thought to myself, this God of ours does not exist, because he shows no love, he does not care, he does not intercede. I renounced the only thing I had in my loneliness. And when I cut my wrists and my father found me, and called a doctor, he said, by the grace of God I found you just in time to save you. And when I said to my father's face, fuck God and his mercy and his grace, he left the room and never spoke to me again.'

'You were molested by a priest.'

'Don't pretend to know, Ode. I will not let my hurt become part of your story. Each day I would take my father lunch to his office in the Town Hall. And he would never acknowledge my presence.'

'Ode, can you drive me?'

'To where?'

'Somewhere. Away from this. Your brother and the warriors. And the house where that girls lives.

'I have a bottle of wine. We could stop somewhere quiet. I am sorry that I left you alone last night.'

'I have to be here for the play. Have you spoken to her?'

'I have. The play is not for a few hours yet. Please don't say no to me. Get the horses ready I shall be back in a moment, I want to get my shawl.'

It had been raining, the road was dotted with little lakes reflecting the sun that had now cleared the sky. Anna was inside the carriage. I hollered to her tender ear over the sound of metal-rimmed wheels on wet flagstones.

'I will find a pleasant spot for our picnic.'

She did not reply.

The land rolled around us green and fragrant. I found it hard to accept that this part of Yurop was so very beautiful.

And I felt ashamed to find it more succulent than the land of my people. I wondered if I had been tainted. Seduced. I spoke their educated language, often better than they did themselves.

I was in love with a white woman.

Once she had said: It is a sport and a pastime is it not, Ode, to imagine the person you have always yearned for. But it is much harder to dream, that you are the one that someone else has been searching for all their life. Much harder to

253

think of oneself as the answer to another person's dreams. It takes a certain self-confidence, which I think neither of us have found easy in our lives. And yet that answer, that perfection is all always clouded by an imperfection.

And my imperfection is the duty I observe towards my brother.

And mine, Ode?

The only imperfection in you, is that you do not understand, nor can condone my imperfection.

There was a rap upon the side door. I reined the horses to a halt. The carriage door opened. Anna with her head covered, stepped out of the carriage and began to run across the fields. Anna was leaving me. So disgusted with my cowardice, and my refusal to challenge my brother.

The father, veeringly drunk, red eyed, cursing in a constant whisper, but unable to look his torturers in the eye, dragged his reserve of wine from the cellar. He removed the corks with an instrument fashioned from a wooden handle and a spiralling wire.

The warriors took the wine without thanks and drank swiftly from the necks.

Those plumescent birds had been run after and caught, their feet bound by wire and looped around small stakes pressed into the lawn. They had no more desire to be there than did the girl.

I spoke badly, my voice was weak and painful. My words were dull.

'My brother, the great warrior came upon a beautiful maid, in a fine garden. She took one look at his magnificence and fell in love.'

And then the girl, dressed in a bonnet with a veil, demurely entered the stage that was her own garden and quite swooned before my brother's presence. She took his hand and they walked in a circle amongst the peacocks.

They strolled and I blabbed. To talk of love, to say these lying words when I had lost my love, a woman to whom I had always spoken the truth. Anna running from me in disgust. Anna who I would never see again.

Damn you, Brother, for bringing me to this.

Not one warrior smiled at this farce. What was this? Were they meant to celebrate that fact that my brother had taken a girl, clearly against her will by all rumour. My father had forbidden rape as part of the conquest and the warriors had followed his edict even after his death. It is not good enough to be as good as the white man. We had to be better than the white man. Stronger, yes, fiercer surely, but also more respectful. If we did not act with honour all the books will ever say about us was that the blacks came to Yurop to rape the white girls. And that is all they came to do. For blacks are animals that have no self-control.

I ceased speaking. A silence fell. This had not been a success. I was slightly pleased at my brother's failure, yet also embarrassed.

And as his daughter strolled nonchalantly from the garden to a small stone arbour, the father came screaming across the grass with the corkscrew in his fist. The warriors had been made so lethargic by this charade that none managed to intervene and my brother was so shocked that he let the man attack him.

The strike was ill judged and merely scraped my brother's throat. Luxxor, the first on the scene, took the father's head in a single blow. My brother called for the girl to be brought back to him.

'Tell her, Ode, tell her, her father's actions have sealed her fate.'

He took the blade from Luxxor, kicked the girl to her knees, the warriors more attentive now, watched him raise the blade. I saw the girl's finger, that ring, and rushing towards her flung my own sweet neck between the steel and the girl.

The warriors had left quickly heading back to their tents, happy to be gone. The father lay dead. And after Anna had risen, taken the bonnet and its veil from her face, stared hard at my brother, and spat upon the ground, she went to the mother and took her inside. Of course she had some good news to tell her about her daughter.

'You fucking idiot, Ode, I could have taken you head off.'

'Better mine than Anna's.'

'Hardly, Ode, you fuckwit. If I had killed her I would have gotten over that soon enough. But if I had killed you?'

'Well you didn't and we don't have to mention it again. I certainly won't bring it up.'

'Brother, you are married to Anna who you nearly gave your life for. I would not have done the same for this girl. I am glad Annette is gone. It would have been a terrible union. Tell Anna that I am not angry with her. If anything, I am indebted to her.'

'Can you not find happiness with anyone?'

'Can anyone find happiness with *me*? Brother, I have hurt so many people and I cannot stop. I am charged with our father's dream. I have a thousand men who risk their lives each day in honour of this quest. At night the dead come for me. Our own men, but also the ghost-faces.

'The change in nature that was visited upon my father, that burden that has been passed onto me, I am as a ball rolling down a hill that never finds a valley. I cannot stop. I cannot stop. I have been chosen to change this world. Unlike you, Ode, I am not a man of great imagination or of learning. My one talent, my one skill learned from when I was four, is combat. I kill men that must be killed because they are our enemy. Because they would kill us if I did not get to them first.

'When I see a white women, Ode, I think your bellies have given birth to the enemy. When I paw one of their pallid paps, I think, this is the organ you used to feed the children that you taught to hate us.

'I think I will commit many more crimes in the course of this quest, Ode. I think I am quite beyond any restraint sometimes. But I think that at the end of this adventure, the world will be a better place. So fuck me and my nightmares of the dead! Our feelings are unimportant. What we are doing will change history. And every man of our race will revere us as their saviours for evermore. And one other thing that you will never understand, Ode. As much as I sometimes even revolt myself, every one of our men look to me as their saviour. I have led the One Thousand half way across the world. Conquered the plague, and the white's run before me shitting their pants.'

'Can you not rest?'

'Ode, I think that if I rest I shall die. How many are we, Ode? Are we still a thousand?

'Brother?'

'Our number, our strength.'

'We are still the One Thousand, yes.'

'How can we be, Ode? We have lost many men and beasts over the duration of the campaign. We have not been able to replenish our forces. So how can we still be a thousand? I cannot count, Ode. How many are we?'

'We are the One Thousand. Brother, in my head and from the end of my pen, we will always be the One thousand. For whatever the white man throws at us, whatever scheme or weapon they prepare to use against us, not one of us has perished. That is the tale. Because we have been chosen for this conquest. The Gods had commanded nature's transmutation and the rhinoceros came to us with a new contract between man and beast. A return in part to the old contract that had existed between us many generations ago. This is as fine a story as the one the white men quote in their one book of invented truths.

'And their God never appears. They paint him but he never turns up to pose. They pray to him, but he never speaks. They write music to him yet he never hums from the sky. Yet our Gods are made manifest in our adventures.'

'How many are we, Ode, in truth?'

'We would be the One Thousand even if it was just you and me and no one else.' I paused. I had been aware of the diminution of our number, and a few days before I had traversed our train and counted heads.

'We are less than our original number, but as strong as our original intention. But, Brother, you must never do something like this again.'

'I didn't have time to think.'

We stood up on a small stone bridge and threw sticks into the water, then rushed to the other side to see whose stick was in the lead. An innocent enough game made slightly fractious by Anna's insistence that the stick in the lead was always hers despite any protests of my part that mine had been the shorter stick and it was the shorter stick that was quite clearly in the lead because it had drifted into the faster current at the centre of the stream.

'Which meant your actions came from the heart. What greater compliment might a woman ask of her man? Should I gush and swoon at you, Ode? Would you like that? I am aware that I have to make this up to you. You have forgiven him haven't you?'

'I think he is truly sorry.'

'Of course you do.'

'So you didn't run from me.'

'I know that you must have thought that it was me. That I had left you. That I ran from you. I was quite deliberate. I wanted to buy time for the girl. How does your brother feel about all this? How angry is he?'

'I told him that the girl had run, and you, in respect offered to take her place so that he would not lose face before the warriors. He admired you for that. He told me that you did the right thing helping her to escape. And he is in your debt. Did you not trust me to keep your secret?'

'Not from your brother, Ode. No two people who are so different, have ever been so close. Sorry, Ode, I did not.'

'Maybe you were right not to. Even the thought of going against my brother is for me a sort of apostasy.'

'Ode. What would you have done, if your brother had succeeded in cutting off my head today.'

'If my brother had cut off your head it would have been *your* fault and not his. He did not know it was you. You were in disguise. How could he be blamed for that?'

'But would you have blamed him anyway?'

'No I would have blamed *you* for breaking my heart.'

'Ode, I am sorry that my question insulted you, but your answer was perfect, and I am happy now.'

We were met with the stench of burned flesh. The road leading into town was blocked with a pile of the blackened bodies of cattle, sheep and goats, roasted beyond eating, a deliberate action. Either side of the road, olive groves were similarly burned to blackened stumps. Beyond a field of tomatoes had been ploughed with feet.

In the town itself, all dwellings had been burned roofless and the floors covered with dung. The church was filled with charred dogs, an awful attack upon the nose. The Khrist had been removed, as had all the gold.

Two warriors took a drink from the fountain and instantly began to vomit.

'There are other towns and villages,' said my brother. 'This is not the only one. We shall ignore this is and carry on with our adventure. A few more miles will not challenge us.'

We were met again with the same sights and stenches. Two small villages a few miles apart, ruined, devoid, putrid.

'No this cannot be allowed,' said my brother, 'we will stop this. This shall not happen again to us. We will not be deprived. We shall find them.'

We rode at speed. Fuelled by anger, resentment, hunger, thirst. Fuelled by my brother's sense of slight. Nothing could be allowed to stand against him. Any insult had to be met.

As Afrik Warriors, used to making our way across open country, we were natural trackers. The Yurop townsfolk left clues that any drunken or blinded man could have followed with ease. We found them cowering in a vale, near a river as the sun began to wane. Chewing twigs and pissing themselves. We rounded them up. They stared at our beasts in horror. The reality of their size and demeanour out-striping the images that had no doubt grown in their minds by rumour.

My brother asked me to translate as always.

'Is there a leader here, a man of high standing that can speak the Latin?'

A tall man came forward. He wore long hair and a face modelled with a thick beard. His clothes, although torn and be-dusted were clearly cut from fine cloth. He wore gold rings on his hands and I wished he hadn't. I could feel my brother reaching for his knife, ready to de-bone the bearer of such riches.

'I am a good Khristan. A father. I will not bow before you, nor genuflect in any way. Not before filthy blacks astride dumb, horned beasts.'

Breaking from my script, I said: 'Take the gold from your hands and place it at my brother's feet.'

'I shall not do any such thing before a dark skinned infidel.'

'Do if for your wife and child. The gold is no longer yours, but you may still save your fingers. Find profit from an act of humility.'

Either age or labour had swollen his knuckles and he fought hard to dislodge them.

'You are far from your mother tongue Afrik. What language do you think in?'

I had never thought of the answer to such a question. And it seemed to me a strange time to ask.

'The voice in your head,' said the man still fighting with his knuckles over the possession of gold, 'what language does he speak?'

'I have three languages in my head. I move easily from one to the other.'

'And do they agree? Maybe one of those voices admonishes you and your kind for what you are doing to these decent people. You have a fine voice, and your Latin has a certain crude elegance. But don't let your own eloquence fool you. The tactics of your people are barbaric.'

They dragged him into the river, the water up to his neck. The water stood to the chests of the warriors that pinned him. His head spoke of his defiance, but we could not see his body, the heaving of his chest the inevitable shaking of his legs.

The rhinoceros, uninterested in the affair, lay on their sides on the grass. Our warriors sat on the ground with their backs against the bellies of their mounts.

The whites had fled with their rich supplies. We had caught up with them both. Our men feasted at last and drank deeply of water and red wine. The captives sat on their knees and prayed in silence.

'You have destroyed your own town,' my brother said, 'your fields, your livestock. You had poisoned the water. How were we to assuage our hunger, flake our thirst? You had left us nothing to sustain us, enrich us, or provide shelter and rest. And then we found the same thing at two villages beyond. This is an idea that must be stopped at any cost.'

'We don't want to sustain you,' said the head in the water. 'We want you to die.'

'Others will no doubt hear of this and will be tempted to do the same. And that shall not be allowed to stand. It will deprive us of our sustenance. The conqueror must be paid his dues.'

'Better that we burn that which is ours by our rights and labour, than to let you take it from us by your force.'

'You shall be punished.'

'Whatever you do to us we shall refuse to accept as punishment. There is no law that says you cannot burn that which is your own. Your attempt to punish us shall be nothing more than your barbarian butchery. What shall you do to us that you would not have done to us anyway? If we had tried to hold our town with all its riches still in place, you would have defeated us. We cannot match your beasts. So there is no incentive for us to stay and fight, so we shall flee before you and leave nothing in our wake. All sustenance will be withheld from you. You will find nothing to satisfy your conquest. You will enjoy no glory when there is no fear, no bended knee, no pleading for mercy. No spoils, no feast. There will only be death and dearth for you to conquer.'

'Physical pain is a powerful tool,' I said in my brother's voice. 'But men tend to faint or go mad when it is at its height. If men were most lucid at the height of agony, such tormenting would be more effective. After a while a tortured man stops praying for his life and starts begging for his death. Is that not so?'

'Then you wish to have me praying for my death. And that shall be your punishment upon us? I do not look forward to those moments. I am sick with fear even as a challenge you with my words, but your actions here today will not stop other towns following our example.'

'There is a deeper pain that can be inflicted on a man,' said my brother. 'For him to witness the pain of those he cherishes whilst watching helpless.

'Ode, take Anna and find some safe distance. You will not approve of what has to be done this day. Don't ask me for detail and do not attempt to assuage me. If I do not put a stop to this now, our father's dream will be ruined.'

And so Anna and myself found what we hoped was safe distance. But we had not gone far enough. Or maybe a cruel wind sought us out and insisted that we hear.

There was a tripartite chorus of absolute horror. The high-pitched screams of children, the weeping pleading of the womenfolk, the low howls of anguish from the men. Then the children stopped their noise and passed the screaming to their mothers, sisters, aunts. Female voices howled and men pleaded and then, the female voices stilled and there was only the sound of the deep weeping of the men.

'This is too much, Ode. Oh, can we not just run? I'm not sure I can bear witness to any more terror.'

'We have to teach them a lesson.'

'But the cries of pain that are being carried on the wind, have you ever heard such anguish? Ode, what is your brother doing to those poor people, these children and the women? What is he doing, Ode? I cannot bear it. I shall have to leave. But *you* won't leave because of your brother. So if I leave I will have to leave you. But, Ode, I too am far from home. I have no money, no means of getting back to my city. I would be a woman alone with miles of men before me. I am safer here, with this army. I am safer close to the bosom of this horror, than alone in peace. What a cowardly and unnatural woman I am to think so much of my own skin and so little of the life of others. I shall have to stay and listen and look. What option do I have? Can we not run you and I?'

'And how can I hide my colour. Where would I be accepted except in the ranks of my own army? The minute I walk away from my brother I am dead. You may run, I will help you.'

The man, his fingers now divested of his golden rings, not bloodied or beaten in any way at all, was brought to me where we sat beyond some trees, among some purple flowers and the bees enjoying nectar and a dance. Anna had fallen into a babbling swoon, in part a relic of her previous fever and in part I imagined by her horror and disappointment in my tolerance of my brother's cruelty.

'Brother, what did we do to the women and the children?' I asked.

'What we had to. Let us not argue. Tell him this.'

'My brother has a message for you. You are free to go. But tasked to travel, to fan out towards the north. Tell the maids to cook fine food and lay it out for us. Tell the ladies to bathe and anoint their pale skins with fine smelling perfumes. Tell the soldiers to store their weapons and wait for us upon their knees in the town squares and markets. Tell the mayors and priests with their fat bellies to be waiting for us lying in the dust. But they must not destroy their towns and run. For if they do. What has happened today, shall happen to them also.'

He held a package wrapped in linen. I could see the red bloom of blood.

'What meat is this that we have given you?' I asked.

'It is not meat, you black cunt. It is the flayed skin from the arms of my daughter and my wife.'

'Brother you have gone too far.'

'Do not tell me of my limits, Ode. And do not talk to me in a peeved voice in front of this white man.'

The man was carried away.

'I would never have countenanced this vile butchery.'

'This idea was your invention, Ode. You wanted to punish the men who killed our father by torturing his family.'

'I wanted to torture him with the *idea* of it. You were the one that actually tortured him!'

'You and your stories, Ode, so afraid of action. Like all educated men, you make up stories while the rest of us are up to our wrists in blood. Ode, we are facing insurrection. If the villagers destroy their food and flee, if they burn their fields and destroy their crops, we will starve. And weakened, the Yuropas will take advantage of us. And we will all be killed. Every single one of us will die here in this foreign land far from the sacred places of our homeland.'

'Then better that we became extinct before the rhinoceros came to our father.'

And in that moment, offending the memory of my father, my brother hit me hard. I fell with all my weight upon the body of Anna.

Anna started from her fevered slumber and pushed me away. She stood clutching her broach. I stumbled to my feet to defend her and put myself before her body. My brother put his hand to my forehead and pushed me over as if I were a post in loose soil. I tumbled backwards into my wife and pinned her to the hard ground.

'Take this white woman away,' my brother said to Mgebe. 'Put his wife somewhere where my brother cannot find her.'

Mgebe looked as if we were about to refuse.

'I will come with you sweet Mgebe,' Anna said. 'I do not wish to see you punished. Ode, do not fight this, it will pass. I will see you tomorrow.'

We sat beside the fire. The sky was black, the wind thin and chill.

Luxxor was drunk and crying hard.

'Why did I do that to the children? Why, Ode?'

'Because my brother told you to. And Luxxor with respect we have killed many children in this campaign of ours. People fall, the rich and poor, the men and women, the old and the young. We grind them all into the dust without exception. When you take a town or village you kill them all. I understand the logic. The men are to be killed because they are either soldiers, or are potential soldiers. The women are to be killed because they will give birth to soldiers. The children are to be killed because they will grow up to be soldiers.'

'Ode, I have killed outright and in the heat of battle and quite carried away I have been. And if I ever have to question my actions after, there are always a few pints of ruby wine waiting to convince me of my perfection. But that slow and excruciating torture, to women and children, and with their pleading eyes upon my face. It will take much wine to blank this day from my memory.'

'Luxxor, maybe it is better that we do not forget.'

Mgebe came to join us.

'Ode, I can hardly look you in the face.'

'Why, what has happened now?' said Luxxor.

'Know Luxxor, that Ode's brother has commanded me to take Anna from him and to hide her somewhere against her will, and Ode's knowledge.'

'Anna is Ode's wife. His brother has no right to take her from him. It is against all tradition and all of law. I will not stand for this. Ode, I can't believe that you allowed this to happen.'

'She tried to stab him with the pin of her broach. I sought to calm him unless he thought of a greater punishment for the challenge against his authority.'

'I am as much to blame,' said Mgebe. 'I am old enough to be this pup's father. And yet I let him command me against my heart and conscience. Ode, I loved your father very much. He was only a few years older than me, yet I looked up to him as my guide. And when he died, on that terrible day, I saw with my two eyes something I will never forget. An image of his soul floated upwards from his chest and descended upon your brow. The soul of your father transferred to *you* not your brother. The rhino got it wrong.'

'Enough of this talk,' said Luxxor wiping his face. 'Where is Anna now?'

'She is in her carriage,' said Mgebe.

'You were commanded to take her somewhere we could not find her and you took her to her own carriage?'

'Lets us say it was the best thing I could think of. Am I to be punished for a lack of imagination?'

'We shall all go, all three. She loves us all. Come.'

As we walked towards Anna's carriage, Luxxor whispered in my ear: 'Ode, when you translate your brother's words to that white tongue, do you embellish? For what your brother says in all reality is nothing more than grunts and threats, arrogance and foul language, and yet you seem to turn his crudity into eloquence.'

Embellish is not the word he used. Nor eloquence. Note that the Kikuyo language is not simplistic. But warriors have no need for such eloquence and embellishment.

What they need is courage and ambition and for all of his faults that is what my brother had. And there I was excusing him again. We were not twins, but we were entwined.

Mphuno lay before my brother's tent.

We had been drinking.

I approached on my knees. Anna started to giggle as I put my head to his cheek.

Mphuno took no notice of me at all. I crawled back to my friends.

'Your brother is the chosen one,' said Luxxor, 'we were fools to think it might be otherwise.'

'Ode, if I am to be banished to my carriage tonight come join me there my husband. And gentlemen join us for more drink before you retire.'

'And Luxxor and myself,' said Mgebe, 'shall fall asleep upon the box. And your brother, in the morning, shall find us in communion but with no fault that he can prey upon.'

'Might it not be an idea,' said Luxxor, 'to leave a husband and wife to greater privacy?'

'I dare not get my husband excited,' said Anna, 'or he simply won't fit inside the carriage!'

And under the dark night we pissed ourselves laughing, in the way that we all do when the reality around us threatens to consume us.

I held her in my arms. Her body was consumed by the most terrible shaking.

'Is this an echo of the plague, or have we made a child together?'

'No Ode, we have not.'

'You have avoided my seed and yet I am sure I placed it inside you. You are still even now, afeared of my deformity.'

'Ode, you look so hard at things that you miss the most obvious and important things. I do not meant to offend you. But I do not wish to become pregnant in this conflict. How do I know if either of us will survive? And we have no home you and me. I cannot come to Afrik, you cannot come to the town where I was born. Any child of ours would never find a home.'

'We have no future?'

'Ode, I lost my future the moment your brother abducted me. Ode, do not make that face. What I have said is true. But I also found you, my love. So for now the present shall be all the future that I need.'

Bundles of straw had been placed around the trees in the orchards. As we entered the town the streets were clear, again bundles of straw sat at the foot of every door. We could hear a preacher intoning in the church.

'They intend to burn the crops and their houses and yet they are still here, Ode.'

'Brother stay our army here and let me listen to this priest's words. Anna will assist me.'

We walked alone along the cobbled street.

We squeezed each other's hand as we appeared before the church doors.

'I just don't want anything to happen,' said Anna. 'I would be happy if this day could just be boring. You are a story maker, Ode. But, can you make this day so dull that it would never be recounted without yawns.'

We opened one of the great doors with great care and slipped inside. The priest spoke from his pulpit. Not from the book, but in the common tongue.

'A northern dialect,' said Anna, 'I may get some words confused.'

The priest was all mouth and Anna struggled, but whispered what she could glean.

'Your sacrifice will not be in vain and you will be seeing each other again so soon, reborn and reunited in the kingdom of heaven.

'There will be no sin attached to your actions. Because you are doing God's work by denying the heathen all hope of help and succour.'

A small child turned around and saw me. She touched her mother on the arm. Annoyed, her mother tutted her but turned her head anyway. She understood my presence and began to scream.

They all turned to view us.

'Any man who strikes and kills this nigga,' cried the priest, 'will have the blessing of our Lord even if the deed is committed in his own house. And we shall burn this white bitch that seems to be his concubine.'

Anna took my arm.

'I am no warrior,' I said. 'But they will not get past me to harm you.'

Oh the sick joy of making promises based not on fact, but on love and fear.

Then the large doors opened behind us and there stood Luxxor and my brother. And I was grateful.

And behind them a sea of horns and black faces.

'The barbarians have arrived earlier than we expected,' said the priest, 'but we know what we must do. We have talked about this.'

The tumult began with one strong man who grabbed his young daughter by the shoulder and the chin and in twisting her to his embrace, broke her neck with an audible crack. This one action became a plague as other parents fell upon their children, strangling them, cracking open their skulls on the stone floor, stamping on their chests.

One man had his son's hair in his hands and his face positioned against the wall.

'I can't,' he cried.

'You must,' said his wife, 'I am not strong enough.'

'Do it father,' said the boy. 'And then mother too and yourself just after, and we shall all be together again in heaven as the priest told us is the truth.'

'Ode, I thought I told you!' said Anna digging her fingernails into my wrists. 'I wanted boredom. Not more screaming. Why are you torturing me!'

One woman holding a limp girl in her eyes demanded of her man.

'Now me, and then turn upon yourself, and we shall be happy everlasting and with the lord.'

He stabbed her in the neck and watched her fall and turned the blade upon his own heart.

It seemed to me at the time, if there truly was an afterlife, such scenes were expressions of love and even joy. The pain of killing those you love would dissolve in moments and they had been absolved of any sin by the words of God in the priest's mouth.

My brother appeared beside me.

'They are killing each other.'

The priest raised the lectern and taking it in both hands came down along the isle at speed, vaulting over the dead and the moaning, coming for us, he raised the heavy, aged, wooden lectern above his head and Luxxor stepped forward with his sword and took both of the priest's arms off at the elbow.

The priest screamed and bled and his congregation turned on each other in greater glory.

My brother watched the spectacle, as he with pleasure, watched the plays.

The men killed their children. Then their wives. And some stabbed themselves in a frenzy whilst others, maybe good friends, helped each other to their afterlives.

Until all were dead except nine children. Four boys and five girls. They seemed thinner than the others. Orphans maybe. They had no one that loved them enough to send them to heaven.

'Ode, tell your brother he must not hurt those children. They are not to be made example of. I cannot stand by and witness the death of more children. That would kill me, Ode. What is left that is womanly about me, will not survive the witness of another atrocity.'

She beckoned them to her. They refused to move. She went to them, clambering over the bodies of the fallen. She smiled hugely, she took a little girl's hand.

I stood beside her. They didn't like me much. The girl cowered.

'This is my friend,' Anna said to her. 'You do not have to be afraid of him.'

The girl frowned and kicked me under the kneecap.

'Children come,' said Anna, 'no one will hurt you when you are with me and my friend. Ode, bring the carriage around to the back of the church.'

I walked past my brother and Luxxor, he still seemed amused by the fact that the townsfolk had killed themselves.

'We had no need of them anyway. The important thing is that they didn't have time to destroy their crops and supplies. Where are you going, Ode?'

'I didn't answer.'

At the rear of the church a stained glass window was split and the children clambering through.

I drove them from the town. Into the countryside.

'What is in there?' said Irin.

'My dresses, would you like to see them?'

'This dress is a piece of shit,' Irin said tugging at her own garment. 'When you got no mum or dad you just get the worst crap. And you work all day, and at the end of it they give you a potato.'

'Well Irin, today I will give you a dress as I have no potatoes to offer.'

'I don't want no mouldy spud.'

'How old are you Irin?'

'Don't know, no one ever tells me anything important. But I guess I've got to be some sort of age.'

'My dresses will be big on you.'

'Do they smell bad?'

'They don't. No.'

'Then I don't care if they're too big, as long as they doesn't smell like puke and poo.'

Anna undid the clasp on her luggage chest and pulled out her dresses one by one, and laid them on the laps of all the children that sat around her in a semi-circle.

Even the boys seemed pleased to handle something of such finery.

Behind them lay a field of bright red flowers.

After much dressing up had been done, by both boys and girls, they went to play. One boy picked the head of a red flower, blew upon it and released a halo of tiny spores. The other's chased them, caught them on the end of their tongues or snapped them between their thumb and finger and stuck them up their noses.

And soon that game caught on and the children sniffed and licked and began to giggle quite wildly.

Anna kept her distance from the game.

'It is gorgeous to see such happiness, but I have to be careful of flowers, their pollens make my eyes stream and I sneeze like a hog. And then my face swells up like a rabbit. I am two animals at once and neither of them very attractive.'

'Then we can include you in an illustrated bestiary next to the basilisks and griffins.'

'Fuck you boy. I will just sit beside you and watch the frolics.'

And so we watched their unbridled joy on a day with a clear sky and high knees and voices.

'Who will look after them, Anna?'

'We could if we stood up to your brother. Which I know you don't want to talk about. We could take these children and go and live in the mountains. But I'm not sleeping in a fucking cave. Too draughty. And you can't trust bears.'

A shrike soared above us.

'With my one good arm I could hardly build a house.'

'No. *I* will have to build our house. And you can sit on your arse and write a story about how hard I worked.'

She grabbed my arm and kissed my shoulder.

'Do I offend you?'

'You have no idea.'

'These children are used to hard work. They are thin, but they are strong and hardy. We could find a place with a stream so we could always have fresh water to drink. Among that flow we could catch fish to bake over a fire. Wild berries, mushrooms. Imagine what feasts we could enjoy, Ode? We can plant potatoes, onions, swede into the ground and watch them grow as the boys and girls grew to young men and women beside us. And we could both teach them to read and write. What joy we could have you and I. You and I, and no one in between us.'

'And am I to walk away from my brother?'

'It is what you would need to do, yes.'

And then there was a shriek. Not an expression of joy, but a cry in the wrong register for a child.

'Shit,' said Anna, 'those two are fighting. Can we not have one day, one hour of peace?'

'I will separate them, stay here. What is "stop now" in their language?'

'Aufhoren or something similar.'

As I approached I clearly saw that they were not fighting as children do, a mad and uncontrollable extension of a game, nor even that petulant violence that arises when one child decides to change the rules.

Timo, the boy with a hair lip and Irin were digging their nails into each other's faces. Another girl was trying to force a twig into the mouth of her sister.

'Aufhoren,' I hollered, the pitch and tempo of voice helping my no doubt feeble pronunciation.

A rush of wind lifted a bloom of poppy and I inhaled. I became almost suddenly euphoric and my member stiffened. All I wanted to do was go to Anna and spread her legs.

It is something to do with the flowers, I said to myself. The spores floating in the air. I recalled what his holiness had said in his sick bed when he thought he might be hurt by us. He said he had distilled the essence of a bright red flower that made him insensate to pain. He did not say it drove him mad after. But then why would he have cared?

Anna appeared behind me with a scarf over her mouth. A protection against pollen, not against the spores of which she was ignorant.

I had already found a moment of bliss, was I about to turn, about to turn on Anna.

I reached down to the field and grabbed a handful of soil and stuffed it in my nostrils. Anna raised her eyebrows.

'It is the poppy that is causing this madness,' I said. 'We have to get them away from this field so they can breathe without this contagion.'

Anna stood there bunching her fists and began to cry.

'The joy they had at first, how happy they were and then it turned to shit.'

She turned and walked away.

'Anna,' I called after her. 'Help me get the kids out of the field.'

She ignored me and carried on up towards the road.

'Anna, help me, I cannot do this on my own.'

I thought I heard her say: And Ode, I cannot do this at all.

Some of the children were still at each other's throats, others were collapsed in sobs and self-clutching.

I grabbed Irin's ankle with my one good hand and pulled the poor child on its belly across the field.

'Anna!'

I made it to the edge of the field of flowers, dropped the child and sprinted after her. The Kikuyo have long legs, we can run, we can give chase. I made the roadside to find no vestigial dust to signify her fleeing soles. The carriage stood unkempt at the road.

Yet what advantage had she used to outrun me?

More shrieking behind me. I turned to see Tomaso who was maybe twelve tearing at the clothes and hair of a much younger girl. Carla I think her name was. If I took time to intervene, Anna would have been even further gone from me. If I did not, I would be unworthy of ever finding her again.

I dragged them one by one from the field. They were spent now. Bloodied and half-conscious. They were hard children. They would repair soon enough. None of them had lost an eye. I hoped that none of them had snapped a bone.

I carefully threw them into the carriage like sacks of potatoes.

I woke the horses and bid them to head North at their best speed. But there was no sign of her. No clue. After ten miles I thought to return to the town we had just taken, if taken is the right word for receiving a town from suicides. Would the children be in danger there?

They are under my protection brother. I am in no mood for argument. Anna has left me.

The children stared at me. We sat in the tent, pitched outside the town. I could not speak their language and they were poor students of the Latin. They were poor students of shoes. They were poor students of cleanliness. But I believe that a child should never be considered ugly. They may not have been beautiful. They may have stunk. But ugliness is a decision that children cannot make for themselves. Ugliness, like stupidity is a thing that has to be learned from your elders.

At night they liked my height. They were not scared of my skin. We all sat in my tent with a bowl of used bones at our centre. They didn't mind my left arm. Irin held onto it as if were a natural thing to do. When I flopped that useless arm around her shoulder she cooed and nuzzled into me. They loved the food I gave them. They drank the half wine and fell asleep leaning against me.

Anna, if only they were ours.

Ode, do not be sentimental. It was you and your warriors that brought this shit down on these children. Hugging a girl-child will not absolve you of the pain that you have brought to this land.

271

I expected to see her at the end of the day. She knew where we were encamped. See wasn't there by nightfall and she wasn't there in the morning. And the army was on the move that day.

'Brother I want to wait here.'

'Ode, listen. I understand. But on your own, one black skinned, who …'

'Who can't defend himself, I know I know.'

'They would kill you. If you stay behind and Anna does turn up, you will be a black man with a white woman, riding cross-country on your own for at least a day, if not more. Someone will find you and they will kill you both for sure. Anna will know where we are by all rumour. And if she headed North as you think she did, rather than back into the waste land behind us, then come with us North, and hope that she returns to us or that you catch up with her. Let logic out-weigh your heart, or your heart will lead you to a cut throat.'

I nodded. He was right.

I watched the children as they swum in the lake.

Maybe, I wondered, had Anna found a nunnery. She had been taken to one in the walled city. She never talked about her time there. A place of safe heaven where she could have been quiet and pious? How she would have hated that.

I used to watch the stars. I used to drink. I used to have a lover. None of you have anything interesting to talk about.

Or she had been taken by hostile forces?

I imagined her slow steps along the dirt road. Her pinched, leather half-boots beneath her. The carefully mastered and cured leather that moulded itself around her instep and toes. Once I had kissed the scuffed tip of one boot when she was concentrating on the cleaning of her underarm.

I could see the sun stroking itself at the sight of her dusty décolletage.

And then I saw the man with his face covered, fast at horse, the gnarled hands that scooped her from her feet and forced her ribs down hard upon the neck of the steed before him. His mates laughing and mother-fucking jeering at her kicking legs and exposed calves.

She was bounty. Famed. The one white bitch running with the pack of dogs.

Or would it only be a matter of time before she came back to me?

Anna, I have something to show you. Those children, I have saved them. There is one little girl that Luxxor carries on his shoulders all day long. The rest stay in your carriage. I feed them.

Anna sat upon the grass beside me, her legs tucked under her. Her skirt covered her feet. She wore her arms bare from just below the elbow.

Why did you leave me? You are my wife.

No Ode, I am not. I am a woman taken against her will. No more valued than a black slave taken from his tribe. It wasn't until I saw those poor children turn on each other, that I fully realised that this conquest of yours has poisoned myself and this world beyond redemption.

That was the effect of the poppy, that was not of our doing.

The Poppy is a response to your invasion. That vile and poisonous plant would never have risen from our soil if you and your army were not here to feed and water it. You are the sun and rain that caused its flowering. I had to walk away.

From *me*!

I can no longer accept the protection of you and you army. You bring such pain and destruction with you. And I play my own part in that to keep my skin in one piece. And so I have turned away from your love and protection and walked madly towards the unknown, out of self-loathing, out of self-hatred.

Leaving me behind bereft?

Ode, you have told me. From birth you hated yourself for how you were born out of the womb. I have learned to hate myself for what I have become over time.

And you have turned against me for my part in your transformation? I was your guardian and your guide and I have joyously taken your hand, and led you into hell?

I walked there on my own. I couldn't breathe any more in your company.

No, I do not believe that. No. And yet I am putting these thoughts inside your head. I am admonishing myself.

That is because you are a writer, Ode. It is what your kind do. You criticise yourself, and by doing so conveniently absolve yourself of any blame you may have caused. You say, I am harder on myself than anyone ever else could be. What self-aggrandising bullshit.

I have caused no harm. I am a writer and a cripple. Do not torment me.

Fucks sake, Ode, you cause harm by celebrating violence.

Damn Anna, I might be making this up in my own head but your words sound just like your own.

And that is because you always paid attention to what I have said. Like no other man I have met before. And I love you, and will think of you forever, if for nothing more than that one simple act of respect that most of your sex find so fucking hard.

Where are you? Lying in a ditch, starved out of your mind. Licking the water out of mud, reaching for worms.

I am wherever you think I am, because I cannot tell you, because I am gone from you.

You cannot be gone. I am in love with you. So you cannot be gone.

Weak romantic nonsense! Fine enough for a poem, but no real way of understanding what it is like to live in this world of shit. And please do not tell me I am your soul mate or I shall puke.

I love you, Anna. In you I found my soul mate.

And I love you too, Ode. And in you I found my soul mate also. Ode, why are you laughing?

I thought that I was crying. Anna, what if you are dead? I cannot push the thought away. It torments me. I followed you from that field and could not find you. How had you run so fast as to outwit me? Or had you fallen foul?

You know that I do not believe in the Afterlife. Not where you are a soul as complete as your flesh once was. And if there is no want in paradise, then there is no reason to strive. And if you have forever, why bother to do one thing this day when there are countless tomorrows in which it could be done. So nothing to do forever, and still your own voice forever in your head. No wine or love could ever fill such a terrifying void.

Yet if there were such a place as your Khristan heaven, where we could both meet again, I would against all judgment strive to believe. But in truth I do not want an eternity with you, I fear we would become complacent with each other, you and I. But twenty years would serve my purpose and my heart and then I would say let us disintegrate, back into the tiny pieces of the world and return to the stars and soil.

Anna, if a small atom of you became ingrained in the hair of a dog, or a drop of you rested in the water that I drank from my cup. What joy that would be.

And Ode, if you were to search you might find a tiny part of me in the jawbone of a horse. I might smell a speck of you in a wine grape that is crushed by a young boy's feet. You may even find me hiding in a fraction of morning dew, perched upon the head of a gargoyle in some great city to the north.

I gestured to the children that we had to go. They pulled themselves out of the water. I looked at their sorry rags.

I took them to our carriage and opened Anna's clothes chest.

I had the telescope taken to the roof of the cabin and set upon its base. And with my eyes to the lens I swept the landscape from North-West to North-East. What did I hope to see? Anna waving? I'm sorry. Come get me.

'Hey,' said one of the girls, 'look at us.'

I looked down. Before me stood the kings and queens of Yurop.

'Beautiful.'

The day had been a day of nothing. A few poor souls stared at us from huts, their fields before them so unkempt and poor that we didn't even deign to abuse them. What pride would there be in watching a man plead for the life of his last turnip? A wife clutching her belly as she handed over a small, wooden bowl of wild blackberries. Her boy licking his lips and crying at the loss of his dreams.

Yet my brother wanted to say a few words before the dark came down upon us like an ending. Something dramatic as the warriors finished their meat and wine and rolled their blankets over them and rested their heads upon the bellies of their beasts.

So flicking back through the pages of my book, I copied speeches that I had already written and jumbled them with little regard or attention to continuity or sense.

We are the One Thousand here on earth and we will be the One Thousand in the Afterlife.

Again, today we have won the greatest battle of all time. The whole earth celebrates our might. Listen to the wind at night! That is the sound of our ancestors singing our praises. The rain that flows from the sky, that is their tears of joy. We are making history but we are also tied into its tide of time. We are particular and immortal."

Ode, are you becoming mad without me?

I am. I never really knew what absence was before. Even after my father died.

Ode, you loved your father.

Yes I did. But I had no choice. It was you I chose. I felt that my father was given, to me or that I was given to my father. You, on the other hand were the magic that I found in this fucked up world. And you walked away from me.

I had no choice.

I know, I do not blame you.

Bollocks, Ode, you blame me for that more than you have ever blamed anyone for anything. More than you blame your brother for his cruelty, or your father for his vision that has led to all this bloodshed.

You cannot talk against my father.

For that is sacrosanct.

Yes. But you are not really here. These thoughts of yours are mine. I am fighting with myself. There are two sets of thoughts inside my head and they are at war.

That is because you are a storyteller, that pain is part of your vocation.

But it hurts.

That is the price you pay for your skill. Washer-women have peeling and dried hands. Your warriors are scarred from chin to knee. The backs of farmers are bent at an early age. Do you think you are, or should be exempt? A woman hosts a child and her poor cunt gets stretched beyond belief to bring life into the family home. Nothing worth having is without pain.

Philosophy, Anna. We could talk all night. Oh Anna, I wish we could talk all night.

We can talk until you fall asleep. When your mind goes to rest, I am like a bedside candle, blown out by your thick, sweet lips.

Did you ever have a child? We never talked about it.

I had a squalling brat from the pathetic cock of a fat priest who forced me as a girl to let him enter me because my father wanted some favour. I drowned it in a bucket and never told a soul.

I hope that is not true.

Did you find me tight and virgin the first night we reached out to each other in our simple bed?

I was too happy to notice. All I remember was the smell of you, the perfection of your flesh under my fingers, your giggles and my overwhelming desire to release myself inside your beautiful body.

As we moved further north it often rained at night. And while my brother and myself and Luxxor all had our own tents, the warriors were happy to sleep under the sky. And if it rained while they slept, they would laugh. I do not need to bathe come morning.

We found a small, cloistered building on a day where the tree-tops disappeared into the grey sky, and a rainstorm froze in the sky and pelted us with tiny, crisp, cannon balls.

I took the children and a hessian sack.

On the large wooden door, there was a wooden ball hanging on a string. I pulled it down and heard a bell ring on the other side of the wood.

A small hatch opened in the door and a pair of eyes scrutinised me.

'Children,' I said, hoping to be understood. The eyes looked down and the bolt was slide back.

A woman stared at me.

'Children.'

'kings and queens.'

I showed the contents of my hessian sack.

'To pay for their food and board.'

The woman nodded noncommittally and opened the door. She put her arms around them as if she had found treasure.

My kings and queens were loath to leave me behind. Tomaso, with strong fingers. Arianna with the gap teeth. Paulo, so small, so bright. Kristen, with the darkest skin. Timo with the hare lip. Irin, who liked to hold my arm. The two sisters, Carla and Bozsi. Arhmonde, sweet eyes, hardly spoke at all.

The soil was dry under my wheels. I drove the empty carriage with care as if Anna was still sat within. I had taken one of her dresses and pinned it to the rear seat. I had lain the night before with it spread across my lap. I had touched it, but I had not soiled it.

Our approach had not gone unnoticed by the old men in their low hovels, those poor souls with more eyes than teeth. Or the young girls halted in a game beside the river, their wet skirts balancing on their knees. Nor the rheumy dogs with their paused leg raised in wonder at our passing might.

We were after all the One Thousand and thunderous in our weight.

I reined the horses.

The whites were waiting for us, maybe five hundred mounted. A dense forest to their left, a rock-ridden, tumbling fall of stream to their right.

Even at a distance they seem to lack shape.

I used the optical device to look closely at their ranks.

'Brother, the men are in rags.'

'It will be no adventure to fight such vermin, Ode. What will you be able to write about in that book of yours at the end of this day?'

'Nowt, Brother. These men are as nothing. They have been thrown at us without regard. To the men who have land and high walls, poor sods like this are nothing more than turnips to be thrown at a dog.'

'We are the dogs?'

'In their eyes, not ours.'

'Then let us pluck those eyes from their heads and feed them to the birds. And, Ode, I have found that I quite like Yurop turnips. With a good wine, a roasted turnip can be a joy.'

'I have found myself more drawn towards lamb and peas.'

'Ode, I could not now live without lamb. Have you seen Luxxor at mealtime? He devours a rack with such concentration, coating it with red jam and pickles. And yet those woollen things, like fat clouds brought to earth, can sustain us in our strength. And even I have taken to wearing their wool over my armour. I often feared this place might weaken us, with its dull skies and skinny beasts, but I am still as strong as I have ever felt. Let us just kill these sad motherfuckers and carry on our way.'

'I would rather we could pass them by, and let them live the rest of their lives in their own peaceful poverty.'

'Yet they stand in our way, and what choice do we have but to exterminate them?'

I stowed the horse and climbed up behind my brother on his beast.

'These poor sods are nothing more than manure for the ambition of their masters,' I said.

When we were maybe five hundred yards from their force they simply turned and fled.

We removed our leather helmets. With so little danger, why hide our faces? Let us breathe. Let us take in the world we are taking as our own with a clear view.

We followed out of habit.

The paws of our beasts pounded the hard earth. Although the sky was dark for early afternoon, there had been no recent rain. Dust bloomed in the dim light. A fraction of a breeze set it to a whirl.

However, although still no match for the speed of our beasts, their horses were faster than I had expected. Coming alongside them, I noticed that despite their rags, the men sat on fine and well-oiled saddles. The horses wore their nosebags, as if eating on the hoof. The men wore scarves across their lower faces. Their brows were smooth and washed.

Why was I so slow to read that which was so clearly before me?

We careened through a field of purple cabbages that seemed to me, against all sense, to vibrate in the dried earth.

The white troops in front of us parted and charged through the five great arches of a viaduct. We followed as was the true course of nature and conflict. Black masses of hanging bats hung under the stone arches and screamed as we flowed underneath.

I caught a sweet and sickly smell ahead.

For beyond the bridge of water sat a vast field of bright red poppy.

'Brother we need to turn about!'

'You are scared of flowers, Ode?'

Charging at full tilt with my arms around my brother's waist, it was impossible to explain.

'Brother …'

'Not now, Ode. We will outrun them, block their retreat, and finish them.'

The careening paws of the rhinoceros flung great clouds of poppy spores into the air. They swum before my eyes and settled down around my nose.

I breathed them in even as I tried to snort them away.

What defilement. And yet what joy.

Then I found a hand around my own waist, another upon the back of my shaved neck. The smell of Anna's sweet scent filled my nostrils. I felt the pressure of her sweet thighs pressing against my own. My mind rushed with the sheer exhilaration and I thought, if we die today, together you and me, Anna, then I will consider this the finest day of all my life.

Anna, hold me tighter. Anna, hold onto me tight. Anna, never let me go. Anna, the blood in my head is like a waterfall.

We veered suddenly to the left, so hard I nearly lost my place. I grabbed my brother harder. Anna grabbed me sweeter.

What is happening, Ode?

'Fuck, Ode, what is this? I have lost control.'

Mphuno skewed wildly from the chase of the fleeing whites, and became a beacon of disorder for the others in our wake.

'What cruel majik is this, Ode?'

We, the One Thousand, the One Thousand men on our fine beasts, we swept in wildly irregular patterns that showed no sign of tactic.

The beasts were ecstatic in the first rush of high, enamoured with their wild frolicking.

I tightened my toes in the laced boots.

Ode, said Anna, they are happy, they are free, but this will not last. We have seen the effect of the poppy before. Joy turns so quickly to utter shit, Ode.

And at her words, Mphuno collapsed. He ploughed the field before him with his knees. And we went to earth on all our shins and shoulders.

Anna, are you hurt, I called.

'Ode,' said my brother, 'why are you chatting shit? Pay attention to our plight.'

Around us charged the beasts, wild figures of eight, and Archimedean spirals of bliss, with their masters, their riders, hopelessly without control. I watched as one by one our beasts fell like grass before the scythe, some losing their front legs, others falling over sideways crushing the thighs of their masters.

Then Anna was on my back, her knees in my sides, her tender hands clawing at the flesh of my neck and drawing blood. I rose myself and toppled her. She lay beneath me, changed beyond any limit of my own imagination.

Her skin was wildly poxed. She spat creatures from between her lips. Hard, black beetles. Crippled, wailing cicadas.

Do you still love me now, Ode? This is the real me. You think this is a delusion? If I look foul to you it is because I have always felt fouled by your attentions. Fool boy, did you think my lies of love were truthful? You think I could love a black and crippled man who only came here to destroy my kind? My only thought was how to survive this horror intact. Now I am going to watch you die.

Foul as she was I fell before her and thought to embrace her, to change her thoughts and words.

'Ode, what the fuck are you doing,' my brother said getting to his feet.

'My love. She has become changed. I shall bring her back to her true nature.'

'Ode, you are kneeling before a dead animal. Try and keep your head, for I swear I am losing mine. We have to get way from this foul place.'

I was sick. I marked the grainy texture in my mouth as the material slid across my tongue. Looking down upon my vomit on the soil I noted the taint of black blood.

There was no Anna, instead a ribcage with vestiges of wool.

The poppy could turn our minds and it entered through the nose.

'And, Brother, we have to get the beasts from this place also,' I said digging soil with my fingers and stuffing it into my nostrils, 'for without them we will be lost forever.'

Since the age of four our warriors had lived a life upon the backs of the beasts that were their hosts and compatriots. It had, for my generation become the natural order. And now all naturalness was in disarray.

I watched with disgust beyond any belief of mine as one of the beasts pounded the skull of the man that had loved and cared for him since his childhood.

And then a man, a warrior, gouged out the eyes of his Beast that had fallen but still breathed and begged.

'Ode, what are we to do?'

And then the men, wilded with the poppy spores, fell to turning on each other.

Our armour, fine as it was, could not parry a direct hit from the point of a blade. They began piercing each other, slicing each other open. Intestines flowed out and danced in the wake of madness. The stink of guts opened to the daylight made the wildlife heave. Clouds appeared above us. Long thin wisps. Tendrils.

My uncle Luxxor, the eldest and most respected of our tribe, began decapitating men he had loved and commanded for years. Men whose flesh he had patiently sewn together again after countless battles, now he undid the precious threads and sutures that his skill had commanded.

I watched the last gurgling of heads absented from the neck. The last spastic dancing of bodies left with no mind to control them.

We were killing our own. The white man's revenge.

'We must get away from here.'

My brother inhaled another dose of the wild red flower. He began to laugh and dance. And my brother does not dance well. And he never lets people see him do things he does not do well.

'Brother we must leave this field.'

'You talk of running? What cowardice is this?

My brother had turned.

'Ode, no brother of mine shall be as feeble to say such words to me. Shall I cut out your tongue here and now to silence you? We run on foot? And what of our beasts?'

He put his hands around my throat. He took my body and my voice in his power. He knocked me over and straddled my chest. All I could do was cry and smile at him in hope.

I was neither in the grip of the initial euphoria nor in the insane phase that followed. Fear calmed me. Fear kept the madness at bay.

'Do not hurt me Brother, you know I cannot defend myself against your strength.'

My brother's fingers were hard upon my windpipe and I thought of death. My mother appeared.

Ode, let me help you clear your mind. Listen, I have come to you because you truly fear that you are about to die at your brother's hands. But that is the moment when I will save you.

Mother, if you come to me as an apparition, does that mean you are absent from the real world?

I died last month, Ode. There was no way of telling you.

Father is …

I know, son. He was waiting for me. Ode, speak to your brother.

It is hard, Mother. My brother is strangling me.

Ode, listen, try and save all your breath for one moment. Wriggle in his grip and tell him I am dead.

I dragged the last air I could between my lips and rasped the truth.

'Our mother has died.'

He froze.

'What? How fucking dare you say such words to me you crippled cunt. I shall squeeze the last breath from your foul mouth.'

But already his hands had fled my throat. His hands waved above his head like birds.

'I saw her,' I said. 'I was about to die at your hands and she came to me.'

'Fuck, Ode, like fuck it what am I doing to you. Shit.'

No, it was not simply fear that ameliorated the second stage of the poppy. It was intensity of mind and feeling. It could be controlled by extremity.

My brother hit his forehead upon the ground as I tried to get my breath back.

'We have to get out of here,' I said.

'How can I command the men, Ode? I have lost my strength and they are beyond reason. How will they listen to me, when they are not even listening to the death cries of men they have known all their lives?'

We both watched Luxxor fall to earth and position a dagger before his own eye. And without much thought, but with speed and deed, we ran at him before he dispatched his sight.

My brother kicked Luxxor's hand as hard as he could, and dislodged the knife from his grip. It did not travel far from his reach.

'Now, Ode.'

We each grabbed a foot and began to drag him across the field.

'Where too?'

'We are going to throw him in the river. We need to terrify him. Bring him to extremity.'

'We have been in the water before, Ode, it does not scare us at all.'

'But only with the rhino beneath us to keep us afloat. The river was calm that time. Here it rages, it is rock strew and perilous, any man would be a fool not to be beset by fear when thrown into this deluge. Luxxor will have to fight for his life, and that is what I hope will save him.'

Luxxor wriggled from our grip and grabbed my brother around the throat.

'You are not your father. You have led us to defeat in a way that your father would never have dreamed of. Useless fucking boy. Your crippled brother is of more use to us than you.'

'Luxxor, I am your master by my father's sad, spilt blood. Do not challenge me.'

'Know this. You are the first born of your mother. You could have been mine. One night I tried to take your mother, newly married. But she beat my head with a pot. But know this, that even if you had been mine illegitimate, I would not hesitate to kill you now for what you have brought us to.'

I reached down to pluck a poppy head. Beat its spores into my palm.

'Luxxor breath this from my palm as a horse may snuffle an offered apple.'

It was such a strange request that he did not fight my advice. He didn't say why should I do such a thing at your command, or fuck you boy, Ode.

He drew the spores into his nostrils, closed his eyes. A moment later he began to laugh. Then he saw his arm around my brother.

'What the fuck. Am I trying to seduce you! Was I about to plant a kiss upon your sweaty lips? What madness has this field of bright red flowers brought us to.'

'Luxxor, you are not yourself.'

'No? Then what am I? A tree? A squirrel?'

'The poppy it robs you of your true nature. There is a short period of bliss and then it turns on you and you begin to act beyond all reason. You are happy now but in a few minutes you will be mad again and trying to kill us.'

'Then what do I do to prevent that?'

'You must dive into the river.'

'Ode, you know I cannot swim. That river is fast and perilous.'

'Luxxor you are the bravest man any of us here have ever met, or ever will meet. In our eyes you are the definition of all courage and honour.'

'And I must dive into the river?'

I did not say yes, and you must face your fear. I did not explain it to him, less the foreknowledge in some way emboldened him.

'It is done. And if I die today, know this, that it has been an honour to walk with you both. You are hardly more than children in my aged eyes, but you are the sons of my adopted brother and the best of men in waiting.'

And then he was off. Like all good men, letting his legs do the thinking.

'Fear of death alleviates the murderous effect of the poppy as does grief?' My brother said.

'I think any sufficiently strong emotion will clear the mind. Remember, Brother, we have trained our warriors not to become overcome with emotion when they fight. We have trained them not to feel so that they shall not be weak. My mind was cleared because I thought I was about to die at your hands, your mind cleared when I told you of our mother's death.

'This flower makes you feel joy then you turn to murder and the only way to feel joyous again is to take more but that will lead you to more murder and so you are trapped in a cycle and the only way to break that is to be absolutely convinced you are about to die. And I don't think that can be faked. The brain cannot be lied to by itself.'

First we stuffed their nostrils with dirt so they would not be re-infected. Most of the warriors were now spent. That was the order of the drug. Bliss, terror, sleep. We grabbed the warriors by their ankles and dragged them towards the river. Me,

284

Luxxor and my brother. Five hands. The warriors shook. There was shit around their mouths. They let themselves be pulled through the flowers.

'I was sure I was about to drown,' said Luxxor. 'It was the greatest fear I have ever experienced, because there was nothing to fight. I do not like the water. And then my mind cleared.'

'There are no men braver than yourself uncle. We shall recover our fellows for sure.'

'None shall drown. But I understand the fear of it will revive them.'

Our One thousand, which in truth had been whittled down to three hundred, were now seventy after our self-destruction. We had to leave the beasts in the field. It became dark. The men were exhausted beyond all experience. We had dragged all those still living into the water and let them fight for their lives and clear their heads.

We moved along the river bank to a place where we thought the poppy would not destroy us in our sleep. The men had to slumber without the comfort of their beasts, a thing they had not done since very early childhood. My brother went around administering large quantities of wine and tobacco.

Luxxor hid under a tree with three empty flagons sat around his knees. He was punching himself about the head. He called me over.

'Ode, what madness brought me to kill those men I loved so much. Such gorgeous boys and fellows, that I would have given my life for. I tore their guts from their sweet bellies. I cannot live with the thought that I have hurt them, yet there are enough of them still alive that I must live to protect those remaining.'

'Uncle, I saw you flailing your sword a great deal. But pardon my disrespect, you had lost all skill at combat in the madness. I don't think a single one of your blows fell fatal.'

He looked at me closely.

'Ode, the storyteller! Go, Ode, leave me to my thoughts and return briefly with more wine if you may. My legs have quite run away from me. But wait! Ode, there is something I must say to you now, because if I do not say it now, I will never be able to say it at any other time. I once did you a great injustice. When you were born deformed, I told your father he was a fool to let you live. I regret that now. And although I did not approve, I am sorry that your white woman has left you. There, that is all the words you will hear from me today. Except to thank you for the wine you are to bring me.'

Many shattered bodies lay among the dew tipped poppies. Our beasts rested there still stupefied. I stood amongst them with a scarf across my face. I kicked a flower, flinched, and noticed that the wetness upon the spores made them fall to earth where they would not be inhaled by any man walking through. Rain or dew would dampen their effectiveness. I looked to the sky, it was dark but with no certain promise of rain. The job needed to be done quickly. But dragging the beasts from the field would cause the spores to be released in enormous number and even damp they would be hard to refute if a man was breathing hard in exertion. Better to raise the beasts where they were and lead them from the field.

But how to raise the beasts? I had not sleep well. But my unsleep had been productive. I had been thinking.

I was not a great lover of wine, although I appreciated the way it made Anna feel, the way it made Anna giggle. And when she was sick the next day and I asked her for the cure, she had said more booze. I was unsure. The thing that will cure you is the thing that has already made you sick?

We stuffed our noses with mud and wore scarves across our mouths.

'Just think,' I said, 'that madness that took the beasts and made them unresponsive to our command. What if we could control that? What if we could administer just the right amount of madness by controlling the dosage.

'We have lost so many of our men. But imagine seventy riders and beasts just the right side of high, with a dose that doesn't lead us to self-destruction. Our reduced seventy would be like the One Thousand again.'

I did not believe that. But to be positive cheered us all.

I knelt and took a poppy head. And bashed the spores onto my palm. With thumb and forefinger I inserted the single bloom at the edge of Mphuno's nostril and let its sleeping breath inhale it.

We waited.

'One makes no difference.'

'Then try a hundred,' said my brother.

'Let Ode experiment. If we overdo the dose,' said Luxxor, 'then Mphuno might die.'

'You both have more patience than me,' said my brother.

'Impatience is the way of youth.'

'Ode is younger than myself.'

'Ode is wiser than us both together. The wise do not get bored so easily. They have their own minds to entertain them.'

I placed another at the edge of his nostril. Our beast breathed it in and did not move.

Three.

'Try four.'

I tried four.

Five. This had all been in the space of a few minutes. Mphuno opened his eyes.

'Try six, Ode.'

Mphuno rose slowly. He put his horn to my chest.

'Come,' I said. 'Let me lead you to the river to drink. We are not far from a field of clover. You can eat after you have slaked your thirst. I have no idea of the workings of your mind, but let us all, man and beast, forget what has happened here.'

And Luxxor began to laugh, and he was not a man that laughed.

'Five,' I said, 'tell the men. If they are poor at counting, tell them one for each finger on a good hand.'

We had begun our journey with one hundred servants. General accident, illness and human foolishness had taken twenty of them over the months. Each still rode upon a female, each now had a male lashed to the pommel of their saddle.

Now we, the warriors were seventy. And our beasts numbered over two hundred.

'Brother, let us arm the servants. Let them wear the armour of the dead, it will double the size of our army. They have known their own beasts and are as close to them as we are to our own.'

'They are not Kikuyo. They were taken from other tribes. You know that, Ode. Why do you insist on being foolish?'

'Can we maybe give them a second status? Men at arms?'

'Absolutely not. It is not our way to grant the servants the special privileges that the warriors have spent a lifetime earning with their graft and pain. It would be a terrible insult to their honour. Ode, you must see that clearly. Would you let one of these lower people stand beside you and tell stories? No of course you would not.'

'We have had to learn many new things on this adventure Brother, let us continue to learn and thrive.'

We clothed the servants in the armour of the dead.

'They will never be like us,' said my brother.

'I agree, but any army we come across will not know that from the sight of them. They are in our armour, they ride the rhino. We are a hundred and fifty together.'

'We used to be the One Thousand.'

We would travel at greater speed than we had ever known for half of the day and then the beasts would slow and we had to rein them in before they collapsed.

No one came anywhere near us. No one stood before us. There seemed to be no villages. Just one endless dirt road, pitted, puddled.

It occurred to me that the road we travelled on had not been made and then traversed. It had been made by the act of travel. Countless journeys, copied and repeated had made the thoroughfare. The fleeing of our enemies had given us a clear path to catch them with.

We found wild onions and mushrooms for the rhino. We ate roasted turnips, hogs. We could find no new wine and Luxxor would take a single spore from the many flowers we had collected, grind it between his thumb and forefinger and place the dust upon the tip of his tongue.

Still we headed north. My brother's desire to circumnavigate the globe was pure fantasy. And yet I could see little alternative.

And then the white ice began to fall and settled on our shaven skulls.

I thought that if we were heading North, it was to certain death. Although I had seen a drawing of northern men in animal skins I had not understood it before.

We wore animal skins too, rational but decorative, part of ritual and adornment, our armour was the skin of the giraffe. Smooth of course, no animals in our home continent had fur or wool conveniently attached to their skins.

I had not fully appreciated the use of fur by the northern men. Because I had no real concept of cold. Landlocked as we were, our seasons were wet and dry and although one season was warmer than the other, neither were cold.

Cold hurts. It had never occurred to me.

Even Luxxor found it hard to bear.

I would rather be stabbed by a blade than by this invisible cowardly thing.

One day he asked me if I thought this cold was a weapon, something devised to destroy us, like the poppy had been cultivated to abuse us. No uncle I said, it is a natural thing.

To me it is not natural, it is unnatural. It gets into my bones and makes them scream. Never before have I felt my age this way.

And as we travel further it will get worse, much worse.

This thing called cold got under the skin and hived it from the inside, it got into the marrow of our bones and made them creak. It slowed the mind. It striped our thoughts of all desire except for the one desire, heat. Heat and meat. Please. Meat warmed us from within. We ate each meal with the finesse and restraint of starving dogs. When we built a fire we would elbow each other out of the way to get closer to the flame. When the fire died, we died with it.

In our tents and under our blankets we were further from home than we ever had imagined.

The cold descended on us and made us moan for comfort.

Our servant came to me one evening, with a sheepskin. Holes had been cut for arms.

It was a perfect fit around the shoulders, but the edges did not meet upon the chest.

The servant took it away thoughtfully and returned an hour later. This time the offered garment was comprised of two skins sewn together, one armhole in each pelt. The two edges met upon the chest and a leather tie held it closed.

'Thank you,' I said to the servant. 'Please make these for all the men. But make them for yourselves also. You should profit from your own ingenuity.'

After that no sheep was safe.

I found my brother in a field talking to a horse. There were birds in the trees. Plumes of smoke in the distance. Two young white children in dun robes hid under a blackberry bush. Their lips were red. They would tell their fathers they had found us there. Send reinforcements. They were no longer scared of us.

We were no longer mighty. The white man had ceased to fear us.

'Brother?'

'Do not think me mad. The rhinoceros came to us remember. Our family was blessed. Whatever the rhinoceros recognised in our father's blood must have passed to me.'

'You wish to tame the horse?'

'I wish to turn the horse against them. The white men are useless without them. The horse is their only advantage. The men are shorter and weaker than us.'

He put his hands on the horse's skull, just between the ears. The animal responded by sneezing into my brother's open, expectant eyes and incensed he took his sword and took one leg at the knee and left the horse howling.

'Come Ode, enough of this shit. The horses are against us. They will regret it.'

As we strode across the wet grass I saw the two white kids tumbling across the field sobbing for the beast.

'We have never found favour with horses, Brother. They have always run from us. We are too tall for them. We are too dark. We remind them of the fearful night. Our smell is too sensual for their senses. Their white riders stink of turnips and onions.

'We have always killed the horse and eaten them. Maybe they have a collective memory. Maybe every horse in Yurop is aware that we prefer to eat them rather than ride them. For all we know, they can send their thoughts amongst their species. Maybe the message of our eating habits is in their whinny. Or they can communicate by smell. They tell their species to hate us by their sweat and the message can travel a hundred miles upon the wind.'

'We do not need them.'

'Brother we could do with any advantage we could find.'

'Our victory shall be all the more worthy of discussion because of these setbacks. The more they turn against us the stronger we become. Do they not know that. Fools. White fools.'

A Yurop man, he came in all humility.

We were sat in snow, high on a hill. Our beasts exhausted. Blankets around our shoulders. We had lit a fire, but it did little to warm the world.

I felt that Anna was beside me, yet when I reached out to touch her shoulder, all I fingered was bracken.

The man bowed before us, knelt in the snow and offered my brother a flagon of red wine, which my brother uncorked and put to his lips.

'You wish a draft, Ode?'

I was not a natural drinker, yet the cold had entered my bones and I thought it might warm and revive me.

'Thank you, brother.'

'I am the Provost to my Lord. I am not here to cause you harm and I ask that you respond in kind. If you are to hurt me, that will dishonour yourself and not me.'

'We have killed enough of your men,' my brother said. 'There would be little reason in adding your single number to the list. Sit by the fire with me. Have a drink of you own wine, take a leg of meat or a wedge of cheese if you prefer. Talk.'

In truth the meat we had to offer were scraps off the bone. In politeness he did not complain, and that made me more attentive to his proposal.

'I am the Provost to a Lord who rules this part of the land. I have been instructed to inform you of recent events. To the south where you landed six months ago, all the destruction you caused has been repaired. The people that you killed in the cities have been replaced by migrant peasants from the countryside. Workers have come from countries beyond our borders and rebuilt the buildings that you burned to the ground. They ask for two things only, enough food to fill their bellies and the granting of citizenship, so that they may bring their wives to join them.

'The fields south of here are full again of turnips, onion. The tomatoes and olives have returned to the trees. South of here the land blooms again and the cities are all abustle with faith and trade. Your conquering did not destroy us. It merely caused us to pause. Everything we lost by your conquest has been replaced. You stole an enormous amount of gold on your way. We have devalued it. You will find that what you thought to be your perfect plunder, has lost its worth. No one will buy it.'

'Of course they will.'

'All trade in gold has been outlawed across the continent on pain of punishment.'

'I doubt you have managed to outlaw greed.'

'You may find some that will still haggle, but any price you will receive will be an insult to your needs.'

'So what have you come to offer me?'

'A position.'

'Under your boot I presume. We will not be mercenaries. We fight for honour, not for the thrill of warfare. You have misjudged us.'

'No, we do not wish to pitch you into battles you may lose. Nothing as crude as that. My Lord has no desire to see you slaughtered, he would rather see you quartered, in comfort at his castle.

'You would be bodyguards to our Lord. You would make an impression on his people, on his enemies. You would not be required to fight so much as to be magnificent. You would be well fed. There are good Khristan girls that would refuse to marry you of course, but not all our young ladies are so sensitive to the teachings of the Lord and the ways of Yurop's finery and manners. You are all handsome men by all standards. I have tasted some of our more adventurous women myself. They may make a man very happy indeed. Any man would be more than thrilled to have such a woman in his bed. And Ode, I think you might find happiness there yourself.'

'I have no need of a lover. I still mourn the disappearance of my wife.'

'Maybe there is no need to mourn.'

I felt icy and leaned nearer the fire.

'Then tell me now what you know.'

'Anna from Napoli. She lives with my Lord. Not as his wife or concubine, but as his guest. He has had in the past some long distance business with her father. She sought him out for sanctuary.'

If she had known her geography and our routes, had that been her plan all along? The minute she neared a place of safety, she bolted. It made sense. I could not fault her.

'How should I believe you?'

'Her name is Anna Savatorre.'

With shock I realised I did not know her family name. She had never volunteered it and I had never asked.

My own family name as son of the Chief Elder was so revered it was hardly ever spoken.

My father was Chief Elder, Sir, Father. Although none of those translations come close to the meaning in our language and the respect my father was due.

And did the Kristan God have a name? His son was called Zhezuss Khrist? Was Khrist the family name? Was God Mr Khrist?

'You may be aware of her name, but that does not prove that you are aware of her person.'

'I thought I might have trouble convincing you. One of my Lord's children, Karl is his name, has been studying the fine arts for the last two years. He has spent a great deal of time drawing hands, which I think he found quite tedious. However recently he has graduated to portraits of the face.'

At this he unveiled a roll of paper from his shoulder bag and unravelled it.

'Is this the woman you have been looking for?'

It was her. Anna. Her likeness. Glorious.

I would have given him a cart of luscious gold for that one piece of paper. But I did not play my hand. Nor did I have a cart of gold.

'Is she well?'

'She is safe, but she is not well. She spends a great deal of time abed. I am not at liberty to discuss private matters of my Lord's business, but it is my understanding that it was her idea to approach you. She must still love and miss you.'

'If you are attempting to fool me, I will command many perverse things done to you.'

'I have no desire to fool you. In no way would that serve my purpose.'

'And what is that purpose exactly?'

'To serve my Lord. But more than that, to use my skills to bring two parties together in such a way as increases the happiness of both. My Lord needs you. You need my Lord. Anna of Napoli needs you and I venture you would like to be reunited with her. And so I bring everyone together, and for my part if I receive favour in return, then that would only seem fair and I would be happy.'

'As bodyguards what would be our function?'

'To defend my Lord.'

'Obviously, but how? Our warriors do not stand around guarding gates as I know many of your soldiers do. When we are not fighting we are training, our men live a life of unrelenting action. That is why we are so fearsome. Do you wish to reduce us to standing fools? A soldier that looks like an extra in a play. Are we to be stared and pointed at? Are we to be curiosities?'

'My Lord will make sure that all challenges and entertainments await you. You will not be bored. You will be challenged. Look, there is a hard winter ahead. Your men can protect us from our enemies and our castle will protect you from the cold. Also the leaves have fallen, the soil is cold. The bracken has turned to brown and begins to flake. The livestock hide under bushes for comfort. It is hard to eat in winter.'

With that last comment I knew that he was aware of our greatest weakness.

'Your men will like these I think. They are a present of goodwill from my lord.'

Tight britches, fur hats with feathers all tumbled in a hessian sack.

'You think that because we are black we will be impressed by gaudy things?'

'My Lord thought you might like to arrive in magnificence.'

My brother was already trying on the hat.

'These will not fit over our armour.'

'What need do you have of armour? You are not going into battle. You have nothing to fear from us. You are a goodly number of fine men on indestructible beasts. My Lord has *twenty* armed men under his command, most of whom are fat and have never drawn blood. My Lord's guards are a disgrace. He feels it keenly.'

My brother was dressed in the pantaloons and was sizing up the leather boots.

'Everything has been especially made to fit your stature.'

'Your lord is rich?'

'My Lord has many lands and many vassals. We may have fine things but we have no fine men. You could change that. We have been at skirmish recently with a bunch of German arseholes. We won our victory but it took its toll. Tell your brother that with your might joined to ours, we shall conquer them in a day and your men may take half of what they have.'

'You are generous with that that does not belong to you.'

'The winter is upon us. There will be food and wine and fires in your hearths and woman to keep your men warm at night. And you, Ode, a woman that you think special is waiting for you and is impatient for you arrival. Only proud fools would refuse such things.'

Remember what I said, Ode.

Yes, Anna.

That time they falsely offered you the chance to teach at the University because they wanted information on the routes to the goldfields. Mistrust any offer that seems to answer your dreams.

Yes, Anna. I know. You are talking in my head again. Looking out for me and advising. But if there is a promise that you are still alive and waiting for me, how could I not follow that? If I am to be fooled again, then so be it. What would I not risk to find you?

'What do you think, Ode?' Said my brother.

'I do not like it.'

'But Anna is there.'

'So this man says.'

'We will not stay long, Ode. A few months maybe. Let us sit out this winter. Take time to cure our beasts. Take stock. Plan for the future. If they displease us in any way we shall have their heads and take the castle for ourselves. I see no danger in their proposal. I see only advantage. And any trick they try and play against us we shall shove it up their white arses.'

'Where are your beasts?' said the Provost at the gate.

Behind him stood the Lord's guards. They were quite pathetic.

'You were meant to come with your beasts. My lord will be bitterly disappointed. He wanted to see them for himself, oh this is not good.'

'I will show you where they are.'

I took my measuring device and let him view them in the distance.

My brother said that we would not enter upon the rhino. They would not be useful in the confined space of such a small castle. Better to be on our feet and ready with our swords. We would invite them in later when we were sure our position was secure.

Also, our beasts were unstable. Without the poppy they were sluggish and dull, with the five spores they were madness itself, barely under our control. Without the power of the beasts we would not be offered this chance to rest and recoup.

The beasts could no longer stand unaided. We had propped them up on mounds of earth.

'There are more soldiers with your beasts. They are invited also. You are all welcome. Come into the comfort and safety of our castle walls, all of you.'

'We heard tell of those German's you said you had defeated. The rhino is not the only beasts we have at our command. White men are right to think of us as different. We are closer to the earth. And skies. The owls talk to us. They are in conflict with the eagle and work against them always. The owls tell us that the Germans are preparing to take your Lord's castle. That is why our beasts and half our army wait outside to repel any attack.'

'They would still be better off, and I think more useful, if they defended us from within.'

'That may be so, but you can tell your Lord that in respect of his reputation and status, they are sworn to protect the path to you Lord's front door. Amongst us, a warriors decision is final, it cannot be assuaged or negotiated.'

'Well I suppose that is to be respected, come in, there is much awaiting you.'

Just inside the gate stood lines of young women of dubious colour, cheeks too red, knuckles too white. They all wore a bright yellow flower pinned to their dresses. The dresses themselves resembled the dun soil that gives birth to the beauty of the flora.

They carried wooden boards as a servant might hold a platter. Across the surface sat cubes of hard cheese, slices of pink, cured sausage. Our warriors dressed in all stupidity, and with their vain hats and soaring plumes towered over these white girls, who fell to curtsy and whinny and kept bobbing their knees in supplication.

Our men grabbed the scraps of food with little subtlety. The Kikuyo have extraordinary fingers. I did not appreciate this until we crossed the sea. And saw how stunted were the maws of the whites.

There was a woman hanging from a gibbet in the square. I could not see her face.

'What sort of welcoming vision is this?'

'Sorry does the sight offend you? We did not know you were so squeamish about death and punishment.'

'You enjoy hanging women?'

'Not generally no,' said the Provost. 'But there are certain crimes that must be met with instruction. I am certain that you conduct your own affairs with a similar regard. Our world is always on the verge of chaos, is that not so? We are the guardians, those of us with power and education. It cannot be wasted. It may be a burden, but we are born to carry it. I do not like to see a woman hanging from a rope. Between you and me it seems such a terrible waste of a nice, warm, homely, prick-pocket. But there it is. Values must be upheld.'

My left arm, dead since birth began to twitch.

'And these barrels?'

'In expectation of your visit. You are tall and lusty by our sight. We gathered wine. I am sure that you can take it. You are hardly feeble women who swoon after a glass.'

'Brother there is something wrong. We need to kill the Provost and his men now before it is too late.'

'Ode! What the fuck! It is too soon in our negotiation to start killing these stinking ghost faces. I thought we had already agreed that we needed their cooperation for a while. And we haven't even met this Lord yet.'

My left arm began to raise itself.

'Shit, Ode, what is going on?'

'I think I have been provoked, Brother.'

'By what?'

I touched the Provost on the shoulder with my dead hand. He flinched.

I have seen this before on white faces. The brow that says fuck you nigger, black cunt, savage. While the lips smile. We may at some point be tolerated, although I doubt that with all my being, but we will never be seen as equal. In their paintings their God is white and their devil is black.

The rich stay indoors, away from the sun and get paler. The poor toil in the fields and get warmer and darken. When the rich leave home, they have a poor man to hold an umbrella over them. For the rich, to show colour, is proof of being of a lower caste. And they think the sun humbly, revolves around their heads. When in truth, the sun is their life giver and we spin, in all humility, in orbit around her.

'You said that Anna was waiting for me.'

'I have not lied.'

I knew.

I went to the hanging woman, put my arms around her hips and rested my head in the small of her back.

There are things in this world which cannot be put into words. Some will disagree. Some will find me a bad storyteller, a weak poet. I might excuse myself and say that I cannot find the words to describe the vision before me, for the floods of tears that rain down in my remembrance make it impossible to see my pen, and the inked words bloom like a cake in the rain before me and become unintelligible.

'There she is.'

I released her, went to my brother.

'Ode, it can't be.'

With my deformed left hand I slide my brother's dagger from his belt and inexpertly stabbed the Provost in the cheek. He gave orders through the blood and pain.

The lids of the barrels popped. They did not contain wine. And we had been fools to think that might have done so.

The fine regalia that we wore had nothing of the resilience of our leather armour. The men in the empty barrels had guns, ready primed and cocked. They shot at us with accurate simplicity. We fell too shocked to wail. And while the men reloaded, lesser men appeared from the corners of walls and unleashed home-made arrows at our flesh.

What fools we were to be led into a white man's castle in vain costume as if we were truly welcome. Every nigger should know in his heart that an offering of opportunity, is a trap.

And Anna swung before me.

And if someone had held before me some scientific device that by application of some turning of a key, would have destroyed the whole world in all its flavour, I would have done it in that moment.

Our men died around me and I would not have complained for arrows to have pierced my eyes and blinded me.

The Provost, holding his cheek slunk through a door in the brickwork.

'Go after him, Ode,' my brother said.

'Me alone?'

'Yes, I am needed here.'

A second volley from the rifles. A rain of arrows, Anna hanging.

The warriors took their wounds, and though many were to prove fatal thereafter, they still had enough of the life force still, and enough of the sheer obstinacy learned in their many years of training, not to simply fall and expire. Taking more shots and with their brothers behind them, using with all love and respect, the body of the near dead before them for protection enough to get through to the perpetrators of this obscene attack, near enough to get them by the throats and gouge out their eyes. Bash them to the ground and stamp upon their foreheads.

'I cannot leave Anna here alone.'

'I'll cut her down myself when we are done,' said Luxxor beside me.

Luxxor peppered with arrows, took some spores from his pocket. Remember Uncle only two, or we lose all reason. He burst into feral laughter. The enemy paused for a moment in surprise. Then he charged. He slammed into a barrel, tipping it, and began to roll it towards the next.

'We will kill them all, Ode,' Luxxor screamed.

'Yes,' I returned. 'Let's wipe this tribe from the face of the earth. They have murdered the one finest example of their kind.'

And from my pocket I took three of the poppy spores. Seconds later my brain exploded with euphoria and for the first time in my life I began to fight. With both my hands on the hilt I cut my way to the door in the wall. If I was poor with a sword, I had Anna at my side to inspire me. I lashed out at every inch of white flesh I could see. Let us see how it opens. Let us see what is inside these creatures that kill my love. And in the depths of despair, I thrilled in the act of killing until I stood before the door. If under the influence of the poppy my moment of euphoria turned to madness, I did not notice, they were indistinguishable.

I put my hand upon the metal rung, pulled, stepped inside and closed it to pitch black. I had never before willingly put myself in such danger.

Ode, I am with you.

No you are not, Anna, you are hanging dead. And I am under the effect of the drug. Anything you say to me right now will be inadmissible.

I'm sorry. I should never have left you.

Shh. I need to concentrate.

I felt my way along a dark corridor of stone.

I was a black skin in black satin and leather. I was made for the dark. As my eyes accustomed to the lack of light, I faintly make out a greyish shadow.

'Provost?'

'I have a loaded gun.'

'But no clear target.'

Very silently I eased myself to the ground and slid along the ground like a snake.

He fired his rifle and the corridor was illuminated for a moment. I saw the distance of his knees and increased my speed. I heard the sound of his back hitting wood. I grabbed his ankles like a supplicant. And with my knife cut both of his Achille's tendons. He screamed just as the door I had entered by opened.

'Ode?'

'Luxxor how goes it?'

'The Lord's men are cowards and have no real desire to fight. Our height and madness shall overcome their careful plans.'

'So we are not yet victorious?'

'Clash of metal and flying blood and forcing metal through flesh. Battle takes its time. There will be no more protest soon enough.'

'How is the poppy in your mind Uncle?'

'I had my moment of bliss and I have vented all my rage upon those that deserve it. I have not shamed myself today. Do you need a hand?'

'No Luxxor I can drag this cunt out on my own.'

'He is not dead, Ode. Do you want me to finish him?'

'No Uncle, I can deal with this.'

'Ode, your love has made a man of you.'

I would rather be a child and know that Anna was still alive somewhere.

I held her. I went to Anna. I kissed her blue lips. I wept on her cheek.

'Anna,' I said, 'we have killed them all.'

Yes I know, she said. I heard the cries.

'Ode, I need you to translate.'

'Not now, Brother.'

'I know but I still need you to translate.'

'Ode,' said Luxxor, 'do what your brother says. Your grief will still be waiting for you. Give her to me, let me clean the vomit from her chin and clothes.'

The Provost was leant against a stone water trough. My brother towered above him.

'Ode,' said the Provost, 'can you give me some water please.'

'No. Fuck off.'

'Where is this Lord of yours?'

'There is no Lord. He died some weeks back. I am in charge.'

'You're in charge of shit.'

'If I had managed to take the rhino from you and turned them to my will, I would have been the most powerful man in this province.'

'They would never have let you ride or command them. That privilege is solely the right of the Kikuyo.'

'I am in great pain. There is flower that you inhale. I noted that.'

'Thank you,' I said.

'For what?'

'I wanted to hurt you but I lacked the idea how to make that spectacular.'

I took charge of his pain. I pressed a very large amount of poppy into his nostril. I Put a knife in his hands. I locked him in the corridor.

After his bliss, he would enter the violent phase of the drugs narrative, and finding no other flesh to harm would have to turn upon his own as Luxxor had once put a knife to his own eyes.

All they had wanted was the rhino.

We walked into a trap and lost so many men.

We burnt all the residents of the Lord's castle in the square with the Provost, what was left of him, tied to a stake in their centre. And then we invited our servants in through the gate, the male and female rhinos trotting along beside them.

'Brother, look. See how comfortable the warrior beasts are with the servants. The rhino want us to train them. We have always been guided by their council.'

Her body lay before me on a cold stone hearth.

Ode, it's fucking freezing in here. Get somebody to light a fire.

'But if I do so, you will rot so much quicker.'

I don't want you getting a fever. I don't want you sick in bed.

I heard the dead echoes of the white women, the ones who washed the Lord's shirts. The ones who boiled his hams and peeled his spuds.

And there had been Anna swinging only yards from their prattle.

They chatted over cheap gin hunched around the one stinking candle, all they had between them for illumination.

Damn, if she had had any self-respect she would have slit her own throat rather than have let those savages paw at her.

She enjoyed it.

Well you never know, such a thing might be a joy.

And where might he put it if it is too big for the usual place.

Oh my God!

Such pictures in my head and me a good girl an all!

It might be a sin to lie with a nigga. And they might be stinky. But who knows. My hopelessly pale husband is a foul piece of dark shit at the end of the day. So who knows. Damn, I would swap my husband for a fox and an onion let alone a big black man that wanted to fuck me. Don't look at me like that. They might be stupid heathens, but I heard tell that they fuck you like a horse. Not that I have tried *that*. Shit, girl, take that look off your face.

Such perversity.

And born a good Khristan too.

There was something wrong with her from an early age.

They said she had a baby by one of them, it was born within two mouths and had to be burned at birth.

I heard the devil himself begged her for a blow job, but she said he wasn't dark enough for her tastes.

I heard she was a cunt sucker and it wasn't until she saw a black wang that she turned. I say go girl. Ha, ha, ha.

Oh Anna, without your senses and good sense to guide me, my imagination runs like a naked fool through fields of pricking gorse and bloodied briar. What I hear about you is crude and lascivious. But I cannot stop these voices. This gee-gaw prattle.

They had discovered that she was my beloved. They had heard tell that she was an admirer of my dark flesh and therefore ripe for punishment. A bitch friend of the invading and murderous army. She survived all the dangers that had beset her during our consort, then in shame of her own protection she had walked into her death. With me lost behind her, dumb and blind.

I tried to talk to her God. He was pretending to listen to his boy. His nailed son kept moaning that he had been forsaken.

Is Anna with you? I asked almost waving for attention. I know she had doubts, I said. But have you shown her the love that you promised in your scriptures? I have read that you celebrate the return of those that turned away from you. Or were those just hollow words?

I received no reply. It is the same with all Gods and heroes. The difference between the sacred and the profane is that the Gods tell you to fuck off without moving their lips.

Is there any way that I can talk to her? I will happily go to my knees and speak any words you ask of me.

You fuckers should have stayed in Afrik, the God father said, turning his gaze on me, where you belong. I never liked your kind. You insisted you were made before my Adam. You think you were around before I even made this earth. Arrogant fucking blacks. Typical. You have always got some complaint. And how many good Kristans died trying to bring you fuckers my true words? And you lot deaf as posts and twice as dumb.

I did not make that place, that continent, your race. That was the work of the devil before I made a new true, pure species of people. You know who Adam was? I had to invent him to counteract the black filth that was about to swarm across my planet.

And there we stayed, boring to death the snows that fell. The warriors ventured out to cut tress with axes that we found in store. And so we set great fires in the hearths. We drank. We ate the cheeses and the cured meats. Some of our servants knew how to make bread. There were barrels of dark flour, pots of yeast. And a drink I had not tried before, called beer. They ventured out and took the sheep from their fields. They opened them for food and skinned them for clothing against the bitter winter.

Luxxor came up with a design for a hat of the same skin, but with the wool on the inside. What? I will tear the throat out of anyone who thinks I have gone soft. But my head is fucking freezing. His idea caught on. Everyone had to have one. The servants sewed while we snoozed in our beer.

Everyone. But how few was that. Such a little number described as all our world and might.

'Once the snows have thawed, Ode. We will head North and return to our homeland without ever once having had to retreat or reverse.'

'It will become colder the further North we go. Brother, we will walk into snow far more treacherous than we have so far encountered.'

'We will be prepared next time. We will wear more furs over our armour and enjoy the novelty. Ode, let us not even think of stopping now. This is but a brief respite to recoup our strength.'

'We shall have to cross more water.'

'We will demand the use of their ships, that is hardly an impediment. You told me of the Yurop adventurers and the Levants, of the Ocipetal people of the Long East. They all find honour in adventure and discovery. Are the blacks to be forgotten and inadmissible from this adventure? Are we forever to be seen to do nothing? Are black people to be the bystanders of this world? We have been called and must listen, Ode. To do otherwise is beyond cowardice. We will circumnavigate this globe and come home with all victory. What is to stop us? We have keen minds and strong bodies. Think, Ode, every plan of the white man to stop us has resulted in their deaths and defeats. We will declare ourselves to be commanders of our own fate.'

'Brother when we entered the castle we were seventy. Now we are only seventeen.'

My brother halted in his dreams.

'Remember, Ode, what you said, if our forces were no more than you and me we would still be the One Thousand.'

'I have a man here, Ode. He wishes to speak to you.'

He wore a long cloak with a hood. He was soaked through and his beard frosted. He carried two large leather bags with metal clasps.

'Come close to the fire. Let me get you a glass of brandy.'

'Thank you, it has been a long walk.'

'Have you no horse?'

'It died, and I am not a rich man to replace it so easily.'

'Remove your shoes and let your feet see the flames.'

I asked for the brandy to be brought.

'Let me introduce myself. I am a scientist of the biology,' the white man said toasting his toes. 'I specialise in animal doctoring. A master of mine once had a baby elephant and white tiger, both of which I was charged with attending. Unfortunately I could not save my own horse. Your rhinos are under the influence of an opiate that makes them unstable, am I correct?'

'No, you are incorrect.'

'The behaviour has been observed.'

'Then the observers are blind fools.'

'What I am about to tell you, may result in my untimely death.'

'Then you should keep your mouth shut and run.'

'The red poppy and its effect, is not a naturally occurring element of nature. I engineered it.'

'So you are responsible for so much of the harm that has befallen us?'

'Yes I am. But if you wage war on us, should we not do everything in our power to destroy you?'

'I cannot deny your logic and your feeling of responsibility to your own race and culture, but if my brother were to hear of this, he would have you flayed.'

Faced with this vile threat, the Doctor remained remarkably composed.

'Look. I may be able to distil a version of that opiate that will calm them, and over time by reducing the dose administered, even wean them off it for good.'

'What do you ask for in return for this service?'

304

'One specimen of your beasts to experiment upon, and if I am successful and it lives, I get to keep it. I have my medical equipment in my bags. You can watch me work if you do not trust me. And if I am successful I ride out of here on one of your magnificent beasts. And then what need will I have for a horse?'

Each day I would wash her. And cover her and smooth her with every unguent I could find. And each day I thought, this day shall be the last, no more of this madness. I shall let her go. I shall put her flesh into the earth, bless her, and weep.

I had fashioned a simple contraption to keep her back straight in the position that I sat her in.

It had always been a thrill to read aloud to her. If my audience had never been more than her own sweet self, I think that would still have been all the inspiration that I would have needed to raise my quill, to put ink to paper. What joy to wake in the morning with balanced sentences already blossoming in my head, and deliciously audition myself before her. Nothing that I ever wrote was written well enough in my estimation unless it had passed the test of Anna's ear.

And even with everything against us and our greatest challenges yet to be faced my brother never wavered in his steadfastness, and the men never wavered in their loyalty to him and his cause.

Was a brother ever loved as much by his own?

What cripple does not adore the fine built man, who is also of his own blood?

Dead Anna rolled her eyes.

But think of it this way. I am correcting the faults in my brother's nature. I, the imperfect boy, am striving to make him perfection.

Better maybe, Ode, to slander your brother. Your brother is a murderer and rapist. Better to write a true account of his deeds.

I cannot.

If your brother is a story, better use your words to murder him before he does more harm. Ode, prop me up, I'm falling over. Thank you. Split yourself in two, Ode. Let one part of yourself write that which your brother likes to hear upon the stage or before his dreams. And let the other part write a true account of his misadventures.

In truth, Anna, I began doing so the day after you left me. I have been sketching out another account. Not for my brother to hear, but to help me remember.

Then read me from that book, Ode.

305

It is the same book, but turned upside down and written from the other end.

This is the true story of our conquest. We have killed many of the enemy and gained nothing. We killed many of the innocent and tarnished our honour. My brother's power is waning. My true love is dead, killed for loving a dark skinned man such as myself.

Holed up in the castle, the servants strive to wean our beasts from the dread effect of the poppy. The doctor of Biology distilled a tincture and brought his offered beast back to health. And it was decided to apply the same treatment to all the other beasts.

In all love and duty, the warriors should be doing this themselves. But a cold, dark misery has descended upon the men. With jars of the tincture at hand, intended for the beasts, and the endless hours, and so little light, and so very little to do to pass the days, they have turned to sipping at the distilled juice themselves, finding great waves of short lived joy, followed, not with sudden bouts of violent madness, but with utter exhaustion and lethargy.

The cure itself was of course designed to defeat us. The scientist of biology had fooled us twice over. He left with his specimen, a knapsack full of gold and our gratitude.

And he left us with the temptation to destroy ourselves.

The snow packs hard the world outside, and the warriors can no longer be bothered to hurry to the fields and kill for meat. We become weaker. And in the face off the loss of our manhood, the warriors, the men, sip more poison and find the time of joy reduced by increment, and the time of disinterest in life greatly elevated.

The servants go after the hogs in the forest and eat them in their quarters. They offer us such meagre shares of bone and offal. Such crushed and mouldy berries. Such hard, frozen turnips. We light a fire in the hearth with the furniture that had once stood before it, for comfort and for warm, for conviviality and the shared talk of men. We suck on the cold hog bones of the day before. The dark marrow as cold as we.'

I raised my eyes from the paper and looked at her lips. I did not see what was truly there. I tricked my mind to see what I had seen before, in happier and quieter times. Her sardonic smile. The film of moisture on the down of her upper lip.

Read me more, Ode. Death is deathly dull.

I myself, am no more immune to the drug and find myself flat out for hours on a dusty bed. Then unstopping the bottle, I write feverishly for as long as I can.

The one true story of our conquest. Our failures and our cruelty. The death of our adventure.

My constant chats with Anna. The way that the drug brought her to me again. Angelic. Transparent. Fragrant.

How she teases and dances before me. And the member of my manhood that she had so admired, had so wanted to caress, no longer works under the influence of the drug. I can no longer even make love to a ghost.'

You can't get it up any more, Ode!

Anna, I cannot.

Shame on you. Well carry on reading at least you can do that.

My brother commands all men to the banqueting room, where our food is meagre and the fire low, and he rants for an hour and then slumps before them.

Luxxor cannot get over the fact that he had killed his own brothers in his moment of madness that first time in the poppy field. He closes the door to his room and weeps and rages. We can all hear him. In the morning his shaven head is covered in bumps and lacerations, from where he had beaten himself about his mind, punished his flesh for his dishonour.

One night he came to me and said: 'Ode, I need to speak to your father, where is he, I cannot find him?'

And when I reminded him of the truth, he said.

'And was his death my fault as well?'

'No Uncle it was not.'

'Ah,' he said, 'so says the storyteller. The king of lies.'

Luxxor killed himself that night, running himself through with a three foot blade.

In truth the warriors had followed my brother because Luxxor had stood at his side. But with his loss, they kept themselves away from the banqueting hall with its paltry mound of hog scraps left by the hunters. And so my brother ranted all alone.

With me as his script-writer and only audience.

There was no carpenter to be found. We had left no one alive to construct that which we might need. But coffin makers make their coffins in advance, knowing that death may cheat the living, but not the coffin maker or his sons. There was a sign hanging above the door, a wooden box from which flowers grew.

Steps down to a workshop and storeroom. Rows of wooden-handled tools attached to the walls. The pleasant smell of newly carved wood. A plate with half a pie. Gnawed and stale. The marks of uneven teeth still upon the pastry. The gelatine, green. A flat jug of beer. I watched a long, black tail disappear into the corner.

Not one of the coffins lined up against the wall would have fitted us.

I chose a simple enough wooden box, and tipped it over. Put my fingers through the leather handle straps. It was fiercely heavy to manage with my one good hand and yet I had no desire to share the task. Dredging it up the stairs from the cellar I was almost blinded with the exhaustion.

Back in my room at the top of a flight of winding steps, I cooed to Anna as I put her across my shoulder.

With Anna's weight inside I could not manage to move her coffin. So I fashioned a harness out of rope, and lashed it to my back. I walked with difficulty to the cold hard ground of a decorative garden within the city walls. There was a bush, I did not know its type or name, but I carefully dug the roots from the earth. The bush itself was bedecked with thorns. I welcomed the blood that poured down to my wrists.

Two hours labour with a spade and my one arm. I was glad of the exhaustion. When I placed her coffin in the shallow hole I crept in beside it.

Ode.

What?

This is my grave not yours.

Sorry.

I went up to my study and began to arrange my papers. Now that I could see the days sitting quiet and still before me, rather than the mess of battle and the lurch of the carriage or the Beast, I could devote the winter to writing.

Two books.

"For my brother, a Story of his Bravery and Conquests as the Leader of our Great Army."

"For Anna, the Truth."

Two books, but one volume. Each story beginning at the opposite end of the pagination. One book with two viewpoints. The book to be turned upside down to be read in passing and contrary accounts. The lies, as Anna called them, only fully came into relief with their juxtaposition.

I went down to the kitchen. The servants were baking bread.

'Can you show me how to do this?'

The servant did not refuse, but I could see his brow and understood the argument against it. I was the son of my father, the late Chief Elder, the brother of the current Master. It was not my place. And somehow I belittled him by assuming to partake of the skill that was his humble own.

When the bread was in the oven I copied another fellow who sliced potatoes and onions and put them in a pot.

I set the glass of watered wine upon my desk. The fresh bread I nearly burned but was saved by another. The bowl of hearty vegetable stew, with dried basil leaf floating on the surface.

A feast, Ode.

But a lonely one.

Eat well, Ode, there is much to be done. Your papers are in disarray. Your mind not much better.

There were three small arched windows in the attic room I had designated as my study. The glass was very thick and although it let in some light, it did not offer a clear view of the rolling, snow covered hills. So I preferred to keep them open despite the cold.

When will the snows thaw?

At this elevation maybe a couple of months from now.

My brother will go insane, holed up for such a time.

But you will thrive and get your thoughts and writing in order. By the time the new green shoots appear you will know what to do.

I found my brother in the great hall. He was killing the air and stabbing dust with a short bladed knife that he slipped back into his belt when he saw me.

'Ode, the servants are plotting against us. They outnumber us now. I shall have to hang half of them to keep the other half in their place. What do you think?'

'Brother.'

'Enough of that, Ode! Ode! It is nice to see you. Give me a hug. Where have you been, Ode, writing or wanking?'

'I buried her.'

He smiled at me like a father and stroked the back of my neck.

'Ode, Anna never loved you. She pretended to. To ensure her own safety. Think of it, Ode, of all of us, who was she safest with? The weakest man amongst us, you. You who were defended in all things, by the strongest man of all, myself. Her love for you, was no more than the part she wrote for herself in this play of ours to ensure her own safety. Ode, where have you *been*?'

'You say this to me? Why did *you* never find love, Brother?'

A small amber bottle of the tincture sat upon the dining table. My brother popped the cork and drank of the tincture like wine.

'If you had not taken her she would still be alive,' I said.

'If I had not taken her she would never have been yours. You would never have known her. She is gone now. But I will find you someone better.'

'There was no one better.'

'You have never had another woman to compare her with.'

'I have no need to compare her to another. I will never forget her face when I made love to her. It is a wonderful thing to be joined with the body of someone you adore. While every white girl you ever screwed wept and screamed and wished herself dead.'

'Don't rile me, Ode. Anna? I never felt she gave me due respect. She lacked humility before the Chief Elder.'

'She could have bowed her head before you or kissed your feet?'

We stood, two brothers in an empty hall with the frost knocking at the bottle glass windows.

'Let us talk of other things. We should be heading North soon. I have been planning it.'

'Brother, can you not see how weakened we are? We shiver in the cold of this room. The snows of the further North will turn our blood to ice.'

The affront to Anna spurned me on to greater disrespect.

'Brother, what if we are labouring under a deception? What if our father was not chosen after all?'

'What the fuck! What the fuck, Ode! Did those words just roll off your tongue? Or were they just put there by some devil?'

He lunged at me and slammed me on the chest so hard that I fell and cracked my head upon the stoned hearth.

'Don't get up again until I tell you to. You disrespect the man who should have killed you at your birth. Nature changed its course and chose our father. How is that in any way deniable?'

My brother had assaulted me.

He had never hit you before?

No.

Not even when you were children? In childish anger or as part of a game?

Never. I have never been assaulted. None of the other boys ever dared, because of my family.

Boys attack each other all the time. And women are hardly immune either.

'And if our father was not chosen,' I said, 'then nor were you.'

'Ode, if you do not silence yourself this moment I will do it for you.'

'And if you *were* chosen, why did you fail?'

'Ode, where has your respect gone? What madness are you exhibiting? I have not *failed*. We are not beaten. We are challenged. That is all. I for one, will rise to that, and prevail.'

'Brother, when you strip away the pretence of this chosen quest, our army is revealed as nothing more than a band of thieves and murderers. We console ourselves with the thought that our actions are justified by the insults and abuse we have suffered throughout history. But where is the glory when we kill a boy hardy yet a man and abuse a girl hardly yet a woman?'

'And is this what you have been writing in that cold room of yours, Ode? I wonder what our father would say if he were still alive. Ode, your brother is brave, and even now when all seems to be against him, he still has faith. But you, Ode, I did not bring you on this quest for you to ...'

Someone sobbed.

'I found them hiding in a panel in the bookcase.'

I walked around the dining table. There in the corner was a woman on her knees holding the body of a young man.

'I could not let him live, Ode. The woman, maybe I will let her entertain me later on, or maybe I will send her to see this young man. It depends on how I feel. I can never be quite sure how things will end when I drink the tincture.'

'Let the woman go, Brother. Let her not be the target of your anger. And let her take the body with her.'

'It is at my discretion not yours.'

'Father would never had an innocent woman on her knees wondering if she were to live or die at his hands.'

'And you know what Father thought, did you, Ode? And how much time did you spend with him? A brief chat maybe when he deigned to put his head into your study. I trained with him every day. So don't fucking tell me what Father would and would not approve of me.'

'If Father were alive he would admonish you for the way you have been of late. He would have protected you against yourself. But I have not. Brother, I have let you stray.'

'No, no more of this arrogance, Ode. I am what I am. I do not need you to be my moral guardian. But no matter. Even if you had each day been in charge of my soul, I would have ignored you and acted as I saw fit. All will be clear. We will succeed. We will be praised.'

'No Brother, we will not. We are finished. Our story ends with abject failure.'

'That is how you see it? You are so sure that your mind is worth more than all the other minds in this world put together. But you don't know the most important thing of all. The most important thing is to *do*, Ode. You don't do. You don't fight. You leave it up to others and then make judgement on their actions.'

He drank of the tincture.

'Brother do not take more,' I said. 'I have tried it myself. I know something of its nature. Our father and our mother are looking down upon us. Do not give them more cause for grief.'

'Yet it is you that insults them. You wish us to return home with the story of our abject failure. *You* insult their dreams. After our father died. It all fell to me. If I have ever been cruel it is because of the weight of the burden I carry. You have no idea at all what that is like.'

'Brother there is little chance of us ever getting home. I know you will not accept that.'

'We will get home, Ode. But you cannot bring the story of failure with you. Would the myth of our conquest not be better than the truth?'

'How will you stop me?'

'I will take your books this night and burn them.'

'But, Brother, I am trained as a Griot. I will simply write it all again.'

'Ode, am I not cursed with your skill of remembering! These last months I have seen many things I am happy to be dull enough to forget.'

'You cannot silence me, Brother. I was born to speak and to remember.'

'Ode, how is it possible to hate someone you love so much? We were born at different times and yet I see us as twins. For fucks sake, Ode, get to your feet. The same Mother and Father. What does a year between us matter? The strength of our father and the passion of our mother made us twins before we even knew how to speak to each other.'

'Brother, throughout our childhood I have watched you every day of my life. Your casual grace. The surety of your body. I often wondered what it must be like to live a life where men and women alike want to know you. Where men wanted to be you. No one ever wanted to be me.

'Our mother's talk was always of you, my brother. How tall you were growing, how all the girls adored you. I could never do anything to make her proud. I would never be able to farm or fight. No girl would ever marry me for fear that my deformity would be passed onto the next generation. It is a hard thing for a young man to bear. A flesh wound heals in weeks. The sewing takes no more than minutes under Luxxor's hands.

'So now, I tell you of my love and admiration and my own sense of worthlessness. Now I shall write what I think of as the truth. I shall write of the exploits of how our tribe *failed* in their attempt to conquer Yurop.'

'The word failed in the very first line, Ode! Who would want to read further?'

'We should have stayed in Afrik and used the power conferred on us by nature's reverse, to build a modest and humane empire there. A proud kingdom, with just laws and fine buildings. And yes, a powerful army of armed warriors on their proud beasts. And any foreign power that thought to enslave us would be ground to dust.'

'It was our father's dream to conquer Yurop.'

'Our father died on the first day of our arrival here, and we should have taken that as a sign.'

My brother leant over me and offered a hand. I took it and he pulled me to my feet. He embraced me in return. But his embrace became a hold, as one might do to pin down an enemy in a fight.

'Brother, so many had to die to satisfy your pride,' I said. 'I know from what I have studied in the libraries of Europe, that this is how history unfolds. The warrior, the king, who can never stop conquering. Feeding his insatiable need, finding excuses to kill others. Too black, too white, wrong God, no God, or praises the right God but in the wrong fashion. Too stupid to be treated as an equal. Too smart with their dangerous views that challenge the mighty import of power. These are the people that must be exterminated.'

My brother's arms around my back forced my chest to his. The more that I berated our cause, the stronger he pulled me to him. I was to be taken to his heart as my breath became more shallow.

'But it is nothing more than excuse Brother,' I said gasping. 'The people don't need to be killed because they are wrong. We find them wrong to enjoy the act of killing them. Brother, during none of this conquest have we shown true heroism. I forged heroism with my words. When the truth is that we are cowards who can only find pride and joy in the pain and suffering of others.'

'Ode, you stupid cunt, all strong people defeat those who are weaker than themselves. What is a contest without the stronger defeating the weaker? What is life without a contest and a dream? Would you prefer to see a world where the weak defeated the strong? Where the aberrations and perverted hold sway?'

'Brother you have a justification for any act of yours however foul. You are never wrong in your own thoughts. You ask the world to conform to the limits and perversions of your own mind. You make the world as you want to see it.'

'As do you, Ode. You want it to be as perfect as a story. You want endings, defensible morality. Crimes and punishments.

'And there is something that I have to do, Ode. Something that will hurt us both. But I have to return to our lands with the news of our victories and I cannot have you contradicting me.'

He took the bottle from the table.

'Drink, Ode.'

'No, Brother. I like its first effect, but then it makes me confused and drowsy.'

'That is not a request.'

We finished it together.

We nuzzled each other and cooed in each other's ears. But even in that joy I knew the short-lived nature of that pleasure.

For he had in his belt that short, dull knife.

There was a knock upon the door of my study. I had my windows open. The cool air on my face eased the pain. I stroked the paper I had before me. But what was the point of trying to write when I could not see what I had written.

Yes?

'Ode, my name is Lhlaka, your servant.'

He had never addressed me before. I was surprised by his voice.

'My name is not Kikuyo. My grandfather was of the Mbezzi tribe. My family has been indentured to yours ever since he was taken. I do not say this to put blame upon you or your family. If the situation were reversed my tribe would have done the same thing to a Kikuyo.'

I had known him all my life and yet never known his name.

'Ode, your warriors are in total disarray, they lie on the floor blathering in their rooms. We the servants, on the other hand have kept ourselves away from this poison. Less than an hour ago your brother, out of his mind, tried to kill Mphuno with an axe. He said he was going to kill them all because the beasts had betrayed him.

'Although it is our place to follow orders and never challenge the Chief Elder, we could not in all conscience allow him to kill the beast that had prostrated himself before your father. We had to restrain him. It took three of us. Your brother was strong.'

Was?

'He is dead, Ode. He struggled violently in our grip and then suddenly collapsed. I do not know what killed him. No blade entered his body. No bones were broken in the fight. We did not strangle him. Ode, with your brother dead, you are now our Chief Elder.'

I heard him take his sword from his scabbard. For one moment I thought he was about to kill me. I was the last of my regal family, far from home and unprotected.

'Ode, I ordered that your brother be restrained. I am responsible for his death. Here, Ode, take the hilt of this weapon in your hand. I am putting the blade to my chest. If I am to be punished, it shall be by you and at your discretion.'

No. No more death, if it can be avoided. And in my heart I could find no blame, no need for punishment. I took the hilt and pulled it towards me away from his chest. Dropped it at my side.

'Thank you, Ode. I am your servant.'

I shook my head.

'I know, Ode, the rhino has not chosen you, but we have. I do not presume to tell you how things should be, but if you will allow me I will make suggestions and wait for your censure or approval. Let me be your advisor and let me see what you can no longer see.'

I nodded.

'Ode, I have some brandy for you, let me pour it into your mouth. It may ease your pain.'

I let him do that for me.

'Ode, when we first arrived here in the castle, the warrior beasts lay there frothing all night long. They were too much work for your men to attend to, especially when drunk and them taking the tincture. It was us, the servants that weaned them off the poison. Giving them a little less each day, till they no longer craved it at all and were free. We were tender with the beasts, carefully removing their armour, washing their eyes, putting water upon their tongues. And I think that they accept us now. A number of us have swung ourselves into their saddles and they have not bucked. We shall ride the warrior beasts and the females that we grew up with will walk alongside us.'

Typical.

Not now, Anna.

Sorry Ode, should I only express myself at your own convenience?

'We are to return, that is our plan. The beasts will take us home. It will be hard and many of us will not survive. But there is no adventure without pain. And we shall not kill unless provoked beyond safety. We shall say, leave us alone. Don't be proud. Just be happy to see our backs.

'But, we wish to return home changed, no longer chained to our lower status. We want to be free. I do not want to raise an invisible child. You are the only surviving son of the Chief Elder, and as such the only male member of the Royal Family of the Kikuyo.

'We would happily protect you and escort you home, if you will by edict, support the elevation of our caste. I know you cannot speak, and anything that you may write would not be understood. But there are nods and signs that many men of different tongues and colours have used to create some brotherhood.

'Your book, Ode. I found it on your brother's desk. I have not opened the cover. I have not pried. It seems right that I should bring it back to you.

Ode, you can do this. Take the story home. Give your people completion. Lay out a future for them. You need to return and this man will help you. For if you do not, your adventure shall become myth and your warriors will become ten feet tall and invincible and kill everyone who stands in their way.

And so I stood and breaking with a tradition that had lasted countless generations I offer my hand to him, a member of the servant class, and he took it.

His breathing became fitful.

'I never dreamed,' he said, 'that one day I would be touched by a Prince.'

Anna broke into giggles.

Oh God, Ode, you have got a fan!

I sat with my book that night open on my lap and caressed the pages.

I took the tincture in great moderation. Yet I took it. Saying to myself, as I always said to myself. This is the last time. But it so helped the pain at the root of my stumped tongue and blotted out the crushing headaches that lay before my absent orbs.

I had dreamed of making my tribe literate. And although that now seemed impossible, nothing could be done at all a thousand miles from home. My people had to know what was in my book. They had to understand me. And the first thing to do was to go home to them.

I imagined the next generation of warriors proudly sat upon the next generation of their beasts.

Let it be known that the Kikuyo educated the known world. A legacy not of sword, but of word.

Ode, they will laugh in your face.

I am the Chief Elder now, they will do as I say.

Ode, they will kill you in the night.

I will say. If we are united with the other tribes and can strive to make ourselves understood to each other, the white man will have no chance against us. If we decide to take Yurop for ourselves, we won't send a thousand warriors. We will send a thousand thousand.

Ode, how can you teach when you cannot talk or see to read?

Anna, are you about to put me in my place?

Yes, Ode, that is what your brother did to you. He did not wish to hurt you, he just wanted you silenced. So that his version of his own life, that would be the version talked about and remembered. He wanted the poet silenced and the braggart heard. The world rejoices in being thick and ugly. History is the story of the foul. Those pure of heart and mind, with love coursing through their veins are forgotten. The myths celebrate brute, uncaring force. Plays are bursting with the acts of murderers. What matter if they die ignoble at the end? Blood and rape are entertainment. And however foul a man, he has his concubine, willing to bask in his bloodied glory. Women may be victims, but we are not innocent. We are defiled by association. Women like to fuck thugs and brutes. And so they breed. The general has more children than the poet. But I was different, and you were different, and I am now nothing more than rot, and you are blinded and rendered mute.

I had to find her grave blind.

On my knees I went amongst the flowers and the bushes until I pricked the back of my hand on a thorn.

Here, I pointed.

I mimed digging.

Lhlaka asked two servants to exhume the coffin. I would take her home. My last act of love to her. Then I buried my brother. He wanted to travel North and this was as far North as he would ever go. Yet it was still a mighty achievement. I did not want to take him home, vanquished, fallen. He would have considered that a retreat.

I could not cry, for there was no longer a conduit for my tears. I could no longer say kind words and tell his corpse of my love. But he was with our mother and our father now. And I thought, Brother, feel free to brag. Tell them you were the hero of their vision. I will be true to myself and Anna's love for me and here on earth will say that we were foolish, wrong and brutal. That no deluded vision of being a chosen race is worth the death and misery of those that we felt had mishandled us. But when I join you in the afterlife, I will concur with you and tell them, tell them all, that we were magnificent and worthy of their trust and love. That we conquered all, and ruled the world. I will tell the story that you wanted me to tell. I shall tell *that* story to the dead.

The green shoots that Anna had spoken of had yet to poke their heads through the snow. Yes there was a mildness in the wind that blew through my windows.

'Ode, if you are in agreement, I think it is time to go.'

Without my asking, Lhlaka presented me with a full inventory.

'Eighty Men at Arms, now in armour, mounted upon warrior beasts. Seventy female beasts in tow. Of the seventeen warriors that had survived the initial battle, your brother and yourself were two.'

My brother dead, me in command. An unimagined history.

'Five have died by succumbing to their addiction. That leaves eight, four of whom, taking neither food nor water had fallen to the common Yurop illness of the chest. They cannot be moved.'

By which he meant for us to leave them there to die. Previously no servant would have thought of such a thing. But now of course they were no longer servants. They were men at arms, men capable of making tough decisions. I did not fight it.

'The last four are able to stand but are quite gone in grief and loss. They will come with us of course, Ode. It would be unthinkable to leave them behind, but I am concerned about them. And I shall watch them closely. For their protection.'

We found a barge that took us downstream for the exorbitant price of five pairs of rhino. There was no ambush, no burning logs across the river. No spilled oil from bridges. Just a silence. We were forgotten and ignored. If my brother had still been alive he would have ranted and gone out of his way to stir a fight and bring them down upon us no matter what the odds. But the servants, more attuned to humility, were I think happy enough to be left alone. Look we are leaving. No more death for now, of our race, or yours.

When the river turned sharply West, we disembarked. Back on dry land we were offered a corridor to the southern boot, one long empty road. Farmers in the fields seeing us approach put down their tools and turned their backs.

There was no last great plan to destroy us. No one wanted to risk their lives. Our force that had once terrified now became boring to our old adversaries.

At the entrance to a village would be a mound of roasted turnip. Eat, pass through, leave us behind. Fuck off. Every door locked, every shutter closed. The smell of cooking the only indication that there was life there at all. Hurry move on. You can walk our high street in five minutes why are you dawdling?

A mile out, I would hear the distant shrieks of children. Back at play. The parents had not let them even take a peek. Black warriors on rhino beasts? We were already becoming nothing more than childish fantasy. Well I never saw one! I think my mum and dad just made it up to scare us. Scrub the floor or the black men will eat your face.

No one tried to kill us. They just wanted us gone.

I wrote the words in Latin, slanted, smudged and unseen. And the priest translated for me.

'My daughter is not with you?'

I explained what had happened as simply as I could. And told him that I had brought her body to be returned to him. And a leather case of books and letters.

'Did she suffer greatly, was she abused?'

She was not. I gave her full protection myself and then later she became my wife.

At this point I expected him to begin ranting, abusing my dark skin, accusing me of raping her. But no. I could hear his measured breathing.

'Did you make her happy?'

Our circumstances were complicated, but she said she loved me, and I told her many times that I felt the same way about her.

'It was all my fault, I should have stood up for her, not just let your people take her, but we had fallen out, she had fallen from God. She grew up without a mother. I was always busy. Regret follows anger. All parents are fools.'

I tried to remember if Anna had ever said something loving or complimentary about her father, something I could offer to comfort him in his grief. But I could not remember one word of respect or of love. And I was loath to invent something lest it ring false.

'I will offer you safe passage through the town. I want no conflict, no fighting and no rowdiness. I will lend you a ship that will take you back to Afrik. It will be a small price to pay for your retreat.'

We will row ourselves. We do not require slaves.

'The winds are favourable at this time of year. What you need is a pilot, which I will provide. You should get home by the wind.'

He paused.

'Ode, have you always looked as you are now? Maybe my daughter felt sorry for you.'

I was not disfigured, nor rendered mute when she knew me, that happened after her death.

'And your arm?

I was born like that. My deformity never upset her. She accepted me for what I was. I will tell you that in all honesty, I was not used to being treated so well by a beautiful woman.

'You were the son of the Chief Elder?

Yes. In your Yuropan terms, I am as a Prince to my people. Now I am the king.

'Anna as a girl dreamed of marrying a Prince, all young girls do, it is a common story in our culture that the girl everyone thinks of as rather odd and ungainly, turns out to be a secret beauty and marries the Prince.'

For myself the story was reversed. I was the one odd and ungainly, she was the Princess. She saved me.

Although the Prince in your stories is never black, I ventured.

'*Never* black. But if Anna found joy in you, does the colour of your skin matter so much? I am not a liberal, Ode. I am not a reformist. It just seems to me that you might have made her happier than any other man I tried to foist upon her may have done. And by your own account it was God-fearing white men, not black barbarians that hung her in their town square.'

I let the comment about barbarians slide.

She often said she loved you deeply.

A lie underlined.

The pilot who spoke Levant said to me.

'I have a message from Anna's father,' he took a piece of paper from his pocket. 'I have already translated it. Go home Kikuyo. Mute as you are, tell your people they must never leave their lands again. You will have to act it out like a child, drawing a line in the dirt, pointing and pretending to cut your own throat. We never want to see the return of your kind.

'I have found some of Anna's letters in her effects that you kindly returned to me. They are written in our tongue and not in the learned voice. The letters are expressed to me alone.

'Dear daddy she says, I miss you so much. How I wish that you and I were sat in our dining room, how I wish I were pouring you a glass of wine. You cannot imagine the grief I feel at our separation. And I have been given over as a slave to the most awful man. A stinking, crippled black that feels that he has the right to paw me. My dream is that you come to rescue me and put this vile beast to death.'

Bollocks.

Thanks, Anna.

When we were within sight of land I asked, by sign and dumbshow for Lhlaka to kill the pilot and throw him overboard.

And so I arrived back upon the soil of my own continent.

I could hear the rhino's huffing impatience. They could smell their own land. Lhlaka's hands grabbed me and placed me astride the neck of Mphuno. Tied my feet and calves into the stirrups, placed my hands upon the pommel.

I knew the porters were Afrik by their accented cries. I knew they were tired by the power of their breathing. I knew they were indentured by the commands of the traders and by unchanging history. I felt the boat shudder against the dock. I smelled the spices of Afrik boiling in their barrels.

The same tired men that had waved to us on our outbound quest, caught our ropes and lashed them to the quayside. We had nothing to offer them. I wondered if they had ever dreamed of our victorious return, with thoughts that they too might benefit from the plunder of our quest. After all they had witnessed our might, seen our resolve. Watched our direction.

Or when you are truly broken, do you cease to dream? For to dream is too imagine, and imagination is the brain at work. And work needs sustenance. Bread and possibility.

I caught the distant sound of wheels riding the cobbled street, and then the rolling of metal across the surface of salt-lashed wood.

'Ode,' called a voice, 'It is Nassir's father. Are you surprised to see me? I have been waiting to see what remained of you and your army. A boy came running to say that the harbour master had spotted you. I have prayed for the day of your destruction. And yet you are still alive. But you have been hurt. Tell me who did this to you and I will have them flogged. Can you not speak? Ah Ode, what is to happen to you now? Your father prized you for your talent with languages. And now silent as a rock. And where is your father now, and where are your eyes? Lying in a Yurop field amongst the turnips?'

I refused to share the truth with him.

'Ode, my son died in the conflict between us and yet it was my fault. I tried to trick you out of your beasts. And I paid dearly for my deceit. But give me three breeding pairs of your beasts now in fair trade and I will help you.'

With a wiggling finger I indicated that I wished the use of a pen.

'I have no paper to hand, Ode.'

I strode to his voice. I heard him reversing his wheels. I got to him before he could escape me. I indicated my hand. He gasped. Did he think I was about to command that we should do to him what we had done to his duplicitous men? I could smell the pungent lunch floating from the surface of his skin. I reached around before him. He offered his hand to mine. I took his palm, and with slow movements wrote these words with the tip of my finger.

~~I have no need of you.~~

'Again, Ode, I did not get that.'

~~I have no need of you.~~

'Really? There is a journey of many weeks ahead of you, maybe months if you encounter difficulties, maybe years if you get lost. What supplies do you have? You will need, pots, beans and dried pulses, cured meats. Earthenware, flagons of watered wine.'

~~We can buy.~~

'You will need your Arab, your Teacher and your guide to find your way home. Without him you will never reach the land of your forebears. Some say that Blacks lack the capacity to orientate themselves in this world. Ode, admit it, you do not even know the whereabouts of your own homeland. You have returned depleted from the north. You have nothing more than the concept of south.'

~~Our guide is waiting for us.~~

'Yes but where? Can you even find him? I did. After you left, he spent some time outside cafes. Enjoying himself. Whilst I wept over my dead son. He visited women. He spent days in the library, reading the classics. He had no idea he was being watched. But after your departure and the death you rained down upon us, he was not popular here. So I took him in and made sure he was safe. Come. Dismount.'

Lhlaka held my elbow. Me the son of the Chief Elder, and him a servant. Life is full of change. Were it not, could we even be bothered to talk about it?

I bought a slate and a nub of chalk from a woman at a stall. Her son bleated in coarse Levant about the emptiness of his belly. I gave her a gold ring from my purse in exchange. The child screamed for yoghurt and lamb.

Lhlaka walked beside me holding my arm like a suitor. Nassir's father wheeled himself along before us.

'I return you your guide. He is of great value to you. You give me five females and five males in exchange,' said Nassir's father turning his head and nearly colliding with a donkey carrying tubs of clementines. Which although I could not see, I could place into this world by hearing and smell.

'Ode. I am sorry to see you so damaged,' said my Teacher.

Lhlaka walked me up the stairs and then left me to my business. Nassir's father was downstairs imagining the riches he would derive from the mating of the rhinos he demanded. He no doubt thought to build an army as we had done.

I chalked my concern.

How have they treated you?

'These many months I have railed and wailed against my fate. You know that bastard has not let me out of this one room once. I have to lean out of the widow to smell the world. For my needs, I have been provided with a pot, a bowl and a cloth.

'But I have been able to read. And there is another world inside the head where we can go to the bathroom whenever we like and take walks among the flowers.'

My Teacher came to me and whispered in my ear.

'Can you kill that man for me, Ode?'

Yes.

'Ode, wipe your answer from the slate.'

I handed him the book from my leather case.

'Ode, is this all your great adventures in delightful ink? Oh Ode, what a fat and fabulous book. This will keep me entertained and appalled for days to come.'

He placed my prize upon his desk and opened the cover. I relished the tickle in my ears of the flicking of pages.

'Oh Ode. Ode. What defacement is this! Your words have been scribbled over by a mad man. Every page. The story is unreadable. Why would you have defiled your own work, Ode?'

Not me. My brother.

I had travelled with the book for many miles with no vision of his frantic palimpsests.

My brother.

'Ode, I am so sorry, there are hundreds of pages here. All ruined.'

No.

You were my Teacher. You taught me to be a scribe. But before that my Master taught me the art of the Griot. The story. All that happened. I remember it all.

'Of course what is writing without memory? Then we will write it all again. How long can it take? It matters not. Write blind. To hell with smudges, leaning scrawl, I will decipher it all. I will read the text back to you for your

324

commendations and rejections. You can nod or shake your head. Then I will make a good copy in my best hand. What a document it will be for future generations. It will take pride of place on the shelves of the library at Alexandria.'

I became quite giddy. How wonderful to find another so enthused by your own dreams.

'Is it to have a title?'

The beast's Biographer.

'Is it to be a histography, a hagiography, or the morbid and salacious truth? If there is enough murder and betrayal in the tale it may even make an entertainment for the common folk. Ode, I am old. This shall be the last great thing I will do with my life.'

Yes, the text could be revived. But I could not.

There will be no one to read the story aloud.

'I have spent much time with you and your people, Ode. Your language surrounded me, in every waging tongue. With greater study I might be able to command it.'

Only a Griot of my tribe can tell the tale.

I could not see his face at this, and a sigh can mean many things. I wiped my chalkboard clean with the edge of my hand ready to say more.

'We shall write it anyway. I shall demand paper and ink from my jailor before you order his demise. We shall begin this day as Nassir's father is buried in his own garden of delights.'

For days on end, the movement of Mphuno between my thighs, forced ranting and howling pains into the sockets of my skull and spat such venom into the root of my throat.

I took of the tincture that Lhlaka offered me. Better to not think clearly, than to be screaming in tongueless pain for so many months of travel.

Journeys end as do lives, tales and seasons.

I recognised the smell of Natal Plum at the entrance to the gorge. I heard a young voice bouncing across the rocks. A Griot in training. Then the vocal exercises ceased and I heard excited feet.

'Ode, is that you? I know you by my sight even though we have never talked. Your father was once kind to mine. When he was unwell. I do not expect you to remember. I am Omayu, the Griot's student. The Griot adopted me after you left him.'

Omayu, do the girls avoid you? Do you find the loneliness crushing and yet you would still not have it any other way. Would you like to learn the Latin? Could you be the blessing I have been thinking of?

'Ode, I can see that your father is not with you. He has always led, Ode, I cannot believe that he is to follow in your wake.'

He is dead. My brother also.

'So few of you returned? What, no Father or Brother? And you badly wounded about the face. Ode, can you not speak?'

I opened my mouth to show him the absence of my tongue. I could not witness his reaction.

'Ode, you have been away for many seasons. Let me escort you home. You are hurt in the wars. Come, Ode, come. I have many things to tell you. Can I ride with you?'

I nodded. I put out my hand for him to grab. I pulled him up to sit behind me. Omayu put his arms around me and spoke into my ear.

'None of the warriors are talking, Ode. Have you all been silenced by the same hideous deed of violence?'

The Servants were dressed in the armour, their faces covered by their helmets, no evidence for the boy to see their lack of our distinctive facial mark. Or hear that that their accents differed very slightly from our standard tone.

'There are no riders on the females. Have the servants all been lost?'

I leant back and tapped him slightly on his thigh to quieten him. Our Servants were no longer to be spoken of so lightly. They were to be elevated to the status of citizens at my command. To be known as Men of War.

'I talk too much, Ode.'

Then I envy you.

'The Wollof are causing trouble again, Ode. They made an incursion into our land last year and … No. But it is not my place to speak of that. I know that we intended to destroy them completely. But some of the Wollof survived. They hid in a cave so I have heard tell.'

We had killed every soul that we could lay our hands upon. Our first act of conquest had entailed the murder of innocent women and children. A crime committed to break the awful cycle of violence. And yet the circle had not been broken. A gaggle of them had survived, vowing upon everything that they held dear, to regroup, become strong again, seek revenge.

'Ode, you will be sad to hear that some months after your army left, the rhino reverted to their old nature.'

For myself and my family, the crossing of the beasts was our legend. My grandfather was preparing to die. His hands reaching out for those of his beloved wife and son. They were to walk together into the world of spirits. And then at the last moment, hours or days before annihilation, nature changed its course. And we became the chosen.

And now the beasts, at nature's command again, had walked away. Could the reversion have coincided with death of my father? Was the dream and contract dead from that day forth?

More foul news to bore into my sockets and my root. More tincture needed to adjust the world to that which I could bear. I felt into my satchel and relieved myself with a draft.

'Even those beasts who had been in training many years, but were not yet mature enough for conquest. They all walked away. We do not know why. One night they were with us, and the next morning they were gone. We espied them in the bush, nuzzling the grass. They had not the ears nor eyes for our presence. We were jilted overnight.

'There is no more giraffe meat now. We are back to maize and cassava. There have been so few babies born this year, Ode. But now you are here amongst us again, everything will return to the way it was! If your father or your brother are not with you, you will command them.'

Yes. The rhino will come back to us now that I am home. I touched my left arm and without thinking Omayu touched it also.

'Ode. Sorry have I offended you?'

I squeezed his hand.

'Ode, you cannot see it, but beside the small toe of my right foot, there is a scar. When I was born there was a small brother growing out from the side like a sapling from a branch. My mother carved that away before she suckled me. My father never knew. When I was twelve years old my mother showed me the tiny bone she had kept as a keepsake.'

Even if I could have spoken, I do not know what I would have said at that very moment.

'Have you brought us riches, Ode? Where is all your plunder, is there a caravan some miles behind you piled with gold and meat? I can see no cloud of dust behind us. Have you returned to save us?'

We stood mounted just outside the gates of my own city. Strangely for a moment, I thought that we were going to have to fight our way inside. For we were met not with cries of joy, but with a stunned and churlish silence.

I knew there was a crowd before us. I had heard the whiney of the opening gates. I could hear the puzzled sandals on the dry earth.

I had Omayu's constant narration in my ear to keep me orientated.

'Your father had promised the return of The One Thousand. The people took that literally. They believed it absolutely. That was our story. They are shocked to see so few in reality. And if you will forgive me, they are shocked to see yourself at the head of the warriors.'

'Remove your helmets,' announced Lhlaka. 'We are home and have no need to hide our faces.'

Their faces had been no obstacle on our long journey home. No Yurops or Levants cared about our tribal distinctions. But home, their difference was appallingly acute.

There was murmuring amongst the Kikuyo.

Not our tribal marks!

'I thought they were the last of our warriors,' said Omayu. 'But the only ones that have returned apart from you are mere servants. Oh Ode.'

They dismounted with all pride and ceremony, but they received no salutations. No wild and vocal welcome.

'Ode, they are not happy to see us,' said Lhlaka. 'We are still nothing to your people, even though we are the only ones to survive, the only ones to cure and return the last beasts unharmed and to bring you home, the last of your Royal Family.'

The women wanted to see the return of their husbands, not their servants. They wanted a man in their bed, not a man sweeping their doorstep.

Lhlaka. If they have ignored you before, they will detest you now.

'The beasts belong to the warriors,' said a man, 'get your filthy, fucking arses off their backs.'

'The warriors are dead,' said Lhlaka, 'we are all that have survived.'

There was an intake of breath. A wave of shock. A servant, an indentured man from another tribe, talking to them like he was their equal. The weak had survived and the strong had perished.

'Ode, you must command them to respect us.'

'You are not permitted to ride the males,' said a man of the crowd. 'Was this not made clear to you when you were a child?'

It was required by our bargain for myself to present the servants now as elevated men. But what crude signing would have been sufficient to overcome the terrible disappointment of the crowd. Such was their palpable anger that I thought they might have killed the returnees on the spot. The Arab, my Teacher sat upon a female behind me kept his quiet, knowing that any intervention in his heavy accent would have brought down great resentment upon himself. I would not bring him to danger by asking him to intervene or explain that which I had already told of him on our long journey home.

'They are staring at you, Ode,' said Omayu in my ear.

Are they happy to see me?

'To be honest, Ode, I do not know what they make of your return, and I am the one with eyes to gaze.'

I needed to communicate with my people and yet under the circumstances I could not. Who and what had I returned to? My father and my brother left behind. My mother dead in my visions. I had no friends awaiting me. Anna gone. Her bones in the ground a thousand miles away.

'We will sleep and rest at the training compound tonight,' said Lhlaka. 'The beasts will be comfortable there. They will be home again. We will go with them and settle them. Tomorrow we will discuss this further.'

Knowing my duty, Omayu led me to the Cave of my Forebears.

Before the campaign my family visited every year. A dark, dank place with lines of carved head on plinths.

It was a long walk and Omayu had to stop me from tripping on stones and rocks.

'Ode, there are four rhinoceros just under a tree to our right.'

Do they take note of us?

'They don't see us anymore. But, Ode, the beasts that have returned, will they remain true to us or revert to the wild as well? Or are the two factions now irreversibly divided. Sorry, Ode, I am talking too much. I am talking out of place.'

I stopped him and touched his mouth.

'You want me to talk?'

I want you to never stop.

I nodded.

329

'Now you still have fifty males and females returned. If they were to breed, would their offspring cleave to their wild nature or would they maintain the contract that they had established with your father?'

As we walked I studied the mathematics in my mind. The gestation period of the rhino is sixteen months. The female may not have a calf until she reaches the age of seven years. The male cannot impregnate the calf until he is twelve. I was seventeen. If fifty females gave birth in sixteen months' time, when I was eighteen, half of them might be males. And they would mature when I was thirty, by which time we would have increased our number of mature males from fifty to seventy five. But of course many calves would have been born over that twelve year period. After that initial wait, a new generation could be ready every two years. I was too sun-struck and too tired from my walk, and still in too much pain to calculate how old I would be when we could again raise a thousand beasts.

'Ode, we are at the Cave of the Elders. I am not allowed to enter as I am not of royal blood.'

I took his hand and dragged him forward. Leading the boy who was now my guide.

Our craftsmen had over the many generations carved the facial likeness of my family. Knowing to start at the end on the very right I felt for them. My father, his face carved before he left for conquest. Oh to feel his face again with the ends of my fingers. I was blind no longer. He was clear before me. As was my mother's beauty, and me unable to weep, for the tears fell not from my absent eyes to my outward cheeks, but inside my frame.

Mother I am the only one that has returned. Father died bravely. My brother died to save me.

I did not mention the hurt he had caused me. I did not know what else to say.

'A year ago,' said Omayu in a whisper, 'a gang of Wollof, a faction of those that had hidden in a cave, came for her at night, passing through our unprotected lands and negotiating the city by luck and stealth. They stuffed rags in her mouth and cut her into many pieces. Sorry, I if have offended you with the truth of it.'

The gates were open to me. Omayu led the way. I moved through my own darkness and the silence of the crowd.

I entered the house I had left many seasons ago. I knew how many steps there were between each room, where to turn and were to find the physical, familiar things. But without my parents and my brother, it was a dead space. And there was nothing inside me to bring it back to life.

Naima appeared behind me. I knew her smell. Burdock root and Wormwood and the sweat under her arms.

I turned round and she gasped.

'Forgive me. Ode, you are changed. I live a simple life. Change is a surprise to me. Forgive my girlishness. You are the only one to return.'

What of the Servants?

'The only true man. Your belly must be empty. Let me feed you. Our fare is not so wonderful of late. No meat anymore, Ode. Still it is easy to complain and harder to continue. And a hard life might be full of blight, but the struggle gives you something to think about and something to dream of. Even if you only dream that one day it might all be over. I have heard that you cannot see, nor speak, nor hear and yet here I am talking to you. But you won't mind me I hope.'

I felt for where I thought her lips must be and touched the end of her nose. She giggled.

I tried again and pointed to her lips and my ears. And she darted forward and kissed my cheek. Then she poked my belly. I laughed silently. That made her happy. I let myself be fed.

For fuck's sake, Ode, said Anna inside me.

What?

Stop feeling so guilty. Enjoy the attention. I cannot be there for you however much I might desire it.

'Ode, Ode, come outside and listen.'

I let the boy lead me. I could feel the heat of morning. With the food that Naima had cooked for me I had even slept quite well without the tincture.

'The servants, Ode. They have come into the city, armed, in armour, uninvited.'

I could hear the breathing of the beasts. The servants were mounted. They sat before us.

'Ode, they have cut their faces, to mimic the Kikuyo mark. And, Ode, the servant Lhlaka is sat upon Mphuno.'

Where are the townsfolk?

'All doors are closed, Ode.'

In fear or simply a refusal to acknowledge the presence of Lhlaka and his men?

'Those homes where we served,' said Lhlaka. 'They will now become ours. It is only our due and right reward for all that we have sacrificed. Ode himself, now head of the Royal family, has promised us full citizenship. I can see him now outside his home. Go to him and ask him if you do not believe what I say.'

A door opened.

'For fucks sake, you dumb shit servile. Ode is mute. He can't tell us a fucking thing. You know this. You could make up any old shit and call it his promise.'

I knew the voice. The Griot.

'Griot, we should be friends,' said Lhlaka. 'Not long from now, you will be telling your people the story of my adventures.'

'I will not speak one fucking word about you or your exploits. You return with not one single warrior alive, and Ode blind and mute. Why should we listen to one word you say? For all we know, you murdered Ode's father and his brother, took Ysoun's Beast as your own and maimed Ode so that he could not tell the truth about your crimes.'

More doors opened.

'Dismount.'

'Return the beasts to those who are warriors in waiting.'

'You talk of elevation,' said the Griot. 'You say that Ode will make you citizens? I will speak with him and demand he indeed changes your status. You shall be The Banished from this day forth for your audacity. You come into our city fully armed and mounted! This shall not be allowed to stand.'

A whistle. A cry. A shriek from Omayu beside me. He grabbed my withered arm. But he was still standing.

A small child crawls into my lap and I embrace it without thinking.

'I thought you might like to cuddle it for a while before I take it home,' says Naima. 'You must be very lonely dumb and blind. It's not mine of course, my own son is running around all over the place back home. Treading on my toes. This child is my sister's. She's gone quite mad, Ode. Since your return alone. No warriors, no husbands, no fathers. Your great loss is also our own. Yet we are the ones left alive to feel it. I can bring the child along some times, if you would like to cuddle it.'

I hold the child as Naima tidies the chaos I make daily in my studio. I can tell the child is a girl from the fragrance of her hair. I fumble for her hand. The hand is a fist. And I gently prise apart the fingers to expose the palm. And I write with my finger, first in Latin and then in Arabic, "Ode".

The child giggles. I am tickling her palm.

I point at myself. Then draw on her hand again.

'That is Ode,' says Naima.

'Otha,' says the child and I nod.

'I must go, Ode,' Naima says. 'You hear what she says?'

I nod.

'I am sorry that I at first thought you deaf as well as blind and mute. I am not used to such things. I have no schooling in such things as this. Children born without hearing or sight are not embraced by our tribe are they? Sorry Ode, I always say things wrong.'

I offer her forgiveness with my smile.

Naima takes my cheeks in her hands and kisses me on the lips.

'I should not do this as I am a widow. You did not bring my husband back to me. But I do not blame you much for that. I did not much take to him. I never dreamed of him when he was gone.'

And she laughs.

And when she is gone I say: Anna, would it be wrong?

It would not.

But she is not you.

No. But she is still warm and there is a heart there behind those breasts of hers. And blood in her veins. What do you think we want from you boys? We dream of your lips and heartbeats, not your pants and balls. And if you mention my name when she holds you, she will never know, because the voice will only be in your head.

Anna, we shall travel west within this continent. We shall take command of the gold fields. We shall rebuff the Arab merchants and their vulturine exploitation. We shall close the path across the dessert.

Gold shall be a thing of value amongst *us*. We will withhold it from the white man. We will make our own land and civilisation proud and magnificent and make the Yurops weep with envy.

And how will they respond? Do you not know?

They will be offended.

They will pour over their holy books to find an excuse to invade and destroy you for having the arrogance to think that that which stands below your feet in your own lands should belong to you and not to them.

Yes. Their God will tell them that we must be condemned for the arrogance of our own skin, as if we coloured it ourselves, against his permission, when the cloud man was not looking. If we can't be controlled and put to work, of what use are we?

They will amass an army and come to take everything that we have achieved from us. They will come and take it all, they will slaughter us, they will not spare the women and children, because each woman is the potential bearer of a future soldier, each child a warrior in waiting.

They will come.

And we will defeat them utterly on our own proud if dusty soil. We will be the one thousand again. Although I will be old by then, and shaky in my counting.

No matter. I shall still be with you. You can use my fingers as an abacus. Each digit for a hundred men.

And if they could find you in the afterlife they would hang you once more for your affiliation.

They could try.

Lhlaka came to see me.

'Ode, how do you fair? How great is your pain? We still have some more of the tincture? Do not be ashamed, Ode. You are not weak to partake of this. You take this to control your pain. Only with your pain controlled are you able to make the right decisions for the future. And you must make those decisions, Ode, I can voice them, but only you can instruct a change in the behaviour of the Kikuyo tribe. I am sorry that the Griot was dealt with harshly.'

Murder. How harsher?

'I need you to make things right. History turns on moments. If we had not contained him, the whole city would have turned against us and thrust us out beyond the walls, with no beasts to bear us. No food or water. I had to act to maintain the safety of my men. Would you have wanted to see our extinction?

'Or, we would have defended ourselves. Our might against the good folks of the city. What carnage might have ensued? Yet all averted by the unfortunate death of one old man. Over the campaign I watched your father and your brother very closely. I learned many things from them.

'Come, Ode. Un-crease your brow. Let us think of the future. Ode, we have healthy males and female rhino, they shall make a new generation. The Men of War will stand side by side with the new warriors. We shall all be equal.

'Ode, we will rise again. We are inevitable. We will learn from the mistakes that have been made in the past. We will not be beaten a second time. The next time we take the Wollof, we will hunt through every crack and hole. Not one shall survive.'

I took his hand. I beamed at him like he was my saviour. I mimed drinking.

'Yes, Ode, let us drink to our new plans.'

He clapped his hands. Omayu brought Cassava brandy. I already had two earthenware mugs at hand. I imagined Lhlaka turning in his direction. I could not be sure. By feel I poured a draft of the tincture into a mug and then gestured to Omayu to give me the wine. I poured.

'Ode, let me do that,' said Lhlaka. 'Sorry. Blind as you are, you have not spilled a single drop.'

We both drained our cups.

Five minutes later Lhlaka was breathing hard about his nose and lolling.

'Ode,' said Omayu. 'Are you going to kill him?'

A movement of my brow.

I have to.

I felt for the knife I had concealed.

'I will help you,' said Omayu.

'Ode, what are you doing?' said Naima. 'Put that down.'

Naima, do not watch. I did not hear you enter.

'A blind man, a boy, a woman. He may still overcome us all.'

I felt for his throat. I held the blade.

I was poised, but I lost the food that Naima had cooked for me the moment the metal touched the blabbering flesh.

'Ode, you are right, these men cannot be allowed to take power.'

They only want equality.

'Women are not fools. Do not ignore my advice.'

'Ode, I shall do it.'

No Omayu, you are still young.

'I'm fourteen. Old enough to kill, don't treat me like a child.'

Omayu, with our Master dead you are destined to be the Griot now. The Griot is not allowed by all law and tradition to cause physical harm. Do not ruin your calling in a moment's anger.

'I want to. I am not a coward, but my Master's spirit would disown me if I harmed a man.'

It fell to me.

The Men of War waited in the square. Relaxing by the fountain. Hoping to return to the houses they had lived in before the quest. And this time, not as servants but as citizens. They gasped at the apparition of me and quickly tried to mount the beasts.

Naima had sawn through the neck. Omayu had placed the head upon a staff.

Without the voice of Lhlaka, the servants were muted. All the townsfolk were waiting. They had weapons and instruments for cooking and tending vegetation.

I mimed that the servants should stay on foot and Omayu beside me spoke aloud my gestures.

I nodded that he had understood me well. The dead Griot would find him a good student. Remove your armour. Return to your old homes but with your eyes to the floor. Whoever is waiting for you there, is your new Master.

'Ode, they are refusing to move.'

I did not blame them. They had tasted freedom. They wished to live, yet not one of the townsfolk would have wanted them in their house lest they began to ferment insurrection. Preparing food, in charge of the young children. How could the Kikuyo ever feel safe with them now? These servants were not, and had never been of their tribe. They had never been chosen.

Omayu lead me.

Omayu lead me down the steps to the central square. I kneeled before Mphuno.

I will be guided by you.

I placed the decapitated head before his nostrils.

Omayu I need your eyes.

'Your Beast does not know what to do with such a foul thing. But the servants are removing their armour in supplication.'

We had not been thorough with the Wollof and they had killed my mother.

I stroked my throat and Omayu translated for me.

'Ode says to kill them all.'

The story will be written. At first the story was of the rhino, when Mphuno came to my father. And now returned home, I was told he was simply happy to graze. The Beast that changed our history.

That is the story I wanted to tell, of the change of nature, the choosing of my father, the opportunities offered to us. And then later the Beast became my brother. His greatest crimes were not the slaughter, for that is war and this is a story about war. You cannot write such a thing and be absolved of compliance, and be appalled by the blood that makes the tale worth telling. The day my brother raped a girl and then tried to force her to play act his lover, was the day he truly became the Beast. For there was no courage in that action and there was no necessity. If my brother mutilated me, I at least understand why. In fact after what I had done and said to him it was almost inevitable. But then the story changed again. Oh, I did what I had to do. The familiar cry of the powerful. But. But that famous word. That abrogation, that deferment. But. If I had not done what I had done, there might have been a profound and bloody battle within the city. If the servants had the rhinos between their thighs, I knew what havoc they could have reaped.

And strangely, during that encounter, the voice of Anna did not speak inside my head at all. Either she was appalled, or I kept the whole episode quite from her knowledge. So I became the subject of my own story. I became the beast's biographer. For I was the Beast.

THE END